Twilight Whispers

Also by Barbara Delinsky

Commitments[*]
Heart of the Night[*]
Twilight Whispers[*]
The Summer I Dared
Flirting with Pete
An Accidental Woman
The Woman Next Door
The Vineyard
Lake News
Coast Road
Three Wishes
A Woman's Place
Shades of Grace
Together Alone
For My Daughters
Suddenly
More Than Friends
The Passions of Chelsea Kane
A Woman Betrayed

*Published by
WARNER BOOKS

Twilight Whispers

Barbara Delinsky

WARNER BOOKS

NEW YORK   BOSTON

WARNER BOOKS

Time Warner Book Group
1271 Avenue of the Americas, New York, NY 10020
Visit our Web site at www.twbookmark.com.

Printed in the United States of America

First Warner Books Hardcover Printing: January 2005
10 9 8 7 6 5 4 3 2 1

Library of Congress Cataloging-in-Publication Data
Delinsky, Barbara.
     Twilight whispers / Barbara Delinsky.
        p. cm.
     ISBN 0-446-52398-4
        1. Murder victims' families—Fiction. 2. Housekeepers—Family
relationships—Fiction. 3. Aristocracy (Social class)—Fiction. 4. Inheritance
and succession—Fiction. 5. Los Angeles (Calif.)—Fiction. 6. Rich people—
Fiction. I. Title.

PS3554.E4427T95 2005
813'.54—dc22   2004042012

Twilight Whispers

To DHG—
historical consultant, sounding board, dad—
with thanks and love.

Chapter 1

THE INTENSE HEAT SENT rivulets of sweat trickling down Robert Cavanaugh's neck. He skimmed them away with the palm of his hand, perversely satisfied that he wasn't the only one suffering. The members of the media contingent around him were just as hot. Shirt backs were damp. Cameramen lowered their equipment from time to time to wipe their eyes and cheeks with their sleeves. More than one reporter fanned himself with his notebook. But this was no press conference, with the bodies packed into a small room made stifling by the heat of television lights.

It was a funeral beneath a blazing July sun, a funeral that attracted as much public attention as the announcement of a new presidential candidate would have done.

When it came to the Whytes and the Warrens, anything attracted attention. That might have galled Cavanaugh under other circumstances, but it didn't bother him now. The press pack was his cover.

Standing among them on a grassy knoll overlooking the crowds of mourners, he was as inconspicuous as a detective lieutenant in the police force could hope to be. His street clothes helped, but then he hadn't been in uniform for years. It seemed like years since he had felt this kind of drive, too, as though everything that had come before in his career had been in preparation for the investigation he was about to lead.

Vengeance was a powerful motive, ugly in its way, but sweet, oh so sweet in anticipation. Cavanaugh's sense of anticipation had been growing ever since that fateful moment thirty-six hours before when John Ryan, a deputy superintendent and the chief of detectives, had summoned him to his office.

"Cavanaugh!"

Cavanaugh had been filling out the report on a rape-murder suspect he'd collared the day before. Hearing his name bellowed across the squad room, he snapped the form from his typewriter, slid it into a folder, and headed for Ryan's office.

"Shut the door," Ryan had ordered in the manner that, to his underling's chagrin, had become even more brusque of late.

Shutting the door, Cavanaugh leaned against a file cabinet as he watched his superior maneuver his bulky form into the worn chair behind his desk. The chair groaned when Ryan tipped it back.

"Got a call a little while ago," he began. His voice was high, as though it were squeezed from his barrel chest. "Two bodies were found on a boat by Lewis Wharf—Mark Whyte and his wife, Deborah Warren."

A sudden rush of adrenaline made Cavanaugh stand straight.

Pleased that he had the younger detective's undivided attention, Ryan went on. "It looked like a murder-suicide to the men who got there first. I want you to take charge."

Cavanaugh nodded.

Ryan raised pudgy fingers to scratch his head, then smoothed his thinning crew cut. "Look for more. It could be something big. There's trouble in those families. Whyte barely talks to his youngest son, and Warren and *his* son have been competing with each other for political support for years. The two who are dead were into some weird things in L.A. They were an embarrassment. Someone may have wanted them out of the way." He arched a brow. "Warren's up for reelection next year. This one smells."

With that succinct analysis, he had lifted a four-inch stack of files and papers from the profusion of empty coffee cups and deli sandwich wrappers on his desk. "Spare time reading. You'll find it interesting. Take your time. You know who we're dealing with, so be careful. And keep me informed. Cavanaugh," he had added in dismissal. "I want to be with this one every step of the way."

Cavanaugh had been flattered at being given the job, then excited when its scope opened before him. It seemed that he hadn't been the only one keeping tabs on the Whytes and Warrens over the years. Ryan's file was far more complete than his own. It went back more than fifty years, documenting the rise of the two families to prominence. Through newspaper clippings, magazine articles, miscellaneous notations and internal memoranda, it told of shrewd business moves, political ambitions, the attainment of power. Interspersed with the admirable, though, were the hints of shady dealings, greed and ruthlessness that Cavanaugh himself had suspected.

For better than fifty years the Whytes and Warrens had cut an ever widening swath through the country's power-elite. Inevitably, enemies had been made along the way, but these weren't to be the crux of Cavanaugh's investigation. Cavanaugh was intrigued by the idea that dissension within the families might have led to the deliberate silencing of two of their number. His fantasies held it to be the ultimate in poetic justice if the Whytes and Warrens were to be caught in a deadly web of their own making.

Now, looking down at the funeral gathering as the public would later see it on television, Cavanaugh knew that any internal deceit would be—indeed, was—well hidden. Sorrow hung as heavy in the air as the heat; treason seemed unthinkable in a group that bore its grief the way these two families did.

Blood boundaries indistinguishable, they stood clustered around the twin gravesights. A Whyte clung to a Warren; two Warrens flanked another Whyte. Belying the antagonism Ryan had mentioned, they were a tight knit group, as, on the surface, they had been for more years than Cavanaugh had been alive.

That, perhaps, was part of their mystique. But it was Cavanaugh's job to see through the illusions to reality, to separate and analyze each Whyte and Warren in search of the weak link that John Ryan, for one, believed existed.

It would be tough. If power was a fortress, these families were protected to the hilt. To find a crack in the wall, then sneak through before it was discovered and repaired, would take time, keen thinking and perseverance.

Ryan had given him the first; he would have all the time he needed to conduct a careful investigation. As for keen thinking and perseverance, Cavanaugh came into those on his own. During the seventeen years he'd been on the force, he had established a reputation for investigative skill and doggedness. He had been his own harsh taskmaster, finding satisfaction in a job well done regardless of the volume of complaints his orders sometimes inspired in the ranks beneath him.

While other detectives sometimes sought the limelight, Cavanaugh had never done so. He believed John Ryan had given him this prestigious job for precisely that reason. While they both knew that success would clinch Cavanaugh's future in the upper echelon of the department, they likewise knew that there would be no grandstanding along the way. Notwithstanding the personal vengeance Cavanaugh sought—and he had no way of knowing whether Ryan was aware of it—the Whyte-Warren investigation would be run in the same plodding, professional manner in which he had run every other investigation he had conducted.

Mindful that the investigation was now underway, Cavanaugh raised the camera that had hung by his side and trained the tele-photo lens on the mourners. He moved from one face to the next, studying and identifying those present. If the heat wilted many of the assembled crowd, the immediate family members seemed impervious to it, sheltered as they appeared to be under a canopy of sorrow. The occasional handkerchief dabbed at a tear, but for the most part the faces were still and pale.

Tripping the shutter of his camera, Cavanaugh captured the tableau, segment by segment, on film. Standing at the center of the group were the senior generation of Warrens and Whytes—Gilbert

Warren, twenty-three-year veteran of the United States House of Representatives, and his wife, Lenore, then Natalie Whyte, pressed close to her husband, Jackson, president and chairman of the board of the prestigious Whyte Estate, which encompassed, among other things, one of the country's major airlines and an electronics division with intimate ties to the government.

They were an attractive foursome, slim, dressed in elegant black, enviable even in mourning.

Their children were no less striking, though in truth they were not children, for they ranged in age from thirty to forty-four. There was the oldest, Nicholas Whyte, somber yet dashing, the heir apparent to the Whyte Estate, and his wife, Angie, a stunning woman who had been the cause of many a broken heart when she had removed Nicholas from the ranks of the eligible ten years before. There was Peter Warren, a lawyer reputedly on a supreme ego trip aimed at a judgeship, and his second wife, Sally. Beside them stood the reserved Laura Warren Garner with her husband, Donald, a renowned plastic surgeon.

Beside the elder Whytes was their youngest daughter, Anne, and her husband Mark Mitchell, both high ranking employees in the Whyte Estate. There was Emily Warren, model-turned-actress and dressed for the part in a dramatic black sheath and veil. She seem weakened by her grief and was supported—appropriately, Cavanaugh thought—by football-hero-turned-gutsy-entrepreneur Jordan Whyte.

Had he not known better, Cavanaugh might have suspected that the families were interrelated by blood. Gil Warren and Jack Whyte had similar shocks of graying hair, and while the Warren profile was more craggy around the nose and chin than the Whyte profile, above average height, broad shoulders and firm jawlines characterized the men of both families. The women had more individual looks; Natalie darker and softer than the lighter haired Lenore; and the female offspring varied in height and coloring, although one was as eye-catching as the next.

They were the beautiful people, individuals, yet not so. Studying them, Cavanaugh realized that it was the dignity of their bearing that created the strongest resemblance. The rich wore grief proudly, he thought with disdain.

Of course, these particular rich knew that they were being photographed and filmed. They were always photographed and filmed. They were a news event, providing fodder with which the media could pique the insatiable curiosities of the average Joe and Jane at home. Cavanaugh was cynical enough to realize that, grief notwithstanding, the Whytes and Warrens were skilled showpeople.

Having captured on film each of the immediate family members, Cavanaugh turned his lens on other mourners. He recognized many of them, and those he didn't know from family-related press coverage he knew from other sources. There were the grandchildren, of course, grouped among other relatives in the background. He also recognized some of Gil Warren's staffers, and members of Jack Whyte's board of directors. The rest of the crowd was made up of numerous prominent members of the political and business communities, as well as representatives of the entertainment world and miscellaneous family friends.

Surveying the crowd, Cavanaugh zoomed in on a captivating model with whom both Mark Whyte and his father had reputedly been involved. Next he focused on a local land developer who regularly contributed to Gil Warren's campaigns—and was as crooked as they came. He snapped a photograph, too, of Gil's personal secretary, whose fourteen-year-old daughter—not present—was of dubious parentage.

Cavanaugh returned his attention to the front row of mourners. He noticed four others standing slightly separate from the rest on the far side of the caskets. He recognized them only because he had been such a voracious student of the Whyte-Warren chronicles. They were the help, Jonathan and Sarah McNee, who had been serving the Whytes for years, and Cassie Morell, loyal housekeeper to the Warrens and an exceedingly attractive woman herself. Almost pixieish in stature, she wore a slim black dress with a white lace shawl collar that might have made a mockery of her occupation had not her mien been properly subdued. Her blond hair was pulled back into a neat knot at the nape of her neck, baring features that were delicate, if a bit drawn.

But it was on the last of the four people that Cavanaugh's focus lingered, on a young woman who was every bit as striking as any Warren or Whyte, though in a softer, more vulnerable way. She was Cassie's daughter, Katia, who had grown up alongside the Whyte and Warren children and had often been photographed with them. Taller than her mother, Katia was fair, with sandy blond hair cut in an artful, shoulder-length style, a delicate, triangular-shaped face and a willowy figure. She wore a stylish light gray dress with padded shoulders and a hip sash, and matching stockings and heels.

Digging into his memory bank, Cavanaugh associated her with the art world—or advertising, he wasn't quite sure. The more he thought about it, the more the latter seemed to fit her sophisticated executive look.

Of those present, he could most readily accept that her grief was genuine. Her head was bowed, hair draping gracefully against her cheek. Her mother had an arm around her waist, but Katia's own were wrapped around herself, almost as though she wanted to keen but was exerting all her control not to.

He snapped several shots of her, then watched while she slowly raised her head, gazed briefly at the ornate brass coffins, then across them, her expression one of pain and confusion. Quickly following her gaze with his lens, he focused on Jordan Whyte, who, as though beckoned by Katia's silent call met her eyes with a matching pain in his own.

Cavanaugh looked from one face to the other. The emotion was real, though its cause was a mystery. Why these two? Why the prolonged visual exchange? It was possible that Jordan and Katia were simply longtime friends sharing their sorrow. It was also possible that there was more to their relationship than even the press had discerned. Were they lovers? Or conspirators? He knew that Jordan, like many other of the Whytes and Warrens, had lost money through deals that the deceased, his brother Mark, had orchestrated. But what was a little money to someone like Jordan Whyte, who had bundles? Where was the motive? And why would Mark's wife, Deborah, have been killed, too? And Katia? Would a creature as innocent looking as she be capable of murder?

The moment ended. Katia looked down again, while Jordan returned his gaze to the coffins of his brother, a recently successful film producer, and his sister-in-law, the dreamer of the Warrens.

Lowering his camera, Cavanaugh wondered about that. A film producer and a dreamer. The official verdict—with final autopsy reports still pending—was that Mark had killed Deborah before turning the gun on himself. The gun was his own. It carried no fingerprints but his. Husband and wife had been alone on their yacht, moored in its slip on the Boston waterfront at the time of the shooting. Though there were many more people to be checked, owners of neighboring boats and residents of nearby condominiums had neither seen nor heard a thing. There had been no sign of forced entry, much less a fight.

But motive? Why would a man who had finally attained a measure of personal success have killed his innocent wife and himself?

Press reports, jumping on the opportunity for speculation, had alternately suggested that the two had fallen in with a bizarre satanic cult in California; that, childhood sweethearts, they had made a pact to die together; that Mark Whyte had been on drugs; that Deborah Warren Whyte had taken a lover on the side and had so inflamed her husband that he had been driven mad.

John Ryan had implied that Mark and Deborah had either been involved in activities or simply possessed information that might have destroyed other members of their families.

It was going to be up to Robert Cavanaugh to find out which of the quickly multiplying theories was true.

Chapter 2

KATIA MORELL LISTENED to the last of the minister's words with only half an ear. She felt numb, had felt that way since she had received the call from her mother telling her of the tragedy. Mark and Deborah—it made no sense. True, Mark had had his ups and downs. True, he ran in a faster lane than the ethereal Deborah might have preferred. But they had been in love. It seemed that they had always been in love.

It made no sense!

Katia had been relieved that the families had decided on a simple service and speedy burial. The press would follow them like hounds until they made it to the island, which she was sure they had every intention of doing once the proper ceremonies had been held in town. The island, their own private refuge off the coast of Maine, was the only place they could be free of the greedy eyes of the world.

With the light squeeze of her mother's hand at her waist, Katia emerged from her thoughts. Looking up, she saw that the families were leaving, heading toward the long black limousines that waited on the nearby drive. She sought out Jordan's head, dark and bowed among the others, and felt the clenching of a dozen fingers around her heart.

It was the first time she had seen him in nearly a year; time hadn't diminished the painful and confusing emotions she harbored. She wanted desperately to go to him but knew that this wasn't the time or place. So she turned with her mother and the McNees toward her own car, one she had rented at the airport when she had flown into Boston from New York the night before.

Without waiting for the others to start off, Katia pulled out of line and went ahead. Caterers had been brought in to provide food for the people who would be returning to Dover with the families. Cassie and the McNees had wanted to be at the cemetery for the service, but they were aware that their supervision was needed at the Warren house, which had been chosen for the reception after the funeral.

The air conditioner quickly cooled the car, making its passengers as comfortable as they could be under the circumstances. Katia concentrated on driving, if for no other reason than to relieve her mind of the heartrending images of those dual coffins. But the McNees and Cassie Morell had no such diversion.

"I still can't believe it," Cassie murmured. Even dazed, she enunciated her words carefully, as she had trained herself to do over the years so that one never knew her native language was French. "So much to live for, and it's gone. All gone." She pressed her fingertips to her temple. "Why? Why did it happen?"

In a flash of memory, Katia heard similiar words from her mother, uttered nearly nineteen years before, when Katia's older brother and only sibling, Kenneth, had died in combat thousands of miles from home. Katia had been only eleven, but she had never forgotten Cassie's pain and bitterness. Now, rather than bitterness, there was simply sadness in her mother's voice.

Sarah McNee was in a daze of her own, her eyes focused blindly on the passing scenery as she tightly clutched her husband's hand. "Mark was such an intense child," she murmured, her brogue, which she made no attempt to cover even in the happiest of times, thicker than usual. "The father couldn't understand him at all, and the missus worried terribly. He was a brooder, had a creative energy and no outlet. He had visions that were different from the others. From the start she knew he'd never make it in the business."

"But he found his own business," Katia pointed out softly, "and he was making a success of it."

Cassie grunted. "Directing films. What kind of business is that?"

"A lucrative one," Jonathan McNee injected, the lilt in his speech coated with dryness.

"But unstable."

Katia shot her mother a gentle, if dissenting glance. "Everything in life is unstable to a degree. If, God forbid, something were to happen to Gil and Lenore today, you could well be out of a job tomorrow. If my company were to be taken over by another today, I could well be out of a job tomorrow. But Mark was onto something good. He'd worked and worked for it, and finally it happened. That's one of the reasons why this is all so hard to believe."

"Directing music videos—you call that good?" Cassie mocked. "I can just imagine the kind of crowd he ran with."

"Mother, Mark was forty-three years old. It's not as though he were a child. He knew what he was doing. The films he made were good, and the music videos were frosting on the cake. God knows they were timely. Ask Jordan. His cable station is devoted solely to showing videos like the ones Mark was putting out, and he's raking it in."

Sarah leaned forward. "Jordan has the golden touch. He rakes it in regardless of what he's doing."

Katia couldn't deny that. Jordan had been phenomenally successful right from the start. Where Nick had been the model son and Mark the distracted one, Jordan, the youngest, had been the aggressive black sheep. He had been determined to strike out on his own, to shun the Whyte Estate and make an independent name for himself. Armed with his father's business acumen, not to mention the quick temper that struck fear into associates and competitors alike, he had proceeded forcefully. There had been times over the years when he had risked everything on a project, when he had weathered odds that had sent others running in the opposite direction, but he'd made it. Tenacity was one of his greater strengths.

"Deborah was pregnant," Cassie said so softly that at first Katia, who had been thinking only of Jordan at that moment, wasn't sure she had heard correctly.

"Excuse me?"

"Deborah was pregnant."

Katia sucked in a breath. "I didn't know!" She shot a glance in her rearview mirror and saw that the McNees were as startled as she, which didn't surprise her. Cassie Morell wasn't a gossip; more than that, she had never fully identified with the McNees. Though employed in the same capacity and seeing them often, she had always remained a bit apart.

"It had just been confirmed," Cassie admitted. "I heard Mrs. Warren telling the congressman about it the other day. Deborah didn't want anyone else to know until she was further along."

Shaken, Katia gripped the steering wheel more tightly. "Do you think it was possible that Mark didn't want the child?"

"I don't know."

"Or that *she* didn't want the child?"

"I don't know."

"Could she and Mark have argued about it?"

"I don't *know.* I only heard one side of the story. Mrs. Warren was frightened. After what Deborah went through with the last one, it's understandable." Desperately wanting a child, Deborah had conceived four years before and carried to term, only to suffer a stillbirth. "They were pleased, the senior Warrens were. They felt that if all went well it would be the best thing for Deborah. It had to have been hard on her, what with Mark running here, there and everywhere."

Katia might have argued that Deborah had known what she had been getting into when she had married Mark, but it seemed pointless. They were dead. Both of them. That fact shocked her each time it registered.

"God, it seems like yesterday that we were kids, so carefree, just playing together . . ." she whispered, letting her words trail off as fragments of the past flashed through her mind. Her passengers grew quiet too, lost in thoughts of their own. Katia was almost sorry to approach Dover and realize that the toughest part was yet to come.

When she had arrived the night before it had been late. Wanting to be with her mother, to console and be consoled, she'd gone straight to the small cottage at the rear of the Warren house where she had lived as a child. She hadn't seen the Warrens or the Whytes other than at the cemetery. Now she would be with them, as she had been for so much of her life. Their grief would magnify her own, she knew. Their devastation would make hers that much more real.

Taking a deep breath, she turned off the main road onto the private way that led, in turn, to a fork. Several hundred yards to the left was the elegant colonial stone farmhouse of the Whytes. Several hundred yards to the right, where she now headed, was the stately Georgian colonial of the Warrens.

As a child, Katia had wondered why two families who shared so much and had even bought abutting pieces of land at the very same time had chosen to build such different style homes. When she had questioned her mother, Cassie had simply said that different women had different tastes, which had puzzled Katia all the more, since even her child's mind saw that Jack and Gil were the ones in command.

Only when she had grown older had she understood that the houses had been consolation prizes. Jack and Gil were indeed the ones in power, basking in the limelight, reaping the glory. Their wives took back seats and were often alone. It was in token deference to them that the men had stood aside when the houses were being designed.

Hence different styles representing different personalities. Natalie Whyte, in her charming stone farmhouse, was a far warmer woman than Lenore Warren, in her more pretentious Georgian colonial, could ever be.

Which was another bit of anguish Katia felt for Deborah. Deborah, who had been gentle and giving, wanting nothing more than to love and be loved, whose mother was stern and whose father was absent, who had wanted a child and had been denied it, twice, by death.

Who said the rich didn't bleed? she asked herself in anger.

Pulling in beside her mother's cottage, well behind the caterers' trucks, Katia parked the car. She sat at the wheel for a minute to regain her composure, then quietly followed the others toward the main house.

At the door, Cassie turned back to instruct her gently, "I don't want you working while you're here, Katia."

"Why not? You are."

"It's my job, not yours."

"But I can help."

"You're a guest."

"A guest in my own home?"

"You know what I mean."

Katia did. In many ways it was the crux of the dilemma she had grappled with for years. Who was she? Where did she belong? On one hand this was her home. She had grown up a Whyte-Warren, the adopted little sister of the others. She had attended school with them, had taken dancing and skating lessons with them. She had had free run of the houses, the grounds, the stables. She had spent Thanksgivings at the Whytes, Christmases at the Warrens. And during the summers she had gone to the island.

She had never wanted for anything. Still, her mother was the hired help.

From the time Katia had been old enough to understand that she and her brother were lower in status than the others, she had wondered at the material advantages she and Kenny had. Cassie had alternately attributed the fine clothes, the skating lessons, the spending money to prudent budgeting on her part and generosity on the part of the Warrens, but Katia came to realize that Cassie would have done most anything in the world to see that her children rose above her own station in life.

Through her high school years, Katia had straddled a socioeconomic fence. She could play the game with little effort, acting the part of a Warren or Whyte. Few people beyond her immediate group of friends knew that she was the daughter of the housekeeper. But she knew, and that knowledge added to the inevitable confusion of adolescence. She felt increasingly awkward eating dinner with the Warrens while her mother ate separately in the kitchen. She felt compelled to help around the house, then self-conscious when she did so. She grew increasingly uncomfortable going to the country club with the others when she didn't belong to it herself.

When it came time for college, Katia knew she had to break out on her own. Rather than apply to Wellesley or Radcliffe or Smith, as her mother had wanted her to do, she applied and was accepted on full scholarship to New York University. There she hoped to find anonymity, and, in time, herself.

New York City was also where Jordon Whyte was.

"Katia?" Her mother urged her back to the present with a gentle shake and a look of concern. "Are you all right?"

Katia stared at her for a moment's reorientation, then smiled. "I'm fine."

"And you *do* know what I mean. You're a career woman now. A *successful* career woman. Your mother may be the housekeeper here, but you—you are on par with any one of the Warrens or Whytes, or, for that matter, any of the guests that may be here today." She touched Katia's hair, stroking it lightly. The gesture was from the heart, emerging as a moment's digression from the dictates of Cassie's brain. Katia had always been aware of that dichotomy in her mother, who loved with extreme gentleness yet was driven by quiet obsession. "I want you to hold your head high."

"I think I'm holding *your* head high," Katia teased, then stood aside as a waiter carried a platter of food in from one of the trucks. Cassie waited for him to pass before responding.

"I'm proud of you," she said with conviction, then enclosed her daughter in a firm hug. "I won't deny that. I have a right to be proud, don't you think?"

Katia took pleasure in the moment's closeness. "I've tried. God knows, I've tried."

"Cassie?" Sarah's slightly frantic call came from the kitchen, her plump figure following seconds later. "They can't find the percolator! I've looked everywhere!"

Cassie reluctantly released Katia, giving her hand a final squeeze before turning to Sarah. "You simply haven't looked in the right place," she answered gently as she went off to unearth the elusive item.

Behind her Katia smiled, as proud of her mother as her mother was of her. It hadn't always been that way. For a time during those high school years when she had questioned her identity so strongly, she had been ashamed of Cassie's position. She had been angry that her mother wasn't a pillar of society, angry that certain guests of the Warrens looked down their noses at them both, angry that she couldn't impress friends by inviting them to the house for dinner.

And she had been torn. There were times when her heart had ached at the knowledge that her mother's fate in life was to make other people's beds. Even when she had reminded herself that Cassie didn't actually do that—there was a maid hired to do nothing but the cleaning, and there was a cook whose veal piccata was as sensational as his Belgian waffles—the hurt remained.

Only when Katia went away to college, when she mixed for the first time with people from all stations in life, did she develop the pride and understanding she felt now.

Cassie's job was to oversee the Warren household and ensure that it ran smoothly. She did that well. She was in control. In hindsight, Katia saw that this facet of her mother's personality had provided a source of stability to Katia's upbringing.

Now, wandering past workers who scurried from room to room in the spacious first floor of the house, Katia marveled at all that her mother governed. The Warren house was magnificent. Each time she returned, she appreciated it more. From the Hepplewhite sideboard and gleaming mahogany table and chairs in the dining room to the double-faced sofas and chintz-covered wing chairs in the living room and the elegant spiral staircase in the huge front hall—it was the stuff of which dreams were made.

Still, Katia was content with her small but stylish apartment in New York. Sinking onto the needlepoint-covered bench by the grand piano in the living room, Katia knew that if she had ever aspired to call these things her own, she did no more. Where once she had thought that the Warrens and Whytes had to be the luckiest people in the world, now she knew differently.

Luck had little to do with wealth and power, and neither of those guaranteed happiness. Mark and Deborah were a case in point. . . .

The sound of tires on the circular drive outside brought Katia's head around. Heart racing, she rose from the bench and hurried to open the front door. A wave of heat struck her, seeming to thicken the pall of sadness cast by the arrival of the ominously black limousines.

The first had come to a stop and the senior Warrens were stepping out. Lenore looked distinctly wobbly. Her son-in-law, Donald, supported her, while Gil turned to help Laura and the children.

Katia stood at the front door, her heart breaking for them all. She hugged Laura, who reached her first, then Donald, and, as the children scampered into the house, she put a gentle arm around Lenore's waist and pressed her cheek to hers.

"I'm so sorry, Mrs. Warren," she whispered. "So sorry."

Lenore didn't return the embrace, though Katia hadn't expected her to. She had never quite accepted Katia as the others had done, and Katia understood. Her heart went out to the woman in more ways than one.

After Lenore passed into the house, there were hugs for Peter, his wife and their two sons, then a prolonged one for Emily. Of all the Whyte-Warren siblings, Emily was closest in age to Katia. They had been bosom buddies once upon a time, and though they had gone their separate ways in the last ten years, the affection they had shared as children remained intact.

"What can I say, Em?" Katia said softly. "It shouldn't have happened."

"I know," was all Emily could manage. Clutching her veil in one hand, she groped blindly behind with the other to draw her companion forward. "Katia . . . Andrew."

Katia nodded, sure that Andrew, beautiful and cocky on sight, was an actor, but equally as sure that he wasn't one she recognized. At that moment, however, she saw Gilbert Warren approach. Apologizing in a glance to Emily and Andrew, she moved past them and descended three shallow steps to meet him.

Her heart wrenching in sympathy, she hesitated before Gil for an instant. He finally moved forward and took her in his arms, hugging her tightly.

"Katia," he breathed hoarsely. "I'm glad you're here."

She felt it then, the special something they shared, and she held him every bit as tightly for a fleeting moment. "I wish it were any other occasion than this, Gil. You know how I felt about Deborah."

For a minute, Gil didn't speak. When he stepped back he studied Katia's face. Then, smiling sadly, he brushed the back of his hand against her cheek. It was a gesture he had made many, many times in Katia's life, as familiar to her as the trace of cherry-scented pipe tobacco that clung to his clothes.

"I'm glad you're here," he repeated brokenly. Taking her elbow, he led her toward the house. "You should have come to see us last night."

"I . . . it wasn't my place to do that, with everyone else here."

"We would have liked it. It's been too long since we've seen you."

"How is Lenore holding up?"

"Not well. My guess is that she'll make it through another hour before she goes on up to bed."

He didn't have to elaborate. Lenore sought the seclusion of her bedroom when something bothered her, and it seemed that something was always bothering her. Which was another thing Katia had come to admire in Cassie, who, along with Natalie Whyte, had been more of a mother to the Warren brood than Lenore. If the world only knew.

"And you?" Katia asked, aware that Gil looked pale and more tired than she had ever seen him. "Are you okay?"

He shrugged, then attempted a smile that failed sadly. "I'll make it."

They were in the front hall. Gil pressed a gentle kiss to Katia's forehead. Then, without another word, he straightened his shoulders and retraced his steps to the front walk. He was going to greet his constituents. Katia should have been dismayed, but she knew Gil too well. Politics was in his blood. One either had to love him as he was or despise him. Katia had simply chosen the former.

The stream through the front door resumed with the arrival of the Whytes. Katia shared heartfelt embraces with each, first Natalie, who looked numb; then Jack, who looked distracted; then Anne, her husband and their four-year-old daughter. Nick and Angie followed with their four children in tow.

And Jordan. Katia held her breath when he stopped before her, then her heart began to hammer. He looked weary, but wonderful. His dark hair was longer than that of either his brother or father, falling across his brow in front, teasing his collar in back. He had already removed his suit jacket, loosened his tie and released the top button of his shirt—less in deference to the heat, Katia guessed, than to the natural energy that filled him. He had never been one to be constrained; even time hadn't changed that. Time had, however, etched tiny crows' feet at the corners of his eyes and slashed rakish grooves by his mouth. They were signs of good humor, though they were pale now in the absence of laughter.

"Oh, Jordan," Katia whispered, her eyes filling with tears. When he opened his arms she melted into them, suddenly overwhelmed by a deep inner conflict. She was so very happy to see him, to feel him, yet so grieved at the circumstances. Clinging to him, she wept softly, not at all surprised that his presence had unleashed her emotions, because it had always been that way for her with Jordan. He had been her idol, her protector. She had adored him from the time she had been four years old. He had always been there for her, never failing to make her feel special.

He held her tightly, absorbing her anguish even as his arms trembled with his own. When her tears ebbed, he brushed them gently from her cheeks, then wrapped his arms around her again and rocked her slowly. She drew strength from him, finding comfort in the sturdiness of his body and the light stroking of his cheek against her hair.

At last she looked up. "Why, Jordan? *Why?*" The beseechful question could have referred to many things in her life, in their lives, but the immediate tragedy was foremost in both their minds.

Jordan took a deep breath, let it out, then spoke for the first time. His voice was as tortured as his expression. "I don't know. God only knows I've asked myself the same question a thousand times in the past day and a half, but for the life of me I can't find an answer." His eyes grew moist as he looked down at her. Then he looked back up and around to see that relatives and family friends had begun to overtake them. A hand patted his shoulder; another squeezed his arm. Each was accompanied by a murmured word or two of condolence before the giver passed by.

"Come on," he said softly to Katia, wrapping an arm around her shoulder and anchoring her close to his side as he began to walk. He gazed down at her. "You've been a stranger for the past year." When she neither tried to deny nor justify the truth of his statement, he went on. "You look wonderful."

"I look awful." She brushed her thumb beneath each of her eyes in search of runaway mascara.

"No, wonderful. You were always beautiful, but you get more so each time I see you."

"And you were always a flatterer, Jordan Whyte."

He didn't argue, because she was right. He had been saying pretty things to women since he was twelve years old. What Katia didn't know was that when he complimented *her*, he meant every word. "I think life as an art director agrees with you." They entered the living room, their conversation now muted by the quiet drone of the gathering crowd.

"It's hectic. Life at any level of an ad agency is, I suppose—and we're far from the biggest. But I like it."

"You've earned your spot. The men aren't still giving you trouble, are they?"

"When they need a scapegoat. But I'll survive." The choice of words had been innocent on her part, yet they evoked more somber thoughts. Her expression grew pained. "Suicide . . . I'd never have expected it of Mark, much less . . . murder. Are they sure? Are they absolutely sure that someone didn't sneak onto the boat?"

Jordan drew her to the same piano bench on which she had been sitting earlier. For as many times in the past as they had sat here, laughing while Jordan had pounded out bawdy tunes on the keys, their thoughts now were sober, solely on the present.

"They're investigating." He snorted. "Famous last words."

"How long does it take to go over one boat?"

"Not long with the naked eye, but much longer in the lab. The preliminary report shows no evidence of foul play by an intruder."

"Did Mark have enemies?"

"We all did—do."

"Any who would kill?"

"I don't know." He frowned, seeming to struggle while he absently stroked Katia's hand. "Mark and I have had our differences. Over the years he's done some really dumb things."

"Those bad investments?"

"Those . . . and other things."

She was about to prod further when a couple approached. Though she didn't recognize the pair, Jordan did. He stood and greeted them quietly. Katia managed a polite smile when he introduced her, but her attention quickly wandered from the solemn interchange.

Across the room, Jack Whyte stood with a group of businessmen, seemingly engrossed in the discussion. By the door, having just entered, Gil Warren was similarly occupied with his followers. They were two of a kind, Katia mused. From the looks of them, the gathering might as well have been a casual cocktail party as a funeral.

Some distance away Natalie Whyte stood with her arm around Lenore Warren's waist. Friends surrounded them, and Katia had to wonder whether the attention was a help or a burden. Jack and Gil thrived on it; it was their world. Their wives, however, weren't as single-minded or resilient. Natalie looked as though she wanted to cry but wouldn't, while Lenore looked as though she needed to cry but couldn't.

Anne, Jordan's younger sister, was quite openly in tears. Sitting in a corner of the sofa, hugging her daughter to her, she seemed to have simply lost control. Katia had so much she wanted to say to Jordan, but this wasn't the time. She met his gaze, then turned a worried glance back to Anne.

Quickly sizing up the situation, he nodded. "See if you can help her," he urged softly. "I'll catch you later." With a soft kiss on the top of her head, he headed off, stopping at nearly every turn to greet one familiar face or another. Katia followed his progress until he disappeared from view, at which point she worked her way toward Anne.

"Annie," she said softly, lowering herself to the sofa and putting an arm around her friend. "Shh. It's all right."

Anne pressed her eyes tightly shut and took a ragged breath, then slowly raised her head and looked at Katia. "I said such awful things to him," she whispered in despair. "It was so unpleasant the last time we were together."

Katia leaned forward and stroked little Amanda's head. "There are all kinds of goodies in the dining room, sweetheart. Why don't you go get some? I'll bet your cousins are already there."

Amanda didn't need any more urging. With the loosening of her mother's arms, she was on her way. Only then did Katia turn back to Anne. "We've all said awful things at one time or another. But there are good times to remember. Wouldn't it be better to think of those?"

"I try, but I keep hearing the other words and wishing I could take them back. But I can't. It's too late. Why did he do it, Katia? What could have possibly been in his mind?"

"We never quite knew, did we?"

"No. Isn't it sad? He was always a little bit odd. And a little bit foolish." She paused. "Poor Deborah. You knew that she'd been in therapy since . . . since the baby?"

"Yes."

"Mark needed it, too. Dad wouldn't hear of any son of *his* having psychiatric treatment, but Mother still suggested it, and Mark hit the roof. It had gotten worse and worse each time he visited."

"What had?" Though she had kept abreast of his activities, Katia hadn't seen Mark in a very long time.

"His talk of money, of fame. He was obsessed with it. Really obnoxious." Her gaze grew pleading. "We weren't ever like that, were we, Katia? You know us better than anyone does. Were we ever obnoxious about what we had?"

"Of course not." If the press had on occasion suggested differently, envy was to blame.

"Money was never a be-all and end-all."

"No." Certainly not among Anne's generation of Warrens and Whytes. "You never flaunted what you had. But Mark went through money pretty quickly at one point. Maybe it became more important to him because of that. He'd been doing well recently, though, hadn't he?"

"I thought so. We all did. He certainly talked enough about all he was making. But when he and Deborah were here a month ago, he came to see me at the house and asked for a loan. When I asked what it was for he wouldn't answer, and when I accused him of being up to his ears in no good, he really blew. That was when . . . when I said those ugly things." Her voice broke. "Maybe if I'd been calmer, if I'd talked with him, tried to understand what he was going through. . . ."

Katia tightened her arm around Anne's shoulder. "You can't

blame yourself for what happened, Anne. Mark was his own person."

"He was my brother." Her eyes filled again. "You had a brother once, Katia. How did you feel when he died?"

Taken aback by the question, Katia considered it for a moment. "Sad. Angry. Confused. I was too young to feel guilt, and besides, it was a different situation."

"Well, I do feel guilt. Lots of it."

"It's unproductive, and you happen to be one of the most productive women I know. So what are you going to do about it?"

Katia's bluntness was just what Anne needed. She stared at Katia for a minute, opened her mouth to argue, then closed it again and sighed. "Nothing. There's nothing to do . . . but go on, I guess." At Katia's nod of agreement, Anne grew more thoughtful. "You're good, Katia. You're a good person."

"So are you. All of you."

"I don't know about that. We've had things our way for so long that we're spoiled. When something like this happens it drives us crazy. There's no way we can buy either Mark or Deborah back, but I swear Daddy would try to bribe God if he knew where to find Him."

"Any parent would do that. Jack isn't unique."

"But you are." Anne quickly turned the conversation back to Katia. "You've done well, and all on your own."

"I had a pretty good start here."

"But beyond that. You could have come to work with us in the business, but you wouldn't. And you refused to go down to Washington and work with Gil."

"I needed to establish my own identity."

"Well, you have. I only hope Jordan sees it before it's too late."

Katia's heart skipped a beat. "Jordan? What's Jordan got to do with this?"

"You'd be good for him."

"I'm like his sister."

"But you're not. There's always been something special between you two. And since you've broken up with Sean. . . ."

Katia sighed. "Anne, your brother has his pick of the most gorgeous women in the world. Every time I see his picture in the paper he's got a different one on his arm. What does he need *me* for?"

"Love, marriage, children."

"Maybe he's not ready to settle down."

"He's thirty-nine, for God's sake. What's he waiting for?"

Katia didn't have an answer for that. Instead she gave a sheepish grin. "To lose his third million and make his fourth?"

Anne found nothing amusing in Katia's attempt at humor. "Are you dating again?"

"Yes."

"Seeing someone special?"

"No."

"Do you love Jordan?"

Katia's gaze skittered unseeingly across the maze of bodies in the room. She was unprepared for this discussion, not so much because she didn't know the answer to Anne's question, but because it was so far afield from the cause for the present gathering. She had wanted to comfort Anne. Apparently she had succeeded too well.

Frowning, she took a deep breath and looked back at Anne. "I love all of you. You know that."

"But isn't what you feel for Jordan different?"

"We live in the same city, but we don't see each other often. He's busy. He travels a lot. So do I."

"You didn't answer my question."

"I can't. Jordan and I—"

"I'm going to speak to him."

"You will *not!*" Katia exclaimed. Then, aware of the people close by, she quickly lowered her voice again. "Please, Anne. Don't."

"Why not? He's my brother. You're right; there's nothing I can do now to help Mark. Jordan is another matter."

"Jordan doesn't need help."

"That's debatable."

"But he's happy as he is."

"He's a fool. If he doesn't grab you soon, someone else will."

Katia wasn't so sure about that. She had tried. Oh, yes, she'd tried. She had dated often over the years, had even nurtured her relationship with Sean for four long years in the desperate hope that it would evolve into love. Unfortunately, neither Sean nor any other man she had met appealed to her as Jordan did.

Of course, she wouldn't tell Anne that. Some things were sacred.

So she resorted to humor. "And what would *I* want with *Jordan?* He's on the verge of bankruptcy as often as not, staking his life's savings on one bizarre project or another. He buys hockey teams that are in the cellar, buildings that are infested with rats, original art that looks like the studio drop cloth. He is totally irreverent and utterly incorrigible. He goes in the out door and up the down escalator. He can't make it through a day without a macadamia nut fix. And beyond that, he's a daredevil in a sailboat, a maniac on a horse, a glutton in an ice cream parlor, and he snores."

"How do you know that?" Anne asked, her eyes narrowed.

"Because he's fallen asleep any number of times on this very sofa, smack in the middle of family parties!"

Anne brushed a finger along her lower lip. "Mmm. You may be right. He's not much of a prize at that, is he?" Slanting Katia a mischievous grin, she started to stand, but after a pause she instead leaned over and gave her a hug. "Thanks," she said softly, and there was a catch in her voice. "Things were pretty hairy at the cemetery. But there is more to life than death, isn't there?"

It was a rhetorical question, one Katia was to repeat silently any number of times during the next few hours. Lenore, as expected, retired to the upper level of the house, while Natalie moved slowly and quietly among their guests. Jack and Gil skillfully worked the crowd, albeit in lower tones and with a moderation of the backslapping that was their usual style. The rest of the Whytes and the Warrens mingled accordingly.

Katia moved from group to group, talking softly with family members, greeting their friends whom she knew and making acquaintances with others. Yes, the deaths were shocking. And tragic. And perplexing. No, there had been no warning of serious trouble from either Deborah or Mark. Yes, it was a useless waste of lives.

She found the air of mourning oppressive and almost wished she could shoulder it as gallantly as Gil and Jack did. Unable to eat, she drank coffee. When her hands began to shake she simply held them more tightly in her lap. When her head began to throb she gulped down two aspirin in the kitchen. And when she had begun to pray for the day to end, Jordan came to her rescue.

She was in the dining room talking distractedly to a friend of Nicholas Whyte's, when Jordan pressed himself wickedly close to her back.

"I need help," he breathed by her ear. "I'm going mad." He looked up at the man who had been talking to Katia. "You'll excuse us?" Without waiting for an answer, he took Katia's hand and strode quickly through the dining room into the kitchen, heading for the back door. She had to trot to keep up, but she didn't mind. The promise of a break—and with Jordan, no less—was wildly welcome.

He didn't stop when he reached the back steps, but continued at the same demanding pace until the house, then the stables had been left far behind and they had entered the apple grove. Only then did his step grow more relaxed, but he kept on walking.

He didn't speak. Words were unnecessary. Katia understood that he needed to expel the nervous energy that had gathered within him, and she found herself doing the same. Even the heat seemed a respite from the gloom in the house, and though the sadness of the day couldn't be completely blotted from her mind, it was lessened by the sweet smell of the grass, the sight of new apples growing in the trees, the buzz of a bee. The world was alive, reassuringly so.

They walked a while longer, through a large stand of lush maples and pines, and then along the low stone fence that bordered the property before returning more slowly to the house. At the back steps, Jordan finally stopped. Dropping Katia's hand for the first time, he propped his forearms on the wooden stoop, hung his head and took several long deep breaths.

Sweat trickled down his cheeks. His hair was damp, curling slightly on his neck. As Katia watched, he flexed the muscles of his shoulders. So broad, she thought. And tense. Still tense.

Wanting only to comfort him, she began to work lightly at the knots in his lower back. His low moan told her that her ministrations were appreciated, which, in turn, encouraged her to continue. She would have done so for hours had the circumstances allowed it. Touching him was a delight.

"Mmm, Katia. You've been the only bright spot in a fucking lousy day."

"This is the worst of it," she ventured softly. "Things will get better."

"I wish I could believe that," was his muffled response. "The press is going to have a field day with this one. It's already started. 'The Romeo and Juliet of the eighties; star-crossed lovers die in each other's arms.' The media loves this kind of thing. I'd lay money on the fact that within a week someone will call wanting to do a book on Mark and Deborah. Or a TV movie. It nauseates me."

"But it's nothing new. They've always been after you."

"After me, I don't care. After Mark and Deborah, who aren't around any longer to defend themselves—that does bother me. And the worst of it is that the one to really suffer will be my mother."

"She's a strong woman, Jordan," Katia said, thinking with admiration of how Natalie Whyte had kept her proud bearing throughout the day.

"You bet." His tone was bitter. "It can't have been easy living with Dad all these years—or without him, which is really more the case. She didn't deserve that, and she doesn't deserve this. She may be strong, but no one can be *that* strong."

"Then we'll have to help her. We'll have to give her back some of the strength she's given us over the years."

Jordan straightened and turned to face Katia. "Come to the island with us," he said with quiet urgency. "We'll be leaving in the morning. Come with us."

Katia swallowed, struggling to find the right words. "I don't know, Jordan. I'd think you'd all want to be alone."

"But you're family."

"Not really."

"Yes!" he said with a sudden fire, then as quickly lowered his voice. "You've been away too much recently, but it doesn't have to be." He paused. "What did you tell them at work?"

"That I wanted to be at the funeral. They'd all read the papers."

"How long do you have off?"

"I have meetings set for tomorrow afternoon."

"Change them," he urged. "You're in a position to do it, and they couldn't possibly find fault, given the cause."

Katia pulled a sarcastic face. "They'd find fault."

"Then screw them! They need you far more than you need them."

"Not true."

"*We* need you." He sucked in a breath, and his tone grew soft and beseeching. "*I* need you. Come to Maine, Katia. Please?"

Held captive by the pleading in his eyes, she knew she had no choice. Long ago she had fallen under Jordan Whyte's spell; neither time nor the distance she had purposely put between them over the past few years had diminished its grasp. If it had been Em, or Anne, or one of the others asking, she would have been able to put up more of a fight. But where Jordan was concerned she was completely unarmed. If he needed her she would go.

With a tiny smile and a swelling heart, she nodded.

Chapter 3

KATIA SPENT THE EARLY HOURS of the next morning procrastinating. It wasn't that she was afraid to call New York, but she wasn't looking forward to the inevitable argument. So she tidied the cottage, though it needed little tidying, and packed her things, though she had precious little to pack. She showered leisurely, washed and dried her hair, then pulled on a pair of shorts and a t-shirt that had been among the few of her clothes still remaining in Dover.

Shortly before nine, with a sense of resignation, she picked up the phone. Roger Boland, her creative supervisor, was at his desk, well into his day as she had known he would be. Of the management people at the ad agency, she was closest to Roger. If anyone would be sympathetic to her cause, she knew it would be he.

But he wasn't. "Hell, Katia, you *have* to get back here! We were supposed to review the storyboards for that beer commercial today."

"I know, but—"

"You have to pick out the bedroom set you want for the mattress ad, and Accounting is expecting a progress report on the perfume commercial."

"I know, but—"

"There's a mile-high stack of portfolios sitting on your desk. You've got to pick the illustrator you want for—"

"The diamond ad. Roger, I *know*. But this is important. It's not as though I'm taking a vacation."

"You went to the funeral. What more do they want?"

Katia clutched the phone tighter. "It's what *I* want that matters, and I want to stay with them for a few days. The storyboards are on my desk; you can look at them yourself. Accounting can wait a little while longer for that progress report. Donna can pick out the bedroom set; she was planning to go with me anyway, and she knows what I want. And the illustrators' portfolios will still be there when I get back. Monday morning, Roger. I'll be in the office Monday morning."

"Did you know he was selling coke?"

"Excuse me?"

"Mark Whyte. He was selling coke."

"That's trash. I don't believe it for a minute."

"And Deborah Warren was pregnant."

"That I did know. How did *you?*"

"It was in the autopsy report."

Katia began to burn. "And how did you find out about the autopsy report?" To her knowledge, the police hadn't been expecting the results until late the previous night.

"It was in the paper. Rumor has it that it wasn't his kid."

"Of course it was!"

"There's no proof."

"*Either* way. So shouldn't we give the woman the benefit of the doubt? She's gone now, dead . . . What paper was this, anyway?"

There was a pause, then a slightly sheepish, "The *Post*."

Katia snorted. "And you thought you were reading Gospel? Come on, Roger. Since when do you read the *Post*?"

"Since I made it my business seventeen years ago. I have to see who's advertising what and how."

"Then look at the pictures, not the words."

"Speaking of pictures, you should see the one on the front page of Mark Whyte hugging a spike-haired singer while his wife looks on in the background."

"Mark *worked* with spike-haired singers, which doesn't mean that he was having affairs with them in front of his wife."

"His father did. Why shouldn't *he?*"

"Jack never had an affair with a spike-haired singer."

"You know what I mean," was Roger's answering growl.

She sighed wearily. "I really don't want to talk about this."

"But don't you see what you're getting into? Those families are rats' nests."

" 'Those families' are my family. And they're my friends."

"Some friends. Did you know that Jack Whyte just made a killing buying up stock for a hostile takeover, then selling it at a huge margin when the company found a white knight?"

"There's nothing illegal in that."

Roger ignored her point. "And Gil Warren spends more tax-payers' money per constituent on mailings than any other representative. Did you know *that?*"

"Gil takes full advantage of the congressional franking privilege."

"He takes advantage of it, all right—to help his own reelection campaign."

"Look, we may not agree with what he does, but it's within the law."

"It may be, but that doesn't mean it doesn't stink. And Jordan Whyte isn't any better. He bought an apartment building on Central Park South and converted it into condominiums, in the process forcing out many of the middle income families who'd lived there for years."

Katia may not have seen Jordan often of late, but unable to help herself, she had kept up with his activities. "He offered them generous deals if they wanted to buy in."

"But they couldn't afford even *that!*" Roger declared. "And while we're on the subject of pressure tactics, do you know what the guy did last week? When one of his biggest cable advertisers—they make fruit juice in those little cartons—threatened to pull out, claiming that the music was increasingly obscene, Jordan had his VJs invite write-ins about the product. The mail room was inundated with positive letters. The advertiser suddenly decided the music wasn't so obscene."

Katia grinned. "Very clever of Jordan."

"Come on. He's an arrogant son of a bitch who wants his own way all the time."

"So do we. We just can't get it as often as he does. Face it, Roger, he's magic."

"Black magic," Roger answered.

"You're jealous."

"You bet I am. They get you there when I want you here. We're up to our ears in clients—"

"Are you complaining?"

"About clients, no. About you taking off, yes. I mean, you should see my desk." He paused, and Katia could just see him waving his hand over what could well be declared a disaster area. "I've got files and reports and mock-ups and sketches, and now you tell me that half of them will have to sit here awhile longer."

Katia was totally without sympathy. "Organization, Roger. That's the key. I've told you so before."

"Organization is incompatible with creativity."

"Mmm. Boland's Law number four-thirty-seven. I can't criticize it, because it works for you, but it doesn't work for me. So," she took a deep breath, "you'll find everything organized on my desk. Help yourself to the storyboards and whatever else you need today and tomorrow, and I'll be back in on Monday to take care of the rest."

"There'll be that much more to take care of by then," he warned sourly.

"One day at a time. That's Morell's Law number one."

Roger had worked with Katia long enough to know when she had her mind set. She was agreeable and generally flexible, but when she dug in her heels, as her tone of voice suggested now, there was no moving her. "You're a stubborn bitch."

"I know."

"Should I tell it to the boss when he wanders in here looking for you?"

"Be my guest."

Roger sighed. "Monday? No ifs, ands or buts?"

"Monday. See you then, Roger."

Six cars filled with Whytes and Warrens made their way to Portland, Maine, later that morning. Katia had left earlier with her mother and the McNees, and while they went to the market to stock up on food, she headed for the nearest specialty shops to supplement the meager contents of her suitcase. The few clothes she had brought with her from New York were far too dressy for the island. So she treated herself to appropriate casual wear, rationalizing the purchases with the knowledge that the few times she had shopped in the city this season had been devoted largely to buying clothes for work.

Skilled at making the most of each minute, she dashed from store to store. Her trained eye quickly spotted items in colors and styles that complimented her—a pale pink shorts outfit, one in mint green, a pair of white jeans, an oversized, hand-painted teal blue and white sweatshirt, a fuschia maillot. Any guilt she felt was not in the size of the bill she ran up, but in the gaiety of the colors she chose.

There was more to life than death, wasn't there?

At the appointed time she returned to the market. No less than three bag boys helped load groceries into the trunk and back seat of the car. From the market it was a mercifully short drive to the pier, where a yacht was waiting to take the family entourage to the island.

The other cars arrived shortly after they did. Suitcases were transferred to the boat and the cars were parked and locked in a private lot nearby. One by one, the various family members who were making the trip boarded the boat. Nicholas Whyte had decided to remain in Boston with his wife and children, as had Laura Warren's husband and the oldest of their boys. The rest of the

Whytes and Warrens were present, along with Carl Greene, Gil's press secretary, who would man the phones at the island.

Sun dappled the deck, as cheerful as the travelers were grim. Though the senior Whytes and Warrens took refuge in the salon below, the others remained sprawled in the lounge chairs they had collapsed onto after boarding. Even the children were subdued in their play.

Katia was at the brass rail on the foredeck, watching the hypnotic motion of the sleek craft slicing through the water when Jordan joined her. He closed his hand over hers and stared ahead where, twenty-five miles to sea, the island waited.

"You called New York?" he asked quietly.

"Uh-huh."

"Everything's okay?"

She paused, then nodded.

"They've seen the papers." Sensitive to the faint twitch of her fingers, he shot her a dry, sidelong glance. "The phones started ringing first thing this morning. Not that the Boston papers were much better. They're jumping on anything they can get."

"How can they do what they do?" she asked in despair.

"It's news, so they say."

"But the autopsy report . . . you'd think that the police department could have waited until . . . until this morning, at least, to release it. Wasn't there anything either Jack or Gil could have done?"

"They considered it. They stood around late last night shouting threats at the walls, but what's the point? There would have been splashy headlines about a court order having been sought, and that would have *really* sparked speculation, which would have been more condemning than the report itself."

"Which said?"

Jordan's face was set in grim lines. "That sometime around one in the morning they both died from single bullets fired at point blank range. That Deborah was pregnant. That they'd each had a drink or two that evening."

His voice hadn't settled. She waited, watching his pained profile, then said softly, "A drink or two wouldn't have hurt. Both of them knew how to hold their liquor. What about drugs?"

"Nothing, thank God."

"Did Mark use them?"

"He snorted coke sometimes, but it looks like he wasn't high at the time of the shootings."

"Did he deal?"

Jordan's gaze shot to her. "Where did you hear that?"

"I . . . Roger mentioned it when I called in this morning. I told him he was crazy."

"Where did *he* hear it?"

"He didn't say. I'm sure it was just rumor."

Jordan faced the sea again, but his profile was rife with tension. He didn't speak, simply gnawed on the inside of his cheek.

"Was it, Jordan? Was it just rumor?"

"I'd like to think so."

"But you're not sure."

There was a pause, then a nearly inaudible, "No."

Closing her eyes, Katia threw back her head and let the brisk breeze wash over her, as though it could dispel her mental torment. "I keep trying to figure out how Mark could have pulled that trigger himself, but I can't. He was—"

"A coward."

She shrugged in agreement. "When we were kids he was always the one to get everyone else into trouble. He'd propose something wild—"

"Like riding bareback through the streets of Dover at midnight?"

"Mmm." A sad smile touched her lips. She had been eight at the time, but she clearly remembered how Emily had crept into the cottage to awaken her and Kenny, how Peter had argued that she shouldn't have been brought along, even as Jordan defiantly boosted her onto the horse's back. "Mark stayed behind. He was tucked safely in bed by the time the police rounded us up and brought us home."

"That was Mark. All talk, no action."

"Did he change so much? I mean, to go ahead and actually pull that trigger. . . ."

"I don't think he did it either," was Jordan's taut reply. "But the alternative is almost as bad." He took in a breath, then grew abruptly silent, seeming to want to say something but deciding against it. "He needed money. There was a particular film he wanted to produce and direct. It was an artsy thing, a long shot, the kind of picture that might develop a small cult following, if that. He couldn't get financial backing on his own, so he approached several of us, but we'd been burned once too often by his wild ideas." He bit his lip and released it slowly. "There's money in drugs. It may be filthy, but it's still green."

"It also attracts enemies."

"Deadly ones. If someone went to the effort of committing a double murder, he must have had a powerful motive. And it wasn't any amateur who stole onto that boat without leaving the slightest trace as a calling card. Whoever it was knew what he was doing."

"Have the police found anything yet?"

"Nothing that they're telling us." He seemed nervous, then angry. "It may be that there really is nothing yet, or that they get their kicks out of being secretive."

"It's their tiny bid for power. Do you know who's in charge of the investigation?"

"A guy named Cavanaugh."

"Is he good?"

"They say he is. I guess we'll have to wait and see, you know?"

He gave her a helpless half smile, drew a gentle circle on her back with the flat of his hand, then left her alone at the rail once more.

The island lay due east of Portland in the Gulf of Maine. When time was of the essence, the families shuttled out or back by helicopter. On this day it wasn't time that was of the essence, but seclusion, which was accomplished the moment the yacht cleared the harbor and entered open sea.

The wind was moderate and the waves accommodating, reducing what might have been upwards of a three-hour cruise to little over two. Katia watched the island materialize from the sea with the same sense of homecoming she always felt seeing it. In the course of her twenty-nine years she had come to associate the island with relaxation and security, and even the more somber circumstances of this particular visit couldn't negate that conditioning. A sense of warmth stole over her when the Cape-style house came into view. Smiling, she took what she felt had to be the deepest, freshest breath she had taken in days.

She wasn't the only one who felt suddenly lightened. Of the four from the salon who had joined the others on deck, Natalie looked relieved, and Lenore was standing under her own power. Jack and Gil were discussing the president's tax proposal with a semblance of their characteristic animation.

The two men had bought the island more than thirty years before. Four-hundred acres of forested land rising steadily to an apex of majestic pines, it had come with an old, two story Victorian cottage that had eventually been razed and replaced by the house now dominating the island's face. A low, sprawling structure, its cedar shingles had aged to blend perfectly with the woods, such that if a person wasn't looking for it it could be easily missed. Only when a person drew close did the house's powerful presence make itself known. So like Gil and Jack, Katia mused.

There was a Whyte wing and a Warren wing, plus a third for the help. Over the years it had been frequently renovated, yielding a home that was modern right down to the large saltwater swimming pool off the back patio.

To one side, nearly hidden by the trees, stood the grounds-keeper's small cottage and on the beach, adjacent to the dock, was a boat house. Miles of narrow paths wound through the island, tentacles that inevitably led back home.

All hands chipped in to carry suitcases and supplies to the house. When Katia had done her share she went to her room to unpack, then quickly changed into the bathing suit she had bought that morning, grabbed a towel and made a beeline for the pool.

She wasn't the only one with that idea. The children were already in the water when she arrived and the skeletal contingent of parental lifeguards was being supplemented by the minute.

Stretching flat on her back on a lounge chair, she closed her eyes and reveled in the healing warmth of the sun, feeling further from the frenetic pace of her life in New York than she ever had before. The outdoor sounds—the gulls, children, the breeze in the trees, more faintly the ocean—were calming, reassuring, restorative. She took them all in, letting her body relax and her mind free itself of thought. She was nearly asleep when a warm hand curled around her shoulder and gently shook her.

She opened one eye to find Jordan hunkered down beside her. "You'll burn," he teased. "Either that or you'll miss all the fun."

Had she not been in such a lethargic state, she would have recognized the mischievous gleam in his eye. But before she could fully rouse herself, he swept her up, strode the few steps necessary and tossed her into the pool. The last thing she saw before she submerged was his broad grin, and it was such a relief from the grimness of the past day that she had to muster every resource she possessed to resurface looking angry.

"Jordan Whyte!" she sputtered, tossing her hair back from her face as she bobbed with her head above water. "You are impossible! I could have drowned! What kind of example is that to set for these children?"

Still grinning, he gave a boyish shrug, then dove smoothly into the water. Knowing him well, Katia headed for the side of the pool, but he caught her short of it. He tugged on her ankle and dragged her under again, then worked his way up her body so that when they resurfaced she was in his arms.

"Too slow, sweetheart," he chuckled. "You'll have to work on that."

"You're an imp," she scolded, but her arms and legs were wrapped around him and she felt unduly happy. He was strong, easily keeping them both afloat, and he was handsome, with his hair streaming into his eyes and his broad shoulders bobbing on the surface.

For an instant his arms tightened around her and his expression sobered. Then, as quickly, whatever it was that passed through his mind was gone as small arms began to tug at him from behind.

"Play with *us*, Uncle Jordan! We wanna be thrown, too!" It was Tommy, Laura's youngest, and he and three other children were suddenly paddling around them in the water.

Releasing Katia, he submerged, then came up with a squealing Tommy on his shoulders. Twisting, he grasped the boy firmly by the bottom and shot him up and into the water. By the time Katia had reached the side of the pool and hitched herself out, he was rocketing a second child from his shoulders.

She watched, smiling, thinking that Jordan would make a wonderful father, wondering why he wasn't one already. Then her smile faded and her thoughts deepened. Climbing back to her lounge chair, she hugged her knees to her chest and continued to watch the play, but she was recalling the way Jordan had held her such a short time before, and she grew aware of a gnawing ache deep inside. It worsened when, laughingly crying for mercy, Jordan hauled himself from the pool. The thick muscles of his shoulders flexed. When he straightened, she saw nothing but the way his dark body hair clung to his bronzed chest, his flat stomach, his legs and the way his suit molded that part of him that propriety demanded be covered. All too well she remembered how naturally her thighs had circled those lean hips.

Her eyes climbed upward, over his body, and met his. She

looked quickly away, then flipped over, stretched out on her stomach and closed her eyes. Even then she felt Jordan's approach, felt him lower himself beside her.

"You shouldn't do that," he said softly.

She kept her eyes closed. "Do what?"

"Look at me that way."

"What way?"

"You know what way," he chided gruffly.

She shrugged, trying to sound nonchalant. "You're a gorgeous man. You must be used to covetous stares."

"They're hard to handle when they come from you."

"Why?" she asked, perversely wanting to goad him on. "Am I that different from other women?"

"Yes! You're—"

"What's this?" The intruding voice belonged to Emily, who was dropping her towel onto a nearby chair. "Is it a private conference or can anybody join in?"

Peter, who had come out to join his wife, Sally, moments before, sat forward. "If it's a family tête-à-tête, I'm game. Are we discussing Mark and Deborah, or have we pretty much chalked them off?"

"Shut up, Peter," Jordan growled as he rose and pulled up his own chair.

Laura, who had been sitting nearby with a drink in her hand, turned her visor-shaded eyes their way, as did Anne, whose husband was busy entertaining the children on the far side of the pool.

Katia had been desperately curious to know what Jordan had been about to say when they were interrupted, but she realized that the moment was gone. So she rolled over and sat up, adjusting the back of her lounge chair accordingly.

"Maybe we *should* discuss them," Peter went on, ignoring Jordan's warning. "After all, they're why we're here."

"That's a dour view." Laura swirled the scotch in her glass.

"We would have come up here at some point anyway. It's been awhile since we've all been together."

Anne agreed. "Laura's right. I feel like I'm totally out of touch with what you've all been doing."

"You're out of touch because you're all but married to the Whyte Estate," Peter countered. "How can you be a wife, much less a mother, when you've got your nose in corporate affairs all the time?"

"I manage," Anne said, not without a trace of defensiveness. "But you're a fine one to talk. How much time can you possibly spend with Sally and the kids when you're either in that posh office of yours pulling strings on the phone, outside some courtroom facing the press on behalf of one client or another, or at a political fundraiser spreading good will?"

"I do what I have to do," was Peter's smooth reply, "and Sally understands."

"Well, my Mark understands, too. And, besides, he's as busy as I am. As for Amanda, it's the quality of time I spend with her that matters, not the quantity."

"Ahh," Peter sighed. "Quality over quantity. The credo of the working woman."

Jordan, who felt that Peter's sarcasm was unnecessary, though predictable, cocked his head to the side. "I respect you, Anne. It can't be easy juggling everything."

Anne pulled a face. "There are times when I want to chuck the whole thing, but then what would I do? I can't imagine spending my life waiting for Mark to come home, like Mom does for Dad. Or living solely for times like these when we can be together for a few days."

"Which brings us back to my original point," Peter injected. "I don't know about you guys, but I sure as hell want to know what happened with Mark and Deborah. I'm not ready to buy suicide, which leaves us with murder."

"Christ, Peter—"

"That's blunt—"

"For God's sake—"

Peter was undaunted. "There's no point in beating around the bush. We've all thought the same things. We've racked our brains trying to understand how Mark could have killed Deborah and then himself, and the pieces just don't fit. Our fathers would very happily blame it on factions trying to cause a scandal that would weaken Gil's chances of reelection next year."

Jordan shifted. "Far easier to blame it on someone else."

"You don't think we should?"

"I think we should, very definitely, but the fact remains that murder is easier to swallow than suicide, which would be a reflection on us all."

"I don't feel guilty about anything," Peter claimed.

Emily snorted. "You wouldn't."

"Guilt isn't the issue," Jordan went on, "if we're talking murder. But even there we're practically without clues. There was a side to Mark and Deborah's life . . ." he hesitated and his eyes grew troubled, "that none of us knew all that well. We can speculate, I suppose. . . ."

"Drugs," Anne offered.

"That's one possibility."

"Money," Peter threw out. "If Mark needed it badly and was stupid enough to approach the wrong people—"

"Why would he ever do *that*?" Laura demanded. "He could have come to us!" She raised her scotch and took a healthy swallow.

"He did," Anne softly, "and we didn't listen."

Laura seemed shocked for a minute. "Well, he didn't come to me."

"Would you have helped him?"

"I . . . maybe. I don't know. Donald was never wild about Mark's schemes."

Peter nodded. "Wise man."

"Was he that badly in need of money?" Emily asked.

"Probably."

"I thought he was making it."

"Not enough."

"But even if Mark *did* go to the wrong people, it still wouldn't make sense," Laura picked up, bewildered. "Why would someone kill him for money? A dead man never repays his debts."

"His estate does," Peter advised, "if they're legitimate debts."

Katia frowned. "But that doesn't make sense either, because if someone like Mark went so far as to borrow money, there couldn't have been much of *anything* in his estate."

"What about Deborah?" Emily asked. "We've been assuming it was Mark who had the problem. Maybe Deborah had the nasty connections."

Even as she said it, the others were shaking their heads. Jordan expressed their views. "No. I just can't see it in Deborah. Mark was the leader; she followed."

"Maybe it was a woman," Peter suggested. "Mark had his share of affairs. Maybe he and Deborah were involved in a bitter love triangle."

Jordan arched a skeptical brow his way. "A woman who expertly stole onto the boat and killed both of them without a fight from one or the other?"

"Maybe they were sleeping."

But Jordan was shaking his head again. "Whoever did this—if there was, in fact, a third party—was an experienced killer, and I doubt a lover would be that."

"What about a *male* lover?" Anne proposed, but Laura quickly nixed the idea.

"Deborah wouldn't have taken a lover. She adored Mark."

"Maybe *Mark* had the male lover," Emily countered. She offered the comment with a crooked smile, but it held the group somber and silent for a moment.

Finally Peter grunted. "That shows where *you're* coming from. The theatrical world is a hotbed of homosexuality."

Anne winced. "Lousy pun."

"And inapt," Emily argued. "It's just that gays are more open

in the theatrical world, a world which, by the way, Mark was involved in. So what about a male lover?"

Jordan had known his brother well enough—on that score, at
least—to answer for him. "No. Mark was a ladies' man all the
way."

"Deborah *should* have taken a lover," Laura reflected in a digression from her earlier thoughts. "God only knows Mark wasn't
faithful, and there are plenty of attractive and available men where
they were."

Peter eyed her speculatively. "You sound envious. I can't believe there's trouble on *your* home front. Donald is as moral as
they get."

Which, totally apart from the sexual, could be very boring,
Katia thought to herself. Though she respected Donald, she had
never considered him an exciting person.

"Donald is fine, and there isn't any trouble at home," Laura insisted. "But when something like this happens, it gets you thinking about your own mortality, about things you might do
differently if you were to live your life over again." Normally the
most reserved of the group, Laura's tongue had been somewhat
loosened by liquor.

"What would you do?" Katia asked, intrigued.

Laura took a deep breath, then looked at the others with a
scotch-bred boldness. "I'd have played around a little before I got
married. No, don't look at me that way, Peter. I'm human. And female. If I were to do it all over again, I'd have experimented to my
heart's content before I settled down."

"So why didn't you?"

"Because times were different when I graduated from college,
and the only thing I wanted to do then was to be a good wife and
mother."

"There's something to be said for that," Katia replied. "It may
be that you're glamorizing the singles scene—a case of the grass
being greener in the other fellow's yard."

"Uh-oh," Peter teased. "Having second thoughts about having dumped Sean?"

"Not particularly."

"But you sound like you want a husband and babies," he added.

"Eventually," she said without shame. She avoided any visual contact with Jordan by turning her attention to Emily. "What do you think, Em? You've been part of the singles scene. Is it all it's cracked up to be?"

Emily gave a naughty smile. "It's not for everyone, but I'm not complaining."

"Hey." Peter looked around. "Where is what's-his-name, anyway?"

"*Andrew* is out jogging."

"Ahh. Good. Nothing like keeping the old—uh, young—bod in shape. Where did you pick him up, anyway?"

"Not that it's your business, but we were introduced by a mutual friend."

"What happened to the other one—was it Jared?"

"Jared," Emily sighed peacefully, "is gone with the wind, which is just as well," she sobered, "because he was a parasite. No guts, much less drive. I swear I could have strangled him at times."

"Which brings us back to square one," Peter announced. "Mark and Deborah. Murder." He tugged at his ear. "I can't help but wonder what the police are going to come up with."

"Getting nervous?" Emily taunted. "Afraid that something will come out to tarnish *your* good name?"

Sally sat straighter. "Peter can stand on his own merits, regardless of what comes out," she said in defense of her husband.

"Then what's he afraid of?" Anne asked, meeting Peter's gaze.

Peter gave an arrogant shift of his shoulders. "I'm not afraid of anything. I'm just curious. That's all. Wouldn't *you* like to know what really happened? Mark was your brother."

"And Deborah your sister," Anne returned. "Face it. They were both a little spacey."

Jordan, who had been somberly, if silently, following the conversation, suddenly sprawled in his chair, stretching his legs forward and tucking his fingertips under the Lycra band at his hips. "It's interesting . . . family dynamics. What made them the way they were, while the rest of us are so different?"

"Are we?" Emily asked with a smirk. "Maybe we're all a little odd."

"Speak for yourself," Laura warned.

"Okay, I will." She tipped up her chin. "I'm odd."

Peter nodded. "I'll say. You were always the emotive one. What are you working on now, Em? Still off-Broadway?"

"I *like* being off-Broadway. Some of the most interesting shows start that way."

He persisted. "But wouldn't you rather be in the big time? You know, top billing at a top theater, your name in lights, center stage when it comes time for the final bows?"

"That's *your* ego talking, Peter," Jordan pointed out.

"And you have no ego?" Peter shot back, but Emily had her own answer ready and wasn't about to miss her chance to deliver it.

"I like being where I am. There's adulation on any stage, and I'm satisfied to work my way slowly to the top. Maybe I'm odd in that, too, because you're all such overachievers. But I'm achieving in my own way."

Peter clearly enjoyed taunting her. "Too bad Mark didn't live to produce that artsy film of his. He might have given you a starring role."

"No, thank you," she responded, her eyes flashing. "I wouldn't have worked with Mark for all the tea in China, not after the charming comments he made about my acting ability last time I saw him."

"He said you'd do fine under his direction," Peter teased.

"I'm doing fine now."

"An actress," Laura mused somewhat wistfully. "None of us tried that."

"Which is maybe why I did. Coming after all of you, I had to do *something* different."

"I understand completely," Jordan offered in the driest of tones.

"Ahh, the baby of the Whytes, out to make good on his own," Peter commented, but without rancor. He and Jordan were close in age, and although they had often been rivals as boys, the fact that they had gone in different directions as adults helped preserve their friendship. "Well, you've done it. I have to hand you that. What is it this week—a polo team? A newspaper conglomerate? Hey, now there's an idea. If you owned a paper you'd be able to control the news. By the way, how can you manage to take the time off from all that to get up here? Aren't you afraid someone will steal a super deal from under your nose?"

Coming from an outsider, such sarcasm would have set Jordan off. But he was more mellow with his family than with others. "I believe in delegating authority," he answered, then gave a devilish smile. "I mean, I *am* the authority, but the people under me are loyal enough to carry it out. They know what I want done. If there's a problem while I'm here, they'll call."

"I'm envious," Laura confessed. "I wish Donald's profession allowed him that luxury. Then he'd have more time to spend with us."

Katia was thinking about the many ways in which Laura's life paralleled her mother Lenore's when Emily verbalized similar thoughts. "You really should do something about that, Laura. Make him take time off. He *should* be with you more. Mother may be too old to change Dad, but you're not too old to change Donald."

"It's Donald's career, just like it was Dad's," Laura said defensively. "And besides, Donald's forty-six and I'm nearly forty-four. Maybe we're both too old to change."

"Long-suffering females," Peter sighed magnanimously. "What would we ever do without them?"

Katia, who was feeling badly enough for Laura without Peter's quips, spoke up thoughtfully. "It's interesting, though. Laura is like Lenore, you're like Gil. Nick takes after Jack—"

"And Jordan takes the best from both of his parents," Emily piped up with a grin.

"Or the worst," Katia added, but she was grinning too.

"So where does that leave Emily?" Peter asked. "Or Mark and Deborah, for that matter? Or *you*, Katia. Who do you take after?"

Katia hadn't been prepared for that one, and while she struggled to answer, Jordan came to her rescue. "Katia has her mother's heart. The rest has come through osmosis. You don't expect that she'd spend so many years of her life with us and not be bitten by the bug?"

Peter was far from satisfied with Jordan's explanation. "What about Henry? What has she got of his?"

Katia thought she heard a subtle challenge in his words, and it made her heart beat faster. What did she have in her of her late father, Henry?

"He liked to cook," Emily offered. "Katia's always taking one gourmet cooking class or another."

"Have you ever sampled her cooking?"

"I have," Jordan cut in, shooting Katia a mischievous grin. "She used to call me when she needed a guinea pig."

"I did not," Katia protested in the same playful spirit, which, if forced, was only for her to know. "I called you when I was so desperate to see your face that I'd have done anything—including slave over a hot stove for the better part of my Sunday preparing French haute cuisine—to get you over. And did I ever disappoint you? Did you ever get heartburn? Indigestion? Ptomaine poisoning?"

"Nope. You're a great cook. I'd come to your place for dinner anytime. It sure beats the crap I stick in my microwave."

"Don't give me that," Katia countered, her eyes narrowing.

"You eat at the best restaurants four to five days out of the week, and when you're not eating out—"

"He's got some *other* woman cooking for him," Anne finished. "You're a bastard, Jordan. Do you know that? You use women like the cave men did. They're good for two things, food and sex."

"That's not true," Jordan argued more innocently than he had a right to given his track record. "I respect women. Didn't I say not more than twenty minutes ago that I respected you? I have witnesses, so don't try to deny it."

"You live by a double standard," was Anne's tart reply.

"Don't we all?" Emily asked. "There are those people we use and those we love."

Jordan was frowning. "But the groups aren't mutually exclusive. Isn't that what love is about? That you can use someone and have them use you back, but the using is productive and rewarding for both?"

"Do you mean to tell me," Anne mocked, "that you've been in love with each of the women who've wandered in and out of your life?"

"Of course not. But what they've given, I've returned."

"That's right," Anne concluded smugly. "Food and sex."

Jordan was about to protest when Emily shot forward in her seat. Eyes widened, she glanced at her watch. "Speaking of sex, I've got to run." She gathered up her towel and the suntan lotion she hadn't used. "If you'll excuse me. . . ." And she was off.

"Is she insatiable, or what?" Peter directed his question at Emily's fleeing form. "I know what really happened to Jared. She wore him out. I hope Andrew has more stamina."

"It's her soap opera," Anne informed him. "She wouldn't miss it for the world."

Jordan broke into an irreverent grin. "Now, who does she get that from? Do you think that Lenore's been watching the soaps in her bedroom all these years?"

"Shh," Katia chided.

Laura sighed loudly into her glass. "No. Mother just sulks."

She drained the last of her drink, then eyed Peter's rising form over the rim. "Where are you off to?"

"Phone call time," he called over his shoulder as he crossed the patio and headed for the house.

"He has to call the office," Sally explained quietly. "And I should relieve Mark M. with the children." Over the years, the families had come to refer to Anne's husband, Mark Mitchell, as Mark M., to help differentiate him from Mark Whyte. The fact that there was no longer any need to do so was something everyone determinedly ignored.

Katia, too, stood. She would have liked to have been left alone with Jordan, but she sensed that Laura wasn't up to budging from her seat for a while, and Anne had stretched back in the sun. "I think I'll wander around. I'll catch you all later."

The rest of the day passed quietly, as did the ones that followed. Introspection seemed the most common pastime among those in self-exile on the island. There was some play, some laughter, but it was always short-lived.

Katia, while deeply feeling the tragedy, was that half step removed from it to be able to watch the others closely. As she expected, Lenore spent most of her time in her room, while Gil was either brooding over papers or on the phone. It wasn't that Gil didn't feel the loss of his daughter and son-in-law, Katia knew, because she saw the haunted look that settled over him from time to time. But work was, and always had been, a panacea for Gil. Katia accepted that, just as, she assumed, Lenore had years before.

Natalie, though having her teary moments, coped with death largely by focusing on the living. She was the one to see that the grandchildren were kept busy when their parents had little inclination to do so. To Katia's surprise, it was Jack who showed the ravages of grief more openly than the other three of the senior generation. He was prone to sudden mood swings, angry at anything and everything one minute, quiet and thoughtful the next. He, too, spent long hours on the phone, for the most part lambasting one or another of his subordinates in Boston. When he wasn't venting his fury on those hapless victims, he was brooding by himself on the beach. Often, at the dinner table or in the living room at night, he would tune out the conversation, only to suddenly look up with eyes filled with anger—or tears—when a question was directed his way.

Katia spent her own time relaxing, working up a tan by the pool, talking for hours with Emily and Anne. Laura, though present, more often than not with a drink in her hand, rarely joined the discussion. Peter was usually on the phone.

To Katia's delight, Jordan frequently sought her out. He conned her into swimming laps with him, though she always tired before he did. He spirited her off on the sailboat, though she wound up clinging for life to the gunwale when the boat heeled at a perilous angle. He took her for long walks along the island paths, talking softly of many things, save the one she truly wanted to discuss.

She sensed that he did need her. He seemed calmer, more at peace when he was with her, though she wondered if that was simply wishful thinking on her part. It occurred to her that she was a masochist, because she treasured his company regardless of what they did, even though it tore her apart to go off alone at day's end.

He had had one chance when she was nineteen, but he had firmly rejected it. He had had further opportunity after she graduated from college, when they were both in the city, free of other commitments. But he had never taken it. He never suggested that he wanted more from her than friendship, and she had far too much pride to push him. So she dated others and eventually took up with Sean. But four years of a live-in relationship had taught her that one man couldn't stand in for another. When Sean had wanted marriage, she had balked and finally faced the truth.

Now, once more, she was free. But the time was wrong for Jordan and her. The circumstances were wrong. She found herself wondering whether they would ever be right. But that thought

upset her, so she simply pushed it aside, something she had become quite adept at doing. Rather than speculate about her hopes
and dreams for the future, as thoughts of mortality would lead her
to do, she spent much of her time thinking of the past.

During one of those periods of reminiscence, while Katia was
meandering through the common living area of the house, she inevitably found herself entering the den. It was a large room that
had always seemed to her to be warmed by the many family photographs and sketches—mostly Gil's—that covered the walls.

The room wasn't empty. The sight of Natalie and Lenore sitting on the rich leather sofa, their laps covered with albums and
piles of loose photographs stopped her short on the threshold.

"Oh! I'm sorry. I didn't realize you'd be here."

While Lenore's eyes remained glued to the pictures in her
hands, Natalie looked up and smiled broadly. "Katia! You have to
see these. It's been so long since we've taken them out, and they're
absolutely hilarious."

Katia hesitated. Lenore didn't look as though she was in the
throes of hilarity, and the last thing Katia wanted was to cause her
distress. But Natalie was insistent, gesturing her into the room.

"Come on. Look." She held out one snapshot and, short of
rudeness, Katia had no choice but to approach.

Taking the picture from the older woman's hand, she studied
it and broke into an immediate smile. "That is precious. Laura and
Em—look at her curls—and Mark and Jordan."

"And you. You couldn't have been more than five at the time."

"God, that was a long time ago," Katia mused, still smiling.
"And my hair was so long, or maybe I was just so short." Unable
to help herself, she bent down to see some of the other pictures in
Natalie's hand. They had been taken at various times, all good
times, fun times. "Oops," she corrected herself, "there I am crying." Then she laughed aloud. "I actually remember that. It was
Peter's birthday party. We were all eating ice cream cones, but the
ice cream fell out of mine and landed on my Mary Janes. I was too
young to be embarrassed. Just heartbroken."

Natalie pointed to the open album in her lap. "And look at these. They were taken after Nick started college, when he was in his 'serious photographer' stage. The way he posed everyone— you all look like you're ready to scream."

"He used to take *forever*. And then when we thought he was all set he'd find that the film wasn't wound right, or the flash didn't work, or he couldn't snap the shutter because the lock was on, and by the time he'd fixed whatever it was someone had moved, so he had to lower the camera and start all over again." She studied the photograph. "We look so . . . formal. Frustrated, but formal. Old-fashioned."

"Old-fashioned isn't necessarily frustrated and formal," Lenore murmured, speaking for the first time since Katia had entered the room. There was a wistfulness to her voice as she straightened a forefinger on one of the pictures in the album before her. "This was taken in the early thirties. Look."

Moving behind the sofa, Katia peered over Lenore's shoulder at a faded photo of Jack and Gil, shoulder to shoulder, beaming at the camera.

"The country was in the middle of the Depression," Lenore went on admiringly, "but those two were irrepressible. That was taken at Amherst. Look at the baggy pants and the hats."

"And the flasks," Natalie noted dryly. "Prohibition meant nothing to them."

"But you didn't know them then, did you?" Katia asked.

It was Lenore who answered. "No. It was another ten years before we came into the picture." She turned another page and pointed. "We couldn't have been more than fifteen when this was taken. Look, Nat. Do you remember?"

Chapter 4

LENORE CRANE WAS A PRINCESS, or so she thought during the first decade of her life. She lived with her younger sister and their parents in a spacious brick home in Boston's Back Bay, a short distance from the bank where her father, Samuel, held the prestigious position of president, and she wanted for nothing.

A beautiful child, she had long, silky blond hair, a small nose, delicately rounded face and the palest of blue eyes. Her dresses were of the softest velvet, hand picked by her mother at Best's. Her shoes were of the finest patent leather, replaced at the first sign of wear. The dolls she played with were from England, and the cups in which she served them tea were miniature versions of the elegant Royal Worcester her mother used when she entertained, which was often.

She was taken to movies at the luxurious Metropolitan Theatre, to parties at the country club, all in the elegant Pierce-Arrow that her father proudly drove. Her piano teacher came to the house once a week, as did a private ballet instructor. She was taught early on how to use the phonograph and had a larger record collection to choose from than anyone else she knew, and if she didn't want to listen to the phonograph, she could turn on the radio, which was the newest and the best, paid for in full at the time of purchase rather than on the installment plan that had become so popular among those of a lesser station.

Never in her life did she dream that anything could shatter such a lovely existence. If her mother's greatest excitement was in frequenting such chic specialty shops as Slattery's and Madame Driscoll's, Lenore only knew that she had the most beautiful, best dressed mother around. If her father's greatest excitement was in defying Prohibition by slipping into the Mayfair after the bank closed each afternoon, Lenore only knew that he'd have a chocolate bunny or some other tempting sweet for her sister, Lydia, and her when he returned.

Unfortunately, imbibing bootlegged liquor wasn't Samuel Crane's only excitement in life. There was a side that he kept to himself, a side that was in stark contrast to the conservative image he upheld at the bank.

Samuel Crane played the stock market, played it with a daring that awed his broker, who soon learned to follow the man's tips rather than offer his own. Samuel would have been fine had he limited himself to investing his own money, but he didn't. He used every cent of his salary to maintain the style of living he found to his liking, so when he needed additional money he embezzled it from the bank.

On October 30, 1929, the day after the stock market crashed, Samuel Crane was found hanging from a noose in the attic of his home. Lenore was just shy of ten at the time, but that day brought about changes in her life that profoundly affected every aspect of her being.

With the sudden death of her husband, Greta Crane was stunned. She barely had time to grieve before humiliation set in, and that was quickly followed by horror when she discovered the extent of the debts bequeathed her—debts that could be repaid only by the sale of everything she had held dear.

The heartrending ordeal was akin, in Greta's mind, to the draining of her own life's blood, and had she not had children to care for she might well have joined her husband in oblivion. For Lenore and Lydia's sakes she pushed on, leaving the Back Bay and moving with the two girls to the upper half of a modest two-family house in Watertown, which she rented for less each month than the amount she'd previously spent on clothes in as many weeks. Gone were the maid, the cook, the Pierce-Arrow and the country club, replaced by an existence that, while stark physically, was even more devastating emotionally.

Disillusionment was a mild word to describe Greta's feelings. She was furious at her husband, at the bank, at the stock market, at Herbert Hoover. She wallowed in shame, living in a purgatory of her husband's making.

Without a source of income, much less the skills to secure one, she took a night job tending a blind woman in nearby Belmont. On the one hand it suited her, for she could steal away to earn her living in the dark, leaving the eyes of the world none the wiser. On the other hand it meant that her small daughters were alone at night and that she, herself, caught what sleep she could during the hours they were in school.

Taking the cue from her mother, Lenore quickly realized the shadow of disgrace under which they lived. She kept her eyes lowered when she went to school, avoided making friends and hurried her younger sister home as soon as class was dismissed to find what little sanctuary she could in the confines of their small apartment.

There was no piano to play, no ballet to practice. Cloistered in the tiny room she shared with Lydia, Lenore took to dreaming. At times she would pretend that her father had been called away on secret business but would one day return to restore his family to its rightful place in society. At times she imagined that she was simply living a nightmare and would awaken once more in the Back Bay, on fine linens beneath eiderdown. At times she would dream of the future, imagining herself swept off her feet by a knight in shining armor who would rescue her from shame and shower her with wealth.

Greta fed this particular dream with the bitterness that had become a mainstay of her personality. "You'll do better than I did," she sternly instructed her daughters on so many occasions that

Lenore learned the speech by heart. "You'll marry men who are careful, men who earn handsome livings without having to resort to gambling. Your father was sick that way, and it is because of him that we have to live as we do. But we'll show them; we'll show them all. You're good girls and beautiful girls. Some day you'll be back on top."

It was easier said than done. Where once Greta would have anticipated her daughters' grand debuts without a worry in the world, now such lavish affairs were out of the question. Not only didn't she have the money, but she was totally alienated from the society of which she'd once been a part, and she refused to mingle any more than necessary with the people of her new and demeaning station.

So she saved every spare penny in an empty oatmeal box on the back of the pantry shelf, intent on providing whatever she could for her daughters when the time came for them to work their way upward once more. She frowned on any unnecessary expense and pushed Lenore into errand running and babysitting jobs as soon as Lydia was old enough to be left alone.

There were times when Lenore wished her mother worked days, for then Greta wouldn't be around to scrutinize every step she took. It became particularly difficult for Lenore when she entered adolescence, when her body made changes that Greta continually editorialized upon.

"No, not that sweater, Lenore," she scolded with a calmness that was deadly. "Lydia can wear that."

"But it's my favorite," Lenore argued, "and the softest one I own."

"Wear the green one."

"The green one itches."

"Then wear a blouse. That sweater is too tight. You don't want to flaunt yourself or you'll attract the wrong sort. It's bad enough that we have to live among neighbors like these, but I refuse to have you stoop to their level."

At times like those, Lenore wondered if "their level" could be half as bad as *her* level. The mother who had once been so indulgent had become a shrew. She rarely smiled and her features were pinched. If there was any warmth in her it was iced over by the rigid will for vengeance that seemed to keep her going.

Lenore needed warmth. She was lonely. Where once she and her sister had been close, the three-year difference in their ages came to seem huge. Lydia was as unsatisfactory company for her as, increasingly, her dreams were, and since Greta discouraged her from making local friends she was frustrated. Even the disgrace she had hidden behind since her father's death began to pale. When her mother spoke of the "wrong sort," Lenore could only reflect that she didn't attract *any* sort, and that bothered her.

The public library was the one spot her mother allowed her to visit during what little spare time she had, and it was there that Lenore met Natalie Slocum. The girls were both thirteen, both alone and craving companionship. What began as a simple exchange of books grew into friendship. While Lenore was at first reticent to open up, Natalie's quiet charm and lack of pretentions soon won her over.

As opposed to Lenore, Natalie had never known wealth. She had been raised in a shabby, wood frame house in an even poorer part of town than the one in which Lenore had spent the last three years, and rather than condemn Lenore for her family's downfall, she was wide-eyed and hungry to hear about life in the Back Bay. It was a dream to her, as it was now to Lenore, and the two sat for hours reveling in it.

Natalie's life had been hard. Her mother had died when she was two and her father had tried his best to raise his only child with the meager means available to him. But he was a milkman, working long busy days, and he was incapable of giving Natalie the guidance she needed as she approached womanhood.

Nonetheless, he had always doted on her, as Natalie was the first to admit. On a cold winter's night he would hold her close beside him and read her stories from the books one of his more benevolent customers had passed down. At the first snowfall of the year, he would wrap her up in layers of clothing and take her sledding on a makeshift flyer. In the spring he would make picnics for them to share beneath the neighbor's oak, which sprawled into their tiny yard with a breath of shade. And in the summer he would always take her to the beach.

The irony of it was that his doting did her in, particularly when she began to blossom and his cooing over her childlike charms was replaced by a more mature, if every bit as intense, praise for her intelligence and beauty. He was her father and as such he was biased, she reasoned; she came to wonder if she had a serious lack that he was desperately trying to cover up.

She wasn't beautiful as he always said she was. The mirror that he had given her for her twelfth birthday told her so. She had dark hair that waved where it shouldn't, brown eyes set too far apart, a nose that had a bump in it, a fleshy mouth and skin the color of the flour paste she used in school. No, she wasn't beautiful, certainly not like Mary McGuire, who lived down the street and was a year ahead of her in school and had everyone in the neighborhood at her beck and call.

Nor was she brilliant. She was smart, perhaps, in a common sense way, but not brilliant. Or, if her father was right and it was so, her teachers certainly didn't think so. They never sought her out for the right answer the way they sought out George Hollenmeister, and they never let her skip reading to help with the younger children the way they let Sara French.

Reaching her own conclusions and being sensitive about them, she kept to herself, which suited her because the books and magazines that were her constant companions didn't mind the way she looked or dressed or that she didn't have a mother or that she would never grow up to be a Ziegfeld Girl.

Just as those books and magazines couldn't talk back to her, though, neither could they provide the human companionship that increasingly, if subconsciously, she craved. Meeting Lenore Crane that fateful day in the library, on the other hand, perfectly fit the bill. The fact that they went to different schools and had never set eyes on each other before gave them each a fresh start. Beyond that, Lenore's insecurity was something with which Natalie could easily identify. The shyness and caution that characterized their initial interactions quickly faded as the need they shared emerged.

They became secret pals, delighting in the knowledge that their friendship was private, an exclusive club for two. Meeting at the library several times a week, they would sit in a quiet corner with books open on their laps while they whispered back and forth about anything and everything.

Natalie told Lenore about the stuck-up Nola Wurtz who always shunned her, and about Mary Melanson, whom she had seen one day behind the school kissing a boy. She told her about doing odd chores for the Belskys on Friday nights and Saturdays for which she received fifty cents a week, and about saving up to buy a pair of saddle shoes. She admitted that she wished she had a mother, or, if not that, a brother or sister, or, if not that, a dog like Little Orphan Annie's Sandy.

In turn, Lenore confessed that having a mother wasn't so wonderful if she was angry all the time, and that sisters were fine until they starting asking questions you didn't want to answer, and that the worst thing about having come from the Back Bay was that you could never go back once you'd left. She asked Natalie's opinion on whether she should cut her hair into a more stylish bob (though it was a moot point, since her mother would *never* have permitted it), whether her sweater was indeed too tight, and whether she thought Greta Garbo was really as beautiful as they said.

The girls saw eye to eye on practically everything, but most vehemently on their plans for the future. They were going to make it, and make it big. They were going to marry well and one day have everything they were missing now. They were going to be respected and admired and sought after by the cream of society. Or so the dream went.

Their friendship, while precious to them both, was viewed as anything but by Lenore's mother.

"You were at the library again today?" she asked with the quiet sharpness Lenore knew so well.

"I do my schoolwork there."

"Was the Slocum girl there too?"

"Yes."

"You spend too much time with her, you know "

Lenore kept her voice low, because she didn't like the way her mother's nose was tightening around the nostrils. A fight was brewing. "I only see her at the library."

"What's the point of it?"

"I like her."

"But she's nothing—"

"You've never met her!" Which was a happy state as far as Lenore was concerned. For once Greta's embarrassment over their home suited Lenore's purpose because she didn't want to subject Natalie to Greta any more than Greta wanted to be subjected to Natalie.

"She *comes* from nothing," Greta specified.

We come from something, and look where we are now, Lenore thought, but she knew better than to say it. As it was she'd raised her voice more than was wise; in a minute Greta would be telling her to be still lest the landlord heard every word. "She has a wonderful father."

"Who has neither money, connections, nor power. When you pick friends, Lenore, you have to pick wisely. If someday you're going to meet a man who can provide for you well, you won't do it through girls like Natalie Slocum."

"Mother, I'm barely fourteen! What difference does it make who my friends are now?"

"Keep your voice down, Lenore, or Mr. Brown will hear every word you say. And in answer to your question, it does make a difference. Believe me."

Lenore didn't, not for a minute, and nothing her mother could say or do, short of penning her in the house, could keep her from seeing Natalie. Their friendship was the brightest light in Lenore's otherwise drab life. It was emotionally rewarding and fun; thanks to Greta's narrow-mindedness, it also satisfied Lenore's adolescent need to rebel.

By the time the girls reached sixteen, they were visiting each other's house regularly. Robert Slocum was warm and welcoming to Lenore, and if Greta was more standoffish with Natalie, at least she was civil. She hadn't given up the war, Lenore knew; she had simply yielded in this one particular skirmish. Which was understandable, because by the time the girls were juniors in high school another major battle loomed on the horizon.

Boys. Lenore and Natalie spent hours talking about them, speculating about who would ask them to the dances, rehearsing seductive smiles, experimenting with their hair, the hemlines of their skirts, the way they walked.

The four years since they had first met had seen changes in them both. Lenore had come to terms with her body, able to appreciate its shapeliness. She had, indeed, cut her hair, and even Greta had had to admit that the pains of curling it were worth the effort. Her once round face had slimmed, emphasizing features that were patrician and fine. She was a stunning young woman, and given the looks she had begun to receive from the boys at school, she knew it.

Natalie was every bit as attractive in her own way. Her once unmanageable dark hair now responded to her skilled hand, falling over her shoulders in gentle waves. She had learned to clip and pencil her eyebrows and add a touch of color to her cheeks, and when she wore deep red lipstick, the mouth she had once considered far too full was luscious.

They were a riveting duo as they walked from class to class together. While Natalie was the more outgoing of the two, Lenore was just that little bit prettier. They complemented one another, gave each other strength, and that self-confidence added a special aura to their looks so that, indeed, they often had company walking home from school.

Which made Greta nervous. She was working as a bookkeeper for a local businessman and was rarely home in the afternoons. But Lydia, a teenager herself and more than a little envious of her sister, was a ready-made spy for her mother, reporting everything that happened and with whom.

"So it was Lewis and Joe today?" Greta asked as she was making dinner. By that time she had taken Natalie under her wing, reasoning that since the two were fast friends what one did affected the other, and since Natalie was without a mother she could benefit from the advice of one older and wiser.

The girls were reading a magazine at the kitchen table. Lenore had actually come to enjoy the times when her mother would lecture the two of them, for the force of the attack was far blunter than it would have been if mother and daughter were alone. She suspected that, as much as Greta had initially resisted, she had grown fond of Natalie, and that gave Lenore, who deep down inside did want to please her mother, a warm feeling. Moreover, when Natalie was there, Lenore had an ally.

"Lewis and Joe?" Lenore repeated, looking smugly up at Natalie. "Uh-huh."

"I don't know about Lewis," Greta went on skeptically. "From what I've heard," and she made it her business to hear everything, "he's been something of a problem in school over the years."

"But he does well, Mrs. Crane. His father teaches at Harvard, and his mother is a Fenwick. You can't find better qualifications than those." Natalie knew just what to say to ease Greta's worry. Not that either she or Lenore were madly in love with Lewis—because Lewis was madly in love with himself—but he knew how to put on a show of chivalry, which, to a seventeen-year-old girl, was something. "He's always polite, and he's very good looking."

"He's a senior, isn't he?"

Lenore nodded. "Uh-huh."

"What are his plans for next year?"

"He'll probably go to Harvard."

"Not on his grades he won't."

"He doesn't *need* grades, Mother. He has money and connections. He's in." There was a faint note of bitterness in Lenore's voice; from time to time she recalled that she, too, had once had money and connections.

Natalie, who understood Lenore well—indeed, often felt bitter about her own lot in life—also understood that Greta wasn't one to be antagonized. She sought to soften her friend's words, saying, "It doesn't matter where Lewis goes to college. He'll be a success. He has the drive."

"Thank goodness for that, at least," was Greta's quiet murmur. She turned to face the girls. "How about you, Natalie? Have you thought about what you're going to do after graduation?"

"I have," Natalie said, frowning, "but my father and I can't see eye to eye on it. He wants me to work because of the money, but I don't see that closing myself off in some office is going to get me anywhere but older."

Greta gave a limp smile. It wasn't that she didn't legitimately feel the smile, just that she had gotten out of practice. But she was pleased now; Natalie was on the right track. "Then you're considering college, too?" That was what Lenore was doing, with her mother's urging. Although it would be costly, it was one way for a girl without status to meet a man with it.

"I'd like to go to Mass. State," Natalie declared. "I can train to be a teacher. . . ."

"Until something else comes along," Greta finished. "That's exactly what I've been telling Lenore. Haven't I, Lenore?" Of course, Greta hadn't been thinking in terms of Mass. State, she'd been thinking in terms of something a little more exclusive, like Simmons. After scrimping for years to save money she wanted her daughter to have the best that it could buy.

"Yes, Mother."

"And it won't be as expensive if you live at home," Greta

added, failing to add that if Lenore lived at home, Greta would be able to sort the good prospects from the bad.

Lenore had other ideas. "I was thinking that it might be nice to live at school."

"Very expensive," Greta drawled in immediate refusal.

"Either that or take a room of my own." She needed to get away from Greta, whose watchful eye and pained expression were like shackles, a constant reminder of where they had once been and how far they had fallen.

"Rooms cost money, too."

"I've been working weekends and summers at the A&P, so I've saved enough to get me started. I can earn extra money by tutoring once I'm at college. Of course," she slowed, lowering her eyes, "if Nat and I were to room together, we could split the rent."

Natalie's eyes bulged. "What a great idea!" Then her face dropped as quickly. "I can just imagine what my father will think of that. I mean, in his heart I'm sure he'd like to see me in college. He wants only the best for me. But the best costs, and he gets nervous."

"If you go off to live somewhere else he'll be alone," Greta pointed out. "That's something to consider."

"Don't add to her guilt, Mother!"

"I was simply making a statement. And it is worth some thought. Besides," she twitched her nose, "nice girls don't live in rooming houses."

"I'm not talking about a *rooming* house," Lenore argued, "but a room *in* a house, or a small apartment."

"You have a room in *this* house, and you don't even have to pay for it."

"It's not the same."

"If you'd like, I could ask you for rent. Some parents do."

"Mother, you're making too much of this."

"I'm sorry, Lenore, but I simply believe that girls your age shouldn't be off on their own."

Lenore couldn't believe what she was hearing, or, rather, she could believe it since it had come from her mother, but she found it laughable. "We'll be eighteen. Half of the girls we know will probably be getting married and having babies right from high school."

"Maybe you will, too," Greta said hopefully. Indeed, she had dug into the oatmeal box for the funds to dress her daughter in the latest styles, and she didn't begrudge the expenditure, seeing it as an investment for the future.

But neither Lenore nor Natalie shared her hope that the investment would pay off so soon. They weren't interested in the boys they knew who were just starting out in life. They wanted to meet mature men, men who were already established, who could give them all they had dreamed about for years. They wanted to live in Louisburg Square and drive Cadillacs and dance their Saturday nights away at the roof garden at the Ritz. They wanted elegant clothes and fur mufflers and servants to do the work they had had to do for years. Above all, they wanted security, which was something that had been relentlessly drummed into their heads.

As the months passed, Greta came to agree with Lenore's assessment of the high school boys. Alex Walter, who took Lenore to her junior prom, was handsome enough, but had neither money nor training and was bound for the Civilian Conservation Corps after graduation, which didn't bode well in terms of ambition as far as Greta was concerned.

Will Farino, who took Lenore to the fall harvest dance, was positively charming, as was his father, a slick salesman who Greta was convinced would eventually find his way into prison. If Greta wanted respect for her daughter, tangling with the likes of the Farinos was not the way to gain it.

Hammond Carpenter, who invited Lenore to go carolling on Christmas Eve and was as beautiful a male as even Greta could remember seeing, had his heart set on entering West Point in the fall. While Greta had no argument with the honor of a career in the military, she had no desire to see her daughter shifted from place to place for a lifetime, much less living on government wages.

George Hastings, who took Lenore to her senior prom, was positively idolized by every girl in the school. Captain of the football team, he was built well, had strong features, a swarthy complexion and thick black hair that ranged over his forehead. He was also nearly illiterate. And when a boy was kept in school solely for his athletic prowess, Greta reasoned, the man that boy would become had few hopes of success—not to mention the fact that his father was a drunk.

So Lenore graduated from high school with a diploma and no husband, which was fine with her, because she was headed for the world. Unfortunately, she was headed for it by trolley, because Greta had her way about her daughter living at home. On the positive side, Natalie had her way about going to college, and had even managed a scholarship, so Lenore and she commuted to Simmons together.

When all was said and done, they were very much on their own, for they left Watertown at six-thirty in the morning and rarely returned before ten o'clock at night. It was easier to feel and act the part of sophisticated women when they were away from the tangible evidence of their modest means, and sophisticated women were precisely what they wanted to be.

Between classes and the jobs they had taken near the college they were busy, but not so busy that they couldn't socialize. There were afternoons spent with friends where the talk over coffee and pastry centered around Brenda Frazier or Alfred Vanderbilt, and movies, where all eyes focused on Clark Gable or Jean Harlow, and parties, where activity revolved around the jukebox and the jitterbug.

And there were men, many of whom were far more exciting than those either girl had known before, but none of whom fit the specifications for Mr. Right. On the one hand each girl had her share of offers, which was some solace, since the prospect of being old maids and having to provide for themselves forever was terrifying. On the other hand they were willing to hold out awhile longer, convinced that it was simply a matter of time before their patience would pay off.

So Lenore and Natalie finished their freshman year, then their sophomore year, and both were still single.

By the summer of 1941 Greta began to worry. Talk of war was rampant, and war would mean the exodus of the best of the available men. "And who *knows* how long a war could go on? You're twenty now and getting older every year. By the time the fighting ends there will be that many more and younger women fighting over the men who come home. I was married by the time I was nineteen."

"And widowed by the time you were thirty-one," Lenore pointed out somewhat dryly. "If I rush to marry now and there *is* a war, I could be left a widow, too, so where would that leave me?"

"It would leave you with whatever estate your husband had."

"Which is why I have to make sure that I find a husband with an estate worth leaving. Don't worry, mother. I'm on your side. I don't want to live this way forever. And I'm trying. Really I am."

Natalie was trying all the harder. She was that much more practical than her friend, and while Lenore continued to work as a tutor, Natalie left her job in the English department and signed on to work spare hours in the office of a young lawyer who had the uncanny knack of attracting wealthy clients. If ever there was an opportunity to mingle with the wealthy, she calculated, that would be it.

Her boss, Gilbert Warren, was handsome and available and very definitely on his way to the top. He took her to dinner from time to time, and though she admired him professionally, he was a little too slick, a little too domineering, a little too arrogant for her romantic tastes.

One of his clients was just right, though. His name was Jackson Whyte, and he was a businessman who had, in six short years, built a flourishing career flying wealthy people from one spot to another in the airplanes that had taken the country by storm the decade before. He was tall and very handsome, soft-spoken but forceful, and when he came near he never failed to set Natalie's pulse to racing.

He also happened to be Gilbert Warren's best friend. The two had met at Amherst, where Jack had been a year ahead of Gil, and, from what Natalie could gather, they were nearly as close as she and Lenore. Jack was in the office often, and during those times Gil was more relaxed than normal. Boisterous laughter would come from behind Gil's door, telling Natalie that the men were discussing far more than the legal brief she had typed for Gil on a matter pertaining to the Whyte Lines the day before. On one occasion Jack even accompanied Gil and her to dinner, and she saw firsthand how well the two men meshed. Where Jack was a brilliant administrator and businessman, Gil had the rashness to think further, making suggestions for growth that might have paled another man but that Jack was more than capable of realizing.

Then the day came when Jack asked Natalie out.

"I'm terrified," she confessed to Lenore that night.

"But you *like* him. You've been waiting for this."

"I know. Still, he's . . . intimidating in a way. He's. . . ."

"Perfect? Your whole face is glowing, Nat. He's perfect!"

"No, he's not. Not really," Natalie answered pensively. "He certainly isn't wealthy, at least, not in the way of old money."

"But he's well on his way there. Do you have any doubts that he'll make it?"

"No. He's smart and aggressive. He took his father's small business and has really built it into something."

"And he's handsome and charming and available. What could be better?"

"He's moving fast. Maybe that's what scares me. Somehow, when I'm with the two of them I get breathless, like I'll never be able to keep up." She smiled sheepishly. "Maybe it's just that he *could* be right in so many ways and I'm nervous that he won't think the same of me."

Lenore grew stern. "Natalie Slocum, that is nonsense. If he didn't like you he never would have asked you out. He's had plenty of time to talk with you, and he knows by now whether he likes what he sees." She grasped her friend's arm and smiled. "This is your big chance, Nat. It's the one you've been waiting for."

Natalie knew she was right, but that knowledge increased her apprehension, because there was so much at stake and she did want the date to go well. It occurred to her that things would be better if she could relax, so she spent that entire night bolstering her self-image, convincing herself that what Lenore had said was right and that Jack had to have liked her to have asked her out. She was sure, she kept telling herself, that she would make Jack Whyte a wonderful wife.

Come morning, she was a bundle of nerves. So the first thing she did when she went to work that afternoon was to walk into Gil Warren's office and tell him about her date with Jack and, by the way, she had a very dear friend who was just her age and absolutely beautiful and wouldn't it be fun if the four of them were to do something together?

The following Saturday night, Jack and Natalie and Gil and Lenore went to the Hotel Brunswick, where they ate dinner, danced and talked the night away. Greta, who had greeted the men when they had arrived and had been as impressed by Jack's shiny new Packard as she had been by the men themselves, was excitedly waiting up for the girls when they were finally delivered home. Natalie was spending the night, as she often did since her father was courting a widow from Chelsea and frequently never made it home at all.

"Tell me," Greta commanded when the girls had stopped bubbling long enough to take off their coats. "Tell me everything."

"He was wonderful!" Lenore exclaimed.

"They both were!" Natatie amended proudly. "They drove right up to the front door of the hotel and left the car with the doorman—did you see the bill Jack slipped him, Lenore?"

Lenore shook her head. "I was too busy matching my steps to Gil's. You should have seen him, Mother. He was so gallant—offering me his elbow, helping me off with my coat, making sure I didn't trip on the steps leading to the restaurant, holding my chair for me. And he knew everyone! The maitre d' greeted him by name and with such *respect*. Wasn't that so, Nat? And the waiter jumped when he raised his finger, and no less than five couples stopped to say hello to us. Did you see the jewels on that one woman, Nat?"

"I swear, we were the envy of every woman there! They kept looking at our table, and it was all I could do to be calm and cool and take it all in as though I've been to the Brunswick a hundred times before."

"But you pulled it off?" Greta asked.

Natalie shared a smug grin with Lenore. "We both did. They were pleased. I'm sure they were." She bit her lower lip to restrain an even broader smile, but the eyes she turned on Greta danced. "We're going out again next weekend. To the theater. The *theater*. Do you *know* who goes to the theater?"

"The best of the best," Lenore answered proudly. "And you can be sure that we won't be sitting in peanut heaven, either."

They sat in the sixth row center, and Lenore and Natalie could have easily spent the evening ogling the intricate crystal chandeliers overhead, the elegant velvet framing the stage, or the finery worn by the other theatergoers. But they diligently paid attention to the show, determined to sound intelligent during the discussion that would surely follow the final curtain. They managed admirably, though they could only sit in silent awe when Jack and Gil launched into a comparative analysis of the many other shows they had seen.

The two young women were on a cloud that night, and there they remained for the next few weeks. Escorted well, they dined at one posh restaurant after another, went to Pops concerts at Symphony Hall, spent days at the beach, took drives through the country. Sometimes the couples were together, other times they went separate ways. Neither Lenore nor Natalie minded that, because each was enthralled with her own special man.

Lenore adored the fact that, when she was with Gil, she felt like a princess again. He treated her as though she were fragile. There was a gentleness in the way he touched her hair, an admiration in his eyes when he looked at her. He told her that she was beautiful, and although she had heard it from other men before, she prized it from one as suave as Gil. She rather liked the way he took control, thinking him not domineering but strong, and if he could be as tough as nails when discussing professional matters with Jack, with her he was unfailingly respectful.

Likewise, Natalie adored Jack. Where once she had been intimidated, his outward affection boosted her confidence. When they were together he was easygoing and indulgent. He hesitated to talk about business when he was with her, as though he wanted to protect her from the more mundane matters of life. Of course, she found his business anything but mundane, since it reeked of success, so she frequently asked him about it, then took delight when he smiled and offered her one small tidbit or another. More than once when they had been with Gil she had seen Jack lose his temper over business matters, yet he was an icon of good humor with her. She truly believed that he was the answer to her prayers.

The Japanese attack on Pearl Harbor in December threw the fate of those prayers into question. Lenore and Natalie spent many a frantic hour wondering what would come of their blossoming romances. Within days of the declaration of war, Jack and Gil made their decisions to enlist, and the women felt that their own futures had been besieged.

Then Jack proposed to Natalie.

And Gil proposed to Lenore.

While the rest of the world seemed to be coming apart at the seams, Natalie and Lenore were ecstatic. Gil's connections with a local judge facilitated the waiving of the standard five-day waiting period, and in a small double ceremony, Natalie became Mrs. Jackson Whyte and Lenore Mrs. Gilbert Warren.

Natalie and Jack went off on a two-day honeymoon in the country, which was a luxury given the circumstances. If Natalie had hoped for something longer, she didn't complain. She had what she wanted; Jack was hers, legally bound. Wildly in love with her husband and the future she envisioned as his wife, she pushed from mind the knowledge that he would be going off to war and immersed herself in his undivided attention.

Her initiation into womanhood was gentle but fierce. She discovered that her husband was as astute in lovemaking as he was in business, exhibiting a keen sense of timing, being daring when daring was called for and conciliatory when conciliatory was wise. She let herself go far more than she had ever imagined she could, but she sensed a need in Jack to stake his claim before he left for the war. With that instinct unique to womankind, she knew that at some point during those two days he had given her a child to keep her company until he returned.

Lenore and Gil stayed in the city. They spent their wedding night at the Ritz, and though Gil had legal business to clear up the next day, he returned to her quickly. In truth, she appreciated the brief respite. Gil was intense, far more so with her than she had expected. Though he treated her with care as she had been given every reason to believe he would, he was a man of passion. Surprisingly, while Natalie had been the one without the mother for guidance, Lenore knew less of what to expect in physical matters than her friend. Greta's sole concern had been with getting her daughter married; once the papers were signed Lenore was on her own.

And that was exactly how Lenore felt, at least when it came to making love. Gil held her and kissed her, touched her slender body with an expertise that did, indeed, arouse her, but he reached his peak of pleasure quickly and was done, leaving her to wonder whether the stories she had heard of shooting stars were merely a fairy tale.

Still, she was happy. She had a husband who was respected, who would see that she was taken care of while he nobly went off to war. And when he returned—for she refused to believe that he wouldn't—she would have the world on a string.

Three days after their weddings, Natalie and Lenore kissed their husbands good-bye. They had both decided, with Jack and Gil's encouragement, to continue at Simmons, but rather than living at home, they moved into Gil's house on Mt. Auburn Street in Cambridge. Natalie had offered to spend her free time in Jack's office, helping her father-in-law manage the airline, which would be running on a heavily curtailed schedule during the war. Likewise, Lenore insisted on doing what she could by way of secretarial chores to assist the older lawyer in whose hands Gil had left his practice.

Within two months after Jack's departure, Natalie's pregnancy was confirmed. She was delighted, as was Jack when he learned of it on his first leave from training camp. Lenore was envious and told Gil as much, then graciously endured his fervent attempts to remedy the situation when it was his turn to have leave.

By the spring of 1942, when both men had completed officers' training and were shipped overseas, the first of the Whyte and Warren heirs were on their way.

Chapter 5

T HEY NEVER SAW ACTIVE DUTY. Either of them . . . the bastards."
Robert Cavanaugh was sitting in the living room of his
Charlestown apartment with a lapful of papers, as he had been
every night for the past ten days.

"You're muttering again, Bob." The gentle scolding came from
the woman he lived with, Jodi Frier, as she strolled in from the
kitchen. Propping herself on the arm of his chair, she studied the
papers. "More history?"

"Mmm."

She slid her eyes from the papers to Bob. His shirt was rum-
pled, collar open, tails out, sleeves rolled to the elbows. He'd
kicked off his shoes and his slim fitting trousers had long since
lost their crease. With his hair curling irreligiously and his jaw
darkly shadowed, he looked like a modern day pirate.

Only he was one of the good guys. Jodi knew that, even if she
sometimes resented his reverent attitude toward the white hat he
wore. She also knew precisely how much the Whyte-Warren investigation meant to him. "Anything interesting?"

"Lots. They came home from the war like conquering heroes,
yet neither of them ever saw the front. They went through officers' training school—Whyte in the navy, Warren in the army.
Whyte spent the war years at Pearl as a procurement officer. His

job was to see that the ships were supplied." Cavanaugh grunted. "Probably had his hand well into the black market."

"Come on, Bob. That's unfair."

"And Warren viewed the war from the safety of a cushy office in England. Pretty easy stuff if you ask me."

"If you ask me, I think you're wishing your father had had it as easy."

Cavanaugh's eyes flew to her face, then he caught himself. He sometimes forgot how perceptive she was. It was one of the things he liked about her. Not having to spell everything out, as he'd had to do for his ex-wife for years, was a relief, as was not being constantly pestered for details—which made it that much more pleasant to offer them. He supposed it had something to do with his ego; he liked to be the one in control. "Damn right I am. He took shrapnel in the back and was in pain every day until he died. A purple heart was small consolation for what he suffered."

Jodi kneaded the tense muscles at the nape of his neck. "You were proud of him, though, weren't you?"

He gave her a wry smile. Her touch soothed him. "I'm not *that* old."

"All right," she drawled. She knew he was sensitive about the twelve years between them. "In *hindsight*. You were proud to know that your father had held his own in combat. And he was proud of himself. I doubt either Gil Warren or Jack Whyte could have felt the same kind of pride."

Only the low drone of the window air conditioning unit broke the silence until he spoke. "Don't bet on it. Minds like theirs are capable of building up any little thing they do to make it seem earth shattering."

"You do have to admit that they've done well in life."

"But at the expense of so many other people!"

Jodi knew from the twist of his lips that he was thinking of his father again. He did that a lot when it came, in particular, to Jack Whyte. She wanted to know what else he was thinking, and while she respected his privacy, she had spent a full ten days watching him brood over his files, so she figured she had earned the right to a few questions.

In addition to which, giving him a neck rub could only do so much. He needed to air his thoughts. And that was her specialty.

"You haven't told me much," she began softly. "When did they get started on their present course? Was it after the war?"

"Uh-uh. It goes back further. Whyte's father was a pilot in World War I. When the war was over he turned to designing airplanes. He was a sharp guy." Cavanaugh made no attempt to conceal his sarcasm. "He saw that there was a lucrative market in building planes for bootleggers who were smuggling stuff in from Canada and Mexico."

"Did Jack play any part in that?"

If only, Cavanauyh thought. It would have been something else to condemn. "He was too young. By the time he joined his father Prohibition was being lifted."

"So?"

"So he took the old man's airplanes, spruced them up, launched an aggressive advertising campaign, and began a legitimate air-passenger service." He paused. "Founded on bootleg capital."

"Which wasn't unusual at the time," Jodi pointed out gently. "Or now, for that matter. There's many a mobster's son who has established himself in a legitimate business with funds from an illegitimate one. It may not be right, or satisfy our belief in justice, but can we criticize the sons who have chosen to straighten up? Often they're the most charitable people."

"Yeah. They use their money to buy respectability."

"But if the money goes to a worthy cause, isn't that something?"

"I think you were right the first time." He looked up at her. "It does offend my sense of justice."

Grabbing a handful of his hair, she gave it an affectionate tug. "That's because you have a super sense of justice. But we're getting off the subject. So Jack Whyte had a going business concern to come back to after the war. What about Gil Warren?"

"Gil had a law practice."

"Before the war?"

"Mmm."

"With someone else?"

"As in someone who handed it to him on a silver platter?" He darted her a look of resignation. "No. His father was a house painter. Gil started from scratch. He was a scholarship student at Amherst, then went on to Harvard Law. But damn," he shook his head in grudging amazement, "the guy had a knack for it. From what I've learned he could put on a show even back then. Not long after he opened his office he was attracting some of the best clients—stole them from prestigious firms, no less. I don't know what it was, whether he was a good talker or a good lawyer or simply a good looker."

"Charisma, Bob. Some people just have it. He did. He does."

Cavanaugh grunted. "You can say that again. Not only charisma, but virility. He may not have seen combat, but he sure saw action of another sort. I mean, the guy was a notorious play-boy before he decided that it would be good for his image to get married, but you can be damn sure that he wasn't spending his nights in England alone behind blackout shades."

"Bob. . . ."

"Okay, okay. I can't document anything but what he did with his wife. Do you know that by the time he got back from England at the end of the war he had two kids, with a third on the way?"

Jodi couldn't help but grin. "I think you're jealous."

"Of a prize stud? Are you kidding? He was probably only try-ing to do one better than his buddy Jack. Besides," he coiled his arm around her waist and threw the issue back at her, "I'd have all the children in the world if you were willing. So who's the source of the problem around here?"

Jodi held her breath for a minute before offering a sheepish, "Me." She wished she hadn't brought the subject up. They always argued about it. She would be more than happy to have children if Bob would marry her, but he wouldn't, so he was as much the source of the problem as she—but to say so would invite war. He had been through a marriage that had scarred him badly, and he had a thing against discussing it.

Jodi was not holding out for marriage on principle; she was a little more modern than that. But she knew Bob wasn't ready to make a total commitment, and until he was she feared bringing their children into the world.

"Do you really think Gil was competing with Jack when it came to children?" she asked in an attempt to nip that more personal discussion in the bud.

"I don't know," Bob said, pondering the possibility as he spoke. "Actually, maybe not. The two of them were closer than most brothers. They worked *with* each other rather than against each other."

"A symbiotic relationship?"

"I suppose you could call it that. It's sick, in some ways. They met at Amherst. Gil went on to Harvard Law and Jack followed him to Cambridge—to the business school—a year later. They both decided to stay in Boston, and once they were working they constantly sent each other business. They married women who were best friends, even had a double wedding ceremony." He arched a brow. "One of those quickie things right before they left for the war." The brow settled. "Jack had two kids of his own by the time he returned from the Pacific, and there were more to come. All told, by the mid-fifties, the tally was four for Jack and five for Gil." He paused, scratching his chin. "But no, I don't think they were competing, because if that were the case their friendship would never have lasted all these years. Something would have come up to tear them apart."

"Maybe the competition was between their wives."

He shrugged. "Maybe."

Jodi sat for a minute longer, gently stroking his hair, before she ventured to speak again. "What do you hope to get out of all these papers?" She gestured toward his lap.

Cavanaugh looked at the files, absently flipping the corner of the pile. "Understanding. Where they came from, what made them tick."

"That's usually my line."

He grinned. "I know. See what happens to a man when he lives with a guidance counselor for three years running?"

She was going to ask if he was complaining, but knew that he wasn't. Their relationship—aside from the issues of marriage and children, which weren't major ones since she was only twenty-seven and had a rising career—worked well, symbiotic in its own way. She gave him tender loving care in exchange for his apartment, his companionship, his affection, and great sex.

"Okay. Let me take a different tack. How does all of this background relate to your investigation?"

That was a tougher one for Cavanaugh to answer. He was having trouble explaining his fascination with the Whytes and Warrens to himself, because in theory he despised them. And he wasn't prepared to tell Jodi that he was looking for internal treachery, because she was an eternal optimist. She'd be on him in a minute.

So he fudged it as best he could. "I'm not sure that it does relate. But every little bit helps."

Jodi was too savvy to settle for that. "The official position still holds that it was a murder-suicide. If you're trying to understand how Mark Whyte could have murdered his wife and then killed himself, why are you concentrating on their parents?"

"I'm not *concentrating* on them. It's just a place to begin."

"That's an awful lot of investigative work for a here-and-now murder-suicide. Isn't it above and beyond the call of duty?"

"Let's just say I'm dedicated."

"Oh, I know that," she teased, but her smile never quite made it. "You're looking for foul play."

His eyes met hers. "What gives you that idea?"

"I know you."

Sliding down in his chair, Bob propped his feet on the small oak coffee table before him. "I'm a detective," he said offhandedly. "It's my job to consider every possibility."

"Some of which are?" When he shot her another, sharper glance, she held up a hand. "Hey, I was just curious. But it's okay. You don't have to talk about it." At times like these she wondered if he didn't trust her. Or if he doubted her intelligence. More likely, he feared she was *too* intelligent and might just upstage him in psyching out a case.

She started to rise, but he dragged her back by a wrist. "It's not that I don't want to, just that there's not much to say." He felt her body slowly relax, so he went on, but more slowly. "On the surface, a murder-suicide could be plausible. Mark Whyte had problems. So did Deborah Warren."

"But we all do, don't we?" The subject interested her. Suicide among the young was a problem on the rise, one she had had to face at the school where she worked. True, the Whyte-Warren deaths weren't exactly the teenage variety, but still . . . "Were either Mark's or Deborah's problems that great to warrant self-destruction?"

"We're looking into it, but we haven't got anything definitive yet. Rumor has it that Mark was having money problems. And drug problems. And sex problems."

"In *your opinion*, were any of those severe enough to explain what happened?"

"What is this, the third degree?"

She caught her breath, stung by his tone. There it was again. His ego. "No. Just me. Wondering."

Something in her voice got to him. Whether it was her softness, her sincerity, or an odd kind of sadness he didn't know. But he felt instant remorse, so he relented. "I don't know the details yet, but from what I've heard . . . my opinion?" His voice lowered. "No."

"Has your investigation turned up any evidence of foul play?"

He stared at the fingernails of his right hand and puckered his lips. "Concrete evidence? Not . . . yet."

He was frustrated. She heard it in his voice, saw it in the downward cast of his head. "If there's something to be found, you'll find it, Bob. You're the best they've got. That's why you were put in charge."

"Yeah. So the best they've got comes up with a big fat zero. What then?"

"Then it really was a murder-suicide."

Cavanaugh considered that possibility for several minutes. When he spoke it was with a touch of bewilderment. "The weird thing is that, in my gut, I *don't* buy the suicide bit. And it has nothing to do with anything Ryan or anyone else might have said." He jabbed his stomach. "It's just here." His bewilderment deepened. "There was something about that scene, about the way the bodies were lying on the bed—no, about the way the gun was in his hand, like the whole thing was staged—I mean, if you were to shoot yourself in the head, wouldn't you lose your grip on the gun as you toppled over?"

He fell silent, grappling with that question. After a minute he resumed speaking with a more forceful inflection. "Those families are strong. I may hate it, but they are. They're doers. They don't sit back and wait for things to happen. I can't believe that they'd stand by and watch two of their number get so thoroughly screwed up that they'd commit murder, much less suicide."

"But mental illness—"

"They're *strong*. They bounce back and wind up on top. Jack Whyte has had setbacks in his day, but for each step back he took three ahead. Mark was his son. That's got to amount to something."

Jodi knew that he was being unrealistic. Genes could only take a person so far. Likewise upbringing and example. At some point circumstance took over. Some of the suicides she had seen had involved the most improbable victims.

"No," Bob went on distractedly. Again it was as though he had forgotten her presence, as though he were reasoning with himself. "I don't buy suicide. But damn it, we have so few leads! We've taken the waterfront apart looking for witnesses, but no one saw or heard anything unusual that night. With the rocking of the boats in their slips there could have been any number of noises that sounded like a gunshot. Mark's prints were the only ones on the gun, but that doesn't mean anything if whoever killed him wiped the gun clean and then put it in his hand."

"A nitrate test?"

"Inconclusive. Could have been from gunpowder lingering on the gun after it was fired."

"The gun was his," Jodi prompted softly.

"Which could mean that whoever used it either stole it beforehand or knew where Mark kept it on the boat. So we could be dealing with a stranger or someone who knew him well." He raked a hand through his hair, then looked up at her beseechingly. "The lab went over every inch of that boat. There were dozens of other fingerprints, apparently left there over a period of time. The only possible clue is a footprint on the threshold to the cabin where they were found. The cabin itself is carpeted, so there was nothing, and it rained the next morning, so any prints on the deck were washed away. Anyway, there's no way to tell if the footprint was from another of those guests who left their fingerprints."

He paused for a breath, calming himself in the process. "I've got the lab doing extra tests on that footprint. If we can find something in it, some unique or characteristic kind of dirt or mud or seaweed . . . something . . . anything. . . ."

"And in the meantime?"

He let out a weary sigh. "In the meantime we search Mark's place in L.A. There may be a clue one way or another. The police out there claim they've already been over it. They weren't thrilled when I told them I'd be sending my own team this week. Can you believe that? It's like they think this is a game and they insist on holding the cards. Hell, we're supposedly working on the same side!"

"Shh," Jodi murmured. "It's okay."

"It's *not* okay, damn it! By the time we get a shot at it half the fuckin' evidence may be gone!"

"I know," she whispered. "I know, but you're doing everything you can."

His features tightened. "No. I'll have my guys tear that place apart, and when they're done they can start questioning people who had any connection with Mark or Deborah. We've already started studying Mark's financial records. His wallet and credit cards were on the boat, so we're checking out every possible lead there."

"Hoping for?"

"Something to explain why the guy would kill his wife and then himself or why someone else would do it. Motive. There's got to be one somewhere. Within the next week or so I'll start interviewing people around here. I haven't rushed it because I don't want to alienate the families."

"Why would interviews alienate them? I'd think they'd welcome anything you do. After all, you're trying to find out whether someone murdered two of their own."

"Scandal, Jodi," he informed her dryly. "As far as the families are concerned it was a murder-suicide. The last thing they want is headlines connecting Mark or Deborah with something ugly. The newspapers are already speculating; something coming from the police would have that much more weight."

Jodi stared at him incredulously. "Do you mean to say that they'd be willing to leave well enough alone simply for the sake of their own reputations?"

"It wouldn't surprise me."

"But aren't you pandering to them by being cautious?" She would have guessed, given Bob's feelings toward the Whytes and Warrens, that he would be more than glad to make them squirm.

"I'm trying to be human," was his quiet response. "To jump right in with wild accusations the day after the funeral would have been crass. I like to think that I'm a step above the sleaze reporter, regardless of my personal feelings."

Jodi's face slowly relaxed into a smile and she hugged him. "That's my man."

He colored under her praise, realizing that he might have sounded self-righteous even though he had meant every word he'd said. "But don't worry," he said more gruffly. "I'll do my investigation. In my own time and way, I'll do it. I'll do whatever it takes until I'm satisfied one way or the other. And if it means that I'll eventually have to grill the Whytes and Warrens themselves, so be it."

Ironically, Robert Cavanaugh found himself on the wrong side of the interrogation table the next morning. Shortly after he reached his desk, he received a call from Jordan Whyte suggesting that they meet for coffee at the Dunkin Donuts on Commercial Street. It was clearly a neutral locale, one where they might be free of curious onlookers.

Cavanaugh, curious himself, quickly agreed and was at the appointed spot thirty minutes later. The shop was nearly empty, but even if it had been packed he would have had no trouble locating Jordan. He was sitting at the counter staring at his hands, which were clasped on the Formica surface. Even with his head downcast and the short-sleeved polo shirt and jeans he wore there was an aura of power to him. Cavanaugh resented that.

Approaching the adjacent stool, he gruffly gestured toward the waitress. "Two coffees."

Jordan looked up. He had never seen Robert Cavanaugh before, and he was puzzled, then wary. In answer to the question in his eyes, Cavanaugh nodded and extended his hand. Jordan met it in a brief shake, but neither man said a word.

Within a minute two mugs filled with hot coffee were deposited on the counter. Cavanaugh cocked his head toward a small booth where they might talk in relative privacy, and only when they had both slid into their respective seats did he speak.

"I'm sorry about your brother and sister-in-law." Death did

sadden him; he wasn't that hardened yet. His enmity toward the families involved couldn't outweigh his sense of common decency. Not to mention the fact that he wanted to play it safe until he had had a chance to size Jordan up.

Jordan gave a single nod in thanks for the expression of condolence, then sat back in the booth, staring at Cavanaugh all the while. He wasn't quite sure what to make of him; he looked clean cut and alert, not exactly the frazzled or slovenly detective Jordan had expected. "I understand you're heading the investigation."

"That's right."

"You're a detective lieutenant?"

"Yes."

"Homicide?"

"That's right." Cavanaugh bided his time. He knew damn well Jordan Whyte had known the answers to each of the questions he had asked. A man like Jordan, coming from a family like the Whytes, didn't approach anything blindly. Cavanaugh assumed that Jordan was using the time to assess him, and he was grateful that he had on his sharp, summer-weight tweed blazer, a crisp white shirt and rep tie. Jordan Whyte should know that he wasn't dealing with a slouch—even if Cavanaugh had splurged on the outfit only at Jodi's insistence.

"I understand that John Ryan was the one who assigned you to the case."

Cavanaugh nodded.

"What happened to George Haas? Isn't he the head of the homicide division?"

When Cavanaugh would have argued that he was more than capable of handling the case, if that was indeed what Jordan was wondering, his pride held his temper for him. "Captain Haas will be retiring by the end of the year. I'm the senior detective under him. Given the need for continuity, Ryan thought I'd be a far better man to handle the case."

Jordan nodded, accepting the explanation. He also accepted the fact that Robert Cavanaugh was well-spoken, his voice showing barely a hint of a Boston accent. He came across as being cultivated, at least relatively so given his occupation. "You think you're in for a long haul, then?"

Cavanaugh gave a negligent shrug. "I'm in for as long as it takes."

Jordan was beginning to suspect that his adversary was not only well-dressed and well-spoken, but shrewd. He wasn't volunteering a thing. "How's it going?"

"It's going."

"Have you come up with anything?"

"As in anything that might suggest that it was something other than what it appeared to be on the surface?"

"That is why you're investigating, isn't it?" Jordan answered disdainfully.

Slowly but firmly, Cavanaugh nodded.

"And?" When Cavanaugh simply stared blankly at him, he prodded further. "Have you found anything fishy?"

"You mean, evidence that someone stole onto the boat and committed a double murder?"

"That's right."

"We're working on it."

Jordan could feel his patience fraying. Getting information from Robert Cavanaugh was like pulling teeth. "Has the lab finished its work?"

"Not all. It takes time."

"How much time?"

"A week, two, three."

"For one lab report?"

"For in-depth analyses of a hundred small details."

Jordan absently batted at a fly that had settled near his mug. "Do you have *any* leads?"

"Not yet."

"What are you hoping for?"

"I'm not *hoping* for anything. Regardless of what you think, a policeman doesn't *hope* for murder."

Jordan sighed. The man obviously had a chip on his shoulder. "Let me rephrase the question, then. What are you looking for?"

"Anything out of the ordinary."

"A murder-suicide in families like ours *is* out of the ordinary."

"That's one of the reasons we're conducting an investigation."

"What are you working on now?"

"Anything . . . everything."

"Look, Detective Cavanaugh," Jordan said, gritting his teeth, his gaze sharp as he shot forward in his seat, "my family has been through enough in the past eleven days to deserve a little more than vague answers." His tone was low, dangerously so, and a muscle high in his cheek twitched. In another less public place he would have exploded, venting the full force of his wrath on Cavanaugh. As it was he was struggling to contain himself. "Two of our members are dead, and we think we have a right to know what you're doing to find out *why* they're dead. We'd like to know exactly what you did yesterday, exactly what you're doing today, and exactly what you plan to do tomorrow."

Cavanaugh couldn't restrain himself. He had too many negative feelings about the Whytes and Warrens to allow Jordan Whyte to try to intimidate him. He too sat forward, his eyes narrowed. "Look, Mr. Whyte, I don't believe I owe you anything. I work for the state, in case you've forgotten, and the only responsibility I have is to investigate this case to the best of my ability and then present my findings to the appropriate authority, which will take any action necessary."

"As a servant of the state you're answerable to the taxpayers," Jordan snapped back. "And I can assure you that my family pays its share in taxes."

"Does it?" Cavanaugh asked with just the right amount of sarcasm. Taxes were another of his peeves, since he firmly believed that, thanks to loopholes of one kind or another, the rich never paid their share.

Jordan wasn't fazed by his question. He went on in an even

more condescending tone. "You obviously haven't done your homework as thoroughly as you'd like to believe or you'd never have asked that."

"And you haven't done your homework as thoroughly as *you'd* like to believe if you think that I haven't done mine!" His eyes were filled with fire. "Forget the fact that Haas is retiring. Forget that I'm the senior man under him. The real reason I got this case is that Ryan believes I can do a better job with it than anyone else in the department. I've had a whole lot of time to prove myself. I worked my way up from the bottom of the force. No one handed me anything for free; my promotions were solely on merit. I work hard, I'm thorough, and I'm a stickler for details. Don't underestimate me, Mr. Whyte."

Jordan was momentarily taken aback. He wasn't accustomed to people standing up to him, particularly when he used his guaranteed-to-have-them-shaking-in-their-boots look, which he thought he'd been using for the last few minutes. Cavanaugh was tough. Cracking him would take a different approach.

He took a deep breath as he slowly sat back, and his arms, which had been propped on the table during his attack, dropped limply to his sides. "You don't like me, do you?"

It was Cavanaugh's turn to be taken aback. He hadn't expected such directness or such resignation. "Whether I like you or not is irrelevant," he said crisply but calmly. "This is a case, just like any other case. Who you are is secondary to the fact that two people are dead. They could have been two vagrants from Pine Street, and if there was reason to think they'd been murdered rather than that they'd drunk themselves to death I'd be carrying out an investigation every bit as intensely."

Jordan, who couldn't help but be impressed by the man's apparent integrity, tipped his head to the side and frowned gently. "How'd you get into police work?"

The question surprised Cavanaugh, but he had nothing to hide. "I served in Vietnam, and by the time I got back I'd developed a fixation on law and order."

"When were you there?"

"Sixty-seven through sixty-nine."

"And you made it back in one piece," Jordan marveled, moments before his eyes grew distant. "You were one of the lucky ones. Four of my college buddies didn't do so well; three came back in boxes and the fourth hasn't made it back at all."

Cavanaugh wasn't about to be upstaged. If Jordan was playing for sympathy, he could match him. "I lost two friends there. We all had college deferments but our luck ran out after graduation. There are times when I wonder if we'd served earlier—or later—whether things would have been different. My friends were in the wrong place at the wrong time."

College. Jordan hadn't expected that. He had assumed that the bulk of the Boston police force, particularly those who had started from the bottom as Cavanaugh said he had done, presumably in the late sixties or early seventies, had signed on directly from high school. "Where did you go?" When Cavanaugh frowned uncomprehendingly, he prompted, "To college."

"University of North Carolina."

Jordan's curiosity increased. "You're younger than I'd expected. When did you graduate?"

Cavanaugh allowed himself a dry smile. "The same year you did. I believe we were rivals."

Jordan had gone to Duke. He grinned. "You bet we were. Did you play football, too?" When Cavanaugh nodded, his grin broadened. "We must have played each other."

"More than once. I knew who *you* were. Everyone knew Jordan Whyte, the star quarterback of the Blue Devils."

"And you?"

"A wide receiver. You wouldn't have heard of me. I was a special team player mostly." Kickoffs and punt returns comprised the majority of the time he had spent on the field. No, no one had heard of him, least of all the star quarterback of the Blue Devils.

"Hey, not bad," Jordan declared. "Not bad at all. Special teams are really important. Some of the most dramatic turns in games happen when special teams are on the field."

"Hey, listen," Cavanaugh cautioned, holding up a hand, "that was a world away. I'm not making apologies for what I did. You don't need to patronize me—"

"I'm not doing that. I meant what I said." His features mellowed as he reminisced. "There was one game we played where we were down by a touchdown with a minute and forty seconds left on the clock. It was a fourth down and punt situation. Our special team came on, the punt was made, and the other team—I think it was Georgia Tech—fumbled. We recovered the ball and ran all the way for the touchdown. Now that was exciting!"

Cavanaugh couldn't help himself. "So did you break the tie and win?"

"Lost by a last minute field goal." He shrugged. "That's the way it goes sometimes."

"Do you ever wish you'd gone pro?"

"Me? Nah. I have weak knees. I'd never have made it in the pros. There's a time and a place for everything; my playing days were well left behind when I graduated."

Cavanaugh knew that he ought to get back to business, but his curiosity got the best of him. "You own a hockey team. Why that instead of football?"

Jordan's smile was lopsided. Cavanaugh tried to decide if he was aiming at self-derision for effect. "Can you see me calling the plays from the owner's box? I'd be impossible to work for; it would be too frustrating to sit still and keep my mouth shut. Besides," he cast a glance at two men who had just settled at the counter and lowered his voice, "buying a football team was exactly what people would have expected from me. I can't be *that* predictable, now, can I?"

Cavanaugh chuckled. "No. You can't. You do enjoy doing the unexpected, don't you?"

"Yes. And it's not only for other people's benefit." Jordan wanted to make that clear. He had been criticized for being a showman once too often. "I do what excites me, and the unexpected does excite me. Which isn't to say that something is automatically exciting simply because it's unexpected. I'm picky in what I choose to do, and I'm lucky in that I can afford to be picky. I'm not as impulsive as some people think. But we all do need breathers. Doing the same blessed thing day in and day out would drive me insane." He paused, thinking. "Isn't it the same for you? Don't you get a little rush when a new and challenging case is dropped on your desk?"

Cavanaugh took his turn swatting at the fly. "I think any detective does. The most exciting ones—maybe the hardest to solve—are those in which the unexpected happens." He looked Jordan in the eye. "It's the little twist here or there that makes things interesting."

If he was trying to make the point that Jordan's involvement in the murder of his brother would be a welcome twist, he failed. Jordan was on one aspect of his wavelength, though. "Which, I suppose, brings us back to the case you're working on now." He'd been fingering the handle of his mug, but looked up at Cavanaugh and spoke softly. "I think we got off on the wrong foot before. It was my fault and I apologize far that. It's just that my family hasn't been able to get many answers, and it's frustrating."

"It's frustrating for me, too," Cavanaugh stated, but his defenses were down. "Things take time. I make calls, but one report or another isn't done. Take the ballistics report. I need the results to show whether the bullets that killed your brother and sister-in-law were, in fact, fired from the gun we found in Mark's hand. But the chief ballistician has been on vacation, and personally, I don't trust the judgment of the guy under him, so we wait."

Jordan took a sip of his tepid coffee, then lowered the mug to the palm of his free hand. "We've discussed it—my brother and sister and the Warrens—and none of us can find justification for the idea of a murder-suicide. We're convinced they were murdered."

Cavanaugh maintained a neutral expression, debating how

much to reveal of his own thoughts. He certainly wouldn't tell Jordan right off the bat that he suspected his family or the Warrens. And he wasn't sure that he did. He *wanted* to, but wanting didn't make a case.

Did he think Jordan was capable of murder? At first impression, no. Jordan seemed to wear his feelings on his sleeve. He appeared to be forthright, quick to spit out his thoughts, legitimately concerned about the case. If he had been a murderer, he would have shown some sign of nervousness; experience had taught Cavanaugh that even the most consummate actors betrayed themselves with the twitch of a lip or the blink of an eye at the wrong moment. No, Jordan wasn't a murderer, unless he was truly pathological—and there was always that possibility.

Cavanaugh couldn't rule it out anymore than he could rule out the vague chance that Jordan had intentionally tossed out the possibility of murder to cover his own involvement.

He decided on a cautious course, revealing only as much as Jordan could learn from another, properly placed phone call. "So far we can't find a motive for murder-suicide either. Money seems to have been a problem—"

"You checked out his credit cards and the bank. I know. We got calls afterward."

"It's my job."

"I'm not criticizing." The fly was by Jordan's ear; he took a distracted swipe at it. "Mark owed a lot but not enough to kill himself over."

"We'll be scouting around L.A. later in the week."

"He dabbled in drugs," Jordan offered, figuring that Cavanaugh would learn it anyway. There were other things Cavanaugh might also learn, but Jordan wasn't about to reveal them at the moment. He wasn't yet sure how far the detective could be trusted. "Cocaine mostly. But he didn't have a serious problem and the autopsy didn't show anything in his blood, so he wasn't wacked out at the time of the shootings, not that casual snorting does that anyway. If he'd been fooling with something hallucinogenic I could understand it. But not cocaine."

Cavanaugh agreed. "And we didn't find any signs of organic disease in either of them. Sometimes if a person is diagnosed as having a terminal illness he decides to end the waiting, but that wasn't the case here." He paused, deciding that he might as well probe while he could. "Do you think there could have been some disagreement between them caused by Deborah's pregnancy?"

Jordan shook his head. "They wanted kids. Mark told me so himself, and even though Deborah had a hard time after the first one died—"

"The first one?"

"Stillborn. Four years ago." He watched Cavanaugh pull a small notebook from his breast pocket, flip it open and jot down a note. "She'd been in therapy to ease her over it, and I'm sure she had to be nervous the second time around, but she did want the baby."

"Could I speak with her therapist?"

"Sure, but he's in L.A. Gil probably has the name and number. I'll get it for you if you want."

Cavanaugh nodded, rubbed a finger on his upper lip as he studied the pad, then returned his gaze to Jordan. "So you do think they were murdered."

"That's right."

"Any specific suspects?"

"No."

"How about the others—your brother, sister, the Warrens? Did they have any suggestions?"

"No. Mark and Deborah spent most of their time in California. Mark kept the boat here and they took it out whenever they came East, but other than holidays and traditional family times we didn't see much of them. Who their friends were, who they worked with, who might have wanted them dead—and why—we just don't know." He looked frustrated again. "We *do* know that they had every reason to live. And," his voice hardened in conviction, "we do know that Mark wouldn't have had the guts to pull that trigger on himself, let alone on Deborah."

They sat in silence for a minute before Cavanaugh finally spoke. "The last of the lab reports may tell us something, and I'll be sorting through the contacts anyway." He returned the notebook to his pocket. "I'd like to speak with other members of your family and the Warrens."

"I'm not sure they'd have anything to add."

"Something they think is totally irrelevant may give me a clue."

"It might be difficult, especially for my mother and Lenore, but if you think it's important. . . ."

Cavanaugh did, but he wasn't insensitive to Natalie and Lenore's plights. "I'll hold off on those two for a while. What about the McNees and the Morells?"

Jordan faltered for the first time, his body going still. "What about them?"

"I'd like to speak with them. Sometimes the help picks up things that those who are closest to the victims miss."

"I suppose that makes sense," Jordan said after a slight hesitation.

Cavanaugh studied Jordan closely. "Katia Morell—she lives in New York, too, doesn't she?"

It was a moment before Jordan answered. "You know that she does. You also know *what* she does."

But Cavanaugh didn't, not in detail, at least. He hadn't gotten that far in his investigation. "She's in . . . advertising is it?"

"She's an art director with an ad agency."

"I'd like to talk with her."

"Is that necessary?"

"I think so."

This time when Jordan sat forward it was with an odd, beseeching look on his face. "Please. Katia is a totally innocent bystander in all this. She's been in New York for eleven years. She has her own life and her own interests."

Cavanaugh wasn't quite sure why Jordan was being protective of Katia, but he remembered the look they had exchanged at the cemetery and the suspicions he had had then. "She's special to you, isn't she?" he asked.

Jordan stared at him. He wondered if he was that obvious about his feelings or if Cavanaugh was simply very perceptive. In either case he sensed that the question had been asked man to man rather than detective to relative of the victim, and it was in that vein that Jordan answered.

"Yes. She's special."

Cavanaugh would have asked more, but something held him back. He felt he was treading on thin ice where this line of questioning was concerned. "If I contact her, will she cooperate?"

Jordan hesitated, then nodded, aware that for whatever his reasons, Cavanaugh was set on his course. But he wanted to make a final plea anyway. "Katia's a good person. I mean really good. She's alone in so many ways. She's like a member of the family, but not like a member of the family. She's one of us, but not. Deborah's death hit her especially hard, and I don't want her to have to relive it any more than necessary. It seems unfair." His gaze met Cavanaugh's. "If she can't reap the benefits of being a Whyte or a Warren, should she have to be saddled with our pain?"

Cavanaugh considered the varied emotions behind Jordan's words. He was protective, willing to fight for Katia's defense, even angry about her lot in life. He could either be hiding something powerful or simply be head over heels in love with the woman. Cavanaugh wondered which it was.

"I'll keep that in mind when I talk with her."

Jordan nodded again, then, as though dismissing that thought, cleared his throat and spoke with greater force. "We do want to help, Detective. My father and Gil have been badgering Police Commissioner Holstrom, but I think they're turning him off more than anything. That's one of the reasons I wanted to see you today. I realize you're busy and that this is only one of many cases you've got to be working on. For that matter, I'm busy too.

I should be in New York and not here. But I felt it important that we meet. It would make things easier all around if you and I could keep in touch—"

"As in telling you what I did yesterday, and today, and tomorrow?" Cavanaugh asked.

Jordan paused for a minute, knowing that he had antagonized the man with that particular comment. "Nah. I was frustrated before, and when I get frustrated I tend to operate on a short fuse." He swung at the fly, which had suddenly chosen to hover by his head. "Goddamned fly! Hell, we don't even have donuts!"

"Maybe if we did it would leave us alone."

Jordan grunted, but calmed quickly. "We're not asking for every little detail, just a general idea of what's going on." His mouth twitched up at one corner in a hint of the same self-derision Cavanaugh had sensed earlier. "We like to feel we're on top of things even when we're not."

Reaching back, he drew his wallet from the pocket of his jeans. "Here's my card. I'll instruct my secretary to make sure you get through." He started to hand the card across the table, then took it back and turned it over. He patted one side of his shirt, then the other. "No pocket, much less a pen. Can I use yours?" He jotted down his home phone number on the card and handed it and the pen to Cavanaugh. "And I know where to find you."

Cavanaugh nestled the card in his own wallet in exchange for money to pay for the coffee.

"Hey, I'll take care of it—" Jordan began, only to be interrupted by Cavanaugh's drawl.

"And let someone think that I'm being bribed? No way, Whyte. I think I can spring for two cups of coffee." He slid out of the booth. "I'll be in touch," was all he said before he left Jordan sitting alone with cold coffee and his thoughts.

Chapter 6

JORDAN RETURNED TO NEW YORK for a quick and hectic twenty-four hours of nonstop business before flying on to Baltimore to watch the Blades drop two home games in a row. While he was there, in addition to brainstorming sessions with the general manager of the team, he spent time with Cheryl Drew, whom he had been seeing on and off for a year. He felt as let down by her company as he had by the losses of his team.

Something had happened to him with the death of his brother: Mortality had hit him in the face. Suddenly he seemed to be seeing his life through different eyes, and he wasn't sure he liked the view. In the professional sphere he had few complaints; teams were bound to lose just as business deals were bound to have setbacks, and those didn't bother him because he knew that there would be wins as well. In the personal sphere, however, he found his life lacking. The role of playboy wasn't all it was made out to be, particularly when one was thirty-nine and suddenly found the thought of a woman in every port tiresome.

It didn't help when, two days after he returned to New York, he took one of those women to the theater and during intermission caught sight of Katia across the crowded lobby. She was with a distinguished looking man who had to be too old for her, Jordan decided—quite irrationally, since he himself was nine years her senior and not that much younger than the man at her side—but she looked as though she were having a grand time, and that upset him.

The following morning he showed up bright and early at Katia's office. She was busy working at her drawing board and looked up, first in surprise, then pleasure, when he turned in at her door.

"Jordan!" Rising quickly, she gave him a hug. "You should have come an hour ago and shared my breakfast."

Leaving his hands lightly clasped at the small of her back, he smiled at her upturned face. "Tell me you're taking a gourmet breakfast course now."

"Actually, I was referring to coffee and croissants from the shop downstairs."

His smile faded. "You eat breakfast at work? What time do you get here, anyway?"

"Seven. Seven-thirty."

It was barely nine. Jordan thought he had been early himself. "After a night at the theater!"

Katia frowned. "How did you—you were *there?* Jordan, why didn't you come over and say hello?"

"It was during intermission and the place was packed. Besides, you looked like you were having too good a time to be disturbed."

Katia heard the faint accusation in his tone and felt an inkling of smug satisfaction. Jordan hadn't said much when she had been going with Sean. She had been free now for a year, yet he hadn't made a move. If he didn't want her there were other men who did. "It was nice. The play was good, didn't you think?"

"Who was he?" Jordan asked quietly.

"Who?"

"The guy you were with."

Moving out of the circle of his arms, she propped her hip against the stool she had been on before. "His name is Alan Montgomery. He's one of a group of doctors who run a private medical center. We've done work for them."

Jordan nodded. He put his hands in his trousers pockets and rocked back on his heels. "Montgomery. Is he here in the city?"

She shook her head. "Long Island."

He nodded again. And rocked again. "A general practitioner?"

Again, she shook her head. "Gynecologist."

It was all she could do not to laugh when Jordan let out a quiet, "Geez." He didn't nod this time or rock back on his heels. "Have you been seeing him long?"

Actually, Alan had been asking her out for months. She had always found him a little too sure of himself and had turned him down with some pleasure. She had agreed to see him only after she had returned from Maine and realized that Jordan was as out of reach as ever.

That, in fact, described her social life to a tee. She had lived the last ten years on the rebound.

"It's the first time we've been out."

"Do you like him?"

She made a pretense of debating the question in her mind. Her mouth turned down in a shrug and she gave a noncommittal nod.

"If he can afford to hire your firm he must be doing well," Jordan reflected.

"He is."

"I bet the women love him." All too well he remembered the man's dashing good looks.

"Jordan. . . ."

"He's probably got an ex-wife or two."

"One."

"And kids?"

"Two. Is that relevant?"

"It is if you plan to marry him."

"Last night was our first date! Aren't you rushing things a little?"

"Just want you to know what you're getting into. He's probably got hefty alimony payments, not to mention child support. And if you did marry him and had kids, he'd be torn between loyalties to his first children and yours." He paused. "Is he *your* gynecologist?"

She did laugh then. "No."

"Thank goodness for *that*," he mumbled and went on more firmly. "You know, a guy like that probably has the hots for half of his patients. It's a big thing today, doctors taking advantage of vulnerable female patients. I can imagine what he pays in malpractice premiums, which is *another* thing you'd better consider—"

"This is absurd, Jordan! I simply went to the theater with the man. I don't have plans to marry him, and if I did, my major consideration would be love, not how much money he has left after his alimony and child support payments, or whether he has adequate malpractice insurance." She eyed him suspiciously. "What's on your mind?"

"You. I worry about you."

Like a big brother. She hated it. "You didn't seem to worry when I was with Sean."

"Sean was harmless."

"You approved of my relationship with him?"

"I knew it wouldn't last."

"Oh?"

"He wasn't strong enough for you."

"Maybe Alan is," Katia suggested, then thought better of pursuing the matter. "But that's beside the point. The point is that I've been on my own for a long time now. Isn't it a little late to start worrying?"

"I've always worried. Maybe I'm getting worse with old age."

Then do something about it, you ass! she wanted to yell, but she simply offered a sad smile. "I'm okay, Jordan. Really I am. And don't worry; I'm not about to jump into something—"

"Katia!" Roger Boland was leaning in at her door, scowling. "I need that storyboard by eleven."

"You'll have it," she answered, knowing full well that Roger hadn't intended on stopping in until he had spotted Jordan through the glass wall of her office. Over the years Jordan had been by enough times for the two men to be acquainted.

Jordan nodded his head in greeting. "Roger."

"How's it going, Jordan?"

"Not bad."

"You're keeping Katia from business."

"I *am* business."

Roger straightened and posted himself more fully on Katia's threshold. "Oh? You're *bringing* us business?"

"Possibly. That's what I have to talk with Katia about."

"I was wondering when you'd get around to it." For every bit as much as Roger disliked Jordan and what he represented, he wasn't about to look a gift horse in the mouth. "You've been using Klein and Wood, haven't you?"

"He's still using Klein and Wood," Katia asserted staunchly.

Jordan looked at her. "Not if you'll agree to do the work."

"Jordan," she warned, "we've discussed this before—"

"That would be great, Katia!" Roger interrupted, but his attention was on Jordan. "What did you have in mind?"

"I'll have to discuss it with Katia."

"And she'll have to discuss it with me, since I'm her superior."

"She may have *nothing* to discuss with you if I don't get a chance to talk alone with her first," Jordan said with a pleasant smile.

Roger knew precisely why he disliked the man. He was smooth and arrogant and stubborn and his smile was about as legitimate as a three-dollar bill. If it hadn't been for the fact that having Jordan Whyte as a client would be a feather in the agency's cap he would have come back with a properly scathing comment. Instead, he held up both hands and backed away from the door. "You've got her," was all he said before he left with an ingenuous smile of his own.

Katia promptly rose from her perch and closed the door. Turning, she leaned back against it and crossed her arms over her chest. "Okay, Jordan. Let's have it."

"I've just bought the old Marshall Arms Hotel and a large parcel of land surrounding it on Martha's Vineyard. I'm going to build a resort and condominium complex there. I want you to handle the ad campaign for me."

Katia studied him for a moment. He stood straight and tall and looked almost irresistible in a tan suit that perfectly offset his dark coloring. She could have melted on the spot if she had let herself, but she didn't. Dropping her chin to her chest, she slowly shook her head. "Other days . . . other projects . . . we've been through this before."

"True."

"You know how I feel."

"I know how you've felt in the past."

She met his gaze. "What makes you think my feelings have changed?"

"You've proven yourself. You're secure now."

"Jordan," she sighed, "that may or may not be the case, but I don't want your help."

"Uh-uh, sweetheart. You have it backwards. My offer has nothing to do with me helping you. I want you to help *me*."

"You've got Klein and Wood."

"For other projects, and they're getting stale if you ask me. I want a fresh outlook for this project. I've seen what you've been doing and I think you can give me what I want."

Pushing off from the door, she paced to the window. "I don't want to do this, Jordan."

"Why not?"

She turned. "For one thing, we're too close. It's a lousy practice to do business with friends or relatives."

"You'd be part of a team. It's not like we'd be the only ones involved. I'm impressed with you *and* your agency."

"If you weren't pleased with the final results it would be awkward."

"But I'd have a say in those final results. There are various rounds of presentations with give and take on both sides. It's not a matter of all or nothing."

"And in the end if you weren't thrilled with what we had done you would get angry—either that or you'd hold it in for my sake and then you'd resent me for it."

He paused, and his voice lowered. "I'd never resent you."

She sucked in a breath, desperately wishing he wouldn't use that soulful tone with her. It was cruel when it could have stood for so much. As though to rid herself of the sound, she shook her head sharply. "It would never work."

"I think it would."

"Of course you do. Whenever you set your mind to something you think it will work."

"Have I been wrong all that often?"

She sent a beseechful glance toward the ceiling. "No, Jordan. You're usually right. But then I've always been looking at what you do from a distance. I've never been on the inside of a working relationship with you before."

"Don't you think it's time you tried?"

"No!" she cried. The thought of working with Jordan and seeing him often was both heaven and hell; she found herself being pulled by both sides, trying simply to survive.

Jordan's expression grew tight. "What is it, Katia? Don't you think you can make it?"

"If you're talking about doing the work, of course I can."

"Then what are you afraid of? Is it me? Are you afraid of having an official connection to me?"

Her mouth dropped open, and she stared at him in disbelief. "Are you kidding?"

"Not at all." He slowly began to advance on her. "It may be me or my family, or the Warrens. It's just possible that you don't want any association with us to sully that reputation for independence you've fought so long and hard for. Do you think we'll swallow you up? Is that it?"

"No—"

"Or that we'll try to rule your life?"

"No—"

"Or that we'll demand some kind of kickback or special favor?"

"Jordan, you're not making sense!"

He stood directly before her, staring down from his formidable height. "Well, neither are you, Katia. You'd bite off your nose to spite your face. I want you to do this project for me because I think you'd do a super job. And if you were honest with yourself you'd agree that the project would be good for your agency. And don't you *dare* accuse me of offering charity, because I'm too much of a businessman for that. Where business is concerned I shoot for the best, and if that happens to be you, I don't give a flying damn who you are or where you come from!"

Katia mutely took in his speech, then, unable to help herself, she broke into a smile. "I love it when you get all riled up," she growled and playfully punched the air with a fist. "Give 'em hell, Jordan."

Jordan stuck his hands on his hips, gritted his teeth, squeezed his eyes shut and counted to ten. When he opened his eyes again, he grinned. "Liked that, did ya?"

"Very impressive. I can see why you're a success."

"Does that mean you'll work on my project?"

She shook her head, only to find it suddenly stilled against Jordan's chest. He wrapped his arms around her. She was his prisoner.

"You'll work on my project," he ordered, his mouth close by her ear.

"No, I won't." She had her eyes closed and was breathing in the scent so unique to Jordan.

"I'll hold you like this forever."

"Your legs would give out long before forever came. Remember those weak knees of yours?"

"I'll lay you down on the floor and ravish you here and now."

"With the whole office looking in?"

"Uh-huh."

She pretended to be considering that, when, in truth, she was simply enjoying the closeness of the moment. Jordan's body was long and firm; her own fit with his perfectly. Couldn't he feel it?

Tipping her head back, she grinned at him. "I dare you." Her hand slid over his chest to his shoulders, then higher. She threaded her fingers through his hair. "Come on, Jordan. *Do* it," she coaxed in a teasing whisper.

Only he wasn't smiling. He was looking down at her with a suddenly intense expression, and while his eyes held hers captive, he moved his hands along her sides until his palms contoured the swells of her breasts.

Suddenly she wasn't smiling either. Her insides had begun a whispering tremor and she felt a tingling in her breasts that couldn't have been greater had her bare flesh been in his hand. More than that, she felt the awakening of Jordan's body, felt it growing against her as it had once, years before.

In a flash of memory that day returned. Katia had been nineteen at the time; it was the spring of her freshman year in college. She had gone from New York to spend the Memorial Day weekend with the families on the island before returning to take final exams and then a summer job in the city.

She had met a boy in school; John was a junior, very attractive, and very much enamored of her. Their relationship had reached the point where physical intimacy was the obvious next step.

All the other girls were doing it. Katia had wondered what it was like. She was attracted to John, but she had put him off repeatedly because Jordan was the one who held her heart. It was only natural that she would want Jordan to teach her what making love was all about.

Or so she reasoned when they found themselves alone one night on the beach. They had been up late talking and, on impulse, had stolen out for a midnight swim in the ocean. The waves had been challenging, and they had been exhausted when they finally flopped down, side by side, on the sand.

"That was great!" Katia gasped. "The water's so cold . . . but invigorating!"

As breathless as she, Jordan rolled to his side and, propping himself on an elbow, looked down at her. "You're great. Do you know that any other woman would have run back out after her toe touched the water? You're a good sport, Katia Morell. Just about the best one I know."

"Coming from you," she teased as she caught her breath, "that's a compliment. I thank you."

"I'm not kidding." He reached up and smoothed wet tendrils of hair from her cheeks. "You are a good sport. And you're beautiful, too."

Katia's breath came faster again, and it had nothing to do with the lingering effects of the swim. "So are you," she whispered as she looked into his eyes. The moonlight glistened off his wet lashes, his hair, his shoulders that were so very broad and suddenly looming directly over hers.

Then he lowered his head and kissed her. Oh, he'd kissed her before, but never like this. It started gently, as though he were sampling her, and apparently he liked what he found, so he opened his mouth and tasted more.

Katia was his for the devouring. For everything he did she returned it in kind. He was no longer like a brother, but a man, and she ached for him as only a woman could.

"Where did you learn to kiss like that?" he murmured hoarsely when at last he dragged his mouth from hers.

"From you," she breathed. "Right now. Jordan, kiss me again."

Her hands cupped his head and brought his lips back to hers, but he was ever the leader, the one in command. He explored her with his lips, his tongue, his teeth, and somewhere in the middle he slid his body fully over hers.

She loved his weight. She loved his firmness, the way the hair on his thighs abraded her smoother limbs, the way his middle pressed into her with each breath he took, the way he arched his back and slid a hand up her stomach until he was cupping her breast.

Her body was his. It swelled to his touch and begged for more. And when he peeled down the top of her tanksuit and closed his mouth over one very taut nipple, she cried out in wonder.

"Katia. Soft . . . sweet . . . Katia."

She was arching her back, offering herself more fully to him. What he was doing to her sent spirals of fire to the tips of her toes, which curled into the sand as her thighs spread further apart. When he cupped the underside of her breast, plumped up her flesh and began to suckle even more deeply, the flame grew.

Katia needed the quenching that only Jordan could offer. "Make love to me, Jordan! Please. I want you so much!"

His tongue continued to lave her and she felt the swelling of his loins. But when she strained closer, he groaned, then stiffened. He raised his head, his breathing rough.

"You're a virgin."

"I don't want to be. Not with you."

He was up on rigid arms, his eyes sliding from her face to her naked breasts and back. He moaned and closed his eyes. "We can't, Katia. It wouldn't be right."

"But you want me. I know you do!" On impulse, almost in desperation, she reached down to touch the proof of his desire, but he caught her hand before it had reached its goal.

"Don't," he commanded hoarsely. "I'll lose control if you touch me."

"I want you to lose control."

"But I don't! I'll hate myself for it, and so will you."

"Why?"

"Because . . . because . . ." He rolled off her and sat up, hugging his knees to his chest as he faced the ocean. "Because someday you'll find a man to love you and take care of you and give you all the good things in life you deserve. And I don't want to spoil that."

"*Spoil* it? How could our making love now possibly do that?" She sat up, and feeling suddenly naked—and angry—she tugged her suit back into place. "Jordan, this is the nineteen-seventies! The double standard is passe. Women aren't 'ruined' if they enjoy premarital sex! Men accept that; they're flattered to know that their wives were desirous to others before them."

His gaze speared her. "Is that what you've been learning at NYU? That you aren't attractive unless you sleep around?"

"I didn't say that."

"You implied it."

"No. I don't want to 'sleep around.' All I want to do is to make love with *you*." Though the fire within her had dimmed somewhat, the embers remained hot. "I want you to be the first. I want you to teach me. And if it's my future you're worried about, just think of how much better off I'll be if I know the score rather than be some pathetic babe in the woods."

"You want to know the score?" he gritted. Even the moonlight couldn't soften the hardness of his features. "I'll tell you the score. I lost *my* virginity when I was fifteen years old, and in the thirteen years since, I've slept with three times as many women as you've got fingers and toes. You don't want to mess with me—"

"But it's *better* that you're experienced. You know what to do. You know what you like and you can show me everything."

"I don't want to mess with *you!*" he yelled, and in that instant Katia's will died a cold death.

She stared at him, then swallowed hard. "I see," she whispered at last, then bolted up and was halfway across the beach before Jordan made a lunge and stopped her.

"No, you don't, damn it," he managed between gritted teeth. She was twisting furiously, trying to free herself from his grip. "Hold still, Katia—"

"Let me go!" She alternately bucked at him with her shoulders and clawed at the sand for leverage. "You've had your say! Let me go!"

Firmly wrapping his arms around her from behind, Jordan

rolled them both to a sitting position and anchored her between his legs. She might as well have been in a straitjacket for the mobility he allowed her.

He bent his head until his cheek was pressed to her temple. "What I said came out the wrong way." He spoke slowly, slightly unevenly. "The reason why I won't make love to you has nothing to do with something being wrong with you—"

"I'm not good enough. I understa—" The abrupt tightening of his arms cut off her words.

"You *are* good enough. You're *too* good. It's me. I'm the problem. I'm not right for you, Katia. If I did what you want—" his voice grew husky, almost pained, "and I could in a minute, believe me, but if I did do it, and then next week, or next month, or next year something went wrong, or we had a falling out or something, it would spoil everything we have now. Don't you see? I cherish you, Katia. I don't *want* anything to come between us."

She didn't know what to say because his tone was so gentle, so caring and sincere, and she respected him so thoroughly, that she couldn't fight him. But she was frustrated; her body still ached. She was disappointed. And hurt. She didn't see why she couldn't have it *all*. She didn't see why anything would go wrong in a week or a month or a year. As far as she was concerned, she was more than ready to commit her entire life to Jordan.

Apparently, he didn't feel the same way about her.

His limbs squeezed her, but playfully. "Friends?" he murmured by her ear.

She brooded for a minute longer, then nodded.

"Good." He hoisted them both to their feet. "Come on. Time to get back."

She had gone with him then, saying good night to him in the kitchen and heading alone to her room. When she saw him the next morning she acted, as did he, as though nothing at all had happened on the beach. She had gone back to school. She had dated John, then other men. For a time after she had graduated she and Jordan had seen each other often enough to stretch the imagination and call it dating, but he had never touched her physically, and she had had too much pride to beg.

The pain and humiliation she had suffered that day on the beach had stayed with her through it all, even through the four years she had spent with Sean. It was the memory of the pain and humiliation that returned to her now as Jordan stood with her in her office, holding her tightly in his arms. In spite of the fact that she wanted him as much as she ever had, she slowly shook her head.

"On second thought," she said quietly, "I think that ravishing me here and now on the floor isn't such a good idea." Carefully she extricated herself from his hold. Stepping back, she straightened her dress. "I've grown fussy with age. I prefer satin sheets and candlelight." She took a resolute breath. "Sorry, bud. No go."

Jordan released her at her first inclination. He had seen a lifetime of emotions pass through her eyes and for a minute he couldn't speak, much less regain his bearings. But only for a minute.

"No go," he repeated dumbly, then took a quick breath. "Okay. I won't ravish you." He returned his hands to his trousers pockets and studied her closely. "But I won't give up on my plan. I want you to do the ad campaign for me. And if you refuse—"

"Don't threaten me, Jordan."

"I wasn't—"

"You were," she insisted, but rather than accusation, her words held understanding. She knew Jordan well, so well. He was the way he was, and though it bothered her at times she loved him anyway. "You were just about to say that if I refuse you'll go to my boss, and you *know* that he'll jump at the chance to do your work." She sighed. "I'll do it, Jordan. But I want you to remember something." Everything about her saddened. "A long time ago you argued against our involvement with each other because you thought that something might happen, that there might be some sort of falling out, and then we'd lose what we had. Well, I'm wondering if what you're suggesting now might very well cause the same thing, and I just want you to know that I've warned you."

Only then did Jordan realize that moments ago Katia's mind had been back on the beach, ten years before.

"Nothing will happen," he said with such force that she was startled.

"Are you that sure?"

"Yes. I won't *let* anything happen."

"Well then . . . I guess I have no choice."

"You do."

"No."

"Why not?"

She thought about that for a minute, finally looking up at him in helplessness. "Because you asked."

"I've asked before and you've turned me down."

"Maybe I am more secure now. Maybe I really do think I can handle it."

In truth, what had happened was that during the short time Jordan had been in her office, she had realized that, for the first time, she wanted to be with him more than she was frightened of being hurt. And she had also gained a certain strength over the years. Hadn't she been the one to step away from him this time? It had been torture, but there had been some satisfaction in it.

"But you will have to speak with my boss," she added. "He makes the decisions on taking new clients."

"There won't be any problem."

"No."

"Good." Jordan had expected to be ecstatic, yet something bothered him. He had the dreadful feeling that he had waited too long, that Katia had grown beyond his reach. Even the knowledge that it was for the best gave him little comfort. He wanted her. Damn it, he always had. In those split seconds of silence he cursed himself, cursed his father, cursed whatever fate it was that held Katia beyond his reach.

"Come on, Jordan," Katia chided. "Where's that victory grin?"

He flashed it, but it was without depth. It reminded Katia of similar grins she had seen over the years on the faces of Jack and Gil, which in turn reminded her of the families.

"How is everyone?" she asked. "I haven't spoken with a soul since I've been back." She felt guilty about that, but she had needed to work out her own feelings about Deborah and Mark's deaths.

"They're okay."

"Your mother?"

"Back in Dover and carrying on as best she can. She spends most of her time trying to comfort Lenore."

"And Jack and Gil?"

"What do you think?" Jordan returned dryly. "They're back to business as usual. The House is in recess until after Labor Day, so Gil is cashing in on the time to muster whatever sympathy votes he can. My father is back to work with a vengeance. From what Nick says he's been more of a tyrant than ever."

"He's upset."

"He's a bastard."

"Ah, Jordan. That's unfair. You saw him at the island. You know how upset he was by Mark's death. So he's taking it out on his work. I suppose he has to take it out on *something*."

Jordan went to stand before the window. "You'd think he'd try to help his wife. She's suffering, too. But no. The man is as selfish as they come. Jackson Whyte is the only person who counts."

"It's just his way," Katia said softly. She came to stand by his side, looking up at his stormy features. "Have you talked with him at all?"

"We have very little to say to one another. You know that."

"But he's just lost one son. Maybe you could help him get over it."

"He and I don't see eye to eye on things. Never have. Never will."

"You could try. You're your own man now. Isn't it much the same thing you were telling *me* a little while ago?"

"No, it's not. With you I was thinking of time and maturity and experience. None of those have any bearing on the differences between my father and me. Our argument is strictly adult to adult."

"You don't like the way he treats your mother, but that's nothing new, Jordan. Your feelings are subjective."

"Damn right. She's my mother."

"She's also an adult, and a thinking one, at that. If she were miserable with her life don't you think she would do something about it?"

Jordan turned his head toward Katia. "She's not . . . miserable. That's not the point."

"Then what is?"

"It's a matter of principle. She's been loyal to him since the day they were married. She's put up with his moods, with business upswings and downswings, with good times and bad, and you'd think that the least he could do would be to be there when she needs him." He returned dark eyes to the city beyond the window. "Instead he buries himself in his work—probably along with one or two very attractive and willing young women."

"At his age?"

"Damn right."

Katia had no retort. She knew that Jack had had his flings over the years. She also knew that Jordan was right in feeling that Natalie deserved better. Still, Jack had to be hurting too, and Katia wished that Jordan could do something to help.

"You know, Jordan," she began in a softly chiding voice, "a lot of what you hear could be pure rumor. Maybe if you got to know the man better you'd be able to separate rumor from truth. Maybe then you'd be able to understand what he's feeling inside. It's possible, just possible that he's not as callous as you think."

A grunt from Jordan was the only answer she got, so she persisted.

"How long has it been since the two of you really talked?"

"Eight years," Jordan said without hesitation. "And that particular 'talk' occurred right here in New York. He was in an accident; the cab he was riding in was hit by another car. Both he *and* his companion at the time were rushed to the hospital. Since I was the only one of us in the city, he called me in to see what I could do about hushing up the entire thing so that the world in general and my mother in particular would never know."

Karia could just picture the scene. "You gave him hell."

"Naturally. He deserved it. At least, I thought so. Not him, though. He wasn't upset at being with another woman, just at being *caught* with one."

"It probably cost him to call you."

"Are you kidding? He thought I'd understand perfectly." He forced his voice deeper in imitation of his father's more gravelly drawl. "'After all, Jordan, you, of all people, can appreciate a man's needs.'"

Katia couldn't resist. "Face it, Jordan. Your reputation preceded you."

"But why me, 'of all people'? I'd really tried to think the best of my father up until that time. I mean, I had suspicions, but I looked the other way."

"You, 'of all people,' because you've had more than your share of women," she said softly.

"Well, shit, I'm not married!" Jordan declared as he raked a hand through his hair. "If I were, I sure as hell wouldn't be trotting from corral to corral like some kind of ageless stallion!"

Katia draped an arm around his waist and gave him a reassuring squeeze. "I know. I know. And it's just one of the ways you're different from your father. But there are many ways in which you're alike, and I suspect that one of them is the anguish you feel over the loss of someone close." She paused for a minute. "Has anything come of the police investigation?"

Jordan wrapped his own arm around Katia's waist, taking comfort in the closeness. "Nah. They're as slow as molasses. Let me tell you, if I ran a business the way they run their investigations I'd be in bankruptcy court before I knew what hit me!"

"If it's to be done right, it will take time," she rationalized. "How's Anne doing?"

"She's okay."

"I've been meaning to call Em, but somehow . . . time just . . . goes."

"Mmm." Jordan looked down at her. He had debated saying anything about Cavanaugh, because the last thing he wanted was for Katia to worry about the police contacting her. Somehow, though, he feared that it would be worse if she was taken off guard. "You may be getting a call from Robert Cavanaugh, the detective in charge of the case."

"Me?" She frowned. "What could he possibly want with me?"

"Routine questions. He's trying to piece together everything he can about Deborah and Mark." Jordan snorted softly. "I think he's trying to piece together everything he can about *all* of us."

"That's part of his investigation?"

"With a stretch of the imagination, I suppose it is."

Katia caught his troubled expression. "Have you met this fellow Cavanaugh?"

"Mmm. We had coffee together."

"Well?"

"He's bright. Educated. And perceptive."

"I'd think that would be good news, but you don't look terribly thrilled."

Releasing her, Jordan began to walk idly around the office. "I don't know, Katia. It's weird. He was really hostile at first, like he despised me . . . or my family . . . or whatever it is he thinks we represent." He was at her drawing board, absently running his fingertip along the edge of the storyboard she had been working on. "He eased up after a time, but I have to think that he's approaching this case with a definite bias."

"So much so that he won't be able to do a good job?"

"No," Jordan answered, but his voice wavered. He scratched the back of his head, then turned a puzzled look her way. "But he's prepared to dig. He's that type. He'll turn over every possible stone looking for the tiniest worm."

"Isn't that good? We all want the case solved."

"Yeah. The question is how many irrelevant worms he'll bring up, and how much dirt will come along with each worm." His gaze grew sharp. "They have a fixation on us, Katia. Guys like that, given a case like this and the kind of carte blanche it offers, would just love to unearth things that the public either doesn't know or has forgotten."

Katia was beginning to understand. "You're afraid that he'll do something to tarnish the image," she said, but without criticism. She was enough of a Whyte-Warren, albeit once removed, to find the prospect of mudslinging as disturbing as Jordan did.

"It's not that the image is squeaky clean, by any means. But every family has its skeletons in the closet; we're not the only ones who'd just as soon keep them there."

Katia went to his side and put a gentle hand on his arm. "He wouldn't spread dirt for the sake of spreading dirt, would he?"

"I don't know. He's bent on interviewing all of us. I think I convinced him to hold off on Mom and Lenore. They'll be the ones who'll be most hurt should anything come out."

"He won't learn anything he doesn't already know," Katia stated softly.

Jordan didn't answer. He simply looked down at the story-board again.

"Will he, Jordan? *Are* there skeletons in the closet—harmful ones?" She was wondering if there were things even *she* didn't know.

Jordan wrapped his arm around her shoulder and drew her close. "Only time will tell, babe. Only time will tell."

Chapter 7

NATALIE WOULD HAVE WELCOMED Jack home from the war with open arms had they been free, but one held three-year-old Nick and the other held two-year-old Mark. Both babies began to scream when the tall stranger took them from their mother and tossed them, each in turn, boisterously into the air. Still, Natalie was smiling broadly, delighted that her husband was back with her for good and that the hopes she had nurtured during the years he had been gone would finally see fulfillment.

When no instant change in her life followed, she was somewhat shocked. The small house in Brighton, in which she had been living with Jack's father and the two boys—Gil and Lenore's house in Cambridge had quickly become too crowded once children had started coming on both sides—seemed that much smaller with Jack's presence. But she didn't have the heart to suggest that they move before Jack had had a chance to get the business back into full swing.

Nor did she have the heart to suggest that Jack was working too hard when he spent fourteen-hour days at the office. She knew that the time he put in was an investment in their future, and since it was a future she badly wanted, she let him have his way.

She did an admirable job of convincing herself that their lives couldn't possibly be a rerun of that blissful two-day honeymoon when they had had time and eyes only for each other. Now there were two demanding toddlers and an even more demanding business to attend to. When Jack finally returned home from work at night he was tired, as was she. Though there were brief times when they came together, sweetly and passionately, in bed, those times were few and far between.

Jack's dedication to his work quickly began to pay off. The airline returned to its prewar status, then leaped ahead. Within a year of its mastermind's return from the Pacific, the Whyte Lines had spread its wings over the eastern third of the country. Though Natalie knew that Jack had borrowed large sums of money to finance the expansion, she felt no qualms when he borrowed a little more to purchase a large brick home on a lovely, tree-lined street in Brookline. This was what she wanted. She was moving up in the world.

Moreover, Lenore and Gil had bought a similar house three streets away.

Lenore and Natalie were as close as ever. During the war years they had continued to share their dreams, along with the joys and the challenges of raising children. Lenore took the greatest delight in her eldest child, Laura, who was well behaved and a comfort to her even after Benjamin, and then Peter arrived, bringing a measure of pandemonium to the house in Cambridge.

If the boys' antics discouraged her from time to time, once Gil returned he didn't mind them a bit. He wanted a large family, the start of a dynasty. The noise and toys and diapers didn't faze him—but then, he was rarely home. His law practice monopolized his time and thought. He had picked up where he'd left off and spent lunch hours, cocktail hours and dinner hours meeting and cultivating new clients.

On occasion he invited Lenore to accompany him, which she did with pride—pride in her husband, in the clothes and jewelry he bought her, in the impressive company he kept. Often on such occasions they were with Natalie and Jack, for, as always, the two men enhanced each other.

Most often, though, Gil left Lenore at home while he concentrated on his career. In some ways she was relieved; Gil was a whirlwind of boundless energy, broad smiles and handshakes. He made it his business to know everyone and to know that everyone knew him. He was adept at even the most banal conversation and was inevitably the center of attention in a group. Lenore, who had somehow not anticipated the amount of work it would take to attain social and professional prominence, found him exhausting to be with.

She was busy herself, first with the children, then with the new Brookline home. She took painstaking care in its decoration, though it seemed that whatever new touch she added was immediately threatened by the destructive power of tiny hands. A crystal vase shattered; a series of crudely etched doodles appeared on a fine mahogany side table; the eyelet edging of the sheer draperies in the dining room was distorted where small fingers poked through it.

Another woman might have taken such innocently inflicted damage less seriously. But Lenore, who was obsessed with preserving her possessions, as though without them she was nothing, nearly fell apart at the seams with each new loss.

She needed help, she informed Gil, who promptly hired a maid. The girl, Cassie, was young, barely eighteen and a wartime refugee from Europe, but what she lacked in experience she made up for in determination. Bright and industrious, she took over the cooking and cleaning chores, leaving Lenore free to manage the children. If Cassie increasingly handled that task as well, Gil didn't complain. He wanted his wife fresh and attractive for those times when he needed her by his side.

And those times grew more frequent as 1947 drew to a close.

"I'm not sure I understand it," Lenore confessed to Natalie one afternoon when she had gone to visit. "For two years now Gil has been satisfied with an evening together every second or third week. Suddenly it's several times a week."

Natalie, who had given birth to a third son, Jordan, the month before, had been slower in recovering from this latest delivery. She, too, had help; Jonathan McNee served as chauffeur, handyman and butler, while his wife, Sarah, was a capable housekeeper. Yet Natalie, who treasured the memories of the time her own father had spent with her, insisted on taking major charge of the children, which left her spent. So rather than go shopping, as she and Lenore had so often done before, they had taken to stealing quiet afternoons together in Natalie's cozy, paneled den while the children napped.

Natalie studied her friend, noting that while Lenore looked tired she also looked classier than ever. Of course, anyone who was slim looked classy to Natalie at that point. "I'd think you'd be pleased," she offered in gentle response to Lenore's complaint about Gil's demands. "He wants your company."

"He wants my *presence*," Lenore corrected with a pinched look that reminded Natalie disconcertingly of Greta. Lenore's mother had seen her younger daughter, Lydia, married several years before and then had remarried herself, albeit not in the style she had once known. "There's a difference. It's not as though we're ever alone."

"But aren't you doing what we always dreamed about? Just this week you've been to dinner at Locke-Ober's, a cocktail party at the Parker House, and to the symphony. Last week it was that party on Beacon Hill and a charity benefit at the Statler. I think it's great, Lenore! I'm green with envy!"

Lenore wasn't so wrapped up in her own worries that she didn't hear Natalie's wistfulness. "But you're still feeling under the weather, Nat. When you're back to snuff you and Jack will be doing the same."

Natalie thought about that for a minute, then sighed. "I don't know. Jack is always so busy. He's off traveling again. To Chicago this time."

"Chicago? Is he going to start flying there?"

"In time—soon, I'm sure. But this trip is something different. He's negotiating the purchase of a hotel."

"A *hotel?* My Lord, that's a far cry from an airline."

"Not really. If people fly into Chicago they have to stay some-where. Jack claims that Chicago is bound to be a major hub for air travel. He feels it's the natural stopover for people traveling from the east coast to the west."

Lenore smiled in admiration of Jack's reasoning. "That's very possible." She gave a slow nod. "So the Whyte Lines is doing well. How lucky you are, Nat. He's in such a . . . *stable* business."

Natalie would have been surprised if the comment had come from anyone other than Lenore, to whom stability and security had always been the highest priority. "It's not any more stable than any other business," she pointed out with due indulgence. "What Gil does is stable."

"Not so. Clients come and go."

"But there is—and always will be—a need for lawyers. And aren't many of Gil's clients steady ones? Before the war he repre-sented many banks and corporations."

"He still does, but it seems he's always out looking for new clients."

"How is his associate working out?"

Lenore shrugged. "All right, I suppose. He's still there." She had only met the man once. He was young and aggressive; she wondered how long he would be satisfied being an associate as opposed to being made a full partner and demanding a larger slice of the pie. The thought made her nervous. "And Gil's thinking of taking in a second one."

"Then he *must* be doing well," Natalie declared with a smile. "See? You're worrying for nothing!"

As it happened, Lenore wasn't. Several weeks and numerous social engagements later Gil informed her that he had decided to run for state representative. They were in their living room, Lenore wearing the sleek dressing gown she favored for an evening at home, Gil still dressed in the tuxedo he had worn to the party from which he had just returned. He had mixed them drinks at the cherry wood bar and had come to stand victoriously before his wife.

"Politics?" she asked in a very small voice.

"Politics," Gil responded with a very large smile. "We've done well over the past few months, you and I. We've charmed them. I've been guaranteed the support of several very powerful party backers who are fed up with the incumbent. I shouldn't have any trouble."

"Getting elected?" she asked in the same small voice.

"Of course. We *are* talking about an election here," he mocked softly.

Lenore continued to stare at him, for once untouched by the devastatingly handsome picture he made with his dark hair, broad shoulders, lean hips and long legs. Her fingers were ominously tight around her old-fashioned glass. "Then . . . that's what all the parties have been about?"

For the first time Gil showed a trace of impatience, but it was only a trace, the slightest flare of his nostrils in an otherwise perfectly composed face. "What did you think they were for?"

"I . . . I thought . . . they were for the sake of your practice."

"Indirectly perhaps. The job of representative isn't a full-time one. I'll be able to maintain my practice on the side." He was looking at her strangely. "I thought you'd be pleased, Lenore. This could be an important first step for us."

Lenore wrapped an arm around her stomach. "*First* step?"

"We have to start somewhere." He looked beyond her, then smiled. "Yes, Cassie?"

"I was wondering if you or Mrs. Warren would like anything before I go up," came the soft voice of the woman standing beneath the broad archway. The vision was equally as soft; neither the long blond hair pulled into a neat knot nor the starchy, slate uniform could detract from the girl's obvious appeal. Over the months in which she had been employed in the Warren household she had proven herself more than capable of her job. The children adored her, which was relief to Lenore, whose primary fear was that Cassie would up and marry the man she had been seeing and leave them. Lenore had come to depend on her.

Now Lenore stared at her blankly. It was Gil who had the presence to answer.

"Thank you, Cassie, but we're fine. You go on up now. Good night."

With a nod, Cassie disappeared, and Gil slowly returned his gaze to his wife. She was a stunning woman, yet the softness he had been so attracted to at the start had seemed to wane. Still, she was the faultless companion when they were in public, and that was what most concerned him.

"You're cut out for this every bit as much as I am," he said in an attempt to compliment her into a more receptive frame of mind.

"I thought we were doing just fine with your law practice."

"Come on, sweetheart," Gil coaxed. "My law practice *is* doing just fine, but this is something really exciting!" Lowering himself to the cushion beside her, he took her hand in his, seeming oblivious to the fact that it was cold. "I start slowly with the House, then move on to the Senate, then maybe to a statewide office. Hell, do you know what opportunities lie beyond that?" His enthusiasm grew with the picture. "Once I get statewide exposure, I can think of running for Congress. *Washington*, Lenore. *That's* where the real power is in this country."

Lenore felt as though the fragile stilts on which she had been trying to build a stately life for the past two years were wobbling badly. "But politics is so . . . so—"

"Challenging! It's what our government is all about."

"Politics is dirty!"

Gil straightened slightly, then shrugged. "I can play rough if the next guy does."

"And the corruption—"

"Only works if one is corruptible. Do you see me as being corruptible, sweetheart?"

Lenore didn't know how to answer that one, because she realized that there were many, many things she still had to learn about her husband. Never in her wildest dreams would she have imagined that he would set his sights on running for public office.

"But politics is such a gamble!" she finally cried, wearing her heart very clearly on her sleeve.

Unfortunately, Gil was myopic where Lenore's deepest fears were concerned. Insecurity was something he staunchly refused to admit into his personal way of thinking. "Everything in life is a gamble, Lenore, if the goal is worth a damn. The secret," he went on, warming quickly to the subject, "is in minimizing the gamble and maximizing the reward. In this case, that's exactly what I've done. I have a thriving law practice with two associates to cover for me during the time I'll be campaigning. In turn, even while I'm campaigning, I'll be attracting new cases. There are some very wealthy people in this district. Once I'm elected my name will be familiar to each and every one of them. People flock to the guy who has connections. My connections will be as good, if not better, than any other lawyer in this state."

Lenore raised her glass to her lips, took a healthy swallow, then mustered her poise. "You're that sure you'll win the election?"

The confident smile Gil bestowed upon her was his only answer. It was the first and last time she would ever ask that question.

In November, 1948, Gil celebrated his election to the Massachusetts State Legislature by throwing a huge victory party at the Parker House. Lenore was by his side wearing a stunning silk dress of royal blue which was nipped in at the waist and hit mid-calf as was the fashion decreed by Christian Dior, a sapphire choker, matching earrings and bracelet, and a brilliant smile. No one ever knew that she spent the next two days in bed.

No one, that is, except Natalie, and, of course, Cassie.

Cassie Jondine was perceptive when it came to emotions. In nineteen short years she had lived a lifetime of them. Born to a schoolteacher and his wife in a small town in northwest France, Cassie—Carmela, then—had been raised in a home where education was the highest priority. That, and love. She had known happiness as a child, coddled not only by her parents but by the older brother she worshipped. Material possessions had meant nothing to her; her father's modest income provided for the family's meager physical needs. And they were rich in the intellectual and emotional commodities that they considered far more precious.

Even as young as she was, Carmela would have had to have been deaf and dumb not to have picked up on the threads of rumor and fear that shimmered through her family's section of town in the late nineteen-thirties. Nonetheless, she had lived under a child's illusion of safety and freedom. She had aspirations of going to the university as her brother had done, then possibly teaching as her father did, or raising a family as her mother did. She loved children and would have been happy to work with them in any manner.

When Hitler took France in June, 1940, her world fell apart. One day her father didn't return home from school and she cried herself to sleep after spending long hours watching her mother wring her hands. The next day her mother was gone from the house for such a long time that Carmela had begun to quake in fear that she, too, had been taken away by the soldiers who goose stepped in small groups through the streets. But her mother did return, pale, drawn and nervous, and quickly set to work packing a small satchel of Carmela's things which she set by the back door. Then she sat with her daughter, retelling her favorite stories, cooking her favorite dinner and watching her eat. Only when the sun had set did she draw Carmela to her.

"A kind, kind woman named Madame Laville will be coming here tonight. She'll be taking you with her, Carmela. You'll be safe as long as you do everything she says."

Carrnela began to tremble. She was astute enough at the age of eleven to hear the finality of her mother's words. "You won't be coming?"

"No, love. Only children are allowed on this trip."

"But why?"

"Because only children will be safe."

"I'd rather be with you. I don't care about—"

"You'll go with her, and you won't question her. She's risking a lot by doing this."

Carmela would have argued further had it not been for the obvious agony on her mother's face. "Where will she take me?" she asked in a tiny voice.

"East. You'll be put on a boat with lots of other children. In time you'll arrive in America."

"But I don't know anyone in America!"

"You will. There will be people waiting for you, looking out for you all the way."

"And will you follow me there?"

Her mother had looked at her then, smiling through her tears as, with fingers bent on memorizing every nuance of her daughter's fine features, she stroked Carmela's cheeks, her nose and mouth, the pale strands of her hair. "I'd follow you anywhere, Carmela. Don't you know that?"

It hadn't been quite the definitive answer Carmela had been seeking, but before she could voice her fears, her mother had crushed her to her breast, where she had continued to hold her and rock her until a quiet knock came on the back door. Carmela had been taken into the dark of night then, with the memory of her mother's softly sobbed, "Bye-bye, baby," wrenching at her, even as a firm hand drew her farther and farther from home.

Nights of stealthy travel had followed that first, breathless movement from one stop to the next, hours of sitting in cold, cramped railway cars, even longer days of hiding in damp church basements or darkened huts. The trip to a safe exit port on the northeast coast of France was prolonged by the necessity for constant vigilance and concealment, and Madame Laville was only the first of many watchful guardians who shepherded the children.

Carmela was numb, both physically and emotionally, desperately wanting to ask questions but not daring to. The presence of the other children was a help in that she didn't feel quite so alone. But there was a negative side to their company too, for fragments of stories of the disappearances of relatives began to emerge, which, with the stretch of the imagination that Carmela was more than intelligent enough to make, coalesced into a terrifying picture of what had been left behind.

Carmela missed her mother, father and brother, and when she wasn't preoccupied comforting and helping subdue the whimpers of the smaller children, she worried about where her family was and how they fared. As for herself, she was old enough to know that her life had taken an irrevocable turn, but she schooled herself not to look farther into the future than what was to come at the end of the particular leg of the journey she was on.

As her mother had told her would happen, Carmela eventually reached the coast and was herded with the others onto a boat for passage across the Atlantic. Though the tension of the preceding days and nights seemed to fade with the shoreline of France, it was replaced by a new one. The unknown lay ahead. Carmela was one of the few children old enough to understand and fear it.

Also, as her mother had told her would happen, there were people awaiting her arrival in New York. They were representatives of agencies geared to placing the young refugees in homes. A travel worn and frightened Carmela, hugging to her chest the small satchel containing the few clothes, books and pictures that comprised her worldly possessions, was transported to western Massachusetts where she met her foster parents, Herman and Leona Marsh.

They were an older couple and they welcomed her with a touch of unsureness. Language was the most obvious barrier; Carmela arrived in America knowing only the sparse English that the chaperone on the boat had tried to teach the children. Neither of the Marshes spoke French, and if they understood it they never let on; from the start they insisted that English would be the only tongue spoken in their home.

Beyond the language barrier, however, was an emotional one. Childless over many years of marriage, Herman and Leona Marsh were inexperienced in the workings of any youngster's mind, much less one who had experienced such intense turmoil in such a short length of time. They accepted Carmela into their home as though she were the daughter of a friend of a relative from the Midwest, choosing to suppress any awareness of the circumstances that had been responsible for her delivery into their care.

They weren't unkind. Carmela had her own room, and, despite the severe rationing imposed by a wartime economy, she had adequate food and clothing. She attended a local school where her struggles to learn English eventually paid off and was given light chores to do around the house. From all outward appearances she settled in well.

But outward appearances didn't reveal the inner trial Carmela suffered.

Everything about the Marsh home was foreign to her. While her own parents had been outwardly affectionate, the Marshes were far more formal. They rarely touched each other, much less Carmela, and for a young girl who had been raised amid hugs and kisses, the difference was stark.

While the Jondine house had always born a pleasantly messed, wonderfully lived-in look, the Marsh house was invariably neat and proper. Never was a lace doily out of place, or a painted china vase dusty, or a newspaper or magazine left lying on a chair. There was a chill to the house that could in no way be remedied by the dull gray radiators that sizzled and sputtered in every room.

While Carmela remembered dinners with her family where each member shared his or her experiences of the day, dinners with the Marshes offered either superficial conversation or silence. At first Carmela assumed that the language difference was responsible, then she realized that Herman and Leona could easily chat with each other but chose not to. Anxious to please, she went along with what was apparently their style; on the few occasions when she forgot herself and burst into an account of something that had happened in school, the mechanical smiles and nods with which her attempt at conversation was met dampened her desire to try it again.

Whereas learning had been as natural as breathing in the Jondine home, in the Marsh home it was considered a chore to be performed, much as one made one's bed or cleaned the house. Carmela's father had only to ask what Carmela was studying in history to spark a discussion that, in turn, fed her enthusiasm for the class. The extent of Herman Marsh's interest in Carmela's classes was encapsulated in his nightly question, "Have you finished all your homework for tomorrow, Carmela?"

Even religion, which had been a low-keyed but steady presence in the Jondine home, was approached more rigidly here, a matter of forced ritual that Carmela came to detest. When she was homesick, lonely and frightened, she had nothing to blame *but* that religion, which in her mind was solely responsible for denying her her parents, her brother, her home and the happy life she had once known.

Worst, perhaps, in Carmela's mind, was the worry. When she asked about her parents, which she did frequently, the Marshes dismissed the question with shrugs of their shoulders—another thing that Carmela came to detest, since she believed that her family deserved more than mere shrugs. Her only hope of news from France came from the local social worker at the placement agency who visited from time to time.

"Have you heard anything?" Carmela would whisper as soon as the Marshes had left the room. She knew that her eagerness would sound like ingratitude to the Marshes.

"No, Carmela. Nothing yet. I promised you that I would tell you if I did hear anything, but it's very difficult getting word from so far."

"What if they've already come and haven't been able to find me?"

It was one of the most common fears the social worker had encountered in children like Carmela. "They'll be able to find you," she said with a smile of confidence. "They'll know to start with the agencies, and we work closely with one another. Don't worry," she repeated, patting Carmela's knee, "we'll make sure they find you if they step foot in this country, and in the meantime we'll continue to try to get whatever news we can." It was a promise that Carmela had to be content with, since it was the only one she had.

In the seven years that Carmela spent with the Marshes, she never quite became one of them. At the start she remained slightly aloof, telling herself that her mother would soon be joining her, even with her father and brother, and that they would find a house like the one they had had in France, and that her father would teach, and her brother would finish his education, and that they would be safe together in America.

As time went on and no member of her family appeared on the scene to claim her, Carmela came to accept that she would be alone awhile longer. She determined to do what she thought would make her parents proud—to study and do well in school, to help out the Marshes in return for her keep, to cause as little trouble as possible.

Then, shortly after the end of the war, the woman from the placement agency came to tell sixteen-year-old Carmela, as gently as was humanly possible, that her parents had died in separate concentration camps and that, though there was no word on her brother's fate, it was to be presumed that he, too, had perished.

For days Carmela went through life in a stupor. Though she had often feared the worst, the confirmation of those fears seemed to kill her spirit in a way that even the Marshes' perfunctory surrogate parenthood hadn't been able to do. She felt more alone than she ever had in her life, and more grief stricken. Hour upon hour she sat looking at the family pictures she had brought with her across the Atlantic; then she would hug them to her chest and re-call the last time she had seen her father and her brother. And her mother.

Bye-bye, baby.

Her sorrow was soul-rending and made all the worse by the pictures and stories that had begun to appear in the newspapers, reporting the atrocities committed in one concentration camp after another. She realized then that her mother had known that last night that they would never see each other again. Her torment over what her mother had to have gone through before her death knew no bounds.

Carmela went through periods of intense anger during which she railed against a God who could permit the annihilation of her family. Herman Marsh's often repeated, "It was God's will. We have to trust that He had a higher purpose in mind," made her wild with rage. She had lost everything she held dear. She was starting with nothing.

It was that very knowledge that finally pulled her through the worst of her depression, or rather the realization that she *wasn't* starting with nothing. She had memories of happiness, and they were something to think about, something to dream about re-creating. She decided that one day she would have a family of her own and that she would give her children the same kind of love she had received, only this time there would be *real* security. After all, Hitler was dead. And she was in America.

Carmela spent her last years in high school nurturing those dreams, to the extent that she was often distracted, both in school and out. Life with the Marshes grew more and more uncomfortable for her. Not only were they the antithesis of what she wanted, but they had little patience for her distraction and seemed to grow more strict by the day. Leona harped on her appearance and the way she did her chores while Herman was never satisfied with her performance in school. He had made it clear that he didn't have the money to send her to college, but he was convinced that without top grades she would never find a good job out of high school.

Carmela learned to tune out their complaints. The focus of her concentration was on graduating from high school, and then freedom. She didn't care what kind of job she took as long as it enabled her to move out of the Marsh house. Only then, she believed, would she be able to clearly plot her future.

Several months before graduation she began to study the help wanted ads in the newspaper. She pondered the range of job opportunities, quickly eliminating those that would be isolating and boring. She didn't want to work in a manufacturing plant or a factory, and though she took secretarial courses in high school, she wasn't sure she would be happy in an office either. She loved children, but she couldn't qualify to teach them without further education, and since Herman had made his feelings on that matter clear and she had little money of her own, teaching seemed beyond her reach.

Then she overheard several girls at school discussing an agency that specialized in the placement of housekeepers. She didn't see herself as a maid, but if a particular home had children in it, it was a place to start. Except that *she* had no intention of remaining in western Massachusetts. She wanted the big city. She wanted Boston.

The reference librarian at the public library helped her find the name of a reputable agency in Boston, and without breathing so much as a hint of her intentions to the Marshes, she wrote a letter and sent it out. The result was promising enough to merit a train ride into the city for an interview, which she skipped school one day to do so the Marshes would never know. She sensed that they would be opposed to her plans, could envision the discussion.

"You can do better than that," Herman would say.

Leona would support him all the way. "Our kind don't hire themselves out as housekeepers, Carmela. Haven't you any sense of social standing?"

The thing was that Carmela no longer identified with the Marshes *or* their kind. She was one girl, very much on her own in the world, and she intended to do things her way for a change. Moreover, it occurred to her that there was little difference between doing the dirty work for some higher-up in an office and doing that for a family who might, just might, have a lovely home and children to care for.

The image she presented to the agency was one of soft-spoken confidence. She had dressed with care, and despite years of enduring Leona's nit-picking, knew that her appearance would work in her favor, as would the fact that she spoke intelligently and with only the slightest hint of an accent. Ironically, in her own quiet way, she was nearly as much of an interveiwer as she was an interviewee. She was concerned about the types of families the agency dealt with because she wanted to work in a home that was warm and happy. And she wanted to work with children. She was well trained to do any manner of household work, she informed the woman with whom she spoke, but her forte was in dealing with children.

Though she had no way of knowing it, her own concerns proved to be as much a recommendation as anything else. The woman interviewing her was impressed, seeing Carmela Jondine as a cut above the usual applicant, and took great care sorting through her cards until she finally selected one, studied it, then smiled.

Two weeks later, a mere three days after her graduation, Carmela began a new life as Cassie by packing up her belongings, taking the train out of Worcester, then a cab from Boston to Brookline, and moving into a small room on the third floor of Gilbert and Lenore Warren's home. The Marshes had been predictably angry, and, Cassie sensed, a bit hurt, but by the time she had informed them of her plans the commitment had already been made.

Cassie Americanized her name when she started her new job to symbolically thrust aside the past and delve into the present. She was hired, first and foremost, as a housekeeper, but she had been so taken by the Warrens when she had gone for an interview that she didn't mind the title. Lenore Warren had never had household help before, which was a plus in Cassie's mind because she wouldn't be following in anyone else's footsteps. Moreover, Lenore made no effort to hide her relief that someone had come to take charge.

Then there were the three Warren children, one more beautiful than the next. Cassie thought they were wonderful, even the two boys with their mischievous ways. She had a gentle way of talking with them, of teaching them that mischief was fine in their bedroom or the playroom or the backyard, but that they had to respect the care their mother had taken with the other rooms in the house. They responded to her soft, coaxing tones and took as much delight in playing with her as she did in playing with them. Even Laura, who was in so many other ways a miniature of her mother, responded to the hugs Cassie bestowed so freely.

And, of course, there was the master of the house. From the very first time Cassie had set eyes on him she had been a little bit in love with Gilbert Warren. He was the epitome of the successful male, exuding an aura of confidence wherever he went. He was unfailingly kind to Cassie, concerned about whether her room was comfortable, about what she planned to do on her day off, about whether she had made friends in the Boston area.

Gil also introduced her to Henry Morell. Henry was employed as a general handyman for one of Gil's friends. He was of French descent, albeit a third generation American. He also didn't speak French, which pleased Cassie, who was determined to be thoroughly American. She thought it sweet that a busy and prominent man like Gil would consider such a small point in his matchmaking attempt.

Cassie saw Henry each time their days off coincided. She liked him. He was easygoing and undemanding, more than willing to escort her to a movie or a light meal or on a shopping expedition. The latter, more often than not, resulted in Cassie buying small things for the children—books or puzzles or sketch pads and pencils. She knew that Gil had artistic talent; she had seen the doodles he left lying on his desk, had even taken some from the wastebasket, flattened out their wrinkles and secreted them away beneath the clothes in her bureau drawer. She didn't know the names to match up with the faces he had drawn, but assumed that the caricatures were of people with whom he worked. In awe of his talent since her own on that score was sadly limited to stick figures, she hoped to encourage one or another of the children to sketch. The fact that they were too young to do more than randomly scribble didn't discourage her a bit.

Cassie had a remarkable amount of freedom in the Warren house. Indeed, there were times when she felt as though she, and not Lenore, were the mistress of the house. She set her own schedule for cleaning, working her chores around the children's needs, and planned menus with little more than cursory approval by Lenore. She did her job well and she enjoyed it, particularly when Gil complimented her on a meal or the appearance of the house or that of the children. She took a pride in her job that she wouldn't have imagined possible, such that it rarely occurred to her that this was to be merely the first stepping-stone for her.

Overall, Lenore proved to be Cassie's greatest challenge. She was generally agreeable and invariably grateful for everything Cassie did, yet she was susceptible to a moodiness that puzzled Cassie, who had a natural instinct for compassion and would have liked to help if she could. But that particular barrier was not to be breached by a housekeeper, Cassie knew, and she felt badly. Lenore held things in and preferred escaping to the solitude of her bedroom when something bothered her. Cassie couldn't help but believe that the woman would be better off discussing whatever was bothering her with someone.

Natalie Whyte was a help. Cassie always felt better for Lenore when she was with Natalie, who had to be, Cassie decided early on, one of the most kindhearted women she knew. Natalie had a comfortable way of looking at Cassie, respecting her as a human being even as she took for granted Cassie's role as housekeeper.

It was Natalie who appeared at the house the afternoon after

Gil's grand victory party; Natalie who climbed the stairs to Lenore's bedroom and spent an hour with her friend; Natalie who then went into the kitchen and tried to explain to Cassie the essentials of what Lenore was experiencing.

"Mrs. Warren needs more help in times like these, Cassie. She's very fragile in her way."

"She's frightened," Cassie offered. "I can see that. But I'm not sure I understand why."

"Politics is much like a career in . . . in the movies, I suppose," Natalie ventured, chosing her words with care lest she betray the confidences of either Gil or Lenore. She had seen how attached Cassie had grown to the Warrens—and how attached they had grown to her—and earlier talks with the girl had convinced her that she was exceptionally bright as well. Natalie's gut instinct told her that Cassie could be trusted, yet too much said was unfair. "A person can be on top of the heap one day and at the bottom the next. It's a precarious business. I believe that's what frightens Mrs. Warren."

"Mr. Warren seems confident."

"Oh, he is, and with due cause. He's a talented man. He'll make a wonderful representative. I have no doubt but that he'll go as far as he wants to in politics. It's just going to take Mrs. Warren awhile to get used to the life he's chosen. She's not an activist, as he is. She does best with an evenly balanced existence."

"A politician's life can never be that," Cassie mused. "It accelerates and accelerates to the point of an election, then plummets immediately afterward, only to start accelerating again when the next election appears on the horizon. With representatives' terms of office a mere two years, that doesn't allow much of a respite."

Natalie arched a brow, but she was teasing. "Where did you learn so much about elections? Your family wasn't involved in politics in France." Some time before, when Natalie had come to give Cassie a hand in the kitchen after a dinner party, Cassie had painted a sketchy picture of her background.

"No, but we always read the papers. I do the same every day. It's one of the best educational tools you can find."

"*If* it's unbiased." She wagged a finger at Cassie. "Be careful about that. Did you see what happened to Frank Sinatra?"

Cassie, whose teenage years had coincided with the rise of The Voice, had indeed seen what had happened to Frank Sinatra. "Do you think that he is in with the mob?" she asked in a conspiratorial whisper.

Natalie shrugged. "The papers reported it, but nothing has been substantiated. He may be perfectly innocent, in which case my point is proven. The newspapers may well be biased. Now that Mr. Warren is attaining a measure of visibility, there are apt to be slanted reports printed from time to time. Be sure to take them with a grain of salt, unless, of course," she grinned, "they're slanted in our favor."

Cassie, too, was grinning, but hers faded quickly. "That must worry Mrs. Warren, too—the thought of having her husband publicly raked over the coals."

"Mmm, maybe." Natalie sighed. "If so, you and I are just going to have to remind her that it comes with the job, and that Mr. Warren can handle it, *and* that it's not so bad, since the very next article will probably be slanted the opposite way. The important thing is that Mr. Warren has the support of the people, and judging from the margin by which he won the election, that is an undeniable fact."

At that moment Cassie made a vow to herself to file for permanent American citizenship so she could vote in the next round of elections. As it happened, she was so busy in the months to come that it was awhile before she gave it further thought.

In February, 1949, Henry Morell asked her to marry him. While she found the thought pleasant it lacked a certain excitement. Henry was nice enough. He was attractive enough. He was bright enough. But Cassie's enthusiasm was wrapped up in the Warrens, and if marrying Henry meant that she would have to leave her position, she doubted she could do it. She felt needed and wanted by the Warrens. For the first time since she had left France she felt she had a true home. She wasn't sure if she was ready to abandon it just yet.

When Henry grew anxious for an answer, Cassie did the one thing that seemed most natural to her. On a rare night when Gil was home, when Lenore had long since gone to bed, leaving him working alone in his den, she knocked on his open door and was promptly waved inside.

He looked wonderful. He was wearing a pair of pleated tweed trousers and a V neck cardigan that lay open over his shirt. In his mouth was a pipe, its mellow fragrance wafting through the air; Cassie had always associated pipes with older men, yet Gil did something superb to its image of studiousness. In fact, the entire image that met her eye was so strikingly male and attractive that for several moments she didn't say a word. Only when Gil leaned far back in his chair and grinned at her did she realize how foolish she must look.

Gathering her wits, she quickly launched into the matter that had brought her to his den.

"Why, that's wonderful, Cassie," he said when she had told him about Henry's proposal. His eyes began to twinkle. "I was hoping for something like this."

Cassie's first thought was that he would be glad to see her go. "Then you aren't pleased with my work?" To discover that she had somehow disappointed Gil was one of her greatest fears.

"I'm *thrilled* with your work. But you're a beautiful girl with a great deal to offer a man."

She blushed at that. His eyes seemed to be taking in every inch of her, and every inch began to tingle. "I'm . . . I'm not sure I should accept," she managed weakly.

"Not accept? Of course you should. Henry is a fine young man." Gil lowered his head and studied her from beneath the shelf of his brows. "Do you love him?"

"I think, well, yes, I guess I do." She wasn't sure if it was love or simple affection. She was in a quandary. On the one hand she had adored her family, but she knew that any love she felt for a man would quite naturally be different. And then there was Gil. She *adored* Gil. But he was married, and even if he weren't, she wasn't sure if she worshipped him as an idol or—though he wasn't all *that* old—as something of a father figure. Of course, her own father had never set her limbs to tingling as Gil had just done with a simple look.

She had a strong suspicion that poor Henry, or any man she might meet for that matter, would inevitably suffer by comparison.

She took a breath. "Henry is very kind. He's trustworthy and dependable. I know that he'll always be there for me."

"If he isn't I'll send the sheriff after him with a billy club," Gil threatened, and Cassie almost believed that he would. "Have you thought of a date?"

"I . . . no. I wanted to speak with you first."

"Well, now that you have you can go ahead and make plans."

"Oh, no. I still have some questions—"

"About Henry? You needn't worry about Henry. My friend Norman Euson will vouch for him."

"No. I'm not worried about Henry. I'm worried about getting married. If I do it would be difficult for me to live here. But I love my job. I'm not willing to give it up."

"There won't be any need for you to give it up," he said calmly and with a confident tip of his head. "I'll simply steal Henry from under Norman's nose and put him on the payroll here with us."

It sounded simple coming from Gil. A warm feeling spread through Cassie. "Would you do that?"

"Of course I would. There's many a day when I could use a driver, and Lord only knows there are enough things to be done by a handyman around this house. Something always needs to be repaired, and there are always errands to run. Henry could help you out when we entertain, and when there are children—"

"Children! I wouldn't have a child just yet! Then I'd *never* be able to work."

"Of course you would," Gil said gently. "Don't you want children?"

"Oh, yes."

"I suspected as much. You're wonderful with ours."

"They're delightful children."

Gil thrust a hand through his hair. His eyes widened for a split second while the rest of his features drew taut. "My wife doesn't always think so. I sometimes wonder . . ." He seemed to catch himself, and when he looked back at Cassie his face had relaxed once more. "But that's where you've been such a help to us. I'm not ready to let you go any more than you're ready to leave." His eyes held hers steadily. "I see no problem whatsoever in your marrying, and then, when you're ready, raising your children here."

She was shaking her head, smiling sadly. "There really isn't room—"

"Not upstairs, but what if I were to fix up an apartment over the garage? You and Henry could live there, and when you do decide to have a child there would be plenty of room. In fact," he went on, rising from his seat and slowly rounding the desk, "I have a secret to tell you." His voice had lowered to a nearly seductive drawl, and Cassie's presence of mind was tested even more when he draped an arm across her shoulders and drew her close. He bent his head. She felt his breath by her temple. "I've started looking for land. Good acreage a little farther out of the city. When I find it, I plan to build my own home, something with twice as much room as we have now." He straightened, tipping his upper body away without releasing her shoulders. "What do you think?"

Cassie could barely think with Gil so close. It took everything she possessed to recall what he had said. "It's . . . I think it's wonderful! But you've been in this house for less than two years." The Brookline house was so much finer than anything Cassie had ever known that she found it hard to imagine anything better.

"And look what's happened in that period of time," Gil returned with typical elan. "My instincts tell me that the time to make a new investment would be soon. People may say that I'm crazy to think of moving out a ways, but I think it's the wave of the future. Every year the population spreads farther from Boston. An investment within the next year or two will pay off when suddenly the rest of the world wakes up to the trend. The value of the land will increase. It's bound to. And I have a car—and, with Henry, a driver. The distance won't bother me."

"But . . . what about your position representing this district? If you move out of it, won't you have to resign?"

He beamed down at her, seeming pleased by her foresight. "Nope. I'll be able to finish out my term. In fact, if I wanted, I could run from the same district again even if I no longer live here. Of course," he drawled, "I wouldn't get too many votes if I did that. Constituents don't like the idea of their rep living elsewhere."

"You'll be up for reelection next year. What will you do then?"

"If we've moved, I'll simply run from my new district."

"Is that *done?*"

"It will be," he said without a blink.

"What does Mrs. Warren say?"

"Mrs. Warren doesn't know." He scowled and batted the air against an unseen pest. "She gets all upset at the thought of the tiniest little change, so I thought I'd wait until I find the land." He lowered both his voice and his head again. "This is our secret. Just between you and me, okay?"

She nodded vigorously.

"So, you see," he resumed in full voice, dropping his arm and slowly moving away from her to return to the desk, "there's no reason at all why Henry shouldn't become part of our family. If my plans pan out we'll have more than enough room. In fact, if everything works out as I see it, we'll have to hire a second girl to help you. There will be that much more to clean, that many more mouths to feed, and we'll be entertaining far more than we do now. Of course, you'd be in charge." He turned to face her, propping his thigh on the corner of the desk. Again his voice lowered. "You're a wonderful manager, have I told you that?"

Cassie shook her head.

"Well, you are. This house hasn't run as smoothly since . . . since . . . hell, it *never* ran smoothly until you came. It's amazing," he murmured. "You're barely twenty. . . ."

She couldn't miss the subtle criticism of his wife, and if it was a comparison he was making, she didn't want it. "Mrs. Warren has so many things on her mind, what with the children and your career and all."

"Mmm."

"And she's the one who supervises me, so I really can't take the credit."

Gil studied her a moment longer, then took a quick breath. "Not only are you a good manager, Cassie Jondine, but you're modest and loyal to boot. I only hope Mrs. Warren appreciates you as much as I do."

So pleased was Cassie with his praise that she had no idea how those final words would eventually come back to haunt her.

Chapter 8

ONE MONTH AFTER her discussion with Gil, Cassie married
Henry. It was, overall, a happy time for her. Though she had invited the Marshes to attend the brief ceremony, which was performed at Gil's insistence in the Warrens' living room by a judge
Gil knew, they had refused, which hadn't really surprised or disappointed Cassie. Gil and Lenore stood as witnesses, and Henry's
employers—or former employers, since Henry would be returning to the Warren house with Cassie—attended in good humor.
The three Warren children, Laura dressed in a ruffled frock and
standing by her mother's side, Ben and Peter tugging at their but-
toned collars and creating whatever other havoc they could, provided intermittent moments of amusement, which Cassie loved.
Sarah McNee had been borrowed from the Whytes to prepare a
light dinner afterward, which Cassie also loved, since she had
never been waited on before.

As a wedding gift Gil gave the newlyweds the use of his car
and a weekend trip to the White Mountains. When they arrived
back in Brookline they moved into the three-room apartment that
had been completed over the garage.

Only two things nagged at the back of Cassie's mind, and they
were far from mutually exclusive. As much as she tried to ignore
it, she knew that her parents would never have approved of her
marriage to Henry. Given the cause for their persecution and sub-

sequent deaths, they would have seen her as a traitor. Cassie had long since eschewed any and all form of religion, yet she couldn't help but feel a twinge of guilt from time to time.

Likewise, from time to time she felt a twinge of guilt on another score. Whereas she had been taught as a child that the love between husband and wife was sacred, she honestly doubted that she loved Henry Morell. Oh, she was fond of him and she was convinced that she could make him a good wife, but she had married Henry for many of the wrong reasons.

She had married him because he loved her. She had also married him because he was harmless, and because by marrying him she could ensure that her life wouldn't be disturbed. She had married him because he was *there*; she eventually wanted children, but she didn't want to have to look for a husband, or a new job, or a new home. Henry was the solution to a problem she didn't care to face in the future.

And she had married him because Gil Warren was already taken.

Therein lay the greatest source of her guilt. In her heart of hearts Cassie knew that she had done Henry a disservice. Her only recourse was to try to give him what he wanted.

What Henry wanted, first and foremost it happened, was a child. He was proud as punch when, two months after their marriage, Cassie learned she was pregnant.

Cassie wasn't quite as delighted. Yes, she eventually wanted children, but she had done her best—without Henry knowing—to postpone that event. But her precautions had failed her. And to make matters worse, Lenore had learned the month before that she was expecting her fourth child, which meant that Cassie's pregnancy couldn't have come at a less opportune time. Lenore did little enough around the house under normal conditions; pregnant, she would do nothing at all. It would be up to Cassie to take over completely. She would have welcomed that idea had it not been for the fear that she would be more limited herself when she reached the advanced stages of pregnancy.

For several months Cassie said nothing to the Warrens. She managed to will away morning sickness and fatigue and worked all the harder in an attempt to prove herself indispensable. To her knowledge Gil hadn't found the land he sought, which was a mixed blessing. On the one hand Cassie wasn't sure she could handle a move and the added work it would entail at this stage, while on the other she feared that the Brookline house would be uncomfortably small once a nurse and a supplemental housekeeper were hired to serve the family's needs while she was indisposed.

Henry was a comfort. He pampered her when she wasn't working, and constantly urged her to slow down. Although he'd have preferred to immediately tell the Warrens of Cassie's pregnancy, he acceded to her wishes on that score.

Most of all, however, Cassie found comfort in the knowledge that her husband was working for the Warrens—especially during times of trepidation when she wondered if, after her baby was born, the Warrens would decide that having a housekeeper with an infant wasn't such a good idea after all. She knew she could do the job, infant and all, yet it was nice to know that Henry would be representing their interests during the brief time of her lying-in.

By October of that year she could no longer hide her pregnancy. Again, as seemed only natural, she approached Gil, though this time far more apologetically than she had the February before.

She should have known that Gil wouldn't be daunted. Nothing discouraged the man, it seemed, least of all the basis for Cassie's worry. He was thrilled for her, even took her in his arms and gave her a hug. Then—to Cassie's astonishment—he spread his palm over her slightly rounded stomach.

"I should have seen it," he said with wonder, looking at the gentle mound his hand shaped. "How could I have missed it?" He raised his gaze to meet hers. "You'll make a beautiful mother, Cassie." His eyes dropped to her breasts, then rose once more. "A beautiful mother with a beautiful baby. How lucky Henry is."

She was touched, and excited, and embarrassed. "You'll have

another child of your own by the time mine arrives," she said in a breathless voice. "And I do apologize. I was looking forward to helping Mrs. Warren with the new baby, but I'm afraid my timing was off. It's just that Henry wants a child badly, but I'm sure he'll work doubly hard during the week or two that I won't be able to—"

"Cassie," Gil chided with exquisite gentleness, "you are not to worry about that. We've monopolized your life for the past two years. You've earned the time off. I don't believe you've taken a fraction of your vacation time in all these months."

"But I enjoy working here. There's nowhere I want to go, no one I want to see. You're the only family I have."

His voice was very quiet, his eyes locked with hers. "You have Henry. And a baby on the way."

"But it's not the same. You all are . . . I don't think I could ever have as much on my own."

"You won't have to," he whispered, stroking her cheek ever so lightly. "You have us. Nothing will ever change that."

Her breath was caught in her throat, and it was a long minute before she could push it forth into speech. "I'll do my best. I promise you I will. Baby or no, I'll see that everything stays as it is."

He smiled then, and her heart turned over. "I'm sure you will, Cassie Morell."

She nodded and took a small step back, but before she realized what he was up to, Gil leaned forward to brush a kiss on her forehead. Heart pounding, she looked up at him in surprise.

"Congratulations, little mother," he whispered so tenderly that she turned and fled to hide the tears in her eyes.

For days to come Cassie repeatedly replayed in her mind that conversation and its accompanying gestures. She told herself that Gil was simply a warmhearted man, that he was affectionate and physical by nature. Yet she didn't see him touching his wife as he had touched her. Nor, even, did he touch his children that way. He seemed always to be breezing from one place to the next with less and less time for his family.

If for personal reasons Cassie wished it differently, she understood the man perhaps better than his own wife did. He was touching bases, solidifying his support for the reelection campaign he would be waging the following year. He had apparently told no one of the possibility of his leaving the district, and if his running for office was vaguely deceitful, Cassie saw it for the shrewd political move it was. Far better, she knew, that Gil should win a second election—she had no doubt that he would—and then, when and if he moved, serve out his term as the law allowed, than to yield the limelight to someone else for a precious two years. Public exposure was critical, and public exposure was exactly what Gil received as a vocal member of the legislature.

She noted many new faces at the series of dinner parties the Warrens threw in the closing months of 1949, and she assumed that they were potential supporters from the outlying suburbs of Boston. Whether Lenore was aware of the reason for these newcomers' presence, Cassie couldn't say. She did know that Lenore wasn't happy about the parties themselves. She saw how the woman drew into herself both before and after each affair. In a sense she couldn't blame her. Lenore had been physically uncomfortable since early fall. She had had hip pains, back pains and swollen ankles, none of which were helped by long evenings of circulating among dinner guests. Still, stylish maternity gown and all, she was a gracious hostess. For that Cassie admired her.

Jack and Natalie Whyte were in attendance at nearly every party. Indeed, they threw several of their own, on which occasions Cassie and Henry lent a hand to Jonathan and Sarah McNee at the Whyte home. Henry, in particular, enjoyed the McNees. While Cassie didn't mix as readily, she always had an open ear to what they had to say.

It seemed, said Sarah, that Mr. Whyte had just acquired his fourth hotel. Fourth! Then the first three had to be doing well, Henry observed, to which Jonathan responded with a shrug and the explanation that Mr. Whyte had a group of investors behind him, and that though one of them had recently dropped out in anger at what he considered to be inequitable returns, there were many more waiting to replace him.

Sarah remarked that the missus had grilled her husband about that one dissenter, and Sarah herself suspected that there might, in fact, be some truth to the rumor that the investment scheme Jack Whyte had put together was decidedly one-sided. Jonathan pointed out that the arm of the law hadn't settled on Mr. Whyte's shoulder yet. When Henry wondered if it was simply a matter of time before that happened, Jonathan quickly informed him that Mr. Whyte had gone through a flurry of sessions with his own lawyers and that steps had been taken to prevent any trouble.

Cassie was disturbed by what she heard since she knew that Jack Whyte had donated a large sum of money to Gil's campaign. She was also disturbed because she respected Natalie Whyte and knew that if Natalie was worried there was just cause. Still, the Whyte Lines continued to grow by leaps and bounds if the reports in the newspaper were correct; Cassie assumed that Jack had to be doing something right.

Of course, she strongly suspected that that something right was limited to the business sphere. If the tiny bits of conversation she caught when Natalie was at the house visiting Lenore were correct, Jack was about as attentive a husband and father as Gil was.

Cassie had to be grateful. For whatever else Henry might lack he was attentive, so much so that there were times when Cassie had to bite her tongue when she thought she would scream. Her temper saw uncharacteristic bouts of shortness as the first of the year rolled around. She was feeling rather like a blimp, and there seemed to be more than ever to be done between the house and the children. Laura and Ben were in school—though Ben for only half a day—and Cassie thoroughly enjoyed little Peter, who prized the time when the others were out to monopolize her attention. But there was refereeing to be done in the afternoons, homework to supervise at night, and baths and bedtime stories, so that when she finally returned to the garage apartment she was exhausted and often out of sorts.

At the end of January Lenore gave birth to a girl. Gil, who had made no secret of wanting another boy, took the disappointment in stride by flying off to Atlanta to visit Jack's newest hotel. Lenore seemed just as happy to have her husband gone, for it meant that she could lie in bed for hours without feeling guilty, which, in turn, meant that the other three children were left solely in Cassie's care—which would have been nothing new had it not been for Cassie's own condition.

The baby, Deborah, was tended by the nurse Gil had hired in advance. Cassie stole into the nursery whenever she could to hold the child herself, but those times were infrequent, given the other demands on her, including the added one of training a girl to fill in for her when she gave birth to her own child.

Unfortunately, the new girl, Mary, was unaccustomed to a busy household like the Warrens. With unswerving perception the children sensed her bewilderment and took advantage of it, casting Cassie in the role of patron saint of new housekeepers in addition to her other chores.

It was a relief, in more ways than one, when, three weeks after Deborah was born, Cassie overcame arduous labor to give birth to a son. She named him Kenneth, in part because she liked the name, in part because no one in her own family had had it. She was well aware of the custom where she had come from of naming a child after a deceased relative and she was determined to avoid it.

Despite her misgivings about having a child so soon, she adored Kenneth from the start. Henry doted on him, and she encouraged him to take part in the baby's care since she knew she would need his help when she resumed her household duties. But she cherished the times when she nursed the child, quietly and alone, for it was then that she could close her eyes and forget she was married to Henry, pretend she was married to Gil and dream that her son would have the very same advantages that every other Warren child had.

That dream received a boost toward fulfillment when Gil insisted that a second crib be set up in the nursery so that Kenny could spend his days there when Cassie returned to work. Cassie was wary at first, convinced that Lenore would object to the scheme. But Lenore, who hadn't been able to shut out the turmoil that had prevailed in the house during Cassie's ten-day absence, would have done just about anything—short of caring for Kenny herself—to get Cassie back in charge.

Over the next few months things did, indeed, settle down. Cassie regimented herself to allow time to spend with Kenny, though Henry took sole command in the evening hours when she was still at the house. Mary, the interim maid, had left for calmer waters, but the nurse stayed on in Cassie's old room. Kenny and Deborah both thrived; the other children had little trouble adjusting to their presence in the house, since, thanks to the nurse, Cassie had as much time as ever to spend with them. Lenore regained the slender figure she prided herself on, and, for the first time in Cassie's memory, seemed to find enjoyment in the older children.

The blooming of spring brought with it Natalie and her three sons, who spent many an afternoon playing in the Warrens' tree-shaded yard with Laura, Ben and Peter. Cassie grew fond of Nick and Mark, clearly seeing that Nick was the organizer and Mark the innovator, and appreciating each for his strength. The chubby three-year-old, Jordan, however, stole her heart, because while he was every bit as adventurous as the others—as a group, the six fed off each other, rendering the level of mischief greater than ever—he had a gentle streak that appealed to her. She assumed that it had to have come from Natalie, though she wasn't sure, since her own contact with Jack had been minimal.

Natalie's contact with Jack was minimal, too, if the number of days she and the children remained at the Warrens through dinnertime was any indication. Eavesdropping on Lenore and Natalie, Cassie learned that Jack had turned his sights on the electronics business, with an eye, in particular, toward cashing in on the advent of television. He was building a plant in Waltham to produce a line of radios and televisions, which, if successful, would grow with the field.

Gil, it seemed, was investing heavily in the project, and

Lenore was predictably nervous. "Where does he get the *money?*" she asked Natalie in bewilderment.

Natalie had no more idea of that than she did of where Jack got his. Investors, he always told her, but she wondered. "From his practice?" she asked with a shrug.

"A lawyer doesn't make *that* much, and what he makes as a legislator is peanuts. He must be borrowing it, and if there's any chance that the project should fail. . . ."

"It won't fail, Lenore. Jack has a keen sense for what the public wants. My only concern is how much more of his time this new project will take. We see him so infrequently as it is. I'm afraid to think what will happen when he adds yet another weight to his shoulders. I mean, we do live well. I love the fact that I can go into Jay's and buy a hat without looking at the price tag, but if Jack is never around to see me wear it, what good is it?"

Lenore wasn't in total agreement on that score. She was more relaxed when Gil *wasn't* around, and what with his law practice, the sessions in the legislature and the social demands that he had been kind enough to exclude her from while she recovered from Deborah's birth, his absence was far more the rule than the exception. What *she* worried about was Gil's gambling borrowed money on something with no track record at all.

When she broached the subject with Gil, he had little patience. "Come on, Lenore. It's investments like this one that will make the difference for us. I can do well with my practice, but only to a certain point. If we want to go beyond that," he lowered his voice accusingly, "and I thought we both did, it will take a little work on the outside."

They were in their bedroom. Gil had just returned from a night on the town and was changing his clothes before closing himself in his den to work. Lenore was in bed, where she had been reading a book for several hours. Now the book lay flat on the blanket and her hands were tightly clenched in her lap.

"But are you taking too much of a risk?"

"On an electronics plant? Hell, no." He tore off his dress shirt and tossed it on a nearby chair, then went to work at the fastening of his pants. "I would have invested in one sooner had the right situation presented itself. Jack's company is very definitely the right situation. You don't think Natalie is worried, do you?"

"No. . . ."

"Well, then?" His pants went the way of the shirt and he turned, wearing only his undershirt and shorts, to take casual clothes from the closet.

Lenore studied his physique. "I'm not Natalie. I just . . . worry."

"Have I let you down yet? Have I ever done anything that's backfired?"

"No." Strange, she mused, how even undressed Gil looked totally invulnerable. He was so hard, arrogant, inflexible.

"You were worried about my taking in a first associate, then a second, but both have been good moves. My gross intake has tripled in as many years, and it's me," he thumbed his chest, "who reaps the bulk of the benefits." He thrust his arms into a sweater and quickly tugged it over his head.

"What about when Robert and Jay want to be made partners?"

"They'll be made partners when I'm good and ready. And when that time comes it will be on my terms."

"And if they object to your terms?"

His speech was barely broken as he smoothly stepped into a pair of trousers. "There are many other lawyers who'd give their right arm to work under me. Neither Robert nor Jay is irreplaceable."

If his view was a callous one Lenore was simply relieved that he intended to hold the reins. Unaware of that relief, Gil was egged on by her lack of comment.

"You were worried about my running for public office, but it's turned out just fine, hasn't it?" Almost angrily, he fastened his pants.

"But now we have to go through the whole thing again—the campaigning and the waiting and the worrying—"

"You're the only one who worries," he declared, moving to stand at the foot of the bed. "I *love* the campaigning, and the waiting is simply a fact of life. It wouldn't be so bad if you could just relax and accept that I'll win."

"You're always so *sure* of yourself."

"That's how I got where I am today." He leaned over the footboard of the bed and propped both fists on the folded spread. "A man is only as good as the way he sees himself. I see myself as a winner. From the day I was fourteen and decided that I had no intention of spending my life painting houses like my father I saw myself as a winner. Because even in that, I was. Simply by deciding to better myself in the world I was a winner." His eyes narrowed. "Growth, Lenore. That's what we're talking here. Growth, financial superiority and power." He tapped his head with a finger. "And if you don't have a mind set for those you're nothing. Is that what you want, Lenore? To be nothing?"

It wasn't so much what he'd said that struck Lenore, but what he hadn't said. *To be nothing . . . again?* Quickly she shook her head, at which point Gil straightened and took a deep breath.

"I didn't think so," he murmured, then turned and left the room.

So the matter was settled. Gil invested in the electronics plant while his reelection campaign went full speed ahead. Though there were fewer parties at home, there were many at local restaurants or at the homes of supporters. Lenore resumed her place by Gil's side, attending each and every one he asked her to. He took his reelection in November for the mere formality it was; the one man who stood a chance of giving him a run for his money decided to bow out of the race at the last minute, leaving a local entrepreneur who only halfheartedly campaigned as Gil's opposition.

Little over a month after that victory Gil presented Lenore with the deed to a tract of land he had bought in Dover, a small blue-blood town some forty-five minutes southwest of Boston.

Simultaneously, Jack presented Natalie with the deed to a similar sized tract of land abutting Gil's. In fact, the two men had been scouting the area together and had bought the land the fall before. Since it would have been too late for Gil to run for the

House from a new district, they had decided to keep the sale quiet until Gil was safely reelected from Brookline.

Natalie was delighted. Jack took her and the children for a drive to see the site. It was a snow-covered winter wonderland, and Natalie fell in love with it on sight, which pleased Jack, who knew that she had been increasingly disturbed by his absences. He saw the purchase of land for a new home for his family as a statement of commitment that he hoped would gain favor in her eyes. It did. And when Jack told her that she would be able to plan the house from scratch, the excitement in her eyes told him that he had bought all the more free time for himself.

Lenore, too, was delighted . . . in her way. She couldn't deny that the land, with its pine groves and apple orchard, meandering meadow and spreading chestnuts, maples and oaks was spectacular. She could even visualize just where she wanted the house to be, picturing a long driveway and an imposing facade. When Gil told her that the design of the house would be up to her, she felt challenged in a way that she hadn't been since she had completed decorating the house in Brookline.

Oh, yes, she wanted to live there. Dover reeked of landed gentry; the thought that she could be part of it was like a dream come true. But . . . so expensive . . . the money . . . a mortgage . . . on top of everything else?

In the end she didn't breathe a word of her doubts to Gil, because she wanted so badly to build a house on this prime piece of land that she let her desires override caution—which wasn't to say that she didn't worry, just that she did her best to reason those worries away. After all, buying land and building a house was a solid investment. They would have something that was *worth* something. Land didn't go bust as a business could. Nor was a house up for reelection every two years. Moreover, the land and the house would be something *she* could enjoy. Lord only knew she didn't find joy in Gil's law office or the House chamber or Jack's electronics plant!

Lenore spent the early months of 1951 with architects and

builders. She was in many ways happier than she had been in years because she had something to work on, some semblance of power. She decided that her house should be a large Georgian colonial, which, in her vision, represented dignity and prosperity. There was to be a three-car garage connected to the house by a wide latticed breezeway, an ample gardener's shed, and a cottage behind the house for the Morells.

When Cassie heard about the last she felt justified in having been so rigid about remaining with the Warrens. She would, literally, have her own house at no personal expense. Kenny, who was about to turn one and was on the verge of walking, would have acres to play in when he grew older, fine schools to attend, and, most importantly, high-standing friends and neighbors. She couldn't have chosen a better environment for her child if she had been a Warren herself.

She wasn't, of course, but Kenny might well have been. He was constantly with Deborah, treated as an equal by their nurse-turned-nanny—and as an equal by the other Warren children. Occasionally, as she had done at the first, Cassie wondered if Lenore was bothered by Kenny's presence. He was, after all, the house-keeper's son. But if Lenore was bothered she never said anything to Cassie, and if she had ever taken the matter to Gil Cassie never knew it.

Cassie did know that Gil was always incredibly kind to her. She could enter the room to bring coffee while he was in the middle of a heated discussion with Jack and he would look up at her with a sudden smile. He liked her. She clung to that knowledge with a swelling heart, knowing that there was nothing in the world that she wouldn't do for Gil Warren if he asked.

There weren't any special requests made of Cassie that spring or summer, not by Gil at least. But the prospect of moving had inspired Lenore's instincts to clean house. She spent hours with Cassie going through each of the children's drawers and closets, making piles of clothing to give to the Salvation Army. Cupboards were cleaned, stale staples and cracked dishes discarded. Cassie didn't mind the extra work since Lenore was in better spirits than she had been in for months. She even opened up a bit with Cassie.

"Laura is becoming such a little lady," she said as she held up a small dress for inspection. "I think that once we move I'd like to start her in ballet classes." She placed the dress aside to be packed away for Deborah. It was a move based solely on habit; chances were that, come the time the dress fit tiny Deborah, Lenore would decide it was old-fashioned.

Cassie grinned, visualizing the feminine Laura spinning around a stage. "She'd make a beautiful dancer."

"I think so. Did I tell you that we're planning on building a stable? We have so much land, and I thought that riding would be a good outlet for the boys."

Cassie visualized another picture, that of Kenny on the back of a horse. "That would be exciting!"

"Mmm. Dover is horse country. Have you ever ridden a horse, Cassie?"

"Oh, yes." She laughed at the memory. "It was an old one, but it did love sugar. It belonged to one of my father's friends, and Michel—my brother—used to take me for rides. There was no saddle, so Michel would lift me onto its bare back and it seemed so high at the time that I'd hold onto the mane for dear life until he'd thrown himself up behind me. Then he'd hold me around the waist, and I'd feel perfectly safe, and we'd amble along."

"You loved your brother."

Cassie stacked several undershirts and set them with the dress. "Oh, yes."

"You have wonderful memories of him."

"That's about all I have of him. That and a picture."

"It's sad," Lenore murmured, but she was thinking in more general terms than the tragedy of the Holocaust. "You loved your brother, have warm, wonderful memories of him, yet he was taken from you. I had a sister—still have a sister—but we were never close. We rarely see each other even now. It's very sad."

"Do you miss that contact?" Cassie asked.

"I miss the sense of kinship."

"But you have your own family now."

Lenore sighed. "True. But there isn't that feeling of a common past. I wonder why it is that Lydia and I never bonded to one another as you did to your brother."

Cassie suspected that Lenore's personality simply didn't allow for it. She knew that Lenore had lost her father abruptly and at an early age, and she wondered if that had affected her ability to form close relationships. She always seemed to place a certain distance between herself and others, as though afraid to risk anything more. Her relationship with Natalie was the one exception.

"You've always had Mrs. Whyte. Isn't there a sense of history in that?"

"In a way, I suppose."

"She's like a sister to you."

"I don't know what I would have done without her. She's a true friend. But still, it's *different*." She was quiet for a moment, then took a breath. "I hope my children always stay close. There's security in a blood relationship. I'd like to think that if anything happens to one of them the others will come to his or her aid."

"I'm sure they will. They do that now in their way."

But Lenore was looking pinched. "Laura is different from the boys, and they're different from one another. As for the baby, who knows what she'll be like?"

"You wouldn't want to have children who were carbon copies of one another. The excitement is in their differences. In time, when they recognize those differences, they'll come to appreciate them. They'll stay close. The experiences they're having now, living and playing with each other, will stand them in good stead."

But Lenore was momentarily distracted, her mind twenty years in the past. "I want them to be in control of their lives rather than having to live life in reaction to things that are *beyond* their control."

"Is that possible? Are we ever free of circumstance?"

Lenore didn't hear her, or, if she did, she chose to ignore the philosophical question. "I want them to be happy. Happy and secure." She returned to the present with a blink. "What do you want, Cassie?"

"For my child? The same things you want for yours. Happiness and security."

"For you. What do *you* want?"

Cassie had to consider that. The past ten years had seen astonishing changes in her life. For many of them she had thought only of the moment. But what did she want in the long run? "I'm really not sure," she finally confessed.

"You're too bright for this job," Lenore blurted out. "You know that, don't you?"

"No. Not at all," she returned quickly and defensively, then grinned. "This job is a constant challenge."

"But you could be doing something even more challenging, and handling it every bit as well as you handle our house."

Again Cassie grew pensive. "Maybe what I like about working here is the stability of it. There's the challenge, but there's also a certain sense of . . . continuity. The children grow and do different things. You and Mr. Warren grow and do different things. But the family remains intact. There's a kind of underlying confidence here that is reassuring." She gave Lenore a contemplative glance. "At one point my life was a huge question mark. Maybe what I'm seeking is normalcy."

"But you could be moving up in the world."

"I guess moving up doesn't mean as much to me as waking up in the morning knowing where I am and what I'm going to be doing, and that I can do it well. I'll leave moving up in the world to Kenny."

For a time Lenore said nothing, simply continued to fold the worn jerseys in her lap. "Funny," she mused at last. "My mother sacrificed everything for the sake of Lydia and myself. I swore I'd never be that type of martyr, and I'm certainly not. I live well. But still I want more for my children. More and better. I went them to have a past, present and future. And I want them to be free of the fear that it could be gone in a minute." The eyes she raised to Cassie's held a subtle challenge. "You know what I'm saying. Don't you."

No question. It was a simple statement. For a split second Cassie wondered if there were more to it than the obvious. For that split second she felt guilty for all the times she had looked at Gil and dreamed. In the next split second, though, she decided to take Lenore's statement at face value.

Putting on her most composed expression, she nodded. "I do, Mrs. Warren. Yes, I do."

By mid-fall of 1951 the houses in Dover were finished and the families moved in. Cassie hadn't underestimated the amount of work involved in moving, but it was another challenge that she met head-on. And, work aside, it was exciting. Everything was new and fresh, including the cozy four-room cottage designated as the Morells'. Cassie had the time of her life decorating it, taking tips from what Lenore had done in the big house, translating them into what she considered affordable, then gradually implementing her ideas. Gil had given them a generous allowance for furniture, which, aside from the bed that they had ordered well before the move, Cassie took delight in searching for slowly. She had never before had such an opportunity, enjoying the shopping—she and Henry, pushing Kenny in his pram, through store after store—nearly as much as the final purchases.

Lenore, too, enjoyed the shopping, but the final purchases were her pride and joy. Indeed, by the time the house was finished inside and out she was convinced it was the finest for miles around. Of course, she never said as much to Natalie, who was every bit as proud of her own new home.

Natalie had chosen to build a replica of an old stone farmhouse, but there was nothing old or rustic about it. Boasting every modern convenience, it was clean and sparkling. It was far more spread out than Lenore's colonial, cushioning well the thunder of six scampering feet. Rather than the high ceilings of Lenore's rooms, it had lower ones that added to the feeling of warmth.

That was what Natalie wanted—warmth. She wanted a home that would reflect her ideal of a family setting. In this she was perhaps remembering the happy days of her early childhood, the closeness she had known with her father, the sense of togetherness. There had been just the two of them then, and they had had the shabbiest of furnishings, but there was a feeling . . . a feeling she wanted to recapture . . . a feeling that would be an enticement for Jack to spend more time at home.

For a while it seemed to work. The house was a novelty to Jack, too, but more importantly, it was a source of pride. He wanted to entertain to show off his prize, and entertain he did. There was a post-Thanksgiving party and a pre-Christmas party and a mid-January party—all lavishly catered, with waiters and bartenders and flowers galore.

Natalie no longer asked whether they could afford it. She had decided that Jack knew what he was doing and that to question him would be to show a lack of confidence in him which, in turn, would evoke his ire, the last thing she wanted to do. She went along with each and every one of the parties, riding nearly as high as Jack so that she was totally unprepared for the scene that took place on the first day of April, barely six months after they had moved to Dover.

The tongue-in-cheek occasion for the party was April Fool's Day, but in fact it was the kickoff for Gil's election campaign in a new district. The Whyte house was packed to the seams. Jack had invited friends, neighbors and business associates, as well as friends of the Warrens, Gil's clients and colleagues, and notable residents of the surrounding communities. Three separate bartenders—one each in the living room, the large heated sunroom and the library—dispensed liquor freely while white-tailed and gloved waiters moved among the crowds with silver platters filled with every hors d'oeuvre imaginable. A buffet dinner was served well into the evening, followed up by after-dinner drinks for those hearty enough to imbibe further.

One guest was, and did. Later, people would wonder who he was. He hadn't been invited, and he hadn't been a guest of a guest.

It seemed that he had been present all evening, though no one knew him. But he knew his host.

"Ja-ack Whyte!" came his sharp cry late in the evening. He had to repeat it several times—in varying intonations—until Jack, who stood across the room with a circle of guests, looked over at the short, stocky man. "I want to propose a toast," the man faltered, squeezing both eyes shut for an instant to clear his head. He raised his glass and held it wavering high in the air.

The busy chatter of conversation in the room had lessened when Jack had looked up, then petered out until now only an occasional murmur broke the silence. Several glasses were raised, but an odd kind of caution prevailed.

"To Jack Whyte," the man began in a voice loud enough to attract attention in the other rooms as well, "who single-handedly choked the l-life out of what would've been a very prosper . . . prosperous business. . . ."

There was a soft gasp from somewhere in the room and the glasses that had gone up came down, but the man continued talking.

"Here's to you, J-Jack Whyte. May you burn in hell, you son of a b-bitch. . . ."

"Who is he—"

"Who brought him—"

"He's drunk—"

"Drunk?" the man bellowed. "*Not* drunk! Only Ja-ack Whyte c-can get drunk on 'nother man's b-blood—"

Jack, who had been standing stock still, was suddenly moving across the room, as was Gil and several of their closest friends. Within seconds the glass had been taken from the man and passed to a waiting hand, and the man had been taken by both arms and nearly lifted off his feet as he was ushered to the door.

"Does anyone know this man?" Jack called over his shoulder. "He's drunk and needs to be taken home." When no one answered Jack called to Jonathan McNee, who came quickly forward. "I want you to drive this man—"

"Don't *want* t-to go home," the drunk man wailed.

Jack spoke gently, aware of his audience. "You've had too much to drink. My man will see that you're delivered home safely. If you have a car here, we'll see that it's brought to you tomorrow." His voice lowered. "Jonathan, take a look at his billfold. We'll need an address."

What Jack also needed was a name, which he had as soon as Jonathan fished identification from the man's wallet. He looked silently at Gil, showed the address to Jonathan, then replaced the wallet in the breast pocket of the man's jacket. Without another word two of Jack's friends guided the man through the door, Jonathan fast on their heels.

By the time Jack turned back to his guests the conversation was slowly picking up again. Jack moved through the crowd, expressing his apology that the evening had been disturbed even for so short a time. By the time he had returned to the circle from which he had come the incident seemed to have been forgotten.

Its impact lingered, though, in Natalie, who was shaking so badly that she quickly excused herself and escaped to the powder room. Lenore, too, had gone so white that someone hastily fetched her a brandy.

The incident's impact lingered in Jack and Gil as well; they retired to the library with their wives the minute the last of the guests had departed.

"Who *was* he?" Natalie demanded.

Jack's gaze met Gil's. "His name is Hiram Buckley. That has to be Buckley Engineering?"

Gil nodded. As the lawyer involved, he knew that many more of the details than Jack. "We took a large government contract from him several months ago."

"Government contract?" Natalie echoed, but she was looking at her husband. "What government contract?"

"For electronic parts. We've been producing them at the plant."

Lenore stirred in the chair into which she'd collapsed. "I thought you were making television sets."

"We are," Jack said, "but we're also doing special work for the government."

"What kind of special work?" Natalie asked.

"Oh," he waved a hand to suggest the insignificance of the issue, "parts for jet airplanes . . . other military things." The Korean War, not to mention the rampant fear of the Russians, who had tested their first A-bomb little more than two years before, was proving to be a gold mine for industry. Of course, Jack had no desire to inform his wife of that. She had weathered the last war well enough, but he knew that she was basically a peace-loving soul.

Gil quickly refocused the discussion. "From what I heard, Buckley thought he had the contract sewn up. He was furious when we got it."

"What's happened to his business?" Natalie asked.

Jack shrugged and looked at Gil, who answered. "It folded."

"Because of one government contract?"

"It was faltering anyway. Losing the government contract was simply the last straw."

Lenore wrapped both hands around her brandy snifter and stared at the tiny bit left in it. What she had drunk hadn't warmed her; she felt as chilled as ever. "Then . . . he has nothing?"

"Hiram Buckley isn't our concern," Gil informed her curtly.

"But he's ruined. Doesn't that bother you just a little bit?"

"It's unfortunate for the people involved when any business folds, but Buckley's would have done it sooner or later even if he *had* gotten that contract."

"It's the way of free enterprise," Jack added. "Survival of the fittest." He turned to Gil. "Which is what concerns me most. Do you think he did any damage?"

Gil rubbed the back of his neck with his hand. "Hard to tell. It was pretty late in the evening. Some people had already left before he created his little scene. I guess it took him that long to get up the nerve."

"Or that much liquor. How the hell did he get in?" Jack was scowling at his wife.

"*I* don't know," she returned. "*You* were supposed to know everyone who came. A full third of them were total strangers to me. How was I to know that one more was there who hadn't been invited?"

Gil stepped between husband and wife and held up both hands placatingly. "There are bound to be crashers at any large affair. I'm sure we've had them in the past."

"But none of them have done what Buckley did!" Jack argued. "Your involvement in our getting that contract was as great as mine. People must know that. Hell, if you're not worried about harm to your campaign, I sure am about my reputation—"

"Take it easy, Jack. He was one crackpot who was very obviously drunk. I think he offended everyone doing what he did after he'd spent the night taking advantage of your hospitality. Besides, there were other businessmen there. They know the score."

"Do they know about Buckley? I think they should. I think we should spread the word that he had run his business into the ground long before he lost that contract."

"And be put on the defensive? That would be exactly what Buckley wants. No, Jack. You're angry. That's all. When you calm down you'll agree that we'd do better to ignore the entire thing. If we make an issue of this, it will only draw attention to something that people may have already forgotten. Besides, we're the ones on top. We know that a worm like Buckley can't hurt us."

Jack gave him an annoyed glance. "I suppose you're right, but that doesn't mean that I wouldn't like to put the guy against the nearest wall and shoot him. . . ."

Chapter 9

ROBERT CAVANAUGH DOODLED a large star on his calendar the day that the department's ballistics expert returned from vacation and took a good look at the bullets that had killed Mark Whyte and Deborah Warren. He called the man twice that morning demanding first priority on his time and was practically leaning over his shoulder when the analysis was finally completed.

"Interesting," Leo Bachynski commented, straightening from his worktable with one of the bullets in his hand. "It's from the same caliber gun as the one you found with the body."

"But?"

"The grooves are distorted." He turned the bullet in his palm. "Similar, but different."

"Which means," Cavanaugh concluded on a note of triumph, "that a silencer was used."

The ballistician agreed. "Looks that way. At least there's nothing to prove that the bullet *wasn't* fired from the same gun. I'd feel safe in saying that a silencer caused the discrepancy in the grooves."

Cavanaugh was already thinking ahead. This was the first concrete lead he had that the deaths were something other than self-inflicted. There was no way Mark Whyte could have shot himself to death, then removed and disposed of a silencer. Still, he wanted corroboration.

His next stop was the medical examiner's office. Unfortunately, the coroner, Nicholas Carne, was at work. The stench in the room was nearly as overpowering as the aura of death. In all his years on the force Cavanaugh had never gotten used to either.

Carne had, of course, and he didn't welcome the untimely interruption. "Can't talk now, Cavanaugh."

"It's important."

"Can't it wait for an hour?"

"If you want me to puke all over your cadaver it can. I need this fast or we'll both be in trouble."

Carne glowered at him over the rims of his glasses, but he did straighten. Snapping off his surgical gloves and tossing them toward a trash bin, he stretched to switch off the mike above the table. Then he pushed his glasses to the top of his head, planted his hands on his hips, and sighed impatiently. "Okay. What is it?"

"The Whyte-Warren case. You did the autopsies, didn't you?"

"My name's on the report."

"You have associates. I want to know who did the actual work."

"You're looking at him."

"Thank you," Cavanaugh said, making no effort to blunt his sarcasm. He had never cared for Carne, who had a chip on his shoulder three miles wide.

"So?"

"New evidence has appeared establishing that it was homicide."

"Sure. Whyte killed his wife."

"No. Someone killed the two of them. I need to take a second look at those autopsies."

"You have the reports."

"They don't tell me a thing, at least nothing that suggests a double murder."

"Then there wasn't anything."

"Can you think back to the autopsies?"

"Jesus, do you know how many autopsies I've done in the last month? Crazies come out of the woodwork during the summer."

"Look, Carne, I know you're overworked, but so am I, and this is important. I need to know if there was anything that might have been strange about those bodies."

"If I'd seen anything I'd have put it in the report."

"I'm talking of something small, something you might have considered insignificant at the time, only now, in light of a possible homicide, you could interpret differently." Sensing imminent rebellion, he rushed on. "I'm not criticizing the work you do. It's just that this is a tough case. You know the families involved. If the department overlooks even the smallest thing we'll never hear the end of it."

As much as Carne resented the intrusion in what he considered his personal domain, he had enough sense to see Cavanaugh's point. He snorted, then tossed his head toward the microphone. "I have transcripts. If you come back in an hour—"

"Now. I need them now." Not that an hour would have made a difference in the case, but Cavanaugh felt that he had wasted far too many hours waiting for the ballistician to return. One more hour was more than he could bear at the moment.

"I won't just hand them over to you," Carne warned in a grumble, but he was slowly walking toward a side office. "You wouldn't know what to make of them. I'm the expert around here. If there's anything to be found I'm the one who'll find it."

Cavanaugh said nothing. He stood patiently while Carne opened a file cabinet, sifted through its contents and tugged out a folder. Setting it on his desk he lowered his glasses from his head to the bridge of his nose and began to scan the notes. He shook his head and turned one page, quickly read the second, shook his head again and turned to the third.

When he wasn't as quick to shake his head, Cavanaugh grew more alert. "See something?"

"I don't know," Carne mumbled. He frowned, looked across the desk at nothing in particular, then returned his gaze to the folder. "Sleep. Could be nothing. There's always the possibility. But if you want to look at it another way—"

"What the hell are you talking about?"

Carne looked up. "There was sleep in Mark Whyte's eyes. Dried mucus. Sand. You know," he stuck a finger under his glasses and made as though he were wiping something from the inside corner of his eye, "the stuff you have to get rid of in the morning?"

Cavanaugh could have done without the demonstration. "Could it have been from an allergy or cold or something?"

"Nope. The guy didn't have anything active in his system."

"If there was sleep in his eyes we'd have to suppose that he'd been sleeping when he was shot."

"We'd have to suppose that he'd been sleeping *at some point* that night," Carne corrected with satisfaction. "He could have been asleep, then woken up and," he straightened a forefinger from his fist and cocked a thumb-trigger, "bam. So you don't really know anything new."

But Cavanaugh did. He knew about the silencer. That, taken with what Carne was saying, was promising. "It's another bit of evidence playing against the suicide theory," he said eagerly. "A guy doesn't go to sleep and sleep *soundly*—which Whyte must have been doing—with the knowledge that he was going to kill his wife and himself. Between the blood workups and tissue studies, we know that he hadn't been drunk or taken any kind of pill or drug—"

Carne interrupted him. "Hold on." He returned to the transcript, read a little further, then set the paper on the desk and looked smugly at Cavanaugh. "It's right here. If you'd read the report, you'd have seen it."

"What?"

"Corneal edema."

"What the devil's that?"

"A swelling of the cornea that normally occurs during sleep. I don't always take that kind of measurement, but where there is a question of drug usage I study the eyes pretty close."

"Did you find the same with his wife?"

Carne flipped through more papers, read a bit, then nodded.

"This edema, could it simply be a function of death?"

"No."

"Could someone wake up, accurately shoot another person, then himself within a minute and still have corneal edema?"

"Possible. Not probable."

Cavanaugh breathed out a sigh. Dealing with Carne had been worth the effort for once.

John Ryan, whom Cavanaugh went to see next, was surprisingly cautious about the two new twists. "Without the silencer itself, you're going on supposition alone. Bachynski could only guess that a silencer was used. Those bullets could have been shot from a totally different gun. And as for Carne, probable versus possible won't prove a damn thing in court. You need more!" he snapped.

"Of course I do. I've just started." And Ryan had originally told him to take his time. Why the impatience now?

"You're going to the coast, aren't you?"

"Monday morning." It was Thursday; as it was, he would have to work late each night to get enough of his other cases out of the way so he could stay in California until he was satisfied that he had searched every nook and cranny. Jodi wasn't going to be thrilled. They had planned to drive to Maine for the day on Sunday, and it looked like he would have to work. Maybe her mother would decide to pop into town for the day, or Jodi would decide to do some Sunday shopping or have an emergency with one of her students to keep her occupied. That sometimes happened on a weekend. . . .

"Good. There's got to be something there."

"If there is I'll find it."

"Go over *everything*. Take his house apart. Look at things that don't even seem remotely connected."

"You know I will," Cavanaugh said, stifling his irritation. He didn't need Ryan telling him how to do his job.

"I'm getting pressure on this one, Cavanaugh. Holstrom has had it to his ears with calls from Whyte and Warren."

"I've been in touch with Jordan Whyte. He's going to try to get the big guys to ease up."

"Jordan Whyte. Sneaky bastard. If he's working to help you he's probably got something to hide."

"If he does I'll find it."

"You do that, Cavanaugh. You know the stakes in this one."

Oh, yes. Cavanaugh knew the stakes in this one. Chief of homicide on the verge of retiring. Someone needed, preferably from the ranks, to take his place. More money, power, prestige.

And revenge.

"Come on, Bob," Jodi argued when Sunday morning rolled around and Cavanaugh informed her that he had to spend at least part of the day at the office. "You promised we'd take off for the day. You've been working overtime all week. Don't you think you deserve a break?"

Unfortunately, Jodi's mother hadn't decided to pop into town. Nor had any other distraction come up to keep her busy.

"What I deserve is one thing," Cavanaugh stated. "What I have to *do* is something else. And what I have to do today is to clean up a stack of paperwork that should have been done yesterday."

"It's not like you to be backlogged."

"It's not every day that I have a case like the Whyte-Warren one."

"Maybe you're spending too much time on it. Maybe you're looking for things that simply aren't there."

Cavanaugh quickly shook his head. "No. Things are there. I just haven't found the right ones yet."

"How can you be so sure things *are* there? Damn it, Bob,

you're still staring at pictures and poring through files and it's getting you nowhere."

"Not nowhere. I'm learning things about those guys that the public doesn't know."

She was disappointed enough about the disruption of their plans—annoyed enough at Bob—to throw caution to the winds. "Like what?"

Cavanaugh felt he had to justify himself. "Like the fact that Gil Warren won some of his early elections by talking his strongest opponents out of running."

"What kind of dunce could be talked out of doing something he wanted to do?"

"A dunce who was promised something even better—like a plum position with one of Warren's friends."

"Whyte?"

"Among others. Of course, who the hell would have wanted to work with Whyte is beyond me. Dirty money from the word go."

"What do you mean?" They had already been through the discussion of Jack's father's bootlegging, but the look of disgust in Bob's eye told Jodi that he had something else in mind.

"In the late forties and early fifties his business expanded too quickly. Where did he get the money?"

"I don't know," she answered blankly. "Where did he get it?"

"Come on. Use your imagination."

"A bank? Investors? Friends? Profits?" She paused, knowing precisely what Bob thought. "Do you have any proof that he got it from the Mob?"

"Proof?" Cavanaugh twitched his nose as though he didn't think proof was relevant, but he answered honestly. "No."

"Then what's the point in suggesting it?"

"Okay," he picked up more boldly. "I do have proof about something else. Come 1951, with the people here so frightened of the A-bomb that children were cowering under their school desks during air raid drills while their parents furiously stocked bomb shelters, Jack Whyte was supplying beta-ray spectographs to the government for use in the development of the H-bomb. More and greater weaponry. He cashed in but good."

"There were those who argued that we needed the more powerful bomb to maintain supremacy over Russia."

"I thought you were a dove! Whose side are you on, anyway?"

"I'm on *your* side, Bob, but I can't help wondering if you're letting your own biases get the better of you in this case." She had seen him, night after night, poring over papers with an intensity she had never seen in him before.

"I'm just pointing out what Whyte and Warren did back then. You can imagine what they've done since."

"But what *relevance* does that have for this case?"

"It has some. I know it does. I'm sure that once I know all the facts everything will come clear. But I can't know the facts of this case until I clear my desk of other cases. I'm heading for L.A. tomorrow—"

"Which is precisely why I want you to myself today," Jodi said plaintively. "You'll be gone for . . . God only knows how long."

"I should have been out there long before now!"

"Don't we have a right to be together once in a while?"

"I'm a cop. Cops don't work nine to five. You knew that *and* what my job meant to me when we first met. My work has to come first. It's as simple as that."

"I see," she said quietly, then turned and very calmly went to the closet where she had hung her pocketbook, draped its strap over her shoulder, and left the apartment.

Cavanaugh left for Los Angeles the next morning, carrying with him not only the burden of the Whyte-Warren investigation but the emotional quandary of his relationship with Jodi.

She had left the apartment before ten the morning before and hadn't returned by the time he left for work at noon. He had painstakingly plodded his way through his paperwork, finding it more of a drudgery than ever. He liked being in the field, working on a case such as the Whyte-Warren one where his intellect was challenged. Filling out forms and filing reports was not his idea of creative police work, though he knew it was necessary. On that particular Sunday it had been doubly frustrating.

He had wanted to be in Maine with Jodi. He had been looking forward to the trip because Jodi was relaxing and fun to be with. They had gone on many day trips in the past, and he liked the way she looped her arm in his as they walked along the beach or talked quietly in a small restaurant over a bucket of fried clams.

He had also been looking forward to the trip because he had known how important it was to her, and he felt guilty. So, after struggling with his forms until he had dispensed with the last, he yielded to impulse, picked up a bucket of fried clams at the waterfront and brought it home to Charlestown.

But Jodi still hadn't returned.

So he got angry. He ate every last clam himself, got indigestion and had to take Mylanta. He wandered through the apartment wondering where she was and when she would be back. He pictured her out with another man and knew jealousy, then fear.

Yet when she returned late that night, giving no explanation of where she'd been, pride prevented him from probing. He behaved as though she had every right to be gone for an entire day without accounting for her time—which he knew she did, though it bugged the hell out of him. They shared their large bed that night, neither touching nor talking, and he left for the airport in the morning with little more than a perfunctory kiss good-bye.

Now, as the plane soared westward, he was suffering. He wanted Jodi. He wanted his job. He agonized, wondering if he could have both under the terms he had set. Jodi wasn't dumb; she was a warm woman with a lot to offer a man, and though she had been understanding of his work for the past three years, he feared she was losing her patience. Maybe he shouldn't have been so blunt in saying that his job came first, but it did, damn it! It was his life!

And Jodi—what was she to him? Hell, he just didn't know.

If the two detectives with whom he was traveling, Buddy Annello and Sharon Webber, thought him particularly withdrawn during the flight, they must have assumed that he was simply brooding about the case, for they didn't bother him. Once the plane landed in Los Angeles, Cavanaugh was fully caught up in the investigation.

So much so that he barely had time to think about Jodi during the five days he was away.

The late August sun brought more people than ever to Martha's Vineyard. Jordan had chartered a small plane—pride prevented it from being one of his father's—to fly Katia and him there from New York. The fact that the regular flights were so crowded had been only in part responsible for that action. He wanted the convenience of setting the timetable. He also wanted Katia to himself. It wasn't that he planned anything illicit, because he was being very careful to avoid that, but because he enjoyed her company enough that he didn't want to share her with even a flight attendant. It was also possible that he wanted to impress her, or, more accurately, make the time she spent with him as comfortable as possible. A chartered plane, at least this one with its plush velour seats and bar and small kitchen, did that.

When they landed they headed directly to the land he had bought. The old Marshall Arms Hotel sat on a prime spot in West Tisbury. It encompassed an expanse of Vineyard Sound beachfront, and, with the adjacent land Jordan had bought, stretched inland to include more heavily wooded areas of pine and oak. Jordan had wanted Katia to see the locale before the old hotel was razed. Now, as they stood before it, she was shaking her head in amazement.

"It's beautiful." Her gaze broadened to encompass the land beyond the hotel. "But that's what's so puzzling. I can't believe that this hotel has been closed for two years and no one has snapped it up sooner. What with the crowds the Vineyard attracts and the fact that this end of the island is so much more peaceful than the other areas around Edgartown and Oak Bluffs it's the natural spot for a resort."

"The last owners of the hotel didn't have the capital to make it into something big. And it isn't that other developers haven't tried to get the land, just that they didn't have the patience or the wherewithal to cut through the red tape. I've been working with the townspeople for a year to get around local ordinances. The people here are possessive of their resources. They weren't wild about the idea of condominiums. They pictured something garish."

Katia squinted through the sun and glanced up at Jordan. Dressed in jeans and a t-shirt, he was every bit as appealing as the land, if in a slightly disreputable way. "What do *you* have in mind?"

"Okay." He set his feet in the sand and gestured with his hands as he faced the aged hotel. "All that is coming down, and the new structure will be set a little farther back from the beach, per the ecologists' wishes. I picture something lower, more modern—"

"Modern? But the charm of the Vineyard is in old New England."

"And every other hotel and inn on the island is that. I want mine to be different. It will be imposing in an understated way," like the house in Maine, Katia thought, "with lots of glass and natural stone. The condominiums will be set back even farther." He pointed toward the woods, first on one side of the hotel, then the other. "I want them low, too. We're not talking high-rise condos here. Two stories at most. More like little townhouses grouped in small clusters. I want them buried among the trees so that the people at the hotel don't see them and vice versa. Privacy is critical. I want this to be an exclusive area."

She nodded, trying to visualize things as he did. Her artist's eye was already forming images for the ad campaign. "Do you have an architect?"

"Amidon and Dunn."

She nodded again, familiar with the firm's work. "Any preliminary sketches?"

"They're working on it. Hopefully they'll have something within the month, but I don't expect we'll see much until after Labor Day. Things are slow now. Everyone's on vacation."

"And then?"

"I'd like to have the razing done as soon as possible. If we can get foundations poured the inside work can be done over the winter. There's a chance we can open by next April or May."

"Which means that you'll want to start advertising by November."

"At the latest. The more units we sell early on the better. As soon as we've done the razing we'll be blocking out the areas for building. As far as the condos go, they'll have to fit in with as little disturbance to the natural landscape as possible. Another demand of the town fathers," he added on a dry note.

"But I can understand their point. It would be a crime to destroy what's been growing for years, and you have to admit that the trees are gorgeous."

"They will make for privacy."

"Mmm. How about price range? Have you thought that through?"

Jordan faced her as though prepared for a challenge. "As I said before, I want this to be an exclusive area. Which means that whoever stays here or buys a place here will pay well for it. Which also means that we'll attract a certain kind of clientele."

"Rich. Okay. What are the estimates?"

"Three-fifty and up for the condos, depending on whatever customizing the buyers want. Two hundred a day at the hotel."

Her eyes widened. "Exclusive is what you're going to get with those prices."

"I'm aiming high."

The corner of her mouth turned up. It was a half smile, one that was both wry and amused. "You'll get it, Jordan. You know that, or you'd never be thinking of asking so much."

"I think we will," he agreed. He seemed to be relieved that she hadn't jumped on his back, but he proceeded with caution. "There may be a snobbish element in what I'm saying, but hell, I'm not in this business for kicks. I've paid a hefty sum for the land here, and with the quality of building I want the costs will be exorbitant. But there is a market for luxury living, and if I don't provide it someone else will."

"It's okay, Jordan," she teased softly, putting a hand on his arm, "I'm not criticizing you. Just don't ask *me* to shell out two hundred a day for a room—unless, of course, the room comes with a Jacuzzi, a personal maid, and an endless supply of champagne and caviar."

"Sorry, babe," he answered in the same teasing tone. "No personal maid. I can give you a Jacuzzi in the executive suite, and I think I can handle the champagne and caviar. But unless you're willing to settle for me wearing a pretty little dress—"

She laughed aloud. "What a great picture! And you'd do it, wouldn't you?"

He simply grinned, then reached for her hand. "Come on. Let's take a walk. I want you to get a feel for the property. That was why I dragged you out here so quickly."

"I was wondering about that." Soon after she had agreed to work with him, Jordan had spoken with the head of her agency. It had been a formality, a mere courtesy. Of course the firm would handle his project. And, of course, Katia would direct the artwork personally. "I don't usually get involved until the architect's drawings are complete."

"But the buildings are only a small part of what we'll be promoting," he said with such boyish enthusiasm that she had to grin. He was holding her hand tightly, leading her across the sand toward the far end of the old hotel. "It's something in the *air*, Katia—something about the way the Sound laps at the shore and the way everything smells of trees and the ocean. The mainland seems a thousand miles away. Down-island, the streets are packed, but here there's just a kind of pervasive tranquility."

"I do know why you dragged me down here so quickly. Within a month that pervasive tranquility will be shattered by the noise of bulldozers and tractors and saws, drills and hammers."

"But only temporarily. Have a heart, Katia. Once everything's done the tranquility will be back."

"There will be people then."

"Of course."

"It won't be like it is now."

"Sure it will. Well . . . maybe not *exactly* like it is now. But the tranquility will be here, and that's what I want to sell. That's where I want the thrust of the advertising to be. Think you can do it?"

Katia knew she could and she told him as much. Ideas were forming in her head—smooth, flowing lines, gentle colors, a soft, ink-outlined sketch—but she momentarily pushed them aside to let her senses fully absorb the scene firsthand. She walked easily beside Jordan; her Reeboks gave her good traction on the sand, then on the mossy earth beneath the trees, while her jeans and the oversized blouse she had knotted pertly at the hip were warm enough, cool enough, just right. Even aside from her positive re-action to the land she felt good. A day away from the city—a Friday, at that, which made for a long weekend—was a treat; though she was officially working, she could never think of being with Jordan as work. At least not today, when she felt so relaxed and happy.

Jordan talked softly as they meandered over every inch of the property. He pointed out where one or another cluster of build-ings would be, shared the details of his plans, invited her feedback and listened to everything she had to say. They discussed various approaches to advertising; in this Katia invited his feedback, for anything and everything she could learn about his feelings would help her when she was back in the office.

As they walked her excitement grew. Hearing his ideas, being in on the ground floor of his plans was stimulating, but then, Jordan himself was stimulating. Surrounded by his aura and that of God's lovely acres, she wondered why she had ever fought working with Jordan.

By the time they had completed the tour and returned to their original spot in front of the old hotel a car was waiting to take them into Edgartown. Jordan helped her inside, then gave the driver the name of a restaurant before he sat back in his seat, looked at Katia, rubbed his hands together and grinned.

"Now we play."

She tried to look stern. "I thought this was a workday."

"It was, but we've done all the work we need to do."

"It's only one in the afternoon. Honestly, Jordan. You're disillusioning me."

"We need to relax."

"If I relax any more I'm apt to fall asleep." Settling lazily into the seat, she looked out at the passing scenery. "This is very definitely a change from an average day at the office."

"I think they work you too hard."

"No. I love it."

"You look tired."

"Thanks."

"Been out with the gynecologist again?"

She smiled but kept her eyes on the window. "As a matter of fact we went to a concert in the park last weekend."

"Tell me he bought a picnic lunch, spread a blanket on the grass and plied you with wine all afternoon."

"Nope. All night. It was an evening concert."

"*All* night? You spent the *night* with him?"

She did look at him then. "And if I did?"

"I don't like him."

"You've never *met* him."

"He's not right for you, Katia. I know it."

"How can you know that if you don't know the man?"

"I feel it in my gut."

She nodded. "Mmm. That's scientific."

"It is. My gut's never guided me wrong."

"No? What about that deal you made a few years back to produce electric cars?"

"How was I to know that the oil crisis would just up and end? Or that people would forget that it had ever happened and pretend that it will never happen again? My idea was good; it was my timing that was off. I'm telling you, someday electric cars will be in. Besides," he added in a final defense, "I saw the problem and got out fast enough to minimize my losses. So my gut redeemed itself in the end."

She chuckled. "Your gut, my foot! It was your financial adviser who redeemed himself."

"Whatever. I still don't like your doctor."

"That's okay. I don't like Little Mary Sunshine."

Jordan, who had delivered his final judgment on the doctor while scowling out his own window, turned his head and eyed her.

"Her name is Mary Sandburg. How do you know about her?"

"I saw a picture of the two of you in the paper."

"What paper?"

"The *Post*."

"Since when do you read the *Post*?"

"I don't. Roger does. He makes it a point to educate me on the finer points he picks up."

"My picture is a finer point? Hell, Katia, I was out with her once, and the damn photographer thought it would be real juicy to suggest a romance."

Katia shrugged. "She's very pretty, and she has money."

"Yeah, from her third husband. She did well that time, but if she's looking for a fourth in me she's nuts."

"You're not interested?"

"No."

"Well, that's a relief." She lowered her voice, well aware of the curious glances cast in the rearview mirror by the young driver. "Her breasts are too big. You know what happens to women with big breasts when they hit middle age? You're stuck with either huge bills for plastic surgery or sagging breasts."

Jordan snagged her neck with his elbow and yanked her close to him. "You've got a fresh mouth," he gritted, but he was trying not to grin.

"Better a fresh mouth than sagging breasts. Course, I could probably use a little more in that department—"

"I like your breasts." His voice dropped to a growl. "Did the doctor like them?"

"The doctor," she stated very slowly and softly, "did not see them."

"You made love in the dark? See? I told you he's not right for you. When two people make love it should be with every light on. They should get as much enjoyment in watching what's happening as in feeling it."

His words and the image they inspired sent a shimmer through Katia. It was augmented by the fact that they had entered Edgartown; somehow, the throngs of people on the sidewalks enhanced the sense of intimacy in the car. She spoke quickly, almost gruffly. "You sound kinky. But that's beside the point. Alan and I didn't make love in the dark. We didn't make love at all."

His stranglehold eased into something less forceful but equally as binding. "You didn't?"

"No. There. Does that set your little brotherly heart to rest?"

Her confession hadn't set anything to rest. In the first place, as much as he tried to make it so, Jordan's heart wasn't brotherly. He had endured the years she had been with Sean because the man's constant presence—in New York, in Dover, in Maine—had kept her solidly off-limits. Now, however, she was free again, back in his life with a vengeance.

In the second place, the thought of Katia making love, period, aroused him. He had seen her breasts once, and though that had been years ago, he could feel them against him now and knew, beyond a doubt, that they were as beautiful as ever.

"It'll do," he said quietly. In the next instant he released her, but not before he had let his hand trail reluctantly down her back. He wanted to touch her. He couldn't help it. But it only made the hunger worse.

With a deep breath he dragged his leg up and crossed it over his knee to hide his arousal. "So," he said, wrapping both hands around his ankle so that his arms could provide an added measure of protection, "what else is new in your life?"

She wished he were still holding her, but took the loss in stride. "Not much since I saw you last. Oh . . . I had lunch with Sandy Kane two days ago." Sandy and she had roomed together during their last two years at NYU; Jordan had taken them both to dinner several times.

"I always liked Sandy. How's she doing?"

"Really well. She's an assistant producer for a TV talk show in Chicago. She was in New York to set up a series of interviews. I don't get to see her often, but when I do it's great. It's like we saw each other just last month, rather than last year. The rapport is always there, you know?"

"She's that kind of person. Curious. Open. Interesting. I can see where she'd be a successful producer."

The driver pulled up at the restaurant just then, interrupting the conversation. Katia climbed out of the car, leaving Jordan to settle his account with the driver. He joined her moments later, and with a light hand at the back of her waist guided her inside.

When they had been seated at a small corner table with menus open before them, Jordan resumed the discussion on a slight tangent. "You enjoyed college, I think."

"After that first year."

"Mmm. How could I forget that first year."

"I don't know. You were always coming to my rescue when I needed it most."

"You were homesick. I was glad to be able to help."

"Homesick was only part of it. Going to NYU was like culture shock. I suppose any large city college would have hit me that way."

"Hey, you weren't from the boonies."

"No, but I'd led an insulated life. Everything had been taken care of for me. Suddenly I had to find my way around a new place, meet new friends, grapple with a checkbook. It was overwhelming."

"It was what you wanted," he reminded her.

"And I'm not complaining. Simply remembering." She leaned forward, elbows on the table, and she was smiling warmly. "You know one of the things I remember most clearly about that first year? Remember the time I was in the middle of finals and I panicked?"

"Do I remember? I still get chills when I think of it. You showed up at my office as pale as a ghost and I could see that you'd been crying."

"I didn't know what to do! I'd had one final, pulled an all-nighter and stumbled through a second, and I felt so sick that I didn't see how I'd be able to study for a third, the one I was supposed to take the next day. You took me back to your place, heated a can of chicken soup and noodles and made me eat it, then put me to bed. Then you woke me up at five the next morning and studied with me for six hours so I could take the exam at noon. And all the time you kept telling me that half of the other freshmen were as panicked as I was. I think you were lying through your teeth."

"It worked, didn't it? You aced the exam."

"Not aced. Got a B plus."

"Close enough. And I wasn't lying; I was guessing. I remember how *I* felt during that first round of exams. I nearly dropped out of Duke."

"Really? You never told me that."

"Pride, Katia."

"So where is it now, that pride?" she teased.

"Oh, I still have it, but it's taken different directions with age. I can afford to talk about my college days, maybe because they're so far behind me."

"You sound like an old man. You're not exactly over the hill yet, Jordan."

"Not yet. But getting there. I'm telling you, my knee was killing me this morning."

"You should have had surgery on it fifteen years ago. Was it pride that kept you from doing it?"

He shook his head. "Stupidity."

The waitress approached, an adorable young woman who looked like she was just in college herself. Katia hadn't glanced at the menu, but Jordan gave it a quick once-over. "Quiche and salad?" he asked. When she nodded he turned to the waitress and ordered two, as well as iced coffees. When the waitress had gone, Katia leaned even closer.

"I thought real men didn't eat quiche," she stage whispered.

"You've been reading the wrong books. I like quiche. Does that make me an unreal man?"

He was unreal, all right, Katia reflected. He was smooth and self-assured, intelligent and positively gorgeous. "It makes you very cosmopolitan, and a free thinker at that. I think you'd eat quiche *because* someone declared that real men don't. You do what you want. I respect that."

"Thank you," he said quietly.

"You're welcome," she answered likewise.

For several minutes they simply sat looking at one another. Katia felt warm all over because Jordan's eyes told her that she was the only woman in the room. Then confusion set in, because if those eyes were telling her the truth, and if she was interpreting that truth correctly, she didn't understand why she and Jordan weren't lovers.

"Haven't you ever thought of marriage?" she asked on an impulse born of frustration.

"Marriage?" He made a shrugging motion with his mouth. "Not recently."

"You never think of it? What about children? Don't you want to have them?"

"I'd like to have children."

"What are you waiting for?"

"The right woman."

She nodded, but her confusion was greater than ever. *What was she doing wrong? Why wasn't she the right woman?* "I thought for a while there that you'd settle down with Donna Parker. She was nice."

"Very nice."

"But?"

"No fireworks."

"Ahh. She was *too* nice."

"As in the sweet and conventional and boring. Yes. How about you? We never really talked about what happened with Sean."

Katia shrugged. "There's nothing to talk about."

"You dated the guy for a year and lived with him for another three. What finally broke it up?"

She wasn't good at lying and didn't even try. "He wanted marriage. I didn't."

"Why not?"

"You said it yourself. He wasn't the right guy."

"And since Sean?"

"Alan?" she teased.

"Forget Alan. No other marriage prospects?"

"I've been too busy."

"A euphemism meaning that no one has come along who meant more to you than your work?"

Oh, that man had come along. He sat smack in front of her. How could she answer? "No euphemism. I've been too busy."

"What do you see in the future? Will you always be too busy or are you going to want to settle down some day?" All too clearly he recalled the conversation in Maine the month before, when Peter had teased her about wanting a husband and babies. Jordan had thought about that a lot in the days since.

"Settle down as in having a family?" She, too, recalled the discussion. Her answer was the same. "Eventually."

Jordan, who had been holding her gaze almost somberly, suddenly grinned. "Remember that guy who took you to your high school prom?"

"Jimmy? Sure I do. You came home right before he was to pick me up, and you dragged me, prom dress and all, to the apple orchard, singing and dancing with me until the hairdo my mother had spent hours arranging was thoroughly wilted by the heat. I had every intention of telling Jimmy I was sick, changing into jeans and insisting that you finish the evening with me. But you had a date."

"Forget my date. You couldn't have stood Jimmy up after he'd gone and rented a tux."

She smiled at the memory. "No. I suppose not. He was sweet. I do remember glaring at you, though. You were lolling there against a tree, so smug with your arms crossed over your chest and your legs crossed at the ankles." She took a quick breath. "Jimmy married a girl from college. Last I heard, he had a house in the suburbs, two kids, a dog and a Cherokee Chief."

"Too conventional for you?"

"Too predictable. He was a really nice guy, like your Donna—"

"But no fireworks."

"None."

Jordan sighed. "I guess we're a pair. Always looking for excitement."

"Not excitement, at least, not all the time. Just . . . fireworks."

"As in endless natural combustion . . . explosive chemistry." He arched a brow. "How did you do in Chem?"

"B minus."

"Same here, and man did I have to work for *that*." He went on to reminisce about those particular efforts, having deftly steered the subject to safer ground. The waitress brought their lunch, and they chatted easily as they ate. By the time they were done and standing in front of the restaurant once more, they were both feeling stuffed.

"How can quiche fill you like this?" she moaned. "I always think of quiche and a salad as a nice light meal."

"When the piece of quiche is a quarter of the pie and the salad has everything but the kitchen sink in it what do you expect?"

He stretched and patted his stomach, which looked wonderfully flat to Katia. She was nonetheless pleased with his next suggestion.

"Let's rent bikes and take a ride."

"Think you can handle it with those knees?"

"Sure I can handle it. Think you can handle it with those thighs?"

She looked down. "What's wrong with my thighs?"

Nothing, Jordan decided, looking at them in her tight jeans. He swallowed hard. "They don't look terribly muscular."

"Thank God for that," she said, and led the way to the nearest bicycle rental stand.

For the next three hours they pedaled around the eastern end of the island. Katia found the ride to be nearly as exhilarating as the look of pleasure on Jordan's face. When they finally returned to the bicycle stand, though, she found that her thighs were not the problem.

"Uh-oh," Jordan said. "Sore?"

She was stretching her legs, but it was her bottom that ached. She would have rubbed it had she been able to do so unobtrusively. "I'm okay."

He walked up beside her and did what she'd wanted to do; his large hand gently rubbed her seat. When she glanced shamefacedly up at him, he grimaced. "Mine's killing me, too. I guess we're both out of shape. Want to try to walk it off?"

"In lieu of hot water bottles that sounds good."

It was. They strolled leisurely along the streets, stopping in shops, browsing, even buying t-shirts. When Jordan announced that he was hungry again, Katia realized that she was too, and that it was easily dinnertime. By mutual agreement they ate at a small French restaurant that was simple but elegant. Whether it was the *acidule de cannette* that sated her, or the bottle of wine she and Jordan drained, or simply his company that made her feel so warm and lazily happy, Katia didn't know. But she had to struggle to pull herself from a pleasant haze when Jordan suddenly leaned forward.

"Let's stay here for the night."

"Jordan, this restaurant closes at ten."

"Not *here*. Here on the island. I don't know about you, but I haven't felt this good in ages. I'm not ready to go back to New York yet."

"But the plane—"

"Is at our disposal. I'm sure the pilot won't mind a night's vacation. We could stay over, have a late breakfast, maybe go to the beach if the weather's good tomorrow, and I'd have you back in the city by dinnertime tomorrow night."

"Jordan, I don't have anything with me!"

"What do you need?"

"Toothbrush, blowdryer, makeup—"

"Toothbrushes we can pick up. You have a hairbrush in your purse, and you don't need anything else. You don't need makeup, Katia. Especially not here."

She was beginning to warm to the idea. It had been a wonderful day; to extend it would be heaven. "We really shouldn't," she said, but her eyes were dancing mischievously. "There are a million things I usually do on Saturdays."

"But it would be fun, wouldn't it?" The feeling in his eyes matched hers.

"Uh-huh."

"Let's do it," he whispered.

"Okay!" she whispered back.

Chapter 10

FINDING A ROOM for the night was harder than they had expected, but neither Katia nor Jordan minded the fact that they had to try four inns before they found one that had space—even if Jordan did have to twist an arm to get the room in the end.

"Now this is style," Katia announced after they had wound their way through the maze of narrow halls and creaking stairways to arrive finally at the attic room they had wangled from the reluctant clerk. The room had one shabby dresser, one rickety chair and one small and lumpy bed. "Ah. A mirror." It was above the dresser and slightly dusty. "How nice."

They laughed, undaunted by the less-than-deluxe accommodations. "See what I mean?" Jordan teased. "My hotel will be in demand."

"That's unfair. The better places were booked solid, and I assume this room is the runt of this litter, if the clerk's hesitance was any indication."

Jordan was emptying the brown paper bag he had carried in, placing toothbrushes, toothpaste and a bottle of wine on the dresser. "Any glasses here?"

Katia found one in the minuscule bathroom and held it out triumphantly. Fortunately, Jordan had had the foresight to have the liquor store attendant open the wine; the room didn't come with a corkscrew. He repopped the cork and filled the glass. "To the Vineyard," he offered, downed a healthy swallow, then passed the glass to Katia, who did the same.

It was the first of many toasts they made, one increasingly more absurd than the next. By the time they had finished the wine they were sitting hip to hip on the floor with their backs braced against the bed. Two hours had passed. They had laughed, reminisced about things they had done as kids, teased each other about things they were doing as adults, and in general had the best time Katia had had in years.

But now Katia groaned. "I think I've about had it, Jordan. My eyes don't seem to want to stay open."

"No problem." He pushed himself somewhat laboriously from the floor until he was on his feet, but bent over with his hands flattened on the bed. He stared at it, then with an effort straightened. "You take the bed. I'll take a blanket on the floor."

"*You* take the bed. *I'll* take a blanket on the floor."

He shook his head slowly. "No, no, babe. Let me be chivalrous."

"You're sure?"

"I'm sure."

As though to emphasize his point—or win another—he extended a hand to her and tugged her up. She sat down with a plop on the bed, then moaned and twisted to one side. "Oh, for a bath," she whispered.

"Go ahead."

"I'd fall asleep in it. Have to wait till morning." Her sole thought was to stretch out on a set of cool sheets, put her head on a pillow and surrender the war with her eyelids. She actually did the latter first. With eyes closed and without thinking, she pulled free the knot of her shirt. She didn't bother with the buttons, but whipped the cotton fabric over her head.

"Katia?"

Her eyelids flickered, then raised. Jordan was staring at the skimpy excuse for a bra she wore. Within seconds he had turned and snatched up the t-shirt he had bought for himself. "Here. Wear this."

She reached for the shirt with a sleepy smile, but before she had a chance to take it he drew it back to his chest. In a single stride he was before her, then hunkering down. He met her gaze, then dropped his own to the tiny catch at the front of her bra. Shakily he released it, peeled the sheer fabric aside and slid the thin straps from her arms.

Even as fuzzy minded as she was, Katia could feel it happening. Her body was beginning to tingle, the sensation centering in her breasts as his eyes adored them.

"More beautiful than ever," came his hoarse whisper. Leaning forward, he touched his lips first to one nipple, then the other.

She closed her fingers on his shoulders and moaned. Her nipples were taut, damp where he had kissed them. She swayed, but Jordan steadied her. With jerky movements he shook out the new t-shirt and rushed to get it over her head. Since it was his size it easily fell to cover her.

Again, however, he had second thoughts. Tugging the t-shirt he had worn all day over his head and tossing it aside, he moved to sit beside her on the bed, slid an arm around her waist beneath the shirt, and pushed it up even as he turned her toward him.

The feel of her bare breasts against his chest was like lightning for them both. Katia sucked in a breath while Jordan made a sound deep in his throat and held her tighter. His eyes were closed; he wore a look of pain. Her own expression was much the same.

"Jordan, I don't think I can stand—"

The words caught in her throat as he roughly cupped her neck and pushed her face up with his fingertips. Then his mouth took hers in a kiss that was filled with fiery passion, and Katia couldn't think, much less speak. His lips angled hungrily over hers, never still, ever searching for more. He thrust his tongue into her mouth, deeply and greedily. There was something about his rush for possession that suggested he would get caught any moment and be strung up by the heels, but Katia only knew that she had ached and ached for the possession too long to either analyze his frenzy or deny him.

With that same odd kind of panic he pushed her back on the bed and moved over her, undulating his fully aroused body against hers as he continued to kiss her. She was dizzy with too much wine and too great a need when he suddenly stiffened, moaned and rolled away.

"I'm sorry, sweetheart! God, I'm sorry!" He threw an arm across his eyes, making no attempt this time to hide the huge bulge at his fly. He was breathing heavily, his muscled chest roughly rising and falling. "I shouldn't have done that. I'll hurt you. I'll hurt both of us."

Had Katia been sober and well-rested, she probably would have demanded an explanation. But she was neither. The best she could do was to grasp the pillow and bury her head, which was spinning madly. Jordan knew what he was doing, some vague fragment of reason assured her. If he had stopped he was probably right. He knew . . . he was probably right. . . .

The next thing she knew it was morning. She came awake slowly, aware of having had a dream . . . or a nightmare . . . unable to decide which. Jordan was sprawled on a blanket on the floor. He wore nothing but his jeans.

Her knight in denim armor.

Aware of a heaviness behind her eyes, then spotting the empty wine bottle and realizing its cause, she carefully worked her way out of bed and crept into the bathroom, where she took the bath she had been too tired to take the night before.

A long time later she returned to the room, where she dried and dressed and realized she felt much, much better. Jordan was still asleep. Love swelled inside her as she looked at him; the frustration she felt was far more emotional than physical.

With a whisper-soft sigh, she walked to the door, closed it quietly behind her and went downstairs in search of coffee.

Jordan was awake when she returned. He stood in the center

of the small room. With his hair mussed and the snap of his jeans undone he looked like he had just that minute awakened, except that his eyes held an expression akin to fear. She stopped on the threshold, confused.

"Jesus, Katia! I didn't know where in the hell you were!"

Relieved, she smiled, closed the door and handed him a mug filled with hot coffee.

"I woke up and you weren't here," Jordan raved on. "I didn't know *what* to think. I searched the room and couldn't find you—"

"It's a pretty small room. Not many places to hide."

"You can take that silly grin off your face. I was *worried*."

"Where could I have gone?" she asked innocently. "You're my ticket out of here."

"I didn't know *where* you'd gone!" He thrust a hand through his hair, then took a drink of the coffee and burned his tongue. "Unh. Shit. This isn't my day."

"You got up on the wrong side of the bed."

"I wasn't *on* the bed."

"Poor baby. Why don't you take a long bath? I did. It helped."

He gave her an annoyed glance before disappearing into the bathroom. But the remedy must have worked, for he was in a better mood by the time he returned from the bathroom. Better . . . but still not up to snuff.

Katia, who remembered—albeit in vague wisps that might well have been a dream but were just that little bit too real—what had happened before she had passed out the night before, wasn't sure what to make of him. During her own long soak she had decided to avoid mention of their brief interlude together on the bed. But the more she thought about it, the more she felt that she was the one who had a right to be angry. He had done it to her again, turned her on, then pulled away. The only thing she could do by way of retaliation was to act as though she simply didn't care.

They ate breakfast in the restaurant downstairs, which was a higher tribute to the inn than its woeful attic room. Katia hadn't expected conversation from Jordan; she knew he wasn't good for much in the morning until he had had two cups of coffee and something solid, but even then he seemed unusually preoccupied.

They left the inn and started to walk, aimlessly she thought, until he guided her onto a sidewalk bench. Then he said something that took her completely by surprise. "Have you heard from Robert Cavanaugh?"

"The detective?"

Jordan nodded.

"No, I haven't heard from him yet." Her eyes were riveted on his grim expression. "What's wrong?"

He stared out toward the harbor, hesitated, then spoke slowly. "There's something you don't know, Katia. Something I don't think anyone in the family knows other than me."

"About Mark and Deborah?"

"About Mark." The muscle beneath his eye twitched. "He was messing around with child pornography."

"Are you *serious?*"

"I wish I weren't, and I sure as hell wish I didn't have to tell you about it. But Cavanaugh has probably been to the coast by now, and if that's the case he knows."

"How can you be sure?"

"Because the police there know. Mark told me so."

"When was this?"

"Two months back. I was out there, so I dropped in to see him. He wasn't thrilled that I showed up when I did."

She shook her head, willing away the image. "Pornography. I don't believe it."

"*Kiddie* porn, and you can believe it. I saw it with my own eyes."

"But why? Why would he get into something as sick as that?"

Jordan's mouth twisted. "Why do you think?"

"He was that hard up for money? But I thought he was doing okay."

"Okay isn't good enough if you want to live in Beverly Hills. He put every cent he had into legitimate filmmaking, and then when he needed more to live on he resorted to . . . to *that*."

"But why children? Why not plain old skin flicks?"

"Because fewer people were willing to do it with kids, so the demand was greater."

Katia closed her eyes and took a shuddering breath. "It's sickening."

"Think of what I felt *seeing* it."

"You talked to him afterward?"

"Yeah, if you can call it that. It was more like a shouting match. I told him he was crazy, and he told me to mind my own business. So I told him that it *was* my business, because he was my brother—even if I wanted to deny it at the time."

"What did he say to that?"

"He said it was already too late, because the cops knew what he was doing. God, Katia, I could have strangled him then and there, and I told him as much, but he didn't care. He said that he had his life and I had mine, and that I should just keep my nose out of his affairs. I mean," Jordan looked at her in bewilderment, "it was like he didn't hear anything I'd said about hurting people, like he was oblivious to hurting even himself."

Katia caught her breath. "Do you think it could have been suicide after all?"

Jordan shook his head firmly. "No. He seemed immune to any and all worry. He was riding high on himself. He was convinced that the law would never turn on him because he was greasing palms right and left." He ran an agitated hand through his hair. "Somewhere along the line the guy became amoral."

Katia sat staring at Jordan for several long moments. Her heart ached for him because she knew he was suffering. His eyes were on the waterfront, but she could tell he saw nothing. His legs were extended limply, his shoulders slumped and his jaw was darkened by the beard he hadn't bothered to shave.

"No one else in your family knows?"

"No one but you."

"Why have you told me?"

"Because if I don't Cavanaugh will, and I want you to be pre-pared. Better you should hear it from me than from him. You may just be able to convince him not to tell my parents right away. I'm going to try to do that, but I don't know which one of us will get to him first."

"Won't your parents have to know eventually?"

"Not if Cavanaugh finds his killer. If the killer is somehow connected with the porno work, it'll all come out anyway. But if there's a totally different connection there's a chance my mother can be spared all that. God, she'll die if she learns what he was up to. She raised her children to respect certain things. You'd think that if he wasn't bothered by the principle of child pornography, at least he'd have been concerned about its illegality."

Katia didn't know what to say. She agreed with every one of Jordan's feelings, and she racked her brain in a futile search to find something to say by way of consolation. In the end she simply took Jordan's cold hand in hers and warmed it between her palms.

"I'm sorry, Jordan. Sorry that you have to bear the weight of this on your shoulders."

"My shoulders are broad enough. I just wonder if Cavanaugh's are. If he's as principled as he led me to believe he won't go pub-lic with what he learns unless he has a good reason to do so. On the other hand, if he gets his jollies out of making people squirm he's got the means. Boy has he got the means."

Cavanaugh was more principled than even he himself had thought. When he learned about Mark Whyte's involvement in child pornography he simply tucked the knowledge under his belt and went on with his investigation. Oh, he was excited; he had something concrete on the Whytes, at last, and the feeling of power that gave him was incredible. But he was also a cop, and a good one, and there was no way he was going to jeopardize his case by leaking something to the press that could later cause problems in a trial.

But where he thought John Ryan would be pleased with what he had done he returned to Boston to find the man disgruntled.

"So you know that Whyte was on the verge of indictment for child pornography. So what? And you know that he was living high off the hog out there. So what? And you know that he had a handful of pretty lousy associates. *So what?*"

"So there's plenty more to investigate *and* plenty of reason why someone may have wanted to kill him. We have a motive."

"What good is a motive without a suspect? And if the porno thing was what got the guy killed, how do you explain why someone killed his wife, too? She wasn't involved in the filming. She was out of it. And if all that took place on the west coast, why the hell would someone fly east to do the dirty work?"

Cavanaugh could feel himself getting angry. He had asked himself the same questions many times; Ryan had to know that. He wasn't sure why Ryan was so upset, but he sensed that it would be better to bide his time than confront the man.

"We interviewed over sixty people while we were out there," he said calmly. "A dozen of them might have had cause to kill Mark. We're looking into them further."

Ryan's pudgy hand hit the desk in annoyance. "Hasn't it occurred to you that one of the Whytes or Warrens knew that there would be an indictment and decided to eliminate the source of the problem? No criminal, no indictment, no trial, no scandal. It's as simple as that."

"Oh, it's occurred to me. But there are ways to do an investigation and there are ways to do an investigation. Personally, I'd like to rule out the possibility of an outside murder before I go pointing a finger at someone within the family."

"What are you? Some kind of bleeding heart? You don't have to protect them, for Christ's sake!"

The more Ryan attacked, the firmer Cavanaugh stood. "I want this done right. I thought you did, too."

"Of course I do."

"Then trust me. There's as much of a chance that one of his associates from the coast killed Mark and his wife as there is that one of the family members did it, and for exactly the same reason. No criminal, no indictment, no trial. It's as simple as that."

"Don't throw my own words back at me, Cavanaugh," Ryan warned, but the worst of his fury seemed to have been spent. "I don't like it."

"I'm just pointing out that you're right." The last thing Cavanaugh needed was Ryan's thirst for blood to mess up the case. "I'll be starting on the families soon enough, but I want to do more work on the coast before that. I left Annello and Webber out there to see what else they could dig up; they'll be calling in every day. If necessary, I'll go back myself."

"Have you looked at the tapes?"

"The porno films? A couple. Buddy and Sharon will be going through the rest. Those films are pretty pathetic."

"What about other tapes?"

"What about them?"

Ryan blew out an exasperated breath. Cavanaugh wondered if the man ate sour pickles for breakfast, too. "Whyte was a film-maker. Don't you think it would be a good idea to take a look at what he's done? There must have been a cabinet in the house filled with his work. All those guys keep private collections."

"He had one, but I didn't exactly have time to sit around and watch movies. The reels in the cabinet had standard labels on them. I doubt we'll find clues to a murder in edited and polished pieces."

Ryan's jaw was set. "All right, Cavanaugh. I put you in charge of this one, so it's your baby. But if I were you I wouldn't settle for standard labels. Anyone as rotten as Mark Whyte—anyone who could hire kids to do obscene things and then film them—is apt to be kinky in other ways. Think about it."

Cavanaugh did, long and hard, and he came up with several new avenues to explore. But what nagged at him more than anything after that conversation was Ryan's impatience with the way he was handling the case. He didn't understand it.

Unable to leave his worries at the office, he broached them with Jodi over dinner. Strangely, he was in the mood to talk, and there was no one he felt was more insightful than she. Moreover, he reasoned, it wouldn't hurt if he tried to mend a few fences. Jodi had welcomed him back from California with a smile, but it had been a cautious one. He knew that she liked it when he shared things with her. And he knew that *he* didn't like this faint wall between them.

"I don't know why Ryan's displeased," he concluded after he had filled her in on the rough details. "I'm going by the book on this one. I'd think he'd be grateful."

"He's looking at the case from the outside. Maybe he doesn't understand or appreciate all the work you've been doing on the inside."

"He should. He was in my shoes once, and it wasn't so long ago that he could have forgotten. Then again, he's always been a little strange."

"Strange?"

"Private. He never opened up to anyone on the force, not about his inner thoughts or about his family. He never mixed socially, kept his home life totally separate. Rigidity in a nutshell. Only it's gotten worse in the last few months. He hasn't been the same since his daughter died."

"They were very close?"

"I don't know. Large family, devout Catholics, I suppose they were close, even though she didn't live around here. I can grant him the right to mourn, but to take it out on everyone else?"

"Maybe he's getting pressure from upstairs on this one."

"Still, he's never been as uptight before."

"He's never had as potentially explosive a case before."

Cavanaugh's eyes grew wide in emphasis. "You can say that again. I'm telling you, if it does turn out that Mark and Deborah were eliminated by someone inside the families to keep the kiddie porn stuff from coming to light, explosive will be a mild word to describe the results."

"Do you think that was what happened? It is rather . . . incredible."

"As in farfetched?" He tried not to be offended, but couldn't help sounding a little defensive. "A jury would go for the motive, especially with families like those. They think they're outside the law. It wouldn't be so incredible to imagine that they assumed they'd get away with murder."

"But to kill two of their own? What kind of people could do that?"

"People to whom power and status mean the world," he said with a smug half smile.

It was that tiny smile that got to Jodi, who, given the circumstances surrounding Cavanaugh's departure a week before, was less indulgent than usual. "They're human, Bob. I saw those pictures you took at the funeral." She held up a hand and raced on. "No, you didn't show them to me, but you left them lying on the table and I looked. That was grief. Couldn't you see it?"

"I'm sure it was grief. The whole situation has to be grievous for them. Can you imagine how your mother would feel if you set out to be a porno queen? That must be how the Whytes felt about Mark."

"Okay. But even if Mark had gone to trial, even if he'd been convicted, the Whyte Estate wouldn't have been ruined. It's huge and powerful. Unless the company was somehow involved in Mark's activities it wouldn't have been threatened. And as far as Gil Warren is concerned, he's been in the House . . . how many years?"

"Twenty-three. Nearly twenty-four."

"Well, the same thing would be true for him. He wouldn't have been hurt by Mark's misadventures unless they'd have incriminated him."

Cavanaugh sighed. "Jodi, we're not dealing with the average

human mind here. Who are you and I to guess why they did what they did?"

"So you've already got them pegged? Cop, judge and jury rolled into one?"

"Goddamnit, that's unfair! I thought we were talking hypothetically."

"Could have fooled me, what with the words you used."

"Just words. I'm trying my best to give them a chance."

"Are you? You know, Bob, I think your problem is that you simply can't conceive of family loyalty. You can't conceive of the idea that people can love one another and still have differences. You can't conceive of the idea that members of a family could stand behind one another even in the worst of times. And there's good reason why you're so blind," she raced on. "Your mother left your father when his business went bust. You and your wife split when things got shaky. You don't have any experience in fighting for those you love, so you can't conceive of anyone else doing it!" She was breathing hard and her fists were clenched. "It's called commitment, Bob, and there are many people who believe in it. So until you know otherwise, wouldn't it be nice to give the Warrens and Whytes the benefit of the doubt?"

Without awaiting his answer, she turned and stalked from the room, which was just as well, because Cavanaugh was, at that moment, speechless.

By the time he had flown to New York two days later and taken a taxi to Katia's office, however, Cavanaugh was fully in command. He had suspected that Jordan would have warned her that he would be coming, so he wasn't surprised when she appeared in the reception area fully composed.

With a pleasant smile she extended her hand. "Detective Cavanaugh, I'm Katia Morell. I was wondering when you'd make it here."

He returned the handshake, noting that she was even more striking close up than she had appeared through the lens of his camera on the day of the funeral, now over a month ago. "I was wondering if we could talk. I know you're working, but if you could spare a few minutes, I'd appreciate it."

"There's a coffee shop downstairs. Let me just leave word that I'll be gone." She went over to the receptionist and spoke with her quietly for a minute, then returned and led the way to the elevator.

Cavanaugh admired her poise, just as he admired the fact that as soon as they were beyond hearing of the receptionist, she calmly asked to see his identification.

"You can never be sure," she said by way of apology as she handed it back to him. Even with Jordan's forewarning, Cavanaugh wasn't what she had expected. He was young, fashionably dressed, and very good looking. Of course, Jordan wouldn't have mentioned that, the rat.

They didn't talk during the elevator's descent. Katia, who was doing her best to hide the vague nervousness she felt, was determined to let Cavanaugh take the lead. Cavanaugh, meanwhile, was feeling slightly awed by Katia's utterly natural elegance.

They took seats at a table near the rear of the coffee shop, and within minutes the waitress had delivered matching orders of coffee and danish. Katia raised the cup and slowly sipped her coffee, studying Cavanaugh all the while. When at last he spoke, it was with disarming gentleness.

"I understand you grew up with the Warrens and the Whytes."

"That's right. My mother has been with the Warrens since before I was born."

"Were you close to Deborah and Mark?"

"We were all close."

"Would you say that you were closer to Deborah than Mark?"

"In that we're the same sex, I suppose so. Deborah was six years older than me, Mark thirteen."

"But you felt you knew him, too?"

"We all played together as kids. Even the older ones, when

they went off to college, came home often. I guess I knew Mark as well as most of the others, though he was very different."

"Different in what ways?"

"More of a loner. Oh, he took part in everything we did, but he was still somehow . . . apart. His mind seemed to be else-where."

"Did the others resent that?"

"No. Mark was Mark."

"Were there any hard feelings as you all got older?"

"We're all different in our own ways. We accept that."

"I understand that Mark and Deborah were sweethearts from way back."

"Uh-huh."

"How did their families feel when they decided to marry?"

"They were pleased. Mark and Deborah were very much in love, and the thought of marriage between the families was wel-comed."

"Was their marriage a good one?"

"Yes. They were alike in many ways." When he raised his brows, inviting her to explain, she did so. "Neither of them was conventional, which isn't to say that they were rebellious or loud, just that they seemed to operate on a different wavelength. They were both artsy, if you know what I mean. They dressed differ-ently, not quite bohemian, but leaning in that direction. It didn't come as a surprise to us when Mark went into filmmaking."

"What about Deborah? Did she ever want a career?"

"Mark was her career. She was happy to go along with what he did."

"Then she had no objections to his lifestyle?"

Up to that point, Cavanaugh's questions had been harmless. This latest, though—or perhaps it was the faintly critical tone in which it had been offered—was the first reference to something negative. Katia tempered the instinctive defensiveness she felt.

"Deborah loved Mark. She had faith in him."

Cavanaugh cleared his throat. He had expected that Katia

would feel a certain amount of loyalty. He wondered how strong it was. "Did you know anything about their lifestyle?"

"You mean in California?"

He nodded.

"I know that it was fast, and that the people they were involved with were even faster."

"Did you ever meet any of those people?"

"No."

"They never brought their friends home with them?"

"To Dover? No."

"Why not?"

"I'm not sure."

"Was it possible that they were afraid of the reaction from their families?"

She shifted in her seat. "It was possible, I suppose. I think it's more likely that there was simply no call for them to bring their California friends east with them. Family gatherings are family gatherings. You must know what they're like, Detective."

"Actually, no," he returned bluntly. "My parents divorced when I was a teenager, and I was an only child."

"I'm sorry."

"No need. I've done fine."

"You just don't know what you've missed," she argued gently, forgetting for the moment who Cavanaugh was and why he had sought her out. "Family gatherings with the Whytes and Warrens are warm, wonderful times. There's lots of talk, lots of laughter, lots of solid camaraderie—even now, when we all lead separate lives."

"You make everything sound very rosy, as though life with the Whytes and Warrens was a never-empty bowl of cherries."

Katia didn't quite understand the whisper of bitterness in his words. "No. Not a bowl of cherries. Not always. There were tense times, such as when Gil was up for reelection—"

"I thought he always knew he'd win," Cavanaugh said with a teasing smile.

Katia couldn't help but smile back. "*Gil* may have known that, but, let me tell you, the rest of us did our share of nail-biting. You'd never guess it, because we all knew that we had to project an image of confidence to the public. I've often wondered if that isn't what the public looks for most—confidence, an air of competence, whether the competence is there or not."

"Do you think Gil has it?"

"Competence? Look at his record."

"Does the rest of the family agree with you?"

"Yes."

"What about Peter Warren?"

"Peter?"

"I understand he's been at odds with his father more than once."

"They're both strong willed. It would be only natural for them to lock horns from time to time."

"I understood it to be more than that. Word has it that Peter's been wooing his father's supporters out from under his nose."

"Why would he do that?"

"He wants to be a judge."

"If that is so—and I'm not in a position to confirm or deny it—there would be no conflict in terms of backers. The same people who've supported Gil could as easily put forward Peter's bid, but even then there's only so much they can do. Spots on the Massachusetts bench are by appointment."

"Political appointment."

"But appointment nonetheless. In the end it's the governor's decision." She shook her head. "Please believe me, Detective. There is no death wish between father and son."

"What about between father and daughter?"

Katia's heart skipped a beat, then began to hammer loudly enough to more than make up for the loss. "Excuse me?"

"Between Gil and Deborah. Was there ever any hard feeling?"

"I'm not sure I see the relevance of that to your investigation."

Realizing both that Katia was very sharp and that he had come on too fast, Cavanaugh held up a hand. "I'm simply trying to understand Mark and Deborah and their families. That's why I've come to you. Other than Jordan, I haven't spoken with the rest yet, because I felt that, with the little bit of distance you have, you'd be able to help me see things more accurately. I've read the papers like everyone else over the years, and if I were to believe what I've read, I'd say that the families were either all good or rotten to the core. There has to be some middle ground. I was hoping you'd help me find it."

Katia's smile was a wry one. "Jordan was right. You are articulate."

"I'm also sincere," he said, and, surprisingly, he meant it. "My job is to ferret out the truth, and that isn't easy when you're trying to read between biased lines. I really do need your help, Ms. Morell."

Katia wasn't sure what it was about the man that appealed to her. She reminded herself that he was a cop, and tried to tell herself that she should keep a stiff upper lip and a certain distance. But Cavanaugh didn't look like a cop, and he didn't act like a cop. He seemed human and deeply concerned with learning the truth.

She inhaled deeply, then exhaled into a smile. "I may be the biggest sap in the world, but for some strange reason I trust you." She arched a brow. "I'm telling you that because if it turns out that I'm wrong, *you* will have the burden of a guilty conscience on your own shoulders. Got that?"

Cavanaugh grinned. He liked Katia immensely. "Got it."

She picked up a knife and cut her uneaten danish in half, then fourths. Lifting one small piece, she took a bite. When she had swallowed and still Cavanaugh hadn't spoken, she set down the remainder of the piece. "Well? Should I pick up where we left off or would you like to start afresh?"

"I'd like to start afresh," he said without hesitation, then extended his hand much as she had done back in the reception area of her office. "The name's Bob. Can I call you Katia?"

Katia started to smile, but checked it halfway. Quickly wiping her hand on a paper napkin, she met his clasp. "Katia is fine."

"Good." He released her hand and propped his elbows on the edge of the table. For several moments he simply smiled, then he dropped his gaze to the danish she had cut. "Are you always so neat?"

"I always watch my weight. Good things last longer if you cut them up and eat them slowly."

"You don't need to watch your weight."

She shrugged, but a smile was tugging at the corners of her mouth. "A woman can never be too thin or too rich."

"Oh, Lord, where have I heard *that* before!"

"I don't know. Where?"

"A friend of mine says it all the time, and in that same smug tone you just used. She's as thin as you are." He sat back in his chair, feeling unusually relaxed. "Actually, you'd like her. She's a guidance counselor in the Boston school system."

"I take it she's not your wife."

"I'm not married. I was once, but my job got in the way."

"I hear it's tough being married to a policeman."

"You've been watching 'Miami Vice,'" he accused, then took delight when she blushed.

"Once in awhile. But I heard it firsthand from a fellow Jack knew. This fellow loved having a wife, but his wife didn't love having a policeman. In the end she couldn't take the strain." Katia paused. "You must love your work."

"I do."

"Do you have any children?"

He shook his head.

"I suppose it's better that way. It's tough on kids when their parents aren't together."

"God, you do sound like Jodi."

His statement pleased her, as did the look of admiration in his eyes. She didn't know why it should be so when Cavanaugh was a cop, here on official business investigating a murder that had hit her own home.

The reminder was sobering. She glanced at her watch. "I really have to get back to the office, but I'm sure there's more you want to know."

"Can we meet later?"

"Sure. How long will you be in the city?"

"I'd planned to fly back tonight, but it's kind of nice being here. I haven't been down in a long time. If I take a shuttle out in the morning, I could go to a show tonight. Any suggestions?"

"Sure. There's *Biloxi Blues*, or Pinter's *The Caretaker*, or you could always see *Cats*. Any of the three are great."

"Anything you haven't seen that I could take you to? I mean, hell, if I'm putting you through all this unpleasantness I'll have to make it up to you somehow."

Forget the fact that he was a cop. Forget the fact that she had been out on three of the four nights since she had returned from the Vineyard, all on the rebound from Jordan's latest rejection of her. Robert Cavanaugh was pleasant and attractive. Why not? "I've been dying to see *A Lie of the Mind*," she said through the side of her mouth. "If you can get tickets, you're on."

Cavanaugh got the tickets, though it took five phone calls and a forty-minute wait at the box office that afternoon. When he called Katia, they arranged to meet for something to eat before-hand. It was at a restaurant on Broadway, over shrimp and steak, that they returned to the matter that had brought Cavanaugh to the city to begin with.

"Tell me about your relationship with the Warrens and Whytes," he asked gently. "I know that you grew up with them and that you're fond of them."

"I love them. They're my family."

"What about your father? I haven't heard anything about him."

"He died when I was nine."

"I'm sorry."

"No, that's all right. We weren't ever close."

"Still, it must have been hard."

"What was hard was when my brother died. I was eleven then, barely old enough to understand war, much less the casualties of one."

"Vietnam?"

She shook her head. "Israel. When my father died and my mother had to make funeral arrangements, we learned for the first time that she was Jewish. She doesn't practice it or identify with it. But Kenny was at an introspective age; once he learned about it it haunted him. When the Arab-Israeli War broke out in '67 he rushed over."

"How did your mother feel about that?"

"Grief stricken. She'd lost her family to Hitler."

Cavanaugh winced. "When you were old enough to understand, how did you feel?"

"You know," she said thoughtfully, "I was really pretty proud of Kenny. He felt something and he acted on it. And I think I understood my mother much better once I'd learned about her past. She was trying to protect us, because there's a little bit of that Hitler's-followers-are-alive-and-well mentality in her, so I can understand why she did what she did. I'm not saying I would have done the same and totally denied my roots if I'd been in her shoes, but then, I've had a totally different life experience from hers. So had Kenny, which may be why he did what *he* did."

Cavanaugh was shaking his head. "I had no idea. Things like this never make it into Whyte or Warren stories."

For an instant Katia wondered if she had misjudged him after all. "I don't want them to! What I've told you is off the record—"

"I know," he said quietly, giving her hand a quick squeeze. "What you've told me goes no further than this table." He withdrew his hand and picked up his fork. "If you lost your father and brother, I can understand why you grew so close to the others."

Reassured that confidentiality would be observed, Katia relaxed again. She liked Cavanaugh. She wanted to talk, wanted him to understand. "Actually, the closeness was there all along. From the first Kenny and I were treated like members of the family. That's one of the things that was so wonderful about the Whytes and Warrens. They always accepted us, and without condescension. Growing up, Kenny and I had many of the same benefits they did. I'll always be grateful to them for that."

"You were fortunate. I can see why you feel so positive about them."

"Please don't misunderstand me," she cautioned. "It's not all gratitude. I love them as family, but also legitimately *like* them. They're individuals, each one of them interesting people. They have faults; we all do. But I have a tremendous respect for their strengths."

Cavanaugh looked down at his food then and took several bites before raising eyes that were more sober. "Mark Whyte was in trouble in California."

Her fork wavered before her mouth; she finally set it down. "I know."

"Do you know what sort of trouble?"

"Yes . . . if you're thinking the same thing I am." She wasn't about to say it first.

"Child pornography?"

She expelled a breath and nodded.

"How did that go across on the home front?"

"It didn't. I mean, they don't know."

That took Cavanaugh by surprise. He wasn't sure he believed it. "How come you do?"

Katia was in a momentary bind. She wanted to keep Jordan's confidence, yet there was no way she could do that without lying. So, albeit with some trepidation, she went with the truth. "Jordan told me."

Cavanaugh's features were controlled, only his eyes darkened. "I didn't know he knew. He didn't mention anything about it when we talked."

"I'm sure he was hoping that you'd find the murderer without having to go into that . . . mess. He's worried about his parents, especially his mother, and what it will do to them if, or when, they find out."

"When did he tell you?"

"Last weekend."

"Did he tell you that Mark was about to be indicted?"

Katia sucked in a breath. "Was he?"

"Yes. Did Jordan know?"

"He said that the L.A. police knew what Mark was doing; Mark had told him that. Mark had also said that he wouldn't be prosecuted."

"But did Jordan know about the indictments?"

"No. At least not that I know of." She read Cavanaugh's face with ease. "If you're thinking that he had an ulterior motive for withholding information from you—or me—you're wrong, Bob. Jordan was sick about the whole thing. I think one of the reasons he told me was that he simply had to share it with someone. Jordan has never had cause to lie to me. He would have told me if he knew that Mark was about to be indicted."

Cavanaugh wasn't fully convinced of that, but he didn't want to risk Katia's confidence. Still, there was something he needed to know. "Are you in love with Jordan?"

Her hand twitched involuntarily. "Where did *that* come from?"

"From the look in your eyes from time to time."

Regardless of the trust she had placed in Cavanaugh, Katia was not about to grant him total disclosure. "Jordan is family. He's like a brother to me."

"He's not a brother. You're not related by blood."

"You know what I mean," was the best she could do.

Mercifully, Cavanaugh seemed to accept it. He pressed his lips together and nodded.

But there was something she had promised Jordan, a plea she had to make. "Bob? Please don't say anything about the pornography unless you absolutely have to. It's going to kill Jack and

Natalie, not to mention Gil and Lenore. They tried, really they did. Jack and Gil may have been absentee fathers for much of the time, but they always wanted the best for their children. And if Natalie finds out what Mark was doing she'll blame herself. She'll agonize over what she did wrong. She doesn't deserve that—none of them do. People may think of them as being wealthy and powerful, but they are human beings. Deep down inside they're not any different from other parents who love their children. They hurt at times. Believe me. They hurt."

Chapter 11

By THE FALL OF 1952 the Whytes and Warrens had become comfortable residents of Dover. Six of their children attended the local schools, and Natalie and Lenore—not to mention the Morells and McNees—had become familiar faces in and around the community. If Jack and Gil's faces weren't as familiar, simply because they were on the go much of the time, their reputations took up the slack. Jack became known as one of the town's most promising rising entrepreneurs, while Gil, whose legal and political expertise preceded him, was a shoo-in for the local seat in the State Legislature being vacated by the longtime, retiring representative.

Natalie kept herself busy with the children, as much to compensate for Jack's absences—he'd been off and running since spring, when the novelty of the house had worn off—as to satisfy herself that her children would know their mother as she had never known her own. She was intimately involved in every one of their activities, a double challenge after December of that year, when she gave birth to a daughter, Anne. Though she hired a nurse to take care of the baby, more often than not as the spring of 1953 unfolded Anne was on Natalie's own hip while she cheered at Nick's Little League games, attended Mark's school plays, and struggled with Jordan's labored attempts to learn to read.

Moreover, she was nearly as involved with the Warren children as she was with her own, since so many of the youngsters' activities overlapped. Lenore was usually present—her heart was in the right place—but when Peter urged his horse into a gallop, promptly tumbled off and broke his arm, she went to pieces, leaving Natalie and Cassie to comfort the boy and see that he had the medical attention he needed. And when Laura developed a sudden and severe stutter, it was Natalie who had the presence of mind to seek out a speech therapist. And when Ben's teacher called to say that he was terrorizing the girls in the class, it was Natalie who sat him down for a long talk.

Lenore was in a perpetual state of nervousness. She worried about anything and everything, from Gil's political stability to Deborah's propensity for the croup to Ben's refusal to drink milk. Where Natalie was happy enough to enjoy all she had at a particular moment, Lenore was obsessed with what she might not have in the future. She envisioned Gil being unseated in the next election or having a sudden downturn in his law practice. She lived in dire fear of a fire or hurricane that might destroy the Dover house and leave them with a major loss.

She worked herself into such a state that migraine headaches became a common occurrence, sending her to bed with the shades drawn, a warm cloth over the bridge of her nose and strict orders that she wasn't to be disturbed. The children weathered her absences well. They had long since learned that either Cassie or Natalie could better handle any problems that arose, and since there was genuine love coming from both of those sources they simply appreciated Lenore when she was with them, and accepted her absences when she was not.

In the fall of 1953 Jack Whyte merged his varied interests into one large corporation, the Whyte Estate. The airline was doing well, swallowing any number of smaller ones in the process. Jack had half a dozen hotels to his name and they too thrived. The electronics plant in Waltham had expanded and was operating under full capacity even after the armistice was signed ending the Korean War.

Cassie Morell learned all this not from Natalie or Lenore but from Gil Warren himself. She made it a point to linger later at the main house on evenings when Gil was there, and though such evenings were infrequent, they were special to her. A pattern emerged. She would put the children to bed, rush to the cottage to kiss Kenny good night, then return to see if she could get something to eat or drink for Gil. He would gesture her into his den and they would talk.

He had all the patience in the world for Cassie, engaging her in conversation on topics ranging from the children's progress in school to his own progress on a legal case to Eisenhower's progress in the White House. He seemed to enjoy himself, opening up to her freely, knowing he could count on intelligent responses, intuitively trusting that what they discussed would go no farther than that room.

At times she felt more like his wife than his housekeeper, and her sentiments on that score were mixed. On the one hand, she felt guilty; she liked Lenore and understood that the woman was of a fragile disposition. On the other hand she felt defiant; Lenore chose to closet herself in her room, away from her husband, who apparently appreciated the company, and if he sought Cassie out for that company—she never thought of it as the other way around—it was his right.

The simple pleasure of Gil's nearness was enough to keep Cassie coming back for more. Not only did he stimulate her mind in a way Henry did not, but he made her feel like a woman as no other man had ever done. It was in his eyes, warm, dark and penetrating, lingering on her face, her hands, her breasts. Though he never made a move to touch her in a way that could be considered improper, she would leave his den feeling as though she had been caressed from head to toe, and the feeling would warm her for days.

Henry, conversely, was leaving her cold. Oh, he was still the same harmless man she had married, but they seemed to have increasingly different tastes. While Henry wanted to spend his days off at the dog track, Cassie preferred to go to a movie, or shopping, or to the Museum of Fine Arts. While excitement for Henry was an evening of watching baseball on a barroom TV with his old

Brookline buddies, Cassie found a good book far more exhilarating. While Henry wanted Kenny to know, even at the tender age of three, that he was *not* a Warren, Cassie was intent on believing that, for all practical purposes, he was.

In time Henry and Cassie simply began to go their own ways. Cassie would have been perfectly happy with the arrangement had it not been for the fact that she sensed an undercurrent of frustration in her husband. Mindful of the vow she had made to herself when she had married him, she dutifully suggested, at least once or twice a month, that they do something together. Though it was a stopgap measure, it seemed to mollify him.

Indeed, she wasn't the only one with mollification in mind. Jack and Gil were ever in the market for appeasements for their wives. In early 1954 they found an ideal one.

While the eyes of the nation were focused on the Supreme Court as it debated the issue of racial segregation in the schools, the two men's focus was on an island off the coast of Maine. They liked the idea of an exclusive retreat for their families. They liked the sound of a private resort to call their own. They liked the location; it was an easy trip and, most importantly, one that would enable them to tuck away their families for summers and vacations while they were free to shuttle back and forth at will.

So they bought the land, did what repair work was necessary to make the old Victorian house there livable, and proudly introduced their families to the site.

Natalie and Lenore, who had secretly had their eye on a summer home in Bar Harbor, quickly decided that having their own island was that much more prestigious. They liked the idea that there was only one house—it rather reminded them of a castle surrounded by a gigantic moat to ward off the riffraff—and since they spent so much time together and their families merged so well the idea of sharing the house appealed to them.

The children were totally innocent of thoughts of prestige or status or appeasement. They simply saw trail after trail to race along, hiding place after hiding place to scrunch up in, endless supplies of sand for castles and mud pies and stuffing down one another's bathing suits. They were in heaven.

If the reactions had been tallied, they would have amounted to a landslide victory for Jack and Gil, which was a good thing, because landslides were hard to come by. Gil had decided to take a step up and run for State Senator, and he faced formidable opposition in the incumbent. Lenore, predictably, was in a state of panic, for which Gil, predictably, had little patience.

"But you're doing just fine in the House!"

"By the time my present term ends I'll have been there for six years. All along I've said it was a beginning; it's time I moved on."

"Maybe in a few more years—"

"*Now*, Leonore. I'm already forty-two. In a few more years I'll be nothing but older. I've gone as far as I can in the House. The Senate is the logical next step."

"Where will you be if you lose?"

"I won't lose."

"But Dover already has a strong senator. Will Crocker is well liked. He isn't about to retire, and he certainly won't graciously bow out of the race. How will you handle him?"

"I'll campaign long and hard."

Not only did Gil campaign long and hard, but his efforts were aided by an eleventh-hour newspaper report that Will Crocker had accepted significant funds from a group of builders who were lobbying in the Legislature for special privileges. Lacking adequate time to defend himself against the bribery smear, Crocker lost the election.

Gil took his seat, but Lenore suffered more deeply from this victory than she had those in the past. She believed that Crocker's timely misfortune was one coincidence too many, and though the source of the fateful revelation was a mystery, she had her suspicions. She remembered her father, knew how quickly and unnecessarily lives could be ruined, feared that Gil, for all his back room maneuvering, would one day be on the losing end of the stick.

And she felt helpless to prevent it. Gil wouldn't listen to her fears. She discussed them with Natalie, who skirted around them in conversations with Jack, but Jack was as wrapped up in ambition as Gil was, and as confident of his success.

The sense of powerlessness that plagued Lenore, the sense of being at the whim of a fate she couldn't see or touch or control, took a tragic twist with the arrival of 1955. Ben took sick. It began with a sore throat and quickly developed into a high fever. The family doctor prescribed aspirin and bed rest, but when the symptoms escalated into muscle pains and spasms, then stiffness, Ben was immediately hospitalized.

Lenore was distraught. Gil spent every free minute he had with his son in the hospital. The other children were frightened. A worried Natalie kept her brood away from the Warren house, though she knew that they had probably already been exposed. Cassie had nightmares of Kenny falling sick. And the newspapers didn't help. They were filled with stories of the epidemic, portraying polio accurately, if dramatically, as the heartrending scourge it was.

Ben had the best of medical care, but even the best couldn't prevent the onset of paralysis, or his death after a valiant ten-day fight.

The funeral was small and private. For once Gil had no thought of public appearances, the only images in his mind being those of his ten-year-old son's body encased in an iron lung, then, and even more devastatingly, in a child-sized coffin. Lenore was no help to him in his sorrow; she was in a world of mourning all her own, one that she allowed no one to enter and share.

For days their grief was compounded by the fear that one or more of the other children would take sick. Even when the incubation period passed and that initial fear subsided, there was the chance that they would pick up the disease from another source, so a more general worry remained.

Brisk winds and occasional driving rains notwithstanding, the island was a particular godsend in the early spring of 1955. Lenore and Natalie rushed the children there the day school vacation began, and there they stayed for a full month. It was the first time since Ben's death that any of them found a measure of peace. While Lenore continued to grieve for Ben, suffering long bouts of depression, she found some solace in the knowledge that the other children were protected while they remained on the island, isolated from the world. Natalie, too, felt safer there, and that sense of security spread to the children, the oldest of whom had been deeply disturbed by Ben's death. Natalie spent long hours with them—with Nick and Laura, who were thirteen, Mark, who was twelve, Peter, who was nearly ten, and Jordan, who was eight—individually and together, trying to explain that Ben was at peace, that life held some tragedies that couldn't be explained, that polio had nothing to do with genetics and that they could not live in fear of its imminent onset.

They seemed to respond to her counseling, or perhaps it was simply time and distance that set them at ease. Whatever the case, they gradually relaxed and returned to a semblance of their spunky selves.

The fact that Jack and Gil joined their families for only a day here or there bothered Natalie and Lenore less than usual. Anyone who had had contact with the outside world was a vague threat. Even Cassie and Sarah, who periodically took turns returning to Dover to see to the men's needs there, were welcomed back to the island with a certain amount of trepidation.

It was during one such trip to Dover that Cassie learned the depth of Gil Warren's grief. She had assumed that he had recovered from his son's death since he was back to work with a passion, and, as was her way, she went to his den to check on him before she turned in for the night.

She had expected that he would be poring through papers, but he wasn't in the den. Driven on by a sixth sense, she quietly made her way to the second floor of the house. The light that beckoned came not from the master bedroom, but from Peter's room, the one he and Ben had shared.

Gil was seated on the bed that had been Ben's. His head was bowed; his arms hung limply by his sides. The toys that had been

Ben's—the trains and soldiers and stuffed dogs—had been long since removed, leaving a starkness that suddenly hit Cassie as it hadn't during the many times she had been in the room since the child's death.

She thought of leaving Gil to his private mourning, but her heart grieved for him too greatly. She knocked lightly on the door-jamb. When he looked up, seeming dazed and distant, she spoke in a near whisper.

"Is there anything you'd like?"

He simply stared at her for a minute, then shook his head.

"Can I help?"

Still he stared, then shook his head again.

She desperately wanted to do something, because his devastation tore into her, but she had to respect his wish to be alone. "I'll be at the cottage then," she said very quietly. Turning, she went back downstairs, then out the back door and across the short distance to her own home.

Without turning on a light she undressed and slipped on her nightgown, then crawled into the bed she had always shared with Henry, who was back at the island. She didn't mind sleeping alone; it was a relief after nights of lying by the edge of the bed to allow leeway for his sprawling form. She had learned to settle for her fantasies to keep her warm, since, for whatever reasons, Henry's body had never quite done the trick.

She was wide awake with her thoughts when a soft knock came at the door. Whether alerted by that same sixth sense that had led her earlier to Ben's room she wasn't sure, but she knew that Gil had come. Without so much as a glance out the window she opened the door and stepped aside to let him in.

He had tossed on a jacket but it was unzipped. His hands were tucked in its pockets and the shirt beneath it lay carelessly open to a point midway down his chest.

Closing the door, Cassie came to stand beside him, where she waited quietly for him to speak or move or do something. He stared at the floor for a long time. His dark hair was mussed, the shadow on his jaw pronounced. He looked exhausted, but it was more than a natural late evening fatigue. She wondered when the last time was that he had had a good night's sleep, wondered exactly how many of his feelings he had hidden over the past weeks.

Gil was an icon of strength; the world, indeed, his own family, saw him as a tower of steel. What Cassie saw now was something different, something every bit as admirable and distinctly human. In a strange way she felt blessed.

Slowly, and with a hesitance she had never seen in him, he raised his eyes to hers. His voice was hoarse, an aching croak.

"I need someone, Cassie. I feel so cold . . . and alone."

It was all she had to hear. She didn't care that someone could have been anyone; the fact was that he had come to her. Given the love she had felt for him for years, she knew what she wanted to do.

Carefully, as though he were wounded on the outside as well as the inside, she eased his jacket from his broad shoulders. "Come," she said then and led him down the short hall to the bedroom. When he was sitting on the edge of the bed she gently unbuttoned his shirt and drew it off. Then she eased him back to the pillow and just as gently removed his shoes, socks and trousers. When he lay in nothing but his underwear she drew the blankets up, slid onto the bed beside him and took him in her arms.

With his head cradled against her breasts, she whispered, "I'll warm you. I'll do whatever you need. It hurts me so to see you this way."

The only sound he made was a choked one as he wrapped his arms around her waist and pulled her closer. And she simply held him, giving him time, willing every bit of the love she felt into him to stave off his loneliness and sorrow.

It was awhile before he stirred. She was stroking his back when she felt the first tentative movement of his mouth near her breast, and almost simultaneously with the loosening of her arms, he did the same to give his lips greater freedom.

Cassie had never felt what she did then, the wild, burning

surge of passion through her limbs. She tried to temper it, but it was hard, because he was using his lips and tongue, stroking her nipple through the cotton of her gown, and she couldn't do anything about the soft moan that slipped from her throat.

She could do something when his hands went to the hem of her gown, though, and she did. Raising her hips, she helped him ease the soft fabric up and over her head. It was the very first time she had ever been naked before a man—Henry took sex as a prim affair—but she was proud of her body, proud that a man like Gil found her attractive. And he did. She could feel it in the way his arms quivered, in the way his stomach tightened, in the way he moved over her and pressed his hips into hers.

She had had enough of primness to know that she wanted to touch Gil all over, and, again, he seemed to welcome it, for he helped her remove first his undershirt, then his shorts. She touched him slowly, savoring the play of hard muscle beneath hair spattered skin, and she felt every one of her senses sharpen to near painful acuity when he touched her likewise.

She let him set the pace, but her thighs were open and waiting when at last he lowered himself and entered her. Whimpering softly at the sheer beauty of it, she held him inside warmly and tightly. And when he began to move she moved with him, letting him guide her to a height of pleasure she had never come near to glimpsing before. She found as much ecstasy in his release as in her own, but she didn't have to wonder why she had never felt such reward with Henry. She never had—never would—love Henry as she loved Gil.

He collapsed beside her and was breathing roughly when he drew her into the curve of his body, but the panting eased quickly as sleep overtook him. It didn't occur to Cassie to seek her customary narrow edge of the bed. The feel of Gil was pleasant and comforting; it was every one of her fantasies come true.

Happily, peacefully, she too dozed off, only to awaken after several hours and find that Gil had drawn back the covers and was looking at her body. Again she felt no impulse to hide herself, and she didn't care if that made her wanton, because she found joy in the way his eyes touched and admired her. Then his hands followed suit, and she discovered that she wanted him again, and if that was wanton, she simply didn't care. She had suspected that Gil had been unfaithful to Lenore more than once over the years, and she had no idea whether he would ever have the desire or opportunity to come to her again, so she had every intention of giving and taking what she could for this one, very precious night.

The only light in the room was that of moonlight reflected off the brittle winter grass, but it was enough for her to see his eyes and memorize the look in them and see his body and memorize its contours. Freer than she had ever been, she touched him and worshipped him, and when he came to her again her climax was even more powerful than before.

This time she was the first to fall asleep, and she had no way of knowing that Gil laid awake for a long time watching her. When next she opened her eyes it was morning, and he was gone. She accepted that, as she did the reality of Henry and Kenny, and Lenore and the children in Maine. So she dressed, prepared Gil's usual breakfast, then cleaned up the house and headed north.

The following month, every newspaper in the country splashed headlines of Jonas Salk's perfection of a polio vaccine. The Whyte and Warren children, as well as Kenny Morell, were among the first to receive it, thanks to string pulling on Gil's part. And though there was a tinge of bitterness that the vaccine had come several months too late for Ben, once the other children had been immunized a collective sigh of relief arose from the Dover homes and life returned to normal.

Normal, that is, in Whyte and Warren terms. Jordan was the one who broke a limb this time—his foot, in a soaring leap from the treehouse. And Peter, this time, was the one whose teacher called home reporting that his practice of throwing spitballs in class was becoming a problem. Laura missed out on the part of the princess in the ballet recital, which set her into a tailspin from which she recovered only after she had been promised the part of the good fairy. And Nick, whose body was growing as quickly as Natalie could buy him new clothes, became the playboy of his seventh grade class.

In June of that, year, shortly before the families retired to Maine for the summer, Cassie received confirmation from her doctor that she was pregnant again. Shortly after that, Lenore learned the same. Cassie was due in December, Lenore in January. Any thoughts Cassie might have had about the irony of it were secondary to the joy she felt. She said nothing to Gil; words were unnecessary on that score, at least. Though they had never discussed what had happened on that cold night in March, they shared an understanding that their lives would go on as they had been.

Cassie weathered the pregnancy well, which didn't surprise her. She had been through one pregnancy and knew what to expect, and the added delight of knowing that she carried part of Gil inside her gave her an enormous amount of strength. Henry coddled her less this time, and she might have wondered if he knew the truth had it not been for the fact that they had been growing apart for years. She had no more intention of throwing the baby's parentage in his face than Gil had of throwing it in Lenore's. It was enough for Cassie to know that she and Gil shared their own, very special secret.

December came and went and Cassie didn't deliver. Yet while everyone else waited eagerly for the new arrival she was calm and at peace. The baby was born on January eighth. Cassie's labor was smooth and short. The infant, a girl, was perfectly formed and beautiful. And Henry, bless his soul, took all the credit.

He didn't take to this child as he had to Kenny, though. He wasn't eager to rock her when she cried, or change her diapers when she was wet, or bathe her when Cassie was exhausted. But Cassie didn't complain, for there was a part of her that didn't want Henry to touch the baby. Katia was hers. And Gil's.

Emily Warren was born three weeks after Katia, and again Gil hired extra help to ease Cassie's work. He also raised the Morells' salaries, and he did something that Cassie thought to be utterly sweet and thoroughly shrewd. When the last of the snow had cleared the ground in Dover, he saw to it that Kenny had a new bicycle to match those of widely varied sizes that he had bought for his own children—bonuses, he called them, for boys and girls who had accepted their new baby sisters with such good spirit.

It was the first of many such gestures, each of which were spontaneous and came at times when they were least expected—and all of which included Katia when she grew old enough to benefit from them. They were silent statements that Cassie's children were to be considered as equals to Gil's own, and though they were well intended, they created a subtle backlash that Gil hadn't anticipated.

First off, there was Henry. He was a man with a family, and though he served Gil without fault—chauffeuring him when his schedule called for it, doing heavy work around the house, supervising the gardener and the groom—he felt emasculated by Gil's magnanimity. He insisted to Cassie that he could buy his children what they needed, and when she explained that it was Gil's pleasure to do what he did, Henry argued that Gil's pleasure was not *his* pleasure. Deep down inside he resented Gil. Cassie never pressed the point.

And then there was Lenore. On the surface she behaved the same toward Cassie as she always had, but there were small things, subtle things, that led Cassie to suspect that Lenore knew the truth about Katia. She felt reasonably sure that Gil hadn't said anything, and there was nothing about Katia's looks—she had Cassie's light hair and her own baby features—that gave her away, but Lenore must have suspected something in Gil's gentleness with the child. He didn't see her often, indeed, less often than he saw his own children, which was far too infrequently for Lenore's satisfaction, but when he did, the tender smiles he gave this particular child were special.

Lenore avoided looking at Katia. If the children were playing together, which was often, since Katia and Emily were so close in age, Lenore's attention would be solely on Emily. It was as though she tried to pretend that Katia didn't exist, but, of course, she failed, because the other children, the nanny and Cassie all adored Katia, who was an affectionate and happy child.

If there were times when Lenore would send Laura or Deborah out with Emily in the stroller, leaving Katia behind in the nursery, Cassie didn't say a word. She had no wish to create a scene; it would only put Gil on the spot, which was the last thing she wanted to do. She had utter faith that if she continued to run the Warren household smoothly Gil would continue to see that her children had all of the advantages in life. As she looked toward the future, that was what she wanted for them.

Lenore, too, was looking toward the future, but in a much more calculating way. She abided Gil's campaigns in 1958 and 1960, compensating for those efforts by investing in clothes and jewels and furs. She loved the respect with which she was greeted in public, but she was tired of the ups and downs of political life, the endless fundraisers, the worry. When Gil informed her in late 1961 that he intended to run for a seat in the United States Congress the following year, she drew her ace from its hole.

"The House of Representatives," she said, nodding. "That's the next step."

"I have the power here, and the backing. It will be a harder race than any I've had in the past simply because of its scope, but I don't see any problem."

Again she nodded, her expression calm. "It will also cost more. Laura's in college; Peter will be headed there in two years. Not only will the campaign be expensive, but if you go to Washington you'll have to give up your law practice. Being a congressman is a full-time job, and it doesn't pay anywhere near as much as you've been earning. Can we afford it?"

"How many times have I told you not to worry about money?" he bellowed, not quite realizing that it was as much her uncharacteristic calm that was upsetting him as what he felt to be a slur on his ability as a breadwinner. "I've worked my tail off for years in that law office, and over time I've made investments that have tripled in value. Christ, Lenore, we're millionaires! Why can't you understand that?"

"Millionaires? Good. Then you can run for Congress or do whatever else you wish." She straightened. "On several conditions."

"Conditions?" he growled. "What are you talking about? We're married, you and I. There aren't conditions between husbands and wives."

"There are now, that is, if you want my cooperation in this race."

It wasn't that Gil wanted her cooperation, but that he *needed* it. She was part of the image, the politician's wife who was gracious and poised and, on the surface at least, eternally devoted to her husband. At forty-one she was a stunningly attractive woman. At forty-nine he was a markedly handsome man. He truly believed that they made every bit as impressive a couple as the Kennedys, who had been in the White House since January.

Gil liked the idea of Camelot; he wanted to be part of it. Yes, he needed Lenore. Unfortunately.

"What conditions?" he asked quietly, but not without a hint of resentment.

"First, I will not move to Washington. I like living here, and I want the children to stay here. You can buy a house in Washington—"

"And support *two* houses?"

"You already support two houses, this one and the one in Maine," which was a new one they had built with the Whytes three years before to replace the Victorian house they had torn down. "If we're millionaires a third house won't make much difference. The children and I will spend time there, but this will be our primary residence. When you need me for important social engagements I'll fly down."

Though it wasn't what he had originally had in mind, it occurred to him that such an arrangement would work to his benefit. He would have the leeway to do what he wanted without constantly having to make excuses for his absences to Lenore, yet she would be on call for those times that mattered.

"All right," he said. "I'll agree to that."

"Fine. Second, I want you to make regular investments—blue-chip stocks and savings bonds—in my name and those of each of the children."

He didn't like the sound of that half as well. "For what purpose? If something happens to me you'll inherit it all anyway."

"I want certain assets to be in our names." She was tired of fearing that Gil would become involved in something sordid, or be sued and lose everything, in which case she and the children would inherit nothing but debts, and history would repeat itself. "Which brings me to my next point. I want the deed to this house to be transferred to me."

He expelled a breath and tried to control his impatience. "For God's sake, Lenore, this is absurd."

"I don't think so. I want it done."

"Why?"

"I'll feel safer."

"Safer against *what?*"

She shrugged. "You never can tell. Personally, I don't see any problem with what I'm asking. You said it before; if anything happens to you, we inherit. Well, why don't you save us the estate tax and simply pass everything on now?"

"Because I don't want to!" he shouted, then lowered his voice. "Because I'm hearing something that I don't like."

"That's just fine, because I've been *seeing* something that I don't like for five long years now."

"What are you talking about?" he demanded, but his voice faltered.

"Katia Morell."

Gil paled instantly. Lenore took strength from his loss.

"Did you think I wouldn't guess? Think I wouldn't know? I might not have if you hadn't fawned over her from day one. But that was unlike you, Gil. You never fawned over *our* children."

Gil didn't even consider trying to bluff his way out. Lenore was too shrewd, and at the moment too dangerous. He could deny that Katia was his child, and she could choose to publicize her belief, causing just enough of a stir to spoil his political future.

"What's the matter, Gil? Haven't got a smooth retort?"

"I don't fawn." It wasn't exactly smooth, but it was the only thing he could think of to say at the moment.

"All right. Maybe fawn is too strong a word. But it's obvious the way you look at her that there's something special between you."

"One night, Lenore. That was all. It was after Ben's death. I was here alone. I needed help."

"You got it. She's loved you for years. Do you know that?"

"Cassie Morell is our housekeeper. She does her job and she's been a second mother to our children. If the fact that she loves me increases her love for them, I can find no fault with it. And I have no intention of dismissing her, Lenore. For the sake of *our* children, I will never dismiss her."

Lenore had thought that out, too. "I don't want her dismissed. You're right. She's a vital part of this household. In fact, you can go to her whenever you want—if you can manage to get Henry out of the way. How does he feel about the little girl, anyway?"

"I assume he doesn't know."

"Like you assumed I didn't know? Give us a little credit, Gil. We're not as stupid as you'd like to think."

"I never thought you were stupid."

"What *did* you think?"

Gil didn't like being put on the defensive, and he had no intention of remaining there. "Very honestly," he began, gaining strength as he went, "I thought—I think—that you found a damn good thing when you found me. You were nothing, Lenore. Oh, you were beautiful, and still are, but back then you were living with your mother in a tiny apartment just waiting for the right prospect to come along. I was the key to your future. In me you found money and power. From the time we were married, even during the war years, you were comfortable. And it's gotten better and better. You have a name that's respected—"

"Feared."

"Respected. You have a house that's furnished to the hilt and a private island in Maine. You have a car, the best clothes money can buy, jewels and furs—and don't think that I don't know what you've been doing. You've been stockpiling. Hell, those jewels and furs alone could support you for years if anything happened to me."

"I've earned them," she returned vehemently. "I've stood by your side and smiled until my face was stiff. On your behalf I've been courteous to some of the biggest bores in the world. I've gone along with your obsession with politics even though from the start I felt it was risky. I've sat here alone on the nights you've found better things to do, and I've raised the family you wanted."

Gil could have argued with the latter, but there were more immediate things on his mind. "Why now, Lenore? Why have you waited all this time, knowing what you know, before mentioning Katia to me?"

"Because I've learned from you, Gil. 'Don't get mad. Get even,' you always say. Remember Donald Whitcomb? He took you down a peg one day in front of the entire House. You said you'd get your revenge in time, and you did. You just happened to take on a client who sued the man for every cent he was worth, and you won. That revenge was three years in the coming. You waited for the right opportunity, and when it came you took it. Well, I'm doing the same. I've saved what I know about Katia Morell until now because now is when that knowledge can benefit me the most."

"God, you've gotten hard."

"It's from watching you all these years. I'd have to have been blind not to see that toughness can be effective."

Gil's eyes narrowed. "Who else knows about Katia?"

"From me? No one."

"You haven't told Natalie?"

"I wouldn't be surprised if she knew, because she's not blind either. But, no, I haven't discussed it with her."

Shifting his shoulders, Gil took a deep breath. His nostrils flared. "That was wise of you, because it would have gone against one of *my* conditions."

"Your conditions for what?" she threw back.

"For the acceptance of yours. If you want to play tough, I'll play tough. We'll make a bargain. I'll give you what you want—blue-chip stocks, savings bonds, the deed to this house—in exchange for two things." He raised his forefinger. "First, I want you never to breathe a word of what you suspect to a living soul. You'll not so much as hint of anything to Henry, or Cassie, or Katia, or to any of our family, or the Whytes, or anyone we know, even distantly—not even to the goddamned blind beggar selling pencils on the corner of Tremont and Park.

"And second," another finger went up accordingly, "I want you to treat Katia—and Cassie—with respect. Katia will never be known as a Warren, but I intend for her to have every opportunity in life to go places. I want her to be accepted by this family. I want her to do things with our children. And I want her to know that she has every bit as much potential as our children, because she does, Lenore. Her mother is an intelligent woman. Katia will do well in life."

Lenore was feeling as though she had placed second in a race she had been sure of winning. But she had won, she told herself. She would at last have the kind of financial security she had always wanted. Still, it was an effort to tip up her chin and eye her husband with something akin to triumph. "We have a deal then?"

"Do we? Will you go along with my terms?"

"If you'll go along with mine."

"Oh, I will. But hear me well, Lenore. If I ever find that you've broken your word you'll lose it all. Jack knows about Katia, and he's going to know about our bargain. There will be a stipulation in my will that if you go against my wishes on the very personal matter that only Jack knows about, anything and everything I've left you will revert to Katia. You won't want that, will you?"

"You know I won't," she answered, feeling something akin to hatred for the man before her.

"Then we have a deal?"

"Yes. We have a deal."

Taken for granted in that deal was that Lenore would do as she had said on the matter of Gil's upcoming campaign, and later, his career in Washington. Sure enough, she was with him through the long days and nights of vying for votes, then the long day and night of the election itself. And when he was sworn in as a duly elected member of the United States House of Representatives, she was in the Visitors' Gallery with the rest of the wives, smiling proudly and looking to all the world as though it were the happiest day of her life.

At the reception afterward, she had more than her share to drink. Indeed, in the months to come, she found that a stiff shot of scotch or whiskey or bourbon—she wasn't fussy—helped her through the tedium of being a political wife. She held her liquor respectably, though, and took satisfaction in the doubting looks Gil shot her from time to time. She wasn't about to embarrass herself. Or him. Of course, Gil didn't know that, and she savored the little bit of power she felt, perverse as it was.

As it happened, Lenore wasn't the only one with a drinking problem. Henry had taken to spending more and more of his free time in the Brookline bar he favored. While Gil was in Washington, which was three weeks out of every four, with the exception of congressional recesses, Henry's driving help was unneeded, so he was relegated to doing chores around the house, which would have been fine had his presence there not struck him as being contrived. There wasn't all that much to do. Specialty work—groundskeeping, carpentry, heavy cleaning—was handled by specialty teams who didn't need his direction or supervision. He felt rather like a third wheel. He knew that he would have long since been let go had it not been for Cassie.

Cassie. His wife. The woman whose affection for him was

about as contrived as his job. Even the children didn't need him. They were in school all day, and when they returned they were busy either playing with the Warrens or doing homework. He missed the times he and Kenny would do things together, but Katia . . . well, Katia had never been his, even in the broadest sense, and he knew it. She was drawn to her mother and the Warrens. Not to him.

So he drank. He hit a tree one night when he was driving home in the car, and Cassie berated him for his stupidity. He slept in most mornings, and she didn't care, because she was busy in the main house, always with something to do, someone who needed her. She refused to keep liquor in the cottage, so he took to stealing nips from the Warrens' well-stocked bar. And if Cassie knew that, she never said a word. Nor did Lenore.

It was a game, albeit a sad one, that Henry played, for he knew that he would never be fired. His wife had an inside line to the master of the house, and precisely because of that the game went on.

It ended on a rainy night in 1965 when Henry had the misfortune of drunkenly staggering across the streetcar tracks on Beacon Street at the very same time that an outbound trolley was trundling by. Though the officials ruled the incident a tragic accident, Cassie Morell suspected that there had been more than a slight suicidal bent to it. Her own fate in life, it seemed, was to feel guilt—guilt that she hadn't perished with her family in the war, guilt that she had driven Henry to the depths of suicide, and guilt that she continued to love Gil.

Kenny and Katia were her salvation, for in them she saw the chance to redeem herself.

Chapter 12

CAVANAUGH LEFT NEW YORK the morning after his theater date with Katia, but returned a week later to see Jordan. He had phoned in advance to set up the meeting, not wanting to arrive when Jordan was out of town, and very definitely wanting to see his office in the hope that it would tell him more about the man.

What the ninth-floor office on Park Avenue told him was that Jordan Whyte was surprisingly unpretentious. The office—actually, a suite comprising roughly a quarter of the floor—was decorated well, but without the showiness Cavanaugh had expected. The furnishings were done in a mixture of light wood and leather, the quality high, the colors muted. There were no gaudy trinkets on coffee tables or self-serving plaques on walls or buxom blondes behind typewriters. In fact, other than an occasional bizarre piece of artwork to add a splash of color, the office was a statement in understatement.

Jordan himself greeted Cavanaugh in response to the receptionist's call and led him down the hall to his private office. "Excuse the mess," he said, gesturing to his desktop, which was covered with blueprints whose corners were weighted down with miscellanea ranging from a jar of paper clips and a small cassette recorder to the telephone. "Those things are a pain to keep rolling and unrolling. I didn't think you'd mind if they witnessed our conversation."

Cavanaugh smiled, but he was busy taking in the rest of the room, which was decorated in much the same style as the outer office, except for the floor-to-ceiling bookshelves and pictures. Photographs, actually. Family photographs. An entire wall of them carefully and identically framed, mounted on the wall in even rows. They were impressive, if one thought of Jordan Whyte as a family man. Cavanaugh didn't want to do that, but when he approached the photos, ostensibly to study them more closely, he saw the fine layer of dust that lay atop each frame.

Which ruled out the possibility that Jordan had manufactured the display for his benefit.

"These cover quite a span of time," he noted as he focused on the faces under glass. They presented a broad assortment of Whytes and Warrens at varying periods. There was more than one shot of Katia Morell.

Jordan was leaning against the desk with his arms folded over his shirt and tie and his creased, trousered legs crossed at the ankles. "I used to have them sitting on a credenza, but it got crowded. When I moved in here I took the old prints and had them framed. I keep extra frames in the stock room. All I have to do is to pull one out when I get a new picture."

Cavanaugh turned then, and Jordan gestured him toward a modern leather-cushioned chair before setting his own long frame into its mate. "What's happening with the investigation?"

"Not as much as I'd like. That's why I'm here. We've been through every one of Mark and Deborah's contacts on the coast and we've come up with zilch. I thought we had someone for a while there, but he managed to produce two witnesses who'll testify to the fact that he was in Reno on the night of the murders."

"Could they be lying?"

"Possibly, but there were hotel and gas receipts. They don't lie."

"No."

"From what we've learned, Mark wasn't pushing dope."

"You're sure?" Jordan asked, half relieved, half skeptical.

"He bought it, used it occasionally, offered it at parties along with booze and chips, but he wasn't pushing."

"Thank God for that."

"Mmm." Cavanaugh's voice lowered. "You didn't tell me about Mark's involvement in kiddie porn."

"No," Jordan answered without flinching. He had known this was coming.

"Care to tell me why not?"

"Didn't Katia?"

"Yes, but I'd like to hear it from you."

Jordan cast a helpless glance at the wall of photographs before returning his gaze to Cavanaugh. "I'm not particularly proud of what my brother was doing. I was hoping you'd never have to know. I'm still hoping my parents never have to know."

"Katia must have told you about the indictments."

"Yes."

"Did you know about them before she told you?"

"No."

"Did Mark know?"

"No. Or if he did he didn't tell me. He assured me that he wouldn't be caught."

"And you believed him?"

"I believed that *he* believed it."

"So you let it go at that?"

Jordan felt his hackles rise and did his best to hold his temper. "If you're suggesting that I thought what he was doing was okay as long as he didn't get caught, you're wrong. I gave him hell."

Cavanaugh crossed one knee over the other. "When was that?"

"Three weeks before his death. I had business on the coast, so I stopped in to see him."

"That was the first time you learned what he was doing?"

"Yes."

"And you argued."

"Damned right we did. I don't condone that kind of stuff,

Cavanaugh. Mark could have been a total stranger and I'd have been disgusted. He was my brother, so it was that much worse."

"Did you see him again after the argument?"

"I took him to dinner that night. I thought I might be able to talk some sense into him."

"But you failed."

"In a big way." The muscle above his cheekbone twitched. "We argued again. Mark stalked out of the restaurant."

"Where was Deborah through all this?"

"She was there."

"Did she side with Mark?"

"She left with him."

"But did she support him in the porno thing?"

"I assume she went along with it, but I don't know what her feelings were deep inside. She didn't say much about it. She has always deferred to Mark."

It was consistent with everything else Cavanaugh had learned about the woman. "Did you see Mark again after that?"

"You mean between that time and his death?"

"That's right."

"No."

"You didn't see him when he came to Boston the last time? I understand they were in town for two days before the murders took place."

"I was here. I didn't see him."

He had an alibi, Cavanaugh mused. But corroboration? "Any proof you were here?"

Jordan's entire body stiffened. He sat straighter in his seat and his eyes were hard. "Are you trying to suggest something?"

"I'm trying to rule something out."

"You're asking where I was at the time of the murders, which tells me that I may be a suspect."

"I'm trying to rule it out," Cavanaugh repeated calmly.

Jordan was anything but calm as he struggled against disbelief, disgust and fury. "You actually think I could have killed my own brother and sister-in-law?"

"I don't think that. I'm simply doing my job by looking at every possibility and eliminating them, one by one. If Mark had lived, and if he'd been indicted, your family—and the Warrens—would have felt the heat. His death spared you all that."

Bounding to his feet, Jordan began to pace the office. "His death spared us? Great. We chose two innocent deaths over a little discomfort." He turned to rage at Cavanaugh. "Man, you are incredible! Do you have any *idea* how much pain those two deaths have caused? Do you have any *idea* what it's like to think of two people, your own flesh and blood being brutally murdered? Two people, two intelligent people, two people who carried a little bit of you in them because you'd spent years and years together," he snapped his fingers, "gone, just like that? No, you don't. You can't, or you'd never be suggesting that we'd benefit from their deaths. What do you think we are—*monsters?*"

"I'm just doing my job, Whyte."

"Well, I'm doing mine as a member of my family by saying that you're way off base! *Way* off base!"

"Okay. Take it easy. I just wanted to run it by you."

"Geez . . ." Jordan scowled at the ceiling, then lowered his head and took a deep breath. When he spoke his voice was calmer. Not quite its jaunty self, but calmer, though his cheek twitched again. "Why don't you try running something else by me? Something sane this time." Hearing his own words, he shook his head. "Okay. You're right. I know that you're just doing your job, but believe me you're barking up the wrong tree." A new thought struck then, bringing a resurgence of emotion. "Hell, you're not going to ask the others to account for their whereabouts that night, are you? They'll be as sick as I am that you could imagine we'd do anything to hurt either Mark or Deborah ourselves."

"I don't know. We're still looking for other leads."

"God, Cavanaugh. Stay away from them. They've been

through so much with this already. My sister Anne is heartbroken that she didn't lend Mark money when he asked for it. My brother Nick, who was closest to Mark as a kid because they were barely a year apart, is sick that he wasn't able to foresee some kind of trouble. Deborah's older sister is going through a mid-life crisis touched off by Deborah's death, and poor Emily is working over-time on the stage so she won't have to think about it." He took a quick breath. "And as for my parents, and Gil and Lenore, they haven't been the same since. They're bleeding, Cavanaugh. Hell, man, don't rub salt on the wound!"

Cavanaugh couldn't help but be affected by Jordan's impas-sioned plea. He told himself that he was a fool, but he believed that the man meant every word he said. "I won't point any fingers unless I have good cause." In another tone the statement would have sounded defensive, but Cavanaugh had offered it with a touch of sadness.

Jordan settled down some. "You won't have cause. I can guar-antee you that. For whatever else you might think of us, we're not murderers."

"What about Peter Warren?"

"Peter isn't capable of murder!"

"But you didn't mention him before. How has he taken the deaths?"

Jordan thought of fabricating a story of boundless grief, then thought otherwise. He had gone with the truth so far; his gut told him it was the best policy. "Peter was stunned. We all were. But he's been able to throw off the shock better than some of the oth-ers. You have to understand," Jordan urged as he sank back into his chair and propped his elbows on his knees. "I love him like a brother, and have a great deal of respect for his legal ability, but Peter is self-centered. In a nutshell. He likes to be the center of at-tention. That's why he enjoys trial work, where every eye in the jury is on him. That's why he wants to be a judge. But take my word for it," he was slowly shaking his head, "there is *no way* that Peter would have raised a finger against either Deborah or Mark.

He loved them too, and he's learned to be very careful with the law. There is no way he'd do anything that would jeopardize his future.

"Besides," he added with a crooked smile, "he hates the sight of blood. It used to be the death of him. When we were kids and someone got a scrape or a cut, Peter nearly passed out. We ribbed him about it. He learned to run in the opposite direction at the first drop of something red. Maybe he's like his mother in that way, I don't know. But I do know that he's turned down cases that are particularly gruesome. No one other than family knows the reason." He took a breath, sighed it out. "Does that sound like a man who could cold-bloodedly shoot his own sister and brother-in-law in the head?"

"No. But then a scandal linking Mark to child pornography might have jeopardized those chances for a judgeship."

"Do you really believe that, Cavanaugh? Would Peter have been held responsible for what Mark did? Come on. Sure, there would have been adverse publicity, and it would have been painful for all of us, but harmful in the sense of affecting our occupational chances?" He shook his head quickly and firmly this time. "I think not."

Cavanaugh had to agree with him, if resentfully. The Whytes and Warrens had power. They could probably have taken a scandal and turned it around for their benefit, though how they would have been able to do that with this particular one was beyond him. Still, Jordan was convincing.

"Well then," he said, "that takes care of Peter."

"That takes care of *all* of us. I'd stake my entire future on the fact that not one of the Whytes or Warrens is capable of doing what you've suggested."

"Did you think Mark capable of child pornography?" Cavanaugh asked.

His point was taken. Jordan chalked one up with his forefinger. "But Mark was different," he cautioned. "Indecipherable in many ways. We've told you that, Katia and I." He paused, sending a more speculative glance Cavanaugh's way. "What did you think of her, by the way?"

"As a murder suspect?" Cavanaugh returned, but the teasing twitch at the corner of his mouth betrayed him.

"As a person," Jordan said, softening up himself.

"She's quite a one. Beautiful, open, warm. I'm surprised some guy hasn't come along and snatched her up."

"So am I," Jordan said, momentarily distracted by the thought.

"Why haven't you?"

"What?"

"Snatched Katia up. You two are obviously close, and you're not related by blood. She's clearly fond of you. I gather the feeling's returned?"

"You gathered that the first time we talked," Jordan reminded him dryly.

"But since then I've met her. I can see how a man could be totally enthralled."

"Were you?"

"I'm a cop. I was interviewing her." He didn't bother to mention the theater date since Jordan seemed not to know about it.

"Don't give me that crap," Jordan said quietly. "You're a man. Did she enthrall you?"

"In a way."

"She told me that you already have a girl."

"Did she tell you *everything* we said?"

"She told me a lot. You impressed her."

"Does that bother you?"

"I thought you said you were a cop. You sound more like a psychiatrist."

"There's a little of the analyst in every good cop. So I'm asking. Does it bother you that she liked me?"

"In that you're a cop, not particularly. I'm not hung up about occupations."

"In that I'm a man. In other words, do you or do you not welcome the competition?"

"I thought you already had someone."

"That's beside the point."

"The hell it is," Jordan returned, growing agitated. "I won't have you chasing after Katia, only to catch her and then leave her for a woman you've got back home."

"Do you want her?"

"Of course I want her!" he yelled. Realizing what he'd done and said, he hung his head, rubbed the back of his neck, then allowed a self-conscious grin to surface. "You *should* have been a shrink. You've got the talent."

"Nah. I like being a cop. And I like the woman I have at home. Katia's safe from me. But I'm telling you, you'd better do something about her before someone else does. Women have only so much patience, even when it comes to the men they love."

Which, in effect, gave them both something to think about.

Cavanaugh didn't have much time to do that in the days that immediately followed, however. He had no sooner returned to Boston when Ryan was on his back. "Well? What have you got?"

"I have a handful of possible suspects on the coast, each with ironclad alibis."

"And the family?"

"Nothing yet."

"If you've ruled out everything else, don't you think that's the way to go?" Ryan demanded, drumming fat fingers on the desk.

"I'm doing it. I met with Jordan Whyte again yesterday. He says he was in New York at the time of the murders. I've put someone on it. We'll see if his story holds."

"What about the others?"

"Nothing suspicious yet. Jordan was the only one who knew that Mark was involved in pornography. He was on the coast, had a couple of arguments about it with his brother."

Ryan looked pleased. "Any witnesses to the arguments?"

"Deborah, but she's gone. We'll have to see if we can find others."

"Anything else interesting?"

"Not particularly."

"What about the tapes?"

"We've been through them. Nothing."

"There has to be something!" Ryan shot at him, then calmed himself. "You viewed all of them?"

"Every one we found."

"Maybe there were others."

"We didn't see any."

"Did you look everywhere?"

Cavanaugh was getting the uneasy feeling that Ryan knew something he didn't. "Just about." He gnawed on his lower lip for a minute. "Did you have something specific in mind?"

"Of course not," the man answered brusquely, or as brusquely as his high voice would allow. "This is your case, not mine. You're the one who knows what the setup is out there. But I read somewhere that filmmakers often get their jollies filming everything. Even visitors in their homes."

"Like Nixon with his recordings?"

Ryan liked that. "Good thought."

"If Whyte did that he hid them. There was nothing with the other reels."

"If he was strange enough to film his personal doings he'd have been strange enough to hide them. Check it out, Cavanaugh. It may be that there's nothing, but damn it, if there's a chance it's worth the effort. We need to make some progress on this one. It's stagnating."

Cavanaugh nodded curtly and left the room before he said something he'd regret. *Stagnating?* Not quite. The investigation was moving along at a reasonable rate. What did Ryan expect? And why was he so impatient? It occurred to Cavanaugh—and was supported by his colleagues—that Ryan's sole interest lately was the Whyte-Warren case. Other investigations were ongoing, but his focus was narrowed on this one. Cavanaugh wondered whether the man had his own personal gripe against one or another of the families. It would certainly explain why he had kept such a detailed file. . . .

Jordan thought a lot about what Cavanaugh had said, but he was in the same bind as always. Katia was his sister—figuratively, and probably literally. He'd always sensed that Henry wasn't her biological father, but he hadn't taken the matter to heart until the fateful day when he had overheard his own father talking. On that day, his world had fallen apart. He positively worshipped Katia, but he didn't know what to do about it. He tried to forget her in Nancy, whom he took out on Tuesday night, in Judy, whom he took out on Thursday, in Alexis, whom he took out on Friday night. And though he had seen Katia under the guise of work twice that week, by Saturday he was aching to see her again.

So he popped over to her apartment at noon that day in the hope that she would take pity on him and share a little of her sunshine.

After her initial surprise she was less than receptive. "I wish you'd called ahead of time, Jordan," she sighed. "I've got a million things to do today." The first of those things was to clean the apartment, which—given the fact that she had stayed in bed until eleven because she hadn't fallen asleep until three—she had been doing when he had rung the bell. She was wearing a pair of ragged cut-offs and an old t-shirt, and she felt like something the cat had dragged in.

"That's okay. I'll wait. In fact, maybe I can help. You look beat."

"Always full of compliments," she muttered, but she left him at the open door, silently bidding him enter if that was what he wanted.

He did. Closing the door behind him, he watched her spray polish on the lacquered coffee table, then rub it for all she was worth.

"Nervous energy?" he asked.

She looked up, startled, then as quickly returned to her work. Yes, damn it. It was nervous energy. And *he* was its cause. During the week she could bury herself in work; even on the weekends she did it at times. This weekend, however, she felt too frustrated to work, too frustrated to do much of anything but take out her grievances on the hapless furniture.

"I thought you'd be in Maine," she grumbled.

"Cassie told me you weren't going, so I decided to stay here."

Katia gritted her teeth. "You should have gone. Your family needs you."

"They need you, too. Why did you stay?"

"I have too much to do."

"Cleaning can wait."

"I have to work." She tossed her head toward the stuffed portfolio that lay on the dining room table untouched.

"You could do it up there."

"Easier to do it here." She shot him a glance. "If you really want to help, you can do this." She dropped the can of spray polish and the cloth, and stalked toward the kitchen. Jordan had started after her when she returned carrying the vacuum cleaner. A self-contained stereo headset was curled around her neck.

"Is something wrong, Katia?"

"What could possibly be wrong?" She bent to plug in the vacuum.

"Something happen at work?"

"Work's fine." She turned on the vacuum, then balanced the handle between her thighs while she put the headphones to her ears.

"Are you having man problems?"

She lifted the speaker from one ear and looked at him. "What did you say?"

"I asked," he repeated more loudly in an attempt to be heard over the steady wheeze of the machine, "if you're having man problems."

She replaced the speaker and started vacuuming. "I'm always having man problems. I think it's my fate in life."

"If someone's giving you trouble—*if someone's giving you— damn it, Katia, I can't compete with music or whatever the hell it is you're listening to!*"

Katia looked up at him, but she neither turned off the vacuum nor lifted the headphones. "I can't hear you, Jordan. I have headphones on."

He swore. But she didn't hear that either. So he strode to the side of the room, pulled the plug on the vacuum, then returned to physically remove the headset from her head.

"Jordan," she protested, "I have to get this done!"

"Not until you tell me what's wrong. You've been like a walking thundercloud since I got here. I want you to tell me what's bothering you."

You, you big oaf, she wanted to yell, but she didn't. Instead she simply put her hands on her hips and stared right back at him. "Nothing's bothering me that a little, good old-fashioned physical exertion won't cure." She had been referring to cleaning. Only after she made the statement did she recognize it for the Freudian slip it was. She hurried on. "It's been a long and tiring week. I'm feeling pressure. Just leave it at that, okay?"

But when she reached for the headset, Jordan held it out of reach. "There's something else. I know you too well."

"If you know me so well you can respect the fact that I want to be left alone."

"You don't usually want to be left alone. It's not like you."

"Then I've changed! Okay?" Again she reached for the headset; he simply held it farther away. "Jordan. . . ."

"What is it, sweetheart?" he asked with such tender concern that she closed her eyes and hung her head.

She stood like that for several moments before whispering a defeated, "Oh, Jordan, I'm so tired of all this."

"All what?" When she simply shook her head, he closed the

small distance between them and folded her into his arms. "Tell me, honey. What's getting to you?"

What was getting to her was the sound of his voice, his gentle endearments, the strength of his arms, the solidity of his body, the heat of him, his smell. And she could do nothing but melt into him. It was the only thing she had ever wanted.

He held her close, stroking her hair with his cheek. He knew what was bothering her. Damn it, he knew. Her need for him was every bit as great as his need for her, except that she didn't know what he did. She hadn't overheard the conversation he had; she hadn't spent the last eleven years of her life waiting for the hand of God to reach out and, by some miracle, make everything all right.

What killed him most was that little bit of doubt that niggled in his mind from time to time. He wished he could confront his father and ask point-blank whether what he had heard had been right, but the two were on the most marginal of speaking terms and such a confrontation would shatter what token peace existed between them. He had even considered approaching Cassie, but when he thought of putting the words to her he cringed. No matter how gently he phrased his thoughts he would be accusing her of infidelity. He didn't have the guts to do it.

Bold, irreverent Jordan—gutless when it came to the one thing that mattered most to him. That thought bothered him, too, but he was helpless to change it. Something had to give, some card had to be turned, some hand shown. He'd tried to keep his distance from Katia, but it was getting harder by the day. Especially now, since Mark's death, when he was so keenly aware of the meaning of life and the passage of time.

"Let's go to Maine, you and I," he murmured into her ear. "The others will already be there. It's Labor Day weekend. We deserve a break."

Katia moaned. She had decided against going in the first place because she was seeing Jordan so often that the painful pleasure of it was killing her. She hadn't enjoyed any of the dates she had been on lately. She couldn't seem to sleep the night through. Work was work. Friends were friends. Cooking was cooking.

And Jordan was Jordan, asking her to subject herself to further torment. What was wrong with him that he couldn't see what ailed her? How could he punish her this way?

"I really should work," she murmured against his polo shirt.

"Like I said before, you can work there. And mix a little relaxation in with it. You're tired. You need a rest."

"If I had any sense I'd take the next plane to an uninhabited island in the Caribbean. Then I'd get some rest."

"Planes don't go to uninhabited islands in the Caribbean."

"Struck out again, did I? Boy, am I getting good at that."

"Come on, Katia," he said, rocking her gently. "Ease up."

Ease up? Any more and she would be a puddle at his feet. She felt like jelly cradled against him this way. "I'm sorry, Jordan," she managed in a weak voice. "You've just caught me at a bad time."

"If you come with me to the island, things will be better. Everyone's there, even Nick and Angie and the kids. Anne and Em and your mother—she doesn't get to see you often. Do her a good turn and visit."

"Guilt trip. Not fair."

"Wouldn't you like to see her?"

"Yes."

"And the others?"

"Yes."

He held her back, his hands on her shoulders, and ducked his head until his eyes were level with hers. "Then let's go. We can fly into Portland and be at the island by dinnertime. Come on, Katia. Say yes."

So many times he had done it this way, and each time she was lost. She moaned once and rolled her eyes, then spoke through gritted teeth. "Yes, Jordan, yes. Is that what you want to hear? Yes!"

His shoulders relaxed and he let out a breath. Two days. Nothing could happen, but he would be with her for two days. Two days. He grinned. "That's my girl. Now—" he looked around, "you go do whatever it is that you have to do to get ready, and I'll just zip around with the vacuum. The place will be spotless by the time you're ready. Everything will be perfect for you to come back to on Monday."

Just then Katia didn't want to think about returning on Monday. Having capitulated—once again—she was determined to make the most of it. And if that meant that she would flirt with Jordan mercilessly, so be it. She knew she could arouse him; let *him* feel the frustration for a change!

The sound of the launch pulling up to the dock brought out the entire island contingent, and there were delighted smiles and hugs when they discovered who had come. Natalie and Cassie, in particular, were pleased. Jordan and Katia's surprise appearance was what they needed to make the holiday special.

And it was special. Katia was the first to admit it. For one thing she had time to spend with her mother. Though she and Cassie spoke weekly on the phone they hadn't seen each other since the funeral six weeks before. Cassie wanted to hear about Katia's work, about friends she had spent time with, about men she had dated, and Katia told her everything. There was a kind of catharsis in it, for she was able to see her life from Cassie's perspective, and, inevitably, she appreciated it more.

Only on the matter of Jordan was she somewhat circumspect. She knew that her mother would love to see her married to him, and though Cassie didn't harp on it or pester her openly, she was always eager to hear about anything and everything regarding that relationship. So Katia had learned to downplay it, particularly now that she no longer had Sean as a shield. She didn't want to raise Cassie's hopes unfairly. And she didn't want to admit that she apparently lacked something that Jordan sought in a mate.

As had always been the case, Cassie seemed to accept that Katia was too career oriented to view marriage as an immediate necessity. Still, she was delighted to learn that Katia was working for Jordan. It was a step in the right direction.

Gil, on the other hand, was far more pensive. Katia had sought him out at a time when all the others were by the swimming pool. He was in his den, sitting quietly. She was immediately worried.

"Gil?" she asked softly.

He raised his chin from his chest and saw her, then broke into a smile. "Katia." He sat forward. "Come on in. You're just in time to rescue me from an old man's morbid thoughts."

"You're not an old man," she chided, walking quietly toward the desk and putting her hand in the one he offered.

"Maybe not in the eyes of a ninety-year-old, but I'm seventy-four. That must seem ancient to you."

"Ancient? You? You're one of the most active and energetic men I've ever known." Which was why she had been doubly concerned to find him sitting alone, neither working nor talking on the phone. Even his pipe sat forgotten in the ashtray, the cherry scent of tobacco barely lingering.

"Sometimes I wonder if I'm running out of that energy," he said, and for a moment he looked every one of his seventy-four years. He was as handsome as always, straight, slim and dignified, but his features were paler than usual and weighted down by fatigue. He looked much as he had when she had seen him after the funeral. She wondered if he had had any peace since.

"Are you feeling all right?"

He dismissed her concern with the wave of his free hand. "Oh, I'm fine. Just not much of a companion for myself." The hand that held hers gave a quick squeeze. "But now you're here. I'm glad you decided to come after all, Katia. It means so much to your mother to see you."

"I know. I like seeing her, too. There are times in the city when I get so wrapped up in everything that it's hard to think of getting away—"

"Don't do that. It's a mistake. Your family is where you come from, what you are. And if you isolate yourself now, some day down the road you'll find yourself alone."

His message was clear, but there was more. "Is that what you're feeling right about now?" she asked softly.

He studied her without blinking. "Could be."

"But you have your work—"

"Ah, yes. And it's always there. Work, people, one fight or another." His brow furrowed. "Now and again, though, I want to get away from it. I've been politicking for better than forty years. There should be something else."

"You have Lenore and your children and grandchildren."

"I'm afraid," he stated slowly, "that I've burned some bridges along the way."

"But they love you."

"Do they like me?"

"I'm sure they do. Oh, you can be intimidating at times," she teased in an attempt to lighten his mood, which upset her, since it was so uncharacteristic, "but then, what powerful man isn't intimidating at times?"

"He shouldn't be. Not when he's with his family."

"Is it possible to turn one's personality on and off?" She settled against the desk, holding his hand now between both of hers. "You are who you are, Gil. You can't change that."

"No, but still. . . ."

"You're thinking of Deborah." Katia knew it beyond a shadow of a doubt. "Gil, you can't blame yourself—"

"If she'd approached me I'd have given her anything she needed. But she was afraid. She was always afraid." He gave a curt laugh. "Funny, isn't it? The world thinks that my kids are spoiled brats, that they only have to wish for something and it's theirs. Then I look at Deborah, who was almost afraid to wish for things for *fear* they'd be hers. Maybe if I'd been around more, maybe if I'd spent more time with her. . . ."

"You couldn't have it both ways. It would have been impossible for you to have accomplished what you have in politics if you'd been with your family every minute."

"Not every minute. Just more than I was. Some men do it. I see them, Katia, some of the younger members of Congress. Sure, they work themselves ragged and sleep on sofas in their offices, but they rush home to be with their families every weekend, and I'm not sure that in the end they won't be just as successful as I've been. More so. Because they'll have that groundwork of love to keep them going."

"You have it."

"Me? No. Ambition keeps me going. That's all." His eyes met hers and grew sharper. "Don't do what I did. I know that your career means the world to you. You're doing well, moving up. But you're alone."

"There are people at work, and friends, and I date."

"That was what I always said, but it's not the same. You should have a family, Katia. A husband who loves you, and children. For a while I thought you and Sean—"

"He wasn't right for me."

Gil nodded, then hesitated, again uncharacteristically. "I've always hoped that something would develop between Jordan and you. He's a fine boy."

"More than a boy," she murmured, blushing.

"So you are aware of him?"

"I've always been aware of him. But he isn't in any more of a rush to settle down than I am."

"He should be," Gil grumbled. "If he waits much longer he'll be enjoying his children from a wheelchair."

She laughed. "I doubt that."

"What he needs is a good kick in the pants."

"He'd rebel for everything he's worth."

"Let him. A little rebellion is good for the soul. It's purging, makes you come to your senses all the sooner."

What Katia had in mind, though, wasn't rebellion as a purgative. Though she spent another hour with Gil, answering his questions about her life in New York much as she'd done her mother's, she was plotting her own personal form of fire starting.

The first match was struck later that morning when she joined the others at the pool. This time she let her eyes wander freely over Jordan's barely clad frame—and precisely at those moments when she knew he'd notice.

Sitting with Anne's daughter, Amanda, on her lap while Jordan chatted with them from the next lounge chair, Katia undertook a survey of his bare chest, focusing on one flat brown nipple that nestled amid a whorl of dark hair. Only until that flat nub rose did her gaze linger, then it skittered away and refocused on Amanda.

Later, she was resting on the same lounge chair, lap empty and legs outstretched while Jordan skimmed pine needles from the pool's surface with the long net he had taken from the shed. She leisurely traced the narrow band of his Lycra suit, raised her eyes to meet his, then dropped them back to his trunks in a blatant visual caress before closing her eyes and lying languidly back in the sun.

Following lunch, when a hoard of Warrens and Whytes were on the patio eating ice cream cones, Katia, who had positioned herself close to Jordan, reached over to wipe a smear of chocolate from his upper lip. Holding his eyes, she brought the finger to her mouth, sucked on it deeply, then immediately turned her attention to the others, offering a timely addition to the conversation.

During the afternoon, when she and Jordan took Nick's two youngest children for a walk in the woods, Jordan boosted little Sean up onto the branch of a tree. Katia stood flush behind him, grinning at the child while her fingers walked a long, slow line down Jordan's spine to its very base. His head shot around in time to see her step back and kneel beside Heather, who was impatiently awaiting her turn for a boost.

That evening, when Jordan was in the family room with Anne, Mark, Peter, Nick and Angie, Katia was the one to bring in a brimming bowl of popcorn. Propping herself on the arm of the chair in which Jordan sat, she directed her eyes to the screen. Meanwhile, she reached into her pocket and pulled out several of the macadamia nuts she had taken from the jar in the kitchen. One by one, with comfortable intervals between, she popped them into his mouth as she watched the movie. When the nuts were gone, she slipped her hand around Jordan's neck and whispered her thumb back and forth over the warm, smooth spot behind his ear. When she felt him tilt his head into her touch, she withdrew it, twisted away to reach into the communal popcorn bowl for a fistful, then slid to the floor to watch the remainder of the show.

Jordan said nothing. He and Katia sat on the patio later that night talking, but he made no reference to the fact that anything might be amiss with her. They ate breakfast together the next morning, during which she drew a ripe strawberry from the jam on her muffin and pressed it between his lips. Then they went for a sail with Laura's husband, Donald, and their daughter, Dawn, and Katia made a point to hang onto Jordan's thigh—his inner thigh, high up—when the boat heeled at a daring angle.

And still he said nothing. Not that she had expected any comment. He had long since proven himself to be a master of sexual self-control when he was with her. But the more self-control he exerted the more determined she grew to test it.

So, after lunch that day—most of the family members, including Jordan and Katia, planned to leave the island by night-fall—she donned her *pièce de résistance*. It was a t-shirt, scooped-necked and sleeveless—practically sideless, the arm-holes were cut so low. Normally, she'd have worn it over another, more traditional t-shirt. Layered, and with matching shorts, it was a chic set. Unlayered, and with the skimpiest of bikini pants, it was nearly lewd.

The pool was the site for her assault. Indeed, the pool was the central point for the families' gatherings, particularly on days such as this when the heat of the sun was something to be gathered in and cherished, then remembered with longing in the long winter months to come.

Katia carefully kept her arms by her sides until she had taken the chair next to Jordan. She had no intention of flaunting herself before the others, and simply tilted her face to the sun as the conversation flowed around her. Only when the children were occupied in the water and the other adults seemed equally preoccupied did she sit forward. Her thighs were spread, her knees bent, her ankles crossed. It was around the latter that she wrapped her hands.

He had a view. He had to have a view. She could feel the warm breath of a breeze against her breasts, and it set them to tingling. She threw her head back, shook it so that her sandy hair billowed, and smiled.

"Mmm. This is nice, Jordan. I'm glad you convinced me to come."

At first Jordan said nothing. She kept her eyes closed, her face to the sun, but her nipples were growing tight.

"Relaxed?" he asked at last. His voice was as tight as her nipples.

"Very. You were right. It is good to see everyone. And we couldn't have asked for better weather. There's many a Labor Day when it's cold and rainy. This is . . . wonderful." The last was said in a purr. Lifting both arms, she drew her fingers through her hair.

"You'll get marks." His voice was tighter than ever.

Katia propped her elbows on her knees. Her eyes stayed closed, her face tilted up. "In my hair?"

"On your body. Where's your bikini top?"

"In my room."

"Lot of good it's doing there."

"This is fine. The sun isn't strong enough to tan much of anything except the soul. Come January I'm going to remember this." As though in reaction to the thought of the cold, she gave a tiny shiver—just enough to wiggle her breasts—then she suddenly lowered her head and opened her eyes. "In fact, the beach will be nothing but a memory then too. I think I'll take a walk there. Want to come?"

For the first time she looked at Jordan. He was sitting with his arms wrapped around his bent knees and would have looked perfectly at ease had it not been for the whiteness of the knuckles of the hand that grasped his opposite forearm. And for his eyes. They were dark, very dark, and smoldering.

When he didn't answer, she popped up from her seat. "See you later, then," she said as she breezed by.

She headed straight for the beach, wondering if he would follow. She refused to look back and spoil her act of utter nonchalance, but she wondered. And listened. And homed in on an ESP she had never possessed but had always wanted.

When she reached the dock she anchored herself against one of the wood pilings. Ankle-deep in the ocean, she shifted until she was looking back at the shore.

He wasn't there. She waited, giving him time, but still he didn't come. He had ignored her bait. He hadn't followed. Coward! she shrieked silently, pushing off from the piling and starting across the rocky beach. She called him an assortment of other names, then turned many of the same ones on herself as she made her furious way toward an outcropping of rocks, which she proceeded to scale in a way that would have been reckless had her anger not endowed her with greater than normal strength and agility.

That strength was spent, though, by the time she had reached a small hollow in the rocks cushioned with beach grass. She had gone there often, both as a child and an adult. Shielded on both sides by boulders, it was a throne from which she could survey her domain.

But at the moment she wasn't feeling particularly regal. Or powerful. She was feeling rather foolish, a mite embarrassed, and very, very frustrated. It occurred to her that the only person she had set a fire under was herself, and it wasn't simply one of anger. Each time she had touched Jordan she had been excited. When she had boldly studied his body her own had stirred in response. And just now, giving Jordan what she had considered to be an irresistible show had only heightened the eroticism in her own mind. If she had the strength or good sense, she mused, she'd climb right back down and take a swim in the ocean. The water was cold; it was always cold. Somehow, though, she knew that it wouldn't help her. The problem was every bit as much in her mind as her body.

She was staring out to sea, feeling sorry for herself, when Jordan's thundering voice rent the afternoon air high above her. "What the hell are you doing up here?" She whirled around to see him towering atop the boulder. "You could have killed yourself climbing up!"

"I've done it before," she said curtly. Self-pity was forgotten, replaced by defiance. "You never knew that, did you? I found your little hiding place one afternoon when I followed you. I was six years old. I couldn't make it up here then, but I remembered just where it was. I've been coming here since I was eight. You're not the only one who likes a little adventure, Jordan. Or a little privacy."

The last was offered pointedly. Jordan chose to ignore it. He sat down hard on the edge of the boulder, gave a push and jumped. It was ten feet worth of jump. Katia rose to her knees in alarm.

"My God, Jordan, look who's talking! That was brilliant! Self-destructive from the word go!"

"And if it was?" He brushed off his hands as he came to his feet. "What's it to you? It's my life, and I can do without your interference!" His eyes narrowed on her. "You've been playing a game, and I don't like it."

"What game?" she asked, wanting to be as perverse as he was.

"Oh, come on, Katia. We *both* know what you've been doing."

"Well that's a relief. I was beginning to think you were deaf, dumb, blind and sexless."

"I am not sexless."

Without guile or the slightest hint of humor, she dropped her gaze to the front of his racing suit. "It's obvious that you've got the goods. Whether they work is something else."

"You know they work."

"How would I know that?" she yelled. "You've never given *me* a demonstration!"

"Is that what you want?" he snarled. Before she knew what he intended, he dropped into a crouch directly before her and took her chin in his palm. Between his thumb and the rest of his fingers, her jaw was immobilized. "You've been taunting me. Little touches here, little looks there. You've been doing it on purpose, Katia, and it's cruel!"

"You don't know what cruel is," she managed to grit out between her teeth.

"And you do? What an innocent you are, Katia. What a sweet, sweet innocent." And with that he took her mouth, bent on destroying her innocence once and for all.

Chapter 13

JORDAN KNEW he would never be able to do it. The instant he put his hands on her his anger began to wane. The instant he covered her mouth with his the anger grew distant, then dissolved completely. In its place was a need so potent that it was palpable and tangible and very nearly audible.

This was Katia, whom he loved. Her lips were still beneath his, but he wanted them open and moving and hungry. So he gentled his kiss to its seductive best, sipping and coaxing and stirring her until she slowly began to respond.

She didn't want to. She wanted to hold herself stiff and unfeeling. She wanted to drive Jordan insane with the same frustration that had been eating her alive for days, months, years. But this was Jordan. She had never had a chance against him, and she didn't now. If his lips were loving her, hers had no choice but to love him back. If his tongue filled her mouth, she had no choice but to offer her own in exchange.

He sighed her name when he came up for breath, but in the next instant he was back, renewing the kiss with even greater ardor. His hands slid up and down her sides, homing in on the large ovals of flesh bared by her poor excuse for a covering. When her hands crept up to thread through his hair, the lift of her breasts was too great a temptation. There was little to bar him; the simple shift of fabric toward the center of her body and he was there. A bare breast, creamy, warm and swelling, filled each hand. He loved them as he continued to love her mouth, stroking, kneading, tugging gently as desire spiraled.

And it did. Oh, it did. He knew he should stop, but in another minute . . . just another minute more. The tiny whispers coming from Katia's throat told him of her pleasure, and if he could give her that, surely he would be forgiven for his sins.

The only sin in Katia's mind was that this explosion of passion had been so long in coming. The wait and its torment had stubbed out any hopes she had of self-denial. After striking that first match she herself was on fire.

The feel of Jordan's long limbs against hers was electric, or so she thought until his thumbs snapped over her painfully taut nipples and wholly new currents of arousal arced through her. She wanted to touch him all over, but feared that if she removed her arms from his neck her trembling knees would refuse to hold her upright. So she simply strained closer and closer, needing the tight fit of his body to ease her pain.

Suddenly he was lowering her to the beach grass, leaning over her, kissing her eyes, her nose, her chin. She felt worshipped, which was exactly how Jordan wanted her to feel. He wanted her to know of his love, though he couldn't say it in words. He wanted her to know that she was the dearest thing in his life and that it hurt him to hurt her, though to tell her that would be to invite questions that he simply couldn't answer for fear of hurting her even more. Instead, he showed her, with his roving lips, his hands and his heated body what she meant to him.

Katia rose to his ministrations by growing greedy. Her palms drew large circles over his chest, his shoulders, his rib cage. She loved the feel of him, and her fingers told him so by raking through the mat of his chest, then following its tapering progression to his navel. They lingered there for just a minute, but there was more they wanted—needed—to touch, and they did. His stomach muscles were rigid, allowing the room she needed to slide her hand beneath the thin band of his trunks.

He was hard and throbbing. She closed her fingers around him, but she no sooner heard his guttural moan when a matching one came from her throat, for his own hand had breached the tiny barrier of her bikini and was opening her and stroking her, clouding her mind with the haze of passion. Her fingers loosened. She couldn't think. What he was doing to her was nearly beyond sensation.

She cried his name, but it was muted in the cavern of his mouth. His thumb was rubbing her while his fingers slipped inside, withdrew, then entered her again. At some point her own hand had left him, because she was clutching his shoulders, digging in her nails, holding on to him as though she were on the verge of destruction.

And it was exactly that in a small way. For after she had writhed up against his hand, after she had caught in her breath and then released it in a series of harsh gasps, after her insides had tightened in spasm after glorious spasm, then finally relaxed, she realized that she had lost. As beautiful as the moment had been, she knew the instant she opened her eyes that Jordan had no intention of possessing her in the most intimate, most total of ways.

Breathing heavily, she closed her eyes and rolled her head to the side. *Why? Why?* She ached to ask, to scream, but she didn't want to hear the answer. She had heard it before. It was too painful.

When a tear slipped from beneath her lid, Jordan moaned, then gathered her in his arms and held her tightly. "Don't cry, sweetheart. It was good."

"Not for you," came a muffled sob from his chest. "Nothing happened."

"I wouldn't say that. I felt a pleasure I've never felt before."

She raised her head then, her eyes beseeching and wide. "Let me do it for you," she whispered and reached for him, but he caught her hand and raised it to his heart.

"No, Katia. Not now. It's enough for me to know what you felt."

His voice came gently through a soft smile, but there was a finality to his words that Katia simply couldn't bear. So she buried her face against his chest and let him hold her until it was time to go. He helped her carefully over the rocks, and they didn't talk as they walked back along the beach, then up to the house.

It wasn't until the following morning, after she had returned to her spotless apartment in New York and spent long hours tossing and turning in bed before finally falling asleep that she was ready to talk. But, of course, Jordan wasn't there.

Jordan wasn't talking to anyone. His associates puzzled at his moodiness, his secretaries gave him a wide berth. The look in his eyes went from sadness to despair to fury, then back many times in the course of the day.

When he flew to Baltimore on Wednesday, he barked at the flight attendant who mistakenly handed his credit card to the passenger on his right. When he jetted from there to Kansas City on Thursday, he snapped at the cabbie whose sensible driving made him five minutes late for his appointment.

And when he returned to New York on Friday, Katia wouldn't see him. Only for business, she said. But they could talk business over dinner, he argued. Only in the office, she insisted. But she had to eat, he pointed out. She had a date, she said, then hung up the phone.

It was only after a weekend that came closer to hell than any he had ever known that Jordan made the concession he had fought and fought for years. He flew up to Boston to see his father.

Oh, they had been together many times in the course of those years, but never to talk, as Jordan needed to now. There were some things on which he and his father had never seen eye to eye; rather than argue, as they had done once, they had taken to skirting around each other. But Jordan knew the time for that was done. Even if his question brought on the most vicious of arguments, the answer he sought was worth it.

Jack Whyte was not the easiest man to find. He never had been, which irritated Jordan every time he thought about it, but it appeared that not even age had slowed the old man down. He

wasn't in his office when Jordan arrived. Nor was he in conference, or at an appointment, or at the men's club, or at the barber
shop. Jordan half suspected that he was at the Bradford, screwing
a dim-witted redhead with mammoth boobs. But he wasn't.

He was, Nick informed Jordan, only after the latter had threatened the staff at the Whyte Estate headquarters with mayhem, in
the Public Garden feeding peanuts to the ducks.

It wasn't quite the setting Jordan had imagined for a show-
down, but it would have to do. He had come too far and gone
through too much grief to postpone the inevitable for so much as
an hour.

What Jordan saw, though, as he entered the Garden from Arlington Street and approached the bench that, according to Nick
and unbeknownst to the public, Jack Whyte had been regularly
occupying for the past seven weeks, was a sad and lonely man.
Jordan stopped for a minute to stare, finding it hard to identify
this figure with the tall, straight-shouldered man he had seen a
week earlier.

This man sat alone. There were no grandchildren on his lap,
as there were on the laps of several senior citizens sitting on
benches across the pond. There was no laughter on his face, no
spirit in his eyes. A fall breeze whipped through his hair, but he
didn't seem to notice, or if he did he lacked the strength or will to
repair the damage, as he would have done in the past. Jack Whyte
was proud of his appearance, his reputation, his status; this man
seemed not to care at all.

Against his will Jordan felt a stab of compassion. This was his
father. There were many things about the man that he didn't like,
but he did love him.

But he loved Katia, too. So he pressed his body into motion,
walking on until he came to the bench. Jack didn't see him at first.
His eyes were focused blindly on the ducks in the nearby water.
His hand was buried in a small bag of peanuts, but it was as un-
moving as the rest of him.

Then, apparently sensing more than a passing presence, he

looked up. His eyes widened when he recognized Jordan, and his posture straightened instantly. A faint tinge of red brushed across his cheeks and he scowled.

Jordan didn't think he had ever seen his father embarrassed before. For all the times he might have wished it, the reality made him more uneasy than he would have guessed. He shifted his stance.

"Nick told me where to find you."

"I didn't know you were in town." His tone was gruff.

"I just flew in."

"Business?"

"I wanted to see you."

"Don't worry," Jack snapped. "I'm not about to die tomorrow. Nick keeps telling me I ought to slow down. I think he's getting impatient to take over the reins." He paused, then grew wary. "What about you, Jordan? You never wanted anything to do with the Estate. What do *you* want from me?"

"An honest answer to a simple question."

Jack eyed him distrustfully, which was very sad when Jordan thought about it. "Sounds too easy."

"It's not. It's a tough question. A touchy one, given some of the things we've said to each other in the past."

Jack sighed, closed his eyes, and rocked his head from side to side as he spoke. "Yes, Jordan, I do love your mother. Yes, Jordan, I care about her. Yes, Jordan, I know that I haven't been a model of the faithful husband. Yes, Jordan, I know that I've hurt her." He opened his eyes. "There. Has one of those answers fit your 'simple' question?"

He obviously remembered their last touchy encounter as clearly as Jordan did. "No. I had another question in mind."

"If you're going to ask me to reform you're wasting your breath. Your mother and I came to terms with our relationship a long time ago. We're comfortable with it as it stands."

"I can't believe she is," Jordan retorted, "but that's neither here nor there. I haven't come here to discuss your relationship with Mother."

"Then why have you come?" Jack bit out. "Say it, boy. Ask your 'simple' question."

Jordan turned his head and stared off toward the far curve of the pond. His father was always impatient with him. He wondered if his decision to shun the Estate had had such a profound effect on the man that it still lingered. But that too was neither here nor there.

Retraining his gaze on his father, Jordan spoke evenly. "Are you Katia Morell's father?"

Jack's eyes flinched, but there was no other change in his stern expression. "What brought *that* on?"

"I need to know," Jordan answered in the same even tone, but there was a sinking feeling inside him. Jack hadn't denied it.

"Why?"

"Because I love her, and I can't do anything about it if she's my half-sister."

Jack seemed to take that confession in stride. His gaze didn't waver from Jordan's face. "Henry was her father."

"I'm talking biological."

"What makes you think Henry wasn't that?"

"I just know it. She's too good."

"Now that's a bigoted statement if I've ever heard one."

"And who did I learn it from?"

"So we're back to slinging insults?" Another reference to their last argument.

"You started it. I'm just pointing out the facts."

"I am not a bigoted man," Jack stated with indignance.

"Perhaps not. But that doesn't mean you haven't made your share of crude statements over the years." Abruptly he grimaced in disgust. "Ah, hell, I don't want to get into this. I'm not putting down what Henry was, just saying that Katia's different."

"Cassie's different. Maybe Katia takes everything she has from her mother."

But Jordan was shaking his head. "No. There are other things. Katia's sharp. She's outgoing and ambitious—"

"So Cassie instilled that ambition in her. And she grew up with the rest of you. She caught on to what it takes to be successful."

Jack was saying nothing more than Jordan had himself said that day in Maine after the funeral. He'd been trying to pacify Peter then. His instincts told him that his father was trying to do the same to him now.

"There's more," Jordan argued, but he had slid down onto the bench, albeit leaving a generous space between Jack and himself. "Take Henry. He was never overly warm to Katia. Kenny, yes. I can remember that well. But I can't remember one instance in which Henry held Katia, or hugged her, or took her aside and spent time with her."

"That was Henry's problem. Things had started going downhill for him by then."

"And why was that? Hasn't it occurred to you that he started to drink soon after Katia was born? Isn't that a strange coincidence?"

Jack blinked, but that was all. "None of us know what was going through Henry's mind. The guy was strictly lower working class."

"Bigoted statement," Jordan muttered under his breath.

Fortunately, Jack missed it. He was lost in his own thoughts. "I never could quite figure him out. He went along for the ride, I guess. Cassie had already become indispensible to the Warrens by the time she married him. He must have walked through those years in her shadow. Poor bugger. I don't envy any man who has to do that."

"Chauvinistic statement," Jordan muttered, again under his breath.

Jack wasn't so lost this time. He turned on Jordan with one gray brow arched high. "Would *you* want to do that? Do you want *your* wife to wear the pants in the family?"

"I don't have a wife, which brings me back to my original question—"

"Don't change the subject. We were talking about Henry. And I was about to say that, for all we know, the man might have made something of his life if he hadn't married Cassie. If he'd been forced to stand on his own two feet, if he'd had a wife who depended on him for food and clothes and companionship—but he didn't. Cassie's life was the Warren household. She worked far harder than he did and earned the bulk of the money they took in. As far as industriousness goes, Cassie had more than enough to pass on to her daughter."

Jordan was growing impatient. "Are you or are you not Katia's father?"

"Are you accusing Cassie of being unfaithful to Henry?"

"That's exactly what I'm doing."

"And you think *I'd* be attracted to Cassie?" He laughed, but it was definitely forced and therefore worried Jordan all the more.

"Cassie is a very lovely woman."

"In her little frocks, with her little white gloves on, walking through a room full of guests carrying a silver platter neatly lined with hors d'oeuvres. . . ."

"You've done worse," Jordan said. He resented Jack demeaning Cassie.

"Ah. So we're back to that."

"No, we're not back to that—"

"This is ridiculous, Jordan! Do you really think that I'd sneak off in the middle of the night, tiptoe through the orchard, steal into Cassie's cottage and take her with her husband lying there watching?" He held up a hand. "No. Don't say it. You pictured something more like a little tryst in the stable. Or," his eyes widened, brimming with mock-horror, "even rape? Maybe *that* thought turns you on."

"It doesn't."

"But you thought—"

"Rape didn't even enter my mind. Now that you mention it, though—"

"Forget I did," Jack growled, crushing the bag of peanuts in his hand. "I have never had to resort to rape."

"Your women are willing. I know."

"Aren't yours? Don't tell me that I didn't pass a *little* bit of masculine charm down to you?"

Pressing the heel of his hand to his forehead, Jordan shook his head slowly. "God, I don't believe this discussion." The eyes he turned on his father were angry. "This is irrelevant! All of it! I just want you to tell me whether or not you're Katia's father. Is that so difficult? Yes or no—that's all I want to hear!"

Jack's voice was as steady as the gaze he leveled at his son. "Why are you asking *me* this? That's what I want to know."

"Because I heard you talking once," Jordan began, offering the one thing that he knew would force his father to take a stand. "It was eleven years ago, when Katia was first starting college. You were in the den with Gil—"

"You eavesdropped on a private conversation?"

"I didn't know it was private, and I didn't maliciously eavesdrop. But you were talking about Katia, so I stood there for a minute because even then everything that concerned her concerned me."

"What was I saying?" Jack asked cautiously.

"You were saying that she should be taken care of. Always. You were saying that Henry, the damn fool—to quote you—hadn't had a penny to leave her, but that that wasn't surprising, given the facts."

"Which you interpreted to mean that he wasn't her father?"

Jordan ignored what he considered to be one more attempt at diversion. "You said," he went on, "that she had good blood in her on both sides, and that if she was to fulfill her potential and make us proud she shouldn't have to worry about things like living expenses or her mother's finances. When Gil pointed out that Katia had already gotten a scholarship you said that we'd just have to compensate for it, that we owed her a responsibility, that—" he paused, then took a breath, "that it was sad enough that her name was Morell when she could have been fully sharing the glory. You *said*," his eyes narrowed in accusation, "that it was a shame she'd never know the truth."

Jack's hesitation was minimal. He was determined to retain the upper hand. "And from that you deduced the truth to be that I was her father?"

"Yes!" In a flash, Jordan recalled the many times growing up when he had been called to the carpet by his father. The situations may have been different—a mediocre report card, an ongoing *thing* with a less-than-reputable girl, a hefty repair bill for the interior of the car that had been ruined when the convertible top had been put down for the sheer joy of riding in the rain—but the defensiveness he felt was the same. He resented it. He was no longer a boy. And the way his father was looking at him made him feel as though he had misinterpreted everything. Which, if it was true, meant that he had lived through eleven years of unnecessary agony and that he had caused much of the same for Katia.

He drew in a shuddering breath as he faced his father. "Is it true?" he asked wearily.

"Eleven years. Why have you waited so long to ask?"

"I didn't think it mattered that much at first. Katia was young. So was I, relatively speaking. I assumed we'd both find other partners, so if it turned out that we were related it wouldn't have been important. Maybe I thought it was puppy love at first, but it survived the years she was with Sean and it's grown. There's been no one else—"

"Come on, Jordan. I know damn well you're no monk."

"Christ, can't you get your mind out of the bedroom?"

"Watch your mouth. I'm still your father."

"And I'm only trying to answer the question you asked," Jordan stated, using every one of his resources to curb his temper. "Sure, I've had my share of women—"

"Your share," Jack snorted facetiously.

"Yes, my share," Jordan returned, passing up the opportunity to make a remark about being a chip off the old block because he knew it wouldn't accomplish anything. "But there's never been one I loved like I love Katia, and you can make fun of that if you want, but it's the truth. And maybe it was Mark's death that brought it all home and suddenly made me impatient—I don't know. I might have come to you sooner if it hadn't been for the disagreements we've had. You know what I think of your lifestyle. And now, basically, I'm accusing you—again—of being unfaithful. But, damn it, I don't care about your philandering anymore. All I care about is Katia."

Jordan had been so emotionally consumed by his monologue that he hadn't noticed the change in his father's face. "Do you miss Mark?" Jack asked. There was no anger, no indignance. Just sadness.

It took Jordan a minute to adjust. "Of course I do."

"So do I. We were never close. I didn't understand him. Maybe I didn't try. But he shouldn't have died that way. No human being should die that way."

Jordan looked at his hands and flexed one. "I know," he said quietly.

"Your mother's taken it hard," Jack went on. His voice was distant, as was his gaze. "I try to talk to her about it, but she's angry, and I guess I can't blame her. I thought I was doing the right thing—working hard, building up the business, providing for my family in the only way I knew how."

He looked at Jordan then. "You don't know what it's like to grow up with nothing. I do. We had to save and scrimp for every blessed thing we had. My father may have been clever, but most of what he earned he pissed away in hush money. He was a crook—a clever one, but a crook. I was sixteen when I literally took over the business." He gave a skewed smile. "You didn't know that, did you?"

Jordan shook his head.

"No one does, and it's a damn good thing. The old man was running bootleg liquor and I was handling the finances. I let him fly his planes and pay his hush money, but I stashed an equal amount away without him knowing it. Part of it went to my mother to buy the things we needed, part of it went into a kitty for college, and part of it went into an account I planned to use when I'd graduated and *really* taken over. It wasn't all that much money, but it was enough for a start."

He cleared his throat, then went on. "My father, rest his pathetic soul, couldn't see beyond a single day. If I hadn't taken over the business, and if he were alive today, he'd probably be doing penny ante drug running from South America. The poor schnook could have been living high off the hog as a major drug retailer here if he'd had the brains."

"You should be grateful he didn't."

"I suppose," Jack mused. "If it hadn't been for your mother, God only knows what he would have done with the business while I was off fighting the war."

"She's a good manager."

"She's a good person. This thing with Mark shouldn't have happened. If I could make it up to her somehow I would."

"I don't think she needs another car. The Mercedes is less than a year old."

The look Jack shot him was caustic. "God, you do think the worst of me, don't you?"

"I only think what I've been led to think." Since this was supposed to be an honest conversation . . . "You define happiness in terms of material goods and holdings. And power."

"You don't seem to be doing so bad along those lines. I don't see *you* donating your entire salary to the Ethiopian Relief Fund."

"I give to charities."

"But you live damn well. Don't try to deny it, Jordan. I can see the clothes you wear, the car you drive. And I've seen that fancy condo of yours in New York. You spend what you want where you want. You're not hurting."

"Not in the material sense."

"Ahh. That's right. You're lovesick."

The muscle high in Jordan's cheek jerked. "And you still haven't given me an answer."

Once more, though, Jack posed a question of his own. "What about Katia? What does she feel about all this?"

"All what?"

"Does she love you the way you love her?"

"I think so."

"She's never said anything?"

"Not in words."

"She doesn't think of you as a brother?"

Jordan hesitated for a split second, then shook his head.

"Have you discussed it with her?"

His eyes widened. "The possibility of our being related? Hell, no! How can I suggest that her mother was unfaithful to Henry? Or that the man she thought was her father wasn't? She may not have been close to Henry—and she may not even have been aware that he treated her any differently than he did Kenny, because all that happened before she was born—but she's never gone looking for reasons. At least, not that I know of."

"Maybe she's the one who's right," Jack said with a shrug. "Maybe she's simply accepted Henry for what he was and gone on with her life."

"But her life—and *my* life—are hinging on what Henry was or wasn't! Can't you see that? Why can't you just look me in the eye and give me a straight answer? It'll never go any further than me. If you tell me that Katia and I are related by blood I'll have to accept it and steer clear. If we're not, I can go on seeing her. In either case she'll never know that we had this discussion."

"If you were to suddenly stop seeing her, wouldn't she wonder?"

"Are you saying it's true?"

"I'm simply asking a question. Wouldn't she grow suspicious?"

"No more so than she is right now." He drew his open hand down his face and left it to mute his voice. "I swear, she must think I'm a eunuch."

Muted or not, Jack heard every word. He had the gall to laugh. "A eunuch? No son of *mine* is a eunuch." He sobered abruptly. "Have you tried it with her? Tried it—and couldn't make it?"

Jordan removed his hand from his face to place it rigidly on his thigh. "I don't think that's any of your business."

"It sure as hell is. I don't want that girl hurt. If something like that happened she might think there was something wrong with *her*."

"There's nothing wrong with her, and there's nothing wrong with me," Jordan muttered. "No, I haven't 'tried it' with her. I've come close, but each time I wondered if I'd be making love to my own sister." His face grew red, but from frustration rather than embarrassment. "Would I have been? *Answer me, damn it!*"

"No. You wouldn't have been."

It came so quietly and with so little fanfare after such a prolonged debate that at first Jordan wasn't sure he had heard right. "Excuse me?"

"Katia is not your sister."

He had heard right, but he was afraid to believe it. "You're not her father?"

"No."

The tight black glove around his heart began to loosen. "Are you sure?"

"For God's sake, Jordan," Jack scoffed, "I'm not *that* indiscriminate that I make love blindfolded! I have never made love to Cassie Morell. Period. That's it."

"That's it?" Jordan's voice was an octave higher than usual, and a slow smile was dawning on his face.

Jack cast his gaze heavenward. "God help me. He's either deaf or stupid or impossibly stubborn."

At that moment Jordan didn't care what names his father called him. He felt as though the life sentence he had been given so many years before had just been commuted. With a drawn out sigh of relief he stretched his legs out and lounged back against the bench. Not even the hard wood could make a dent in his euphoria.

"An imbecile," Jack was saying, scowling sidelong at his son. "But so help me, if I've given you the go-ahead to do what you want with her, what you want had better be good. That girl deserves a kind husband and a good home. I don't want to see her get anything else. And if she says that she loves you too, and if you two decide to get married, if I *ever* hear that you've been un-faithful to her, I'll *personally* see that you're whipped."

"Double standard?" Jordan mused. His head was back, his eyes shut. He was thinking of the irony of his father, who had cheated on his mother for years, making such a statement.

Jack followed his thoughts precisely. "Where Katia's concerned, yes. I feel that way about Anne, and I feel that way about Katia. Even if she's *not* my own daughter," he tacked on for good measure, but that good measure brought one of Jordan's eyes open a slit.

"Whose daughter is she?" he asked nonchalantly.

His father's response was equally as nonchalant. "Henry's."

"Then why would you feel a responsibility toward her?"

"Because she's been practically a member of the family since the day she was born. Because she's a lovely girl. Because your mother loves her. Because *her* mother helped us out many times. Because—"

"All right," Jordan interrupted with a raised palm and a grin. "I get the point." For the moment, he did. He didn't believe for a minute that his father actually thought Henry could sire as fine a person as Katia, but it was enough to know that he was free, that she was free, that they were free . . . so hard to believe. "You are telling me the truth, aren't you?" he asked in the last flicker of a fading skepticism. "There is no blood relationship between Katia and me?"

Jack pushed himself up from the bench. "I have to get back to work," he growled, "and I've already answered your question. If you want to sit here asking it a dozen times more, I'm sure the birds and ducks and squirrels would love to listen."

With that he turned his back and set off for Arlington Street, leaving Jordan to savor the sweet smell of freedom.

Robert Cavanaugh was feeling distinctly boxed in. The room—a private screening room on the ground floor of Mark

Whyte's Beverly Hills home—was dark. It was stuffy, thanks to the cigarette that Sharon Webber had only moments before stubbed out. It was warm, since the central air had been off until they had arrived two hours before.

"Okay," he sighed, uncrossing his knees and pushing himself from his chair. "Let's label that one and take a look at the next." He ejected the VCR tape from its slot, tossed it to Sharon, then knelt and fished a new one from the random assortment in the slide projector case.

A slide projector case. Who would have thought that it hadn't contained a slide projector? He had come across it late the afternoon before, after he and Sharon had spent hours searching the house for something they might have overlooked. Ryan had been right, damn him. There *were* tapes. Private tapes. Whyte must have had the same delusions of grandeur Nixon had had. Either that or he had been obsessed with his trade. He had filmed any number of private exchanges in his home—in the living room, the bedroom, the kitchen.

Personally, Cavanaugh couldn't understand why his guests had allowed it. There was enough incriminating evidence on the tapes to send more than a dozen people to the can on cocaine charges alone. He could only conclude that they hadn't known they were being filmed, which was incredible to Cavanaugh, who was uncomfortable whenever a camera was aimed his way, but also made some sense given the personalities involved. These people were every bit as arrogant as Mark Whyte must have been. They loved being filmed. They loved flaunting the law.

But wouldn't they have been worried by such concrete evidence of felony? Wouldn't they have wanted to get their hands on the tapes, if not before, then after Mark's death? Granted, Mark's hiding place had been clever. But wouldn't they have ransacked the house in their search?

Apparently they hadn't known the tapes existed, which, the more Cavanaugh thought about it, could be rationalized. With a guy like Mark, a filmmaker by profession, the presence of a tripod-mounted camera in the room might well have been taken for granted. It was a silent participant. No one had to know that the film was running.

Mark Whyte may have known that the tapes gave him the power to wheel and deal with the cops if he was ever arrested himself, but he had evidently kept that knowledge to himself. So far, Cavanaugh recognized the faces on the tapes as belonging to people that either he or Sharon or Buddy had interviewed. There were airtight alibis all around. Coupling that fact with the absence of any signs that someone had come after the tapes, Cavanaugh had to assume that neither the existence of the tapes nor their contents were related to the murders.

Of course, Deborah had to have known about the tapes, Cavanaugh mused. But even if she had been disturbed by their existence, even if she had argued with Mark about them, even if she had threatened to use them in some context herself, there was no reason why Mark would have resorted to murder. He could have simply destroyed or erased what he had so clandestinely captured on film.

With more force than necessary he shoved the next cassette into the machine, then stepped back, sank into his chair, propped his elbow on its arm and his fist against his mouth.

"This is getting pretty boring," Sharon said, shifting in her own seat. "Do you really think we'll find anything?"

"Dunno." His reply was muffled. "Maybe."

The oversized television screen lit up then, and they both focused on the picture. After several minutes, Cavanaugh gave a growl of disgust. "An orgy. I don't believe it. Of all the fuckin' stupid things to film."

Sharon smiled. "Sit back and enjoy it. The kiddie things were worse. And be grateful Scrumfitz isn't here. He'd be putting on a show of his own."

Cavanaugh snickered. Scrumfitz was the lecher of the department. With antennas attuned to anything and everything sexual, he knew the minute the latest newly seized smut tape began to roll. With uncanny precision he homed in on the interrogation room being used for the showing. He sat back and stared. While other cops offered ribald comments, he never said a word. Just squirmed. And breathed hard. Then raced for the men's room the minute the show was done.

Scrumfitz would have enjoyed this one. Naked bodies were everywhere, a writhing mass of arms, legs, buttocks and breasts.

"Recognize any of 'em?" Cavanaugh joked against his fist.

"Hard to see faces when there's so much else."

"You've been away from home too long, Shar. When this is over you'll have to take that husband of yours and lock yourselves into a suite at the—" He sat forward. "Who is that?"

"Which one?"

Snatching up the remote control, he rewound the tape for several seconds, then let it roll again. "The brunette . . . there . . . way on the right, with the dark-skinned guy."

"Like her looks?" Sharon teased.

"She looks familiar. Have we seen her somewhere?"

"We haven't interviewed her."

"Maybe she's been on TV, or in a commercial?" He repeated the rewind-advance sequence. "I feel like I ought to be able to place her, but I can't."

Sharon shrugged. "Just another pretty California face."

"Nothing rings a bell with you?" For a third and final time he replayed the scene.

"Nope."

"Okay," he sighed, letting the tape continue on, but holding the remote ready in his hand.

He didn't use it again. Not for that tape or the two that followed. By the time the next tape was midway through he was too enthralled with what he witnessed to even think of the control, at least, not until the tape had run its course. Then he rewound the entire thing and played it a second time.

"Jordan told me he had argued with his brother," he said when the second showing was over. "That was putting it mildly."

Sharon reached back to switch on a light. "We've got a death threat, Bob. 'So help me,'" she quoted, "'if any of this gets out I'll kill you.' The tape will stand up in court. A jury will go for it."

Cavanaugh should have been elated, but he wasn't. He had come to respect Jordan. He could have sworn the man was being honest when he declared that he would never have lifted a finger against his brother.

"And his alibi's shaky," Sharon went on. "Jordan left his office at five-thirty on the night of the murders. No one knows where he was between that time and the time he showed up at the office at nine the next morning. That would have given him plenty of time to drive up to Boston, do his thing, then drive back."

Cavanaugh nodded slowly. Strangely he was thinking of Katia, of how she would be crushed to learn that Jordan had done anything deadly. Though Cavanaugh had meant what he had told Jordan, that he had no personal designs on her, he couldn't deny the protectiveness she inspired in him. He remembered that day at the funeral, how her hair had shielded her face, how she had looked up at Jordan with such pain in her eyes. . . .

"Well," he said, taking in a large breath, "it's a possibility."

"Possibility? It's the strongest thing we've come up with so far! Between that tape—"

"Words, Sharon. How many times have you been so furious at someone that you've threatened to kill him?"

Sharon paused, then pulled a face. "Sam and I talked about buying a new car last week. I told him that I'd kill him if he got a pickup. But it was just an expression, Bob. Sam didn't think any more of it than I did."

"But you've made my point."

"Come on. Buying a new car is slightly different than being run in for making vulgar films of kids."

"Still, people say things in anger that they don't really mean, especially to people they're close to. You can't get much closer than a brother. Jordan and Mark probably said the same thing to each other a million times while they were growing up."

"They're not growing up now. They're not arguing about who reached first base first or who called who a name or who was going to tell on who when a window broke." She pointed to the blank TV. "On that tape they're arguing about something very adult, very dangerous and potentially far-reaching. The motive is there, Bob. Between that tape and Jordan's questionable whereabouts at the time of the murder we could have him cold."

"Circumstantial evidence. We've got no one who saw a thing on or near the boat that night."

"Many a conviction has been based on circumstantial evidence."

Cavanaugh looked at Sharon. "You're pushing it."

She looked right back. "You're evading it."

"Uh-uh. I'm only trying to give the guy the benefit of the doubt. There's still plenty of doubt here."

"There's always doubt. But *reasonable* doubt? A jury will have to decide whether what we've got goes beyond that."

He rose from his chair and headed for the VCR. "Right. But we're not at that stage yet. There are still," he rummaged through the slide projector box, "five more cassettes in here. I think we ought to see them through."

Sharon shrugged, let out a long sigh, then reached for a cigarette. "It's your game. You're the one who's calling the shots."

Unfortunately, Cavanaugh knew that wasn't completely true. When push came to shove, Ryan had to be considered. He would have to see the tape, though Cavanaugh knew what his reaction would be. Unless he came up with something else soon, Cavanaugh feared that the Whytes and Warrens were in store for far greater pain than that which Jordan, for one, maintained they were feeling now.

Chapter 14

HENRY MORELL'S DEATH wasn't Cassie's only source of grief in 1965. The war in Vietnam had begun to heat up, and her reaction to it was visceral. Her stomach knotted during the evening news; her palms grew moist over the morning paper. She suffered flashes of memory—leaving home in the darkness, running from one hiding place to another, fearing for those left behind, terrified of what was ahead—and she identified with the peasant families who were feeling the brunt of the conflict.

The Warrens weren't. Nor were the Whytes. Gil carried clout with the head of the local draft board, who had guaranteed him that, even when their student deferments expired, none of the Whyte or Warren boys would be called to service.

Natalie was greatly relieved. Nick was twenty-four and in business school, with every intention of joining the Whyte Estate when he graduated. Mark, at twenty-three, had a degree from Haverford under his belt, but was floating from one bohemian colony to the next, trying to decide what to do. She found his lack of direction worrisome enough; she was grateful not to have to worry about his being trundled off to war. As for Jordan, he was nineteen and a sophomore at Duke; she didn't mind that he was living it up at his fraternity house, as long as he did it there rather than in a seedy bar in Saigon.

Lenore worried about Peter incessantly. It didn't matter that

Gil had assured her he would never be drafted; she feared it nonetheless. He was twenty-one and still in school, but she was convinced that the day after graduation he would be taken from her. His thick, brown hair would be reduced to a pathetic crew cut. He would be forced to dress and act exactly like every other draftee. And, like Ben, he would die without her being able to do a thing to prevent it.

Her fears were heightened all the more when, at the end of the first semester of his senior year, a call came through from one of the Dartmouth deans that Peter had been caught cheating on an exam. The first thing she did was pour herself another scotch; the fact that it was her third of the day was irrelevant to her pressing need for it. The second thing she did was place a frantic call to Gil in Washington to give him the news. The third thing she did was go to bed.

Gil handled the problem with characteristic finesse. He spent the rest of the day on the phone, first with the dean who had originally called Lenore, then with several other deans, then with the professor of the course in question, then with Peter. Gil vehemently agreed that Peter should be penalized by having to retake the exam and, even then, receiving a significantly lowered grade in the course. He whipped out his checkbook and sent off a sizable donation to the faculty endowment fund. Then he called Lenore to tell her that the mess had been very neatly cleaned up.

Cassie, who was quite naturally biased, believed that Gil had done the right thing. Peter was young. He had made a mistake which, given the fright he had had, he was sure not to make again. She could only hope that Kenny would be either smarter or as lucky.

Kenny was a junior in high school, and she was concerned about him. Since his father's death he had been different. He didn't talk with her as he used to, and though Natalie assured her that withdrawal was common, even necessary, in teenagers, Cassie was uneasy.

Kenny had been shocked to learn that she had been born a

Jew. When he had been younger and had asked about her child-hood, she had told him about her early days in France without any particular mention of religion and she had been truthful up to the point of the reason for her flight. Then she had claimed that economic conditions had brought her to America; only after Henry died had she told her children the truth. She explained that she hadn't wanted them to worry, to think that the same thing could happen to them, for it couldn't, she assured them. They were Americans, and they were free.

Kenny had studied the horrors of the Third Reich in school. Though Cassie hadn't dwelt on the details of her own story or the fate of those she had loved, she sensed that Kenny had taken as much from what she hadn't said as from what she had. He knew that she detested war; he also knew, despite her disclaimers, that she was slightly paranoid. Her greatest fear was that, out of spite, he would graduate from high school and promptly enlist.

In an attempt to prevent that from happening she began to talk of college, to push it far earlier than many of Kenny's friends' parents did. Through it all, though, she sensed that Kenny was merely going through the motions of listening. His mind was else-where. She didn't know where, and it drove her to distraction. She had dreams of her son becoming a lawyer like Gil, or a business-man like Jack, or a prominent doctor, or a noted scholar. She wanted him to have power of his own, because only then would he be in command of his fate.

She breathed a great sigh of relief when, in the winter of his senior year, he finally submitted applications to Oberlin, Lehigh, American University and Brandeis.

Lenore wasn't breathing any sort of sigh of relief. Deborah claimed she didn't want to go to college at all. What she wanted to do, she said, was to be with Mark, who was at that time living in a commune just north of San Francisco. Lenore was horrified. She nagged Gil to talk with the girl, but it seemed that whenever Gil was home Deborah was out, and whenever Deborah was home Gil was in Washington. So Lenore drafted Natalie to sit down with

Deborah, but Natalie was in a bind, because she was desperately trying to convince herself that Mark's taking time to "find himself" was an important part of his growth. At wit's end, Lenore even enlisted Cassie, whom she knew felt much the same way she did about the importance of a college education. But Cassie struck out, too. In her own, rather wispy way Deborah was determined to do her own thing.

So, it appeared was Kenny. In June, 1967, several days before his high school graduation, he called Cassie from a pay phone at the airport to say that he was flying to Israel. He wouldn't be allowed to fight, he said with some regret, but he could help out on the sidelines. He felt that, as a citizen of Israel by heritage, he had an obligation, and that if the Israelis were as good as they were reputed to be, he'd be back in time to enter Lehigh in the fall. Before Cassie could do more than catch her breath, his money ran out and they were cut off.

It was the last time she ever heard his voice. Two weeks later, on a morning so sunny that Cassie was later to think God had been smirking at her, a telegram arrived saying that Kenny had been killed while shuttling supplies to troops on the Golan Heights.

Cassie stood on the doorstep of the stately Warren home in Dover and watched the Western Union car drive off. She didn't sway. She didn't cry. She just stood there, oblivious to the passage of time, until Lenore found her.

"Cassie?" She was coming down from her bedroom, slightly fuzzy from yesterday's drink, and paused, puzzled, on the stairs. "Was that a delivery?"

Cassie nodded, but otherwise didn't move.

So Lenore approached, looking for whatever it was that had arrived. She was expecting a sweater she had ordered from Bonwit's, but there was no sign of it, much less any other package. Then she spotted the yellow paper Cassie held. She took it—without effort, since Cassie's fingers were limp—and read it. Her fuzziness cleared instantly, but it was several minutes before she could speak.

"Oh, Cassie . . ." she whispered in sympathy. "Oh, Cassie, I'm sorry." Any grievances she might have had against the woman were momentarily forgotten. Lenore could easily substitute Peter's name for Kenny's and know precisely what Cassie was feeling. Indeed, in that instant she wouldn't even have fought Deborah's choice of a commune.

Slipping an arm around Cassie's waist she guided her from the doorway. It was the first physical gesture she had ever made toward Cassie, but Cassie was too crushed to appreciate it.

Lenore gently escorted her through the house to the back door, then over the gravel path to the cottage. Twice along the way she held up a silencing hand, once to the cook who was baking rolls in the kitchen, the second time to the laundress who was stretching freshly washed blankets across a line in the back yard.

Cassie refused to think, as though by shutting down her mind what she had read on the yellow piece of paper would be blotted out, erased, nullified. She let herself be led into the cottage, down the hall to the bedroom, then to the bed itself. She sat down at Lenore's urging, lay back at Lenore's urging, closed her eyes at Lenore's urging.

But what had always worked so well for Lenore didn't work so well for Cassie. As soon as she closed her eyes her mind opened. So she quickly raised her lids and sat up to see Lenore standing by the door wringing her hands.

"Is there . . . is there anything I can do?" Lenore asked nervously. She had a headache. She needed a drink.

Cassie shook her head. Without a word she stood up and returned to the small living room where she awkwardly lowered herself into a chair and sat stiffly. Lenore, who had put the telegram on Cassie's dresser, followed her.

"Don't worry about work," she said hurriedly. "The others will take care of everything. You just rest."

Cassie nodded, her eyes wide, focused unseeingly on the floor.

"Katia will be home later."

Cassie nodded.

"Is there anyone you can call?"

Cassie shook her head.

"No friend or—" She was about to say minister, then realized that it would be a rabbi, then realized that, knowing Cassie, it wouldn't be anything at all. "Maybe I should call Gil—"

Cassie's head came up so fast that Lenore swallowed the word in her throat. But she knew that was the thing to do.

"Yes. I'll call Gil now," she said and practically ran from the cottage. She stumbled into the house and made straight for the den to put in the call.

Gil wasn't in his office. She babbled out a message, saying that there was an emergency at home and that he should return her call as soon as possible. After helping herself to a drink from the living room bar she returned to the den and waited.

It was nearly an hour before the phone rang. "Gil," she breathed when she heard his voice. "Thank God."

"What's happened?" he asked sternly. He had grown used to Lenore's frantic calls. On occasion they had concerned nothing more pressing than a pesty reporter or a mishap with the car, in which case he simply had to reassure her, or direct her to the proper insurance representative. On occasion they had required more of an effort, as had happened the summer before when Laura and Donald had been on their honeymoon and been stranded in Europe thanks to an airline strike. They had had to work back and forth with Jack until they had finally secured seats for the couple to return in time for the party celebrating the opening of Donald's new medical office.

"It's Cassie," Lenore said quickly. "She just got word that Kenny's been killed."

"*Killed?* In Israel? He wasn't supposed to be fighting!"

"He wasn't," she raced on. "He was helping move supplies to

the troops. I don't know what to do, Gil. Cassie's in the cottage, sitting in a chair staring at the floor. She won't cry. She barely talks—"

"Katia's still in school?"

"Yes."

"Good. Look, Lenore, I'm going to fly right up. I may not make it there before Katia gets home, and if I don't, I want you to catch her before she sees Cassie. Break the news to her gently. I'm asking—begging you—to do that—"

"I'm not an ogre, Gil—"

"I know that, and I do appreciate your calling me."

"Cassie didn't ask me to do it."

"She wouldn't. Is Natalie home?"

"She was going downtown to shop."

"Have her come over as soon as she gets back. Once you've told Katia, let her go to Cassie, but I want either you or Natalie to stay with them until I get there. Can you do that for me?" Unspoken was the promise of a reward for Lenore if she complied.

"Of course I can do it," Lenore snapped back, for once annoyed by the tit-for-tat nature of their relationship when she was trying to rise above the quarrels of the past and be humane.

"Good. I'll be there in a couple of hours."

True to his word, he was in Dover by mid-afternoon to take over. He talked softly with a very upset and confused eleven-year-old Katia, spoke with the representative from the Israeli consulate who came by to confirm Kenny's death, made arrangements to have Kenny's body returned to the States, and then, with Katia safely entrusted to Natalie, sat down with Cassie.

They didn't say much. Cassie hadn't moved from her chair. For a long time Gil simply squatted beside her, holding her cold hand, unsure if she even knew of his presence.

"Talk to me, Cassie," he said at last, but very, very softly. There hadn't been many times in his life when he had felt impotent, but this was definitely one. "You're bottling it all in."

"What good will talking do?" she asked in a hoarse whisper.

"He's gone." She took a truncated breath. "Just like my parents and Michel."

"They died for a cause. So did Kenny."

"No! It was a waste! He should never have gone! He's a citizen of *this* country!"

"But he felt an allegiance to Israel—"

She shook her head firmly. "He was rebelling. He was angry because I hadn't told him sooner."

"No. He felt *called* upon to do what he did. He was a man—"

"He wasn't even eighteen. He must have lied to get over there."

"But he was acting as a man, doing what he thought was right."

"He was too young to know what was right and what wasn't." The harsh sound she made didn't come near to qualifying as a laugh, though its sarcasm came through loud and clear. "And I was worried about Vietnam. . . ."

"Cassie, Cassie, don't do this to yourself. You raised a wonderful boy whose heart was in the right place. You should be proud that he died doing something that meant the world to him."

"He was a little boy jumping on a bandwagon." Her composure began to crumble. "He must have thought it would be an exciting thing to do."

"He thought it was the *right* thing to do. And it doesn't matter what you think or what I think or what anyone else in the world thinks, Cassie, but if Kenny believed in what he was doing—even in his little boy's mind—then that's all that matters."

Sucking in an uneven breath, Cassie lay her head back against the chair. When she didn't say anything further, Gil could only hope that she was thinking about what he had said.

"Can I do anything for you?" he murmured helplessly.

Cassie's eyes remained closed. "Katia. Where is Katia?"

"With Natalie."

"I want her." Her voice cracked. "Will you bring her here?"

"Right now." He wanted to ask about the funeral arrangements, because he had every intention of making them for her, but he knew that it was too early for her to think about that. It would be several days, at least, before the body made it back home. They had time. "I'll stay in Dover for the rest of the week—"

"You'll be needed in Washington."

"I have aides to take care of things there. This is important."

"But Lenore—"

"Lenore was the one who called me. She understands that you're alone. She'll do anything she can to help." He straightened and looked down at her. "You've been good to both of us over the years, Cassie. Just tell us what to do."

For the first time in the twelve years that had elapsed since Ben's death, Cassie held out her hand to Gil. It was a small gesture, the only way she could thank him for being there. Holding his hand, she looked up at him.

"Katia," she whispered. "Please."

So Gil went to get Katia and brought her to the cottage. He left mother and daughter alone to deal with their grief in whatever manner they could, but he remained available, returning to check up on them from time to time. He called the few friends Cassie had and saw that meals were brought to the cottage. At one point, while Cassie slept, he took Katia for a long walk in the woods.

When, very late that night, he returned to the main house, Lenore was waiting for him. "Is she all right?"

Gil shrugged, hands anchored in his trousers pockets. "She finally cried." Soft, soulful sobs while she held Katia to her breast. The heartrending image would stay with him forever. "She needed it."

"Is Katia asleep?"

"Yes." He had just come from the child's bedroom, where he had stood for a long, long time gazing down at her.

"And Cassie?"

"Not sleeping, but lying down."

Lenore looked down at the velvet sash of her robe, twisting it around and back with her fingers. "You can go to her," she whispered. "She needs you."

"No, Lenore," Gil said quietly. "Cassie doesn't need me—at least, not in that way." Indeed, he had offered himself moments before, wanting desperately to comfort her, but she had refused him with the saddest of smiles. "She's strong. She retreats into herself and finds what she needs there. I want to help with the funeral plans, though she could probably handle those on her own, too." He took a deep breath. "She's a very moral person. What happened between us after Ben's death was done for my benefit. Even if I'd gone back to her after that one night she probably would have turned me away. Cassie may love me, but she recognizes that you're my wife. She never meant to come between us."

In her heart Lenore knew that Cassie had been the least of the things to come between she and Gil. Granted, the one night in which Cassie had given herself—and its very concrete result— had been the weapon Lenore had needed to obtain what she needed, but she didn't hold Cassie to blame for the distance between Gil and her. No, there were other women. There was Gil's unremitting arrogance, his unfailing confidence. There was his greed for power, and his career.

And, if Lenore were truthful, there was her own insecurity. It had abated somewhat in the past few years. She felt economically stable now. But there was always the fear, always the fear that some disgrace would be visited upon the Warrens that would lead to their downfall. It had happened to Lenore once; she wasn't sure if she could survive it again.

The day after Kenny was buried Cassie returned to work. Gil and Lenore both protested, but she was vehement about picking up where she had left off. The fact that she didn't—from that time on she was less smiling and more stoical—was something that no one seemed able to remedy. But she ran the Warren household as capably as always and in that no one could find fault.

*   *   *

The sixties ended and the seventies began. Gil moved steadily into a position of congressional prominence, landing increasingly prestigious committee assignments, receiving more than his share of press attention. Lenore wasn't oblivious to the murmurings of a possible presidential run, but the murmurings never came from Gil. She often wondered why it was so; she would have assumed that he would grab for as much as he could get, and she fretted accordingly. But, lest she put a bug in his ear, she said nothing while he defended his seat every two years, seemingly content with the solid niche he was carving for himself in the House of Representatives.

Jack, meanwhile, was carving a similiar niche for himself in the Fortune 500. The Whyte Estate had become a large and powerful corporation. Its chain of hotels grew regularly, spreading through the country, then on into the Caribbean. The single plant for the production of television sets had spawned a network of plants producing micro-electronics and computers. And the airline, with its clever advertising and its frill-filled service, had become one of the nation's most prominent.

With the last of her children off to college, Natalie found she had more time on her hands than she knew what to do with. Jack rarely needed her. He was wrapped up in the world of business, spending no more than two or three days out of the week at home. Nick was working with him, but if Natalie had thought that her son's presence would free up her husband she had been wrong. Jack was busier than ever.

She had to give him credit; when Jordan had been playing ball he had made a point to attend every game. He had likewise made himself available for Anne's graduation and subsequent matriculation at Smith. But, other than an occasional dinner at the country club or a theater engagement or a party, he had little time for Natalie.

To counter the superfluity she was feeling Natalie became active in civic causes. She volunteered her time to work at the flower shop at the Deaconess, helped plan fundraisers for the

New England Home for Little Wanderers, became active on the board of the Museum of Fine Arts. If Jack made the occasional disparaging comment regarding the long-range usefulness of these endeavors she ignored them. She had discovered that it wasn't enough to have things and be someone. She needed to be needed.

Lenore didn't need to be needed as much as she needed to be loved. She came whenever Gil called, ostensibly because of the agreement they had made, but also because a small part of her still wanted to please him. She wanted to do the same for her children, but too often her nerves were her undoing. When Laura's toddlers contracted the chicken pox she hovered over them in such a state of worry that their faces would be permanently scarred that Laura finally sighed and sent her home. When Peter asked her to tutor his disgruntled wife on the fine points of living with a lawyer, Lenore could think of nothing to say and ended up simply treating the young woman to lunch at the Ritz. When Deborah became engaged to Mark Lenore bought them a complete set of Baccarat crystal, then went into near hysterics when they exchanged it for two Nikons and a camper. And when Anne came home from school madly in love with her math teacher, who was twenty-four, a notorious playboy and, by the way, married, Lenore was the one who went to bed.

Cassie watched it all quietly, aware of the remarkable irony of the situation. Lenore Warren and Natalie Whyte were regarded by the overall public as two of the luckiest women alive. Yet neither was totally happy. Neither had quite found what she had been seeking.

The public didn't know about the weeks of tension that plagued the Whytes in 1971 after Jordan informed his father that he was going out on his own.

"I won't walk in your shadow!" Jordan shouted when tamer reasoning had failed to produce results.

"Nick is part of the Estate, and he's not walking in my shadow!" Jack shouted right back.

"Like hell he's not!"

"Don't swear in front of your mother!"

"Why not? She's heard it from you often enough—"

"Natalie, can't you talk some sense into your son?"

"You do swear, Jack—"

"Not about swearing! About joining the business!"

Natalie found herself right in the middle. She ached for Jack, whose idea of an empire called for the involvement of his sons, but she also ached for Jordan, who had turned down acceptances at Yale and Columbia to play football at Duke, where he felt he had a chance of shining on his own, much as he wanted to do now. She was tied up in knots as the argument went on, and for days after, even when Jack had offered token surrender, she was torn.

The public didn't know, in 1972, of the behind-the-scenes maneuvering Gil had to do to bail Peter out of a land development scheme whose organizers, unbenownst to Peter, were connected with the Mob. Lenore knew, however, and for days she awaited word that a hit man had done his thing.

The public was totally unaware of the uproar in the Whyte home when, in 1973, Nick announced that he had decided to promote his most attractive secretary to the position of his administrative assistant. Jack's arguments against the move were so thorough and vehement that Natalie suspected he had either had or wanted the young woman for himself—and not in the capacity of administrative assistant.

In 1974 Emily Warren threw her family into a tailspin by taking up with the head waiter at a two star restaurant in New York, but the public didn't know about that, either, because while it added more gray hair to Gil's head than he cared to count, the affair was brief and hushed up. The waiter in question quite readily accepted a position at a four star restaurant in Dallas, leaving Lenore to explain to Emily why that restaurant in Dallas just happened to be in one of Jack Whyte's hotels.

The public did know, however, of the tragic airplane crash

that took the lives of a hundred and sixty-two people in 1975, and about the eventual finding by the FAA that weather conditions rather than negligence on the part of Trans-Continental Airways, as the Whyte Lines was now known, had been its cause.

The public also knew that Gil Warren won reelection in 1976 by his largest margin ever, and that in 1977 he played a backseat role in negotiation of the new Panama Canal treaties, and that in 1979 Whyte Electronics received a three-hundred-million-dollar contract for computer parts from the Air Force.

No one—not the public or Jack Whyte or Gil Warren or any of their offspring—knew, though, of what took place in the attic of the Warren home in Dover on a heavily overcast day in December of 1980. Cassie had been restocking the second floor linen closet when she noticed that the door to the attic was open. She went to close it, then paused and on impulse slowly began to climb the steps. What she saw at the top stopped her cold.

Surrounded by dusty cartons, used baby paraphernalia and beloved but crippled furniture was Lenore. She sat on an old chair, staring fixedly at her hands, and if she had heard the creak of the steps she made no sign.

"Mrs. Warren?" Cassie held her breath for a moment, but there was no response. "Are you all right?"

At first there was silence. Then, very slowly, Lenore raised her head. "I'm . . . not sure."

"Are you feeling ill?"

Lenore thought about that, then shook her head. "I just . . . came up here." She sent a disconsolate glance at the rafters. "My father died in an attic like this one." Her eyes fell to Cassie's. "He hung himself. Did you know that?"

Cassie shook her head. Her insides were quivering, and the fact that she saw no sign of a piece of rope or other potential noose in Lenore's hand was small solace. "Maybe you should come downstairs. It can't be healthy to be brooding about that."

"I can almost understand why he did it," Lenore rambled on, oblivious to Cassie's words. Her eyes were on the rafters again.

"He felt that he couldn't face tomorrow. It was sudden in his case. He'd been playing with fire for years, but he thought he'd never be burned. Then, in one shot he was. He couldn't handle the pain."

"You're much stronger than he was, Mrs. Warren," Cassie said with a calm she didn't feel. The fact that the woman might be considering suicide chilled her to the bone. "You've lived with pain and you've overcome it."

"Overcome? I don't know about that."

"Please, come downstairs. It's drafty here. I'll make you some hot tea—"

"I want a drink."

"There's plenty downstairs."

"Could you bring me something here? I'd appreciate that."

Cassie's mind was working quickly. She refused to leave Lenore alone, but she couldn't refuse the woman's order. Turning, she quickly descended the steps. At the bottom, she called out for the maid, who, if she was doing her job, would right about now be dusting Lenore's perfume tray. "Isabel? Isabel!"

The thin girl appeared at the doorway of the master bedroom.

"Isabel," Cassie instructed, her voice little more than a whisper, but filled with urgency, "I want you to go down to the kitchen. Call Mrs. Whyte and tell her that Mrs. Warren needs her right away. Then make a cup of tea with lemon and honey and bring it to me."

"Tay? Lemoon an howney?"

"Yes, girl. Tea—boiling water with a tea bag—no, just tell cook to do it—tea with lemon and honey. But call Mrs. Whyte first. The number is at the top of the list by the kitchen phone. This is *important*, Isabel. Can you do it?"

The girl nodded. "I do et," she said and ambled toward the stairs.

"Quickly!" Cassie whispered. "Run!"

Only when she was sure that the girl had increased her pace did Cassie hurry back to the attic. She feared what might have happened even in those few short minutes she had been gone, and breathed a small sigh of relief when she found Lenore still sitting in her chair.

"Isabel's gone for something to drink. She'll be back shortly."

Again it was as though Lenore hadn't heard her. "Do you know what it's like not to want to face another day, Cassie?"

In other circumstances Cassie might have been evasive. But she was determined to keep Lenore interested and talking. "Yes."

"Is that what you felt when Kenny died?"

"Yes. And when I learned what had happened to my parents and brother. I didn't think it was fair that I should have to live without them. I would have exchanged my life for Kenny's in a minute."

"But you didn't."

Sliding onto the corner of a carton, Cassie gave a one-shouldered shrug. "I couldn't. He was dead. Not even self-sacrifice would have brought him back."

"And you had Katia to live for." Lenore's eyes were on Cassie again, but Cassie ignored their sharpness.

"Just as you have Mr. Warren and your children and grandchildren."

"Ahh, but they don't need me. They're all involved in their own lives. I'm the one who's marching out of step." She frowned and spoke gruffly. "Where is that drink?"

Cassie wasn't as concerned about the drink as she was about Natalie. The more she talked with Lenore the more reassured she felt, because Lenore certainly wasn't catatonic and she didn't sound depressed to the point of self-destruction. Still, she was obviously disturbed. Once Natalie arrived Cassie would feel better. "Isabel will bring it."

"She's so slow, that girl. I sometimes wonder if she's on another planet."

"In another country sometimes, I fear," Cassie said more lightly. "But she'll be along. She's really a good girl."

Lenore sighed. "You do look to the brighter side of things."

"Do I have a choice? Do any of us? If we think only of the dark side we get nowhere."

"If there's nowhere to go it doesn't matter."

"You can't be talking about yourself, Mrs. Warren. You have a full life." Between the occasional trip to Washington and the more regular ones to Maine, not to mention local visits to Laura's house and Peter's house, Lenore was often on the go. Of course, she was often home, too.

Lenore moved her head in short shakes. "The children are all on their own. They have their own lives. I'm in the way."

"That's not true! You and Mr. Warren are the cornerstones of the family. Look at the Thanksgiving we just had. If either of you hadn't been there there would have been a void. And Christmas is coming up. It'll be the same then. The children may be on their own, but their lives are fuller knowing that they can always come home."

Lenore seemed to consider that for a minute, but when she spoke again it was on a different tangent. "Do you miss Katia?"

Cassie adjusted quickly. Though she hadn't often discussed her with Lenore, Katia was her favorite topic. "Very much. But she's busy, and she's happy."

"Mr. Warren wanted her to go to Washington."

"She needed to be on her own," Cassie explained, then offered a guilty half smile. "I'm afraid I coddled her for a long time."

"After Kenny's death, you mean?"

"It was hard not to. She was all I had. In some ways Kenny's death was harder for her later on than when it happened." She kept talking, buying time. "I wanted to protect her from grief, so I minimized it and tried to act as if nothing had happened. Only I couldn't pull it off. Katia knew that I was different and she was afraid to say anything for fear of upsetting me more. It was a full two years after that telegram came before she and I really talked about Kenny. She cried that night like I couldn't remember her ever having done." Her voice cracked. She had to take a deep breath before continuing. "After that I felt even stronger about protecting her from anything upsetting. Seeing her smile means the world to me."

"She is a happy girl," Lenore admitted quietly. "She has a kind streak in her." What Lenore might have said was that Katia had always been kind to *her*, even when given little encouragement. But she didn't say that, for it verged on thoughts better left unsaid.

"I tried," Cassie went on. "I wanted her to be kind and good and successful. I'm not sure she appreciated the nights I spent drumming the importance of studying and then working into her head. There were many times she would far rather have been out with her friends."

"Like Emily was."

"Katia adores Emily. She's glad they're in the same city now."

"I worry about Emily. She's so . . . impulsive."

"She's an actress. Isn't that part of the image?"

"I suppose, but still—"

"Lenore! Are you up there?"

Lenore recognized her friend's voice instantly. After sending a quick frown Cassie's way, she called back. "I'm here." Under her breath she muttered an impatient, "Where is Isabel?"

Then Natalie was at the top of the stairs, taking in the scene. Cassie tried to warn her with her eyes that Lenore was upset, but Natalie sensed it on her own. "What are you doing up here?" she asked gently. She extended the cup and saucer she held in her hand.

"What's this?" Lenore asked, regarding the innocuous drink as though it were poison.

"Tea. Isabel sent me up with it."

"I wanted a drink. Not . . . *this*."

"You do *not* want a drink, Lenore. You haven't had a drop in two years and you don't want one now." She thrust the cup and saucer toward Lenore, who had the choice of taking it or being scalded when Natalie plunked it on her lap. She took it.

"I just wanted a little something, Nat," she simpered. "It wouldn't hurt."

"It *would* hurt," Natalie insisted softly. "One little something would lead to another little something, which would lead to more of something, and before you knew it you'd be right back up there. Come on, Lenore," she coaxed, lowering herself to a carton on the opposite side of Lenore from that on which Cassie sat, "you spent six weeks drying out, and you felt so much better about yourself afterward. Do you really want a drink that badly that you're willing to undo all you've done since?"

Cassie, who was well aware of the treatment Lenore had undergone, even if no one outside the immediate circle of Warrens and Whytes knew of it, was beginning to feel uncomfortable. With Natalie there her presence was unneeded. But when she started to rise, Lenore caught her wrist. "Don't go, Cassie. I'm not sure I can handle this woman on my own."

A touch of humor. Cassie felt better. "Of course you can," she said with mock sternness. "We may not always agree with her, but Mrs. Whyte has a good heart. Indulge her. And drink your tea." Again she made to leave, but it was Natalie this time who stayed her.

"Don't go, Cassie. Tell me what you and Mrs. Warren were discussing."

"We were discussing," Lenore began boldly, "my daughter Emily and her impulsiveness. But now that I think of it, she's no worse than the others. Peter is as arrogant as they come. He's already dumped one wife, and if he doesn't get off that high horse of his his second will dump *him*. And Deborah—good Lord, is she ditzy. There are times when I wonder whether the hospital switched babies on me. She's so *odd!*"

Natalie laughed.

"It's not funny," Lenore argued. "Are my feelings about Deborah any different than yours about Mark?"

"My feelings are the same as yours," Natalie replied.

"And doesn't it upset you?"

"Of course it does. But there's absolutely nothing I can do about Mark. He has a mind of his own and a life of his own. If I were to try to change him, it would only drive him away, and he's far away enough already."

"Then you're happy with the status quo?"

"Happy? No. I wish things were different, at least where Mark is concerned."

"What about the others?" Lenore asked with a hint of belligerence.

It had become a free-for-all, Cassie mused, and she wasn't sorry. Lenore needed to spout off much more than she had ever needed to drink.

"Do they give you pleasure?" Lenore was demanding.

Natalie considered that for a minute. "Overall, yes."

"And that's why you have to bury yourself in causes?"

"I don't *have* to. I *want* to. I could be sitting around feeling sorry for myself like you are, but—"

"Feeling sorry for yourself?" Lenore interrupted her. "Why?"

Natalie gave a tiny toss of her head. "There's always something. Life isn't perfect. Take Nicholas. He's married now, the perfect picture of the family man, but do you honestly think he doesn't still have his eye peeled for a shapely pair of legs?"

"He's not fooling around behind Angie's back, is he?" Lenore's voice was low, secretive, almost excited.

"I don't know. So I worry. I think I'd feel better if his hair began to thin, or if he developed a pot belly." She took a quick breath. "And then there's Jordan. He doesn't show *any* signs of wanting to settle down. Instead, what does he do? He does crazy things with his business. One minute it looks like he'll lose it all, and I can see Jack sitting in his office waiting to say, 'Ah-ha, I told you so!' The next minute he salvages everything. And through it I sit chewing my nails."

Cassie saw that for the figure of speech it was. Natalie had beautiful nails—long, well shaped, manicured on a weekly basis. Much like Lenore's.

"But you have Anne," Lenore pointed out. "She has to be rewarding for you and Jack."

"And you have Laura. I could say the same thing there."

"Laura is exactly like me. She's boring."

"You are not boring. You're well read. You're knowledgeable about what's happening in the world. You're charming and per-sonable—that is, when you're not wallowing in self-pity."

"Is that what I'm doing now?"

"Yes."

Lenore turned to Cassie. "Am I wallowing in self-pity?"

Cassie drew back. "I really shouldn't be here."

"Yes you should," Lenore returned crossly. "You know as much, if not more, about this family than anyone does. So I want you to tell me—honestly—if you think I'm wallowing in self-pity."

"I, well, you do have some legitimate concerns—"

"*Am* I wallowing in self-pity?"

Cassie took a breath. "Yes."

"Thank you," Lenore said firmly, then looked from Natalie to Cassie and back. "Why is it that neither of you are doing it? God only knows you've both got the right."

"No one has that right," Cassie said softly.

Natalie agreed. "It's counterproductive."

"Counterproductive to *what*? What else is there?"

"You have to *do* something," Natalie said. "Cassie and I have things to keep us occupied. If you had something to wake up for every day—"

"I should go to work? At my age?"

"For God's sake, Lenore. You're only sixty. Okay, it may be a little late to enter a profession, but there has to be *something* that interests you."

"Being with my husband interests me," Lenore blurted out, then went on without realizing, or caring, that Cassie was there, "but he doesn't want me around. He never has. He's perfectly happy to stay in Washington and call me down whenever there's a social engagement that calls for my presence, but he doesn't want my company. He's made that clear."

"That's not what I see," Cassie said, quietly but bluntly. Both Lenore and Natalie turned to look at her. "I think he'd very much like to have you around, but he's felt you haven't *wanted* it."

Natalie nodded. "Of course, Cassie's right. You've always chosen solitude over him. You'd rather hide in that bedroom of yours—"

"I go there when I'm upset," Lenore argued in her own defense.

"But you're upset all the time, and about the wrong things. Honestly, Lenore, you can't let every little thing bother you. There's no point to it. Maybe if you spent more time in Washington with Gil—I mean, you could always do something in his office, even if it meant stuffing envelopes."

"I don't like Washington. I feel safer here."

"Safer? Against what?"

"Against . . . against . . . oh, I don't know! There are so *many* things."

"Maybe you should start analyzing them one by one. My guess is that you'd find there weren't so many things, and that the ones that do exist aren't really all that threatening."

"I'd be a thorn in his side."

"Not if you were your charming best."

"But a woman shouldn't *have* to be her charming best all the time, *especially* in front of her husband."

"That's where you're wrong, Lenore," Natalie cautioned. "A man needs to see the charm directed at him sometimes. It's not enough that the only time it shows is when there are others around."

"But I can't compete! I can't compete with all those lovely young things who work for him!"

"Ahh. That's it, then. You're going to give it all up without a fight."

"There isn't much left to give up. And you're a fine one to talk, Natalie Whyte. Jack isn't home any more than Gil is. What do you think *he's* doing for his daily dose of charm?"

Natalie was silent. Cassie wanted to wither into the carton she sat on. The air in the attic seemed suddenly colder and very stale. Even Lenore seemed to have run out of words.

Lips pursed, Natalie studied the oval tip of one of her perfectly manicured fingernails. "I've known about Jack's escapades for years. I . . . accept them."

"And you're going to give it all up without a fight?" Lenore asked, repeating Natalie's own words but more gently.

Natalie raised her head. "I'm not giving it all up. When Jack is with me he's with me."

"But is that often enough?"

"No. Not for me. But I can't change him, Lenore. All I can do is change myself to adapt to him."

"You shouldn't have to do that. *I* shouldn't have to do that."

When Natalie spoke again, she wore an expression of profound sadness. "What we should or shouldn't have to do in life is sometimes irrelevant. It's what circumstances dictate we do that matters."

Lenore debated silently for a minute. "I'm not sure I like that idea," she whispered at last.

"Neither do I," Natalie answered, "but that's the way it is."

Cassie could do no more than offer a sad nod of agreement.

Chapter 15

AFTER THE VISIT WITH HIS FATHER, Jordan returned to New York. He didn't snap at a single flight attendant or chew out a single cabbie, though either of those must have thought him soft, what with the silly smile he wore. He spent every free minute dreaming, conjuring up the most exquisite seduction. If Katia wanted satin sheets and candlelight, satin sheets and candlelight she would have. If she wanted champagne and caviar, or a bed of roses, or a goddamned Bedouin tent, he'd get those for her, too.

Unfortunately, she wouldn't know beforehand, so he would have to use his own judgment. He wanted their first time together to be a wonderful surprise.

He was in for the surprise, though, when he went to Katia's office the following morning. Oh, she was there, all right. She was bent over her drawing board as he had seen her many times before. But there was no smile on her face when she saw him. She neither stood to give him a hug nor held out a hand.

"Jordan," she said with a short nod in greeting.

The chill in her tone brought back their phone conversation of the Friday before. Jordan had been so delighted by what he had learned from his father that he had completely forgotten that Katia was angry with him.

No sweat, he told himself. She would come around in no time. She always had. After all, she loved him.

"I brought the architects' preliminary drawings," he offered on a light note as he crossed her office to place them in front of her.

She promptly tossed the large envelope of drawings onto her desk. "I'll take a look at them later. You say they're only the preliminaries?"

"I pushed for even these."

"You shouldn't have bothered. If they're only preliminary they won't do me much good. I can't plan artwork around sketches that are bound to change. I'll wait for the final ones and save myself some work."

"I thought . . . well, maybe these will give you some ideas."

"I already have some ideas. When I get the final drawings I can do something with them." Pen in hand, she returned to her board.

"Working on something good?" he asked in his most congenial tone.

"I hope so."

"What is it?"

"A soup ad."

"Mmm, mmm, good."

"Cute." But still she didn't smile.

"Ah, listen, Katia. I know you're pissed at me."

Her pen went to work. "No I'm not."

"You are. I can tell."

"I'm busy. That's all."

"Then maybe we can meet later and talk." He pictured a lunchtime rendezvous at his place. He would supply the lunch, but they would never get to it because they'd be feasting on each other.

"It's a bad day, Jordan. I'm sorry."

"Tonight, then. I don't care how late."

"I'm really bushed. It was a busy weekend."

"Busy . . . how?" he asked with caution.

"Use your imagination."

His imagination was lethal. "Katia, we have to talk," he stated gruffly.

"Go ahead," she offered breezily.

"I love you."

"So what else is new?"

He shot a glance behind him, then stalked to the door, closed it, and returned. "I love you, man to woman."

Her pen stayed in motion. "That's nice."

"I've never told you that before," he protested. "All I get is a 'that's nice'?"

"What else would you have me say?"

"You could say, 'I love you, too, Jordan.' Or, 'Do you really mean it, Jordan?' Or, 'Oh, Jordan, I've been waiting so long to hear you say that.'" He'd given each possibility a properly excited inflection, but Katia appeared to be unmoved, and that frustrated him tremendously. It also frightened him. "Katia, do you *hear* what I'm saying?"

"I hear."

"And it means nothing? Is it every day that a man tells you he loves you—damn it, put down that pen. *Is* it, Katia? Don't you have *any* reaction to what I've said?"

Katia sighed and hung her head. "I feel very sad, if you want to know the truth."

"Sad?" he asked on a note of panic. "What do you mean by—"

"Katia!" Roger opened the door and stuck his head through the narrow gap. "We've got a problem on the mattress thing. I need you. Now."

"She's busy," Jordan growled.

But Katia was capping her pen. "It's okay, Roger. I'm on my way."

"But what about me?" Jordan asked.

"What about you?" She stood and straightened her skirt.

"I'm business, too."

She glanced around the office as though checking to see if

there were anything she wanted to take along for her meeting with Roger. "Is that what this has all been about, business?"

"No, you know that, but—"

She passed him on her way to the door. "I have to run, Jordan. Let me know when you get those final sketches."

Jordan opened his mouth to speak, but before he could get a word out Katia was gone. So he closed his mouth, frowned down at the storyboard, and tried to take in what had happened. He replayed the conversation, wondering what he had done wrong, finally deciding that Katia simply hadn't been in a receptive mood.

Maybe it *was* a bad day. Maybe she *was* bushed. Maybe— though the thought bugged him—she *had* had a busy weekend. He would simply have to catch her later. That was all.

She did love him. He knew it, and he knew that love didn't end with a single falling out. Okay, so it was more than one time he had turned her away. She thought he was trying to manipulate her. But she would understand in time. She was a reasonable woman. He would simply have to keep trying.

As he left the office something else occurred to him. It was a ray of hope, a flicker on the bright side. Other than the instant when she had glanced up from her desk to find him at her door, Katia hadn't looked at him. She had staunchly avoided his eyes. It was, he thought in the psychoanalyst's mode, a very good sign.

Jodi Frier, who should have been even more adept at psychoanalytical thinking than Jordan, was stymied. Cavanaugh had returned from the coast looking disgruntled. When she asked about his trip he simply grunted. When she asked if he'd come up with anything new he turned away. He spent most of his time at home—surprisingly more than usual, which made it, ironically, all the harder for her—sitting in a chair with his legs sprawled out, his shoulders slumped and his eyes troubled. She knew that his mood had to relate to the Whyte-Warren case, but after three days of enduring his brooding presence, she also knew that this wasn't how she wanted to live. If she could glimpse what was on his mind she could be sympathetic. But he wouldn't talk, and her patience waned.

Late on that third night, as she was getting ready for bed—alone—something inside her rebelled. Tossing a robe on over her nightgown, she stalked back into the living room.

"You must have run into a tube of super glue out there," she remarked caustically.

"Hmm?" He didn't look up.

"Your frown is set. Permanent. Immovable."

"Not now, Jodi. I'm thinking."

"You've been thinking night and day since you got back. Well, I've been thinking, too, and it occurs to me that you could just as well do your thinking without me around. The bare walls won't complain. Neither will an empty bed."

He did raise his eyes then, and they pleaded with her as he spoke. "Please. Jodi, I've got problems. Don't do this to me now."

"Damn it, Bob. You have to be one of the most selfish people I know. Your problems always come first." She held up a hand. "Okay. I know. You warned me at the start. But all of a sudden I'm realizing that I can't live this way. You've got problems. Fine. In any kind of meaningful relationship, people try to work problems out together."

"My problems have to do with my work."

"So do mine. *Your* work is making me a little crazy. You sit around here like a mummy—a *disgruntled* mummy—and you won't give me the slightest clue about what's eating you."

He pushed himself straighter in the chair. "My work is confidential. I can't be blabbing my thoughts to the world."

"I'm not the world. I'm me. Just one person. You've told me confidential things before. You *know* I keep everything to myself."

"What do you want me to do?" he snapped. "Lay my case out in every minute detail so you can go over it with a fine-tooth comb?"

"I don't want details. Just the overall drift—if that's what will help me understand why you've been so withdrawn."

"Don't nag me, Jodi," he warned.

"Because I'll sound like your ex-wife?" She was angry enough to be reckless. "You know, I'm beginning to side with her more and more each day. A relationship demands trust, but you obviously lack it. That's enough to drive *any* woman away. Maybe she was smarter than me, because she hounded you more instead of brooding off by herself. Well, I'm *tired* of brooding by myself. I'm tired of brooding, period!"

"No one's asking you to brood."

"No one's giving me any reason not to."

"You're pushing me."

"Likewise."

Squeezing his eyes shut, he rubbed the bridge of his nose with his thumb and forefinger. "I can't take this now, Jodi," he said in a voice that warned of imminent explosion.

Which was exactly what Jodi wanted, she was that disgusted. "I can't take it either, Bob!"

He stood abruptly, as angry as she. "Feel free to leave!"

"I will!" She whirled and would have started off, but he caught her arm.

"Don't."

She didn't look at him, but her voice lowered, as his had. "Why not?"

"I don't want you to. I want you here."

"So I can watch you agonize over your case while I agonize over mine?" Unspoken, but understood, was that he was her case.

Hands on her shoulders, he slowly turned her to face him. "I don't want you agonizing. I don't want to agonize either, but, my God—" he looked away and shook his head, "I feel so torn."

"About us?" she asked more timidly than she would have liked at that moment.

He shook his head again, but this time he was looking at her. "About this case. It's killing me."

"I can see that, which is why it's so hard for me to stand by and watch. What's happened? It wasn't so bad before. Challenging, yes. Sensitive, yes. But something happened on this last trip that's knocked you for a loop. Tell me, Bob," she urged softly. "Maybe I can help."

A gruff sound came from his throat as he put his arms around her and drew her to him. She didn't know whether it was his case or their relationship that made him hold her so tightly, but just then she didn't really care.

"Ahh, Jodi. What a mess."

She held her breath. "Us?"

He chuckled softly against her hair. "No. You were right. I have been like a mummy. Everything's bound inside. It's not fair of me, but it's hard to change sometimes."

"Change is easy if you want it."

"That's not true. When you've lived your life one way you get stuck in certain ruts. Maybe if you'd come along when I was twenty-one—" he caught himself. "But then you'd have been nine, so nothing would have come of it."

"Do you want to change?"

"I don't want to lose you," was his hoarse response.

She ignored the way his hands had begun to roam her back. "Then you'll have to change, at least a little."

"I'll try." He was cupping her bottom, urging her hips to his.

"Do you mean it?"

He breathed deeply of the faint lemon scent lingering in her hair. It turned him on. "Let's go to bed," he murmured.

Jodi closed her senses to the pull he had on her. "And forget it all with a good romp?" she croaked.

"If you want to help me, that'd be one way."

"Like putting a finger in the dike?"

Cavanaugh's hands came to rest on her hips. "I wasn't thinking of it that way. I thought . . . I wanted to show you what you mean to me."

Drawing her head back, she framed his face with her hands. "If you want to show me what I mean to you, you can sit down and talk to me," she whispered. "That's what I need more than anything."

His lips thinned, and for a moment she thought he was going to refuse her. He closed his eyes briefly, and his frown was back in place. But when he looked at her again she knew that the pain reflected in his eyes was caused by something else.

"What is it, Bob? What is upsetting you so?"

"This case," he said at last. "Things are pointing in the direction that I thought I wanted them to go, but suddenly I'm not so sure of my own feelings." He let himself be led to the sofa, then seated. Jodi came down close beside him, never taking her hands from him. "I've hated those families for years. I've read stuff in the paper about how wonderful they are, how powerful they are, how successful they are. It always seemed unfair to me that they should have so much when others had so little."

She pondered that, as well as Bob's reasons for saying it. "I've guessed that you blame Jack Whyte for your father's demise—"

"With reason!" Bob interrupted. "The man *ruined* my father!"

Jodi was slightly stunned by his bluntness. It was a minute before she could ask, "What happened exactly?"

He blew out an uneven breath, diffusing his sudden spurt of anger. "You know the gist of it. After he was hurt in the war he insisted on going back. They wouldn't let him fight, so he stayed in the background, working with machines mostly. By the time he left the service he'd had a taste of electronics. He saw it as a field that had nowhere to go but up. So he collected every cent he could, took out a slew of loans and started a business, and it was really going well, more employees every year, more contracts. But when he got what he thought would be the first of many lucrative government contracts, he went a little wild with expansion. The very next year he lost the contract to Whyte Electronics."

"Fair and square?"

"Who knows? Warren was still in local politics, but he had friends in high places. Between Whyte's business acumen and Warren's pull, a pattern emerged. My dad's story wasn't unique.

He was far from the only victim. Whyte drove other companies out of business in precisely the same way—by stealing a critical contract."

"But it was only one contract . . ."

"It was the one he needed. Without it he found himself so heavily in debt that the only thing he could do was sell out."

"To Whyte?"

"Not voluntarily. But Whyte had already stolen away several of his top men, and without them no one was about to make a reasonable offer. Not that Whyte did. He gave him shit, which was exactly what my dad felt like from that day on."

The rest Jodi knew. "When you first got this case you were aching to pay someone back for all that. Is the problem now that you can't do it—that you've come up with something to make the families look like martyrs?"

Cavanaugh was silent for a minute before admitting quietly, "Just the opposite."

"I don't understand."

He looked her in the eye. "The evidence we have points to Jordan Whyte as a murderer."

"*Jordan Whyte*? Killing his own brother and sister-in-law?"

"That's what the evidence suggests."

There was much she didn't understand, but what immediately concerned her was Bob. "Then . . . where's the problem? I'd think you'd feel as though justice were finally being served."

"I'm not sure it is justice. That's the problem."

"What do you mean?"

Sliding his arm around her shoulder, he held her closer. Far from being sexual, the gesture reflected the need he had for encouragement. What he was about to say—and the fact that he had to say it to Jodi—was hard, because he had been wrong, damn it. He had been wrong.

"I really did want to believe the worst. When Ryan suggested that there might be some funny business going on inside those families I couldn't have been happier. Then I started to learn about them—you know, all those files and documents I read—and I was angrier than ever. The Whytes and Warrens have gotten away with hell over the years. When one of Whyte's planes crashed in seventy-five, he and Warren managed to fix it with the FAA so that the cause of the accident was listed as the weather rather than shoddy maintenance. Whyte and Warren arranged more junkets between businessmen and politicians than you could count. Warren's lobbying was what got Whyte Electronics its huge contract with the Air Force in seventy-nine, even though there were other bids that were better and lower. They've come this close," he held his fingers a fraction of an inch apart, "to being caught, and they've always escaped."

"But?" she urged him on. There was another side to the negative; she knew it, and right now she knew that Cavanaugh did, too.

"But then I read further. Not just the papers Ryan gave me. Many of those nights you thought I was at the station I was really in the library digging up obscure little articles, or talking with people who at one time or another had known the Whytes or the Warrens. I told myself that I wanted to have all the facts at my fingertips. And—I know what you're thinking—maybe there was a thirst for vengeance, and even a little bit of fascination that went along with it, but in any case I saw the other side of the coin, the one the public doesn't often see, and I realized that life hasn't been all hunky-dory for those families, either."

He paused, absently stroking her shoulder. "I'm not sure," he resumed slowly, "that those kids had any more of a life with their fathers than I had with mine, or that Natalie Whyte's marriage has been much better than my mother's was. Or that Lenore Warren—do you know that she's an alcoholic?"

"No!"

He nodded. "They covered it up well, but in the late seventies she spent time under treatment at a sanitarium. She's been dry since then from what I can gather, but there must have been something very wrong with her life to drive her to drink."

"Which goes to show that PR can be misleading."

Cavanaugh was staring off toward the window. "And along comes this thing with Mark and Deborah. I've spoken with all the brothers and sisters now. To a one they can't understand what happened. I met with them separately, so it wasn't a case of them putting words in each other's mouths, though I suppose they could have fabricated something beforehand."

"What about Jordan?"

"The damnedest thing." He gave a quick, almost angry shake of his head. "I actually like the guy. I wanted to despise him, but I can't. Maybe he just turned on the charm—but I can't even say that, because some parts of our conversation were pretty heated. When I suggested that Mark and Deborah's deaths might have been an inside job he hit the roof, and it wasn't just righteous indignation. I've seen the reactions of criminals when they're caught, even white-collar criminals, but I've never seen such legitimate *anger*." His voice dropped. "At least I thought it was legitimate."

"Is the evidence conclusive?"

"No."

"But it does point a finger at Jordan. What does Ryan say?"

"Ryan's delighted—which bothers me, too. I mean, hell, I'm the one who has reason for wanting revenge, but he's even more obsessed with the case than I am. He managed to put together in-depth files, and it was like he knew the tape existed that would incriminate Jordan. He told me to take my time, but he's the one who's put on pressure for the rush. I'm willing to look at the whole picture with an open mind. Not Ryan. He wants me to run to New York and arrest the guy."

"Will you?"

"Not yet. There are still a couple of things I've got to work out."

"What did Ryan say to that?" Jodi asked, as if she didn't know.

A small smile tugged at Cavanaugh's mouth. "He was furious.

Threatened to have me removed from the case if my stalling gave Jordan a chance to leave the country."

"Would he do that?"

"Remove me from the case? You bet."

"Not that, Bob. Would Jordan leave the country?"

"I can't see it. I'd post bond for him myself, I'm that sure. His family means too much to him. And his work. And Katia."

Jodi hadn't missed the slight softening of his voice. "Katia?"

"Katia Morell."

"The housekeeper's daughter. Very attractive from what I saw in those pictures." She was watching him closely. "Have you talked with her?"

Cavanaugh held her gaze, pleased to see an inkling of jealousy. "Uh-huh."

"And?"

"She's lovely."

"That wasn't what I wanted to hear."

For the first time in days he smiled. "I know." He gave her a squeeze. "But you don't have anything to worry about. Jordan's in love with her and he's very protective."

"*That* wasn't what I wanted to hear, either," she came back with a pout.

"Okay. She's lovely. She's beautiful. She's personable. But the chemistry just wasn't there between us."

"It got *that far*?"

"Jodi, it didn't get anywhere! That's what I'm trying to tell you! I liked her very much, which isn't to say that I want to go to bed with her."

Jodi relaxed against him. "But Jordan does."

"I didn't ask the man whether he wants to, or already has for that matter. I was a cop interviewing him for the investigation. It was enough that I dug out his feelings for her, because that's all that's really relevant. I can't see him leaving Katia, any more than I can see him dumping a scandal in his family's lap and taking off. If he's guilty. Which I don't think he is." Again, that angry little headshake. "Damn it, I don't. But I'm almost afraid to trust my instincts. They've been so biased in this case. If only I had *facts* to work with."

"Can you get them?"

"I don't know. Ryan gave me a week to come up with something. If I'm empty-handed at the end of that time I'll have to bring Jordan in."

"Do you have any possibilities?"

"Not many." He screwed up his face in frustration. "There are little things that smell—I mean, things that may or may not be relevant but that just aren't setting right. I've got this uncomfortable feeling that I'm missing something, but for the life of me I can't figure out what it is."

"It'll come to you if you think hard enough."

"That's what I was trying to do when you ruined my concentration."

"I'm sorry," she said, but she was teasing and not a bit contrite.

He arched a brow at her. "Are you?"

"Of course. Now that I know the reason behind that corrugated brow of yours."

"But the corrugated brow is gone. My concentration's shot for the night. See? You've stripped me of all my defenses, made me feel like a sentimental idiot. So what are you going to do about it?"

Jodi knew a challenge when she heard one. She looked up at him, grinned, and before he could say another word swung around to straddle his thighs. Her robe and nightgown had risen in the process, but that was all right, because she had every intention of baring him as well. Her hands were already at work releasing the button of his pants. "I'll just have to restore your sense of masculinity," she murmured against his lips.

If Cavanaugh had indeed feared that he had shown a weak side that night, he rose to the occasion and corrected the image.

*   *   *

Jordan had no occasion to rise to. In the two days succeeding the day he'd seen Katia he tried to contact her, but call after call proved fruitless. He phoned her at the office, but she was either at a meeting or in the field. When his timing finally clicked and he caught her at her desk, she refused to discuss anything but business. He phoned her at home only to find that no one answered, that the line was busy, or that he had woken her from sleep and she was, she claimed, too groggy to talk. Elaborate plans of seduction notwithstanding, he was contemplating taking firmer measures—such as posting himself at her door and refusing to budge until she had let him in and talked—when something happened that momentarily took his mind off her in a way that the pressing demands of his own work hadn't been able to do.

Cavanaugh appeared unannounced at his office, looking tired and grim. Immediately Jordan sensed that something was wrong.

"Have you got a VCR around here?" Cavanaugh asked.

"Sure. Why?"

"I need to show you something."

Puzzled, Jordan led him down the hall to a conference room, in a concealed portion of which was a TV and VCR. He took the cassette Cavanaugh handed him, loaded it into the machine, then started it off. Twenty minutes later he had seen enough.

"I can't believe he filmed that!"

"He filmed everything. You should've seen what we found."

"Other private conversations?"

Cavanaugh nodded.

"And none of the participants knew they were being filmed?"

"Looks that way."

"Nuts. He was nuts!"

"Maybe not," Cavanaugh said with care. "If he'd ever been nabbed on cocaine charges, he'd have had a hell of a lot of people to bring down with him. The tapes would have been insurance. He'd have been able to cop a tidy deal for himself."

But Jordan was thinking beyond cocaine. He spoke slowly, warily, looking at Cavanaugh all the while. "If you'd brought those other tapes to show me, I'd be asking whether you thought someone on the tapes killed Mark to get them. But you didn't bring those tapes. You brought this one." He paused and watched Cavanaugh look down at his shoes.

"You did threaten to kill him."

"I was furious at the time. It was an idle threat, the same kind any person makes in the heat of anger. Hell, you've seen me blow up, but I calm down right afterward, don't I?"

"That's what I've seen."

"But whoever killed Mark and Deborah had to have planned it. The boat had to have been staked out, as well as the area, because whoever stole onto that boat did it when there weren't any witnesses around. It was premeditated. Do you honestly think me capable of the premeditated murder of—forget my brother—anyone?"

"No. But you did have a motive."

Jordan made a harsh sound and thrust his hand through his hair. "We've been through that. I did not have a motive, at least not one that I'd consider valid." He stood straighter. "Am I under arrest?"

"No."

"Why not—if the evidence says I'm the prime suspect?"

"Because I'm not convinced you did it."

"Why not?"

Cavanaugh shot him a slanted smile. "Maybe for old time's sake, 'cause you were one hell of a player at Duke."

"More than one football player has served time."

"Well then, let's just say that I'm not ready to book you. There are still too many questions that haven't been answered."

"Like what?"

"Like where you were at the time of the murders. I asked you that once before and you said you were here, but I don't know exactly where 'here' is, since we got off the subject."

"Here is in New York. Mark and Deborah were in Boston."

"Where in New York?" He took the small notebook from his pocket.

"On Eighty-Second Street between Third and Lexington."

"Doing what?"

Jordan looked him in the eye. "Screwing a woman who will gladly tell the entire world that you questioned her and why."

"Which answers my next question." It also told Cavanaugh something else. If Jordan were guilty he wouldn't be so concerned either about his image in the press or the hurt any publicity would bring to his family. He was a smart man. If he were guilty he would *know* that the publicity would come sooner or later. "So you don't want her involved. She will have to be, you know."

Jordan did. "Just tell her . . . tell her that . . . ach, use your imagination and make up some story, but so help me, if she goes to the papers I'll hold you," he pointed, "responsible."

"Will she back you up?"

"She sure as hell better! That was no *phantom* who serviced me that night!" His statement was punctuated by the tic in his cheek.

"Why weren't you with Katia?"

"Katia and I don't have that kind of relationship."

"But you're in love with the woman."

"So?"

Cavanaugh scratched his head. "Let me get this straight. You're in love with Katia, but even in this modern age you don't sleep with her. So you take out your frustrations on other women."

It was as much the detective's nonchalance as the callousness he suggested that rankled Jordan. "You've got it wrong, Cavanaugh. I don't use other women, at least, no more than they use me. And as far as the 'modern age' goes, it has nothing to do with what I feel for Katia. I would have taken her to bed years ago, but I didn't think I could—" His nostrils flared. "This is really none of your business."

"Maybe not. But I'm trying my best to help. My boss, John

Ryan, would have liked to have hauled you in two days ago. If he'd had his way you'd already have been booked, processed and arraigned, and if it's publicity that scares you—"

Jordan held up a hand in surrender. "I get the point. What do you want to know?"

"Your relationship with Katia. What is it exactly?"

"Funny you should ask that," Jordan said with open sarcasm, "because I'm trying to work that out myself."

"What do you mean?"

"I love her. You've got that much, right?"

Cavanaugh nodded.

"I've loved her for a long time, but, well . . . listen, Cavanaugh, what I'm telling you is strictly confidential. I don't want anyone to know about it, *least* of all Katia. I'm trusting you, man. Are you with me?"

"I'm with you."

"Well, you see," he lowered his head, and his cheeks grew red, "up until last Friday I thought Katia and I might be related." He looked back up, raising his voice accordingly. "I know that sounds stupid, and it turns out that it isn't true, so there's no point in going into it further, but I'm trying to get Katia to see me now, only she won't. So. We don't have *that* kind of relationship."

"Yet."

"Right."

"I can buy that." What Jordan had said made sense. Cavanaugh knew of Jack Whyte's philandering. Before he had only sympathized with Jack's wife; now it appeared that Jordan had done his share of suffering for it. Still, Cavanaugh was curious. He tipped his head to the side. "You really thought that Cassie Morell and your father—"

"I overheard a conversation once and jumped to conclusions," Jordan grumbled. "I was wrong. Forget it."

"How do you know you were wrong?"

"Is this necessary to clearing my name?"

"No."

"*Then forget it.*"

Cavanaugh let out a long breath. "Okay. So Katia and you don't have *that* kind of relationship. I take it you've seen lots of different women in the past."

"You've read the papers."

"Right, and now I'm asking you. Have you seen different women?"

"Yes, I've seen different women. What does that have to do with anything?"

"I'm just wondering how come you remembered so fast exactly who you were with on the night of the murders."

"It was easy," Jordan said far from easily. His back was stiff, his eyes hard as they bore into Cavanaugh's. "When I learned about the murders I agonized just like the rest of my family. I conjured the image of Mark and Deborah sleeping peacefully on that boat until someone came aboard and shot them dead. And one of the first things I did was to think about what *I* was doing at the same time that my brother's life was being snuffed out. If you think I'm proud of the fact that I was covered with sweat on a fancy bed, fucking a woman who doesn't mean a goddamned thing to me, you're crazy!"

More than ever before, Cavanaugh believed in Jordan's innocence. There was no way a man could put that kind of self-disgust or raw pain in his eyes just for show. Unless he was an actor of award winning caliber—then again, there was the possibility that he was truly psychotic, which Cavanaugh had considered once before but was willing to stake his entire career against.

"I'm sure you're not proud," Cavanaugh said, humbled himself.

Jordan scowled at him, then at the VCR. "I'm telling you, that threat didn't mean a thing. I'd never have hurt my own brother. And I told you right off that we'd argued."

"I spoke with a waiter at Morton's." That was the posh restaurant in Hollywood where Jordan had taken Mark and Deborah after the scene at Mark's house. "He confirmed that you argued there, too."

"If he told you that I raised a knife during dinner and aimed it at my brother's heart he was lying."

"No, he didn't say that."

"Praise be," Jordan said, shooting a dark glance toward the heavens. But Cavanaugh's next question brought him quickly to earth.

"Do you own a gun?"

"No."

"Have you ever?"

"No. I've never even held one in my hand."

"Did you know that Mark owned a gun?"

"No. So where does that leave us?"

"Asking questions and questions and more questions."

"Of whom?"

"People on the waterfront again. Someone has to have seen something."

"Yeah. A black blob in the middle of the night. You won't get any identification there."

"Do you do any snorkling or scuba diving?"

"What do you think." It was a statement, not a question, and was offered reproachfully. "I've tried just about everything that's physical and a little dangerous, but the only diving or snorkling I've done has been in the Caribbean. I don't own any equipment. You can search my place. Of course," he speculated, "it's possible that I rented the stuff. You could check around the sports shops in Boston. But then you'd have to check with the places here, too, because if I drove from New York that night I might well have rented equipment before I left."

He was wallowing in scorn when a more constructive thought struck. "I drive a bright red Audi Quattro. Not exactly nondescript. Maybe someone saw it parked near the Boston waterfront. No," he rubbed a finger along the straight line of his nose and spoke pensively, "I wouldn't have parked it there if I was going to board the boat from the water. Are you sure that's what the murderer did—came out of the water?"

"I'm not sure of anything. No one saw a person approach the boat from the dock, but I guess I could check on the car. There was a damp footprint just inside the cabin, so I'm assuming that whoever it was came from the harbor."

"Which means that I'd have parked elsewhere. You could check out the possibilities. A car like that, with New York plates reading JSW-1 would be hard to miss. Then again, I could have rented a car that wouldn't be noticed. Check out the rental agencies."

"Thank you for the hint. I'd never have thought of it on my own."

Jordan might have appreciated Cavanaugh's wry grin had the circumstances been different. "Maybe either Deborah or Mark showered before going to bed."

"The footprint was different. It didn't match theirs. Besides, the lab found traces of muck from the harbor."

"Then you definitely have a crazy on your hands. The only ones who knowingly go into *that* water are police divers looking for bodies embedded in cement."

"Or men who want their storming of a boat to go undetected."

"One-footed men. What happened to the other footprint?"

"Pretty much lost in the carpet, for purposes of identification at least. The guys have kept at it and have found microscopic traces of the same muck leading in a trail through the cabin to the bed." He paused. "Do you use foot powder?"

"No. Why?"

"There were traces of it in the rug, and neither Mark nor Deborah had any on their feet. How about your shoe size?"

"Eleven."

"Consistent with the footprint."

Jordan looked at Cavanaugh's shoes. "What size are those?"

"Eleven. Point taken. Hey, I'm not saying that a competent defense attorney couldn't get you off."

"Defense attorney," Jordan echoed, closing his eyes for a minute. "I can't believe this has gone so far." His eyes opened. "Should I be speaking with one?"

Cavanaugh considered that before answering reluctantly, "It wouldn't hurt to have someone on call just in case."

"Do you think I'll need one? I want your honest opinion, Cavanaugh."

Again Cavanaugh considered the question, and again he answered with reluctance. "I think you well may. I'm trying my damnedest, but whoever did this planned it well. It's even possible," he said as the thought dawned, "that you've been intentionally framed. Whoever did it may have known about those arguments you had with Mark and about the tape." He rubbed his temple with the heel of his hand. "God, I should have thought of this before."

"Yeah. The only problem is that we're still without motive and suspect. All we know is that we're dealing with a shrewd cookie, if what you're suggesting is the case. He couldn't have feared what was on the tapes if he was hoping they'd be found, so it has to be someone connected with Mark or Deborah in another way. Who could have known about the arguments? Who else saw those tapes? And why the devil would he want to frame *me*?"

Cavanaugh was as perplexed as Jordan. "It's possible," he began slowly, "that you were simply a handy patsy. On the other hand. . . ."

"What?"

"Maybe we've been on the wrong track. Maybe the motive relates to you rather than Mark."

"You mean someone slaughtered my brother and sister-in-law to settle a gripe he had with me?" Jordan couldn't believe it, or maybe the thought sent such a chill through him that he simply couldn't give it credence.

"It's possible. Do you have enemies?"

"None who'd kill like that."

"*Think*, Jordan. Anyone who ever threatened you or let word get around that he'd get even one day or simply had *reason* to be that angry at you?"

"No, damn it! I've had differences with people, but nothing like *that!*"

"Someone? Anyone?"

"No!"

Cavanaugh let out a breath and pushed off from the table against which he'd been propped. "Okay. Let's let it go for now. But keep thinking. Please."

"What are you going to do?"

"First I want to check out your alibi. Can I have a name and exact address?"

Jordan gave him the information. "Once you've spoken with her, will I be in the clear?"

"Assuming she backs up your story—"

"She will."

"Assuming she does, it'll make my case with Ryan a little easier. But he's out for blood," Cavanaugh warned. Tiny murmurings sounded at the back of his mind, but he pushed them aside. "If I don't come up with something else he'll go with the charge, alibi or no. He'll take the chance that the alibi witness can be discredited on the stand."

With a slow nod, Jordan confirmed his assumption. "She can be discredited. She's scatterbrained. A great lay, but scatterbrained."

"Again, a good defense attorney could help you there. If the prosecutor tries to discredit her he can probably have it stricken from the record."

"After the jury's heard it."

"The jury will be instructed to forget it."

"Come on, Cavanaugh," Jordan said with disgust. "I'm a realist. Once the jury's heard it they've heard it." He paused, and his voice fell. "Shit, I can't believe we're talking trial and jury. There has to be something we can do. There has to be something *I* can do."

"Just stay close. Don't try to run."

"Hey." He stood straighter. "I'm not a runner. Even aside from the matter of honor, running would be a sign of guilt. And I'm not guilty."

"I believe you," Cavanaugh said quietly. "And it's been a help talking. Between the two of us we may have latched on to something that may lead us somewhere. I'm not exactly sure where, yet." There was that nagging at the back of his brain, but he wasn't quite ready to pin it down. "I'll do my best to find out." Sliding his notebook back in his pocket, he started for the door.

"Cavanaugh?"

He turned. "Yeah?"

"Thanks for the show of faith. I appreciate it."

"Yeah, well, maybe I'm trying to prove something to myself."

Jordan didn't quite understand that, but his mind was in too great a turmoil to try. "You'd never make it as Kojak. You're too softhearted."

"Tell that to anyone," Cavanaugh said, pointing a finger, "and I'll testify against you myself."

Jordan was in agony. He felt angry one minute, terrified the next. He racked his brain for the identity of someone who held a grudge against him strong enough to kill Deborah and Mark and then frame him for it but he came up with nothing. His mind wandered, jumping ahead, imagining himself being arrested, booked and arraigned, imagining the torment that would cause his family. And Katia.

Why now? *Why now?* Just when he was free to pursue her. But she wouldn't see him. And he had no one to talk with. He felt more alone than he had in his thirty-nine years.

The rest of the day was a waste of effort as far as work was concerned. Jordan left the office at four-thirty and wandered the streets of Manhattan for hours trying to make some sense out of what was happening. He thought back on his discussion with

Cavanaugh, but even the fact that Cavanaugh was on his side was small solace when the other side was so menacing.

Only when his knee began to ache did he go home, but he found little rest there. For hours he sprawled nude on his bed with an arm thrown over his eyes, but what he saw behind his lids was so unsettling and infuriating and downright unjust that he finally bolted up and spent what was left of the night pacing the floor.

By morning he had worked himself into a state of desperation. He knew he couldn't go to work, and he didn't want to walk the streets again. He couldn't go to Boston because his family would know that something was wrong, and he couldn't go to Katia because she wasn't seeing him.

There was only one place left. Picking up the phone, he put in a long-distance call to Cavanaugh. He had no idea whether the man had returned to Boston the night before, but it was worth a shot.

For once things went his way. "Cavanaugh, it's Jordan Whyte."

"Think of anything?"

"Nothing. Did you check on my alibi?"

"She's out of town."

"Shit."

"She'll be back in two days."

"Oh. Okay." He squeezed his eyes shut against the throbbing in his head. "Listen, I just want you to know that I'm going up to Maine. I know you said to stick around, but I think I'll lose my mind if I do. I need fresh air."

"Where in Maine? The island?"

"Yeah. You can call me there if you need me." He gave Cavanaugh the number. "And if you want to come up for some reason, contact Anthony Oliveri in Portland." He supplied that number as well. "He'll take you over."

"Got it," Cavanaugh said, putting down his pen.

"Want me to call in when I get there?"

"You're not under arrest."

"I'm trying to show you that I'm acting in good faith."

"I trust you. How long do you think you'll be there?"

"I have a couple of critical meetings set for Monday. If I don't make it back by then my business will be shot to hell."

"Three days. Sounds like a nice vacation."

Jordan answered him with a harsh, guttural sound.

"Okay. I get the point," Cavanaugh said. "Are you going to be alone up there?"

"Yeah."

"Maybe you shouldn't be."

"I've got no choice, pal. Right about now I'm not fit company for anything that lives and breathes. I wouldn't wish myself on a dog."

"That bad?"

"That bad."

"Listen, don't do anything drastic."

"Like slit my wrists? I hate the sight of blood. But I didn't tell you that, did I? Peter isn't the only one with the problem, but if you ever tell him I told you so I'll kill you."

"Really?"

"Really."

"Then I guess I'll have to keep it to myself." He paused. "Take it easy, Jordan."

"I'd say the same to you, but I'm counting on you to come up with something, Cavanaugh."

"I know. I'll try."

It was Jordan's turn to pause before offering a very quiet and heartfelt, "Thanks."

Chapter 16

 JORDAN WAS IN MAINE by mid-afternoon. The fact that it was pouring did nothing to brighten his spirits, not that anything would have just then. He felt as though everything he had ever wanted in life was dangling by a thin thread above his head, within reach yet not, because every time he stretched up and made contact, he set the thread to swinging elusively.

Heedless of the rain, he walked through the woods, but neither the rich smell of wet pine nor the brisk late September air nor the ever-present and rhythmic crash of the waves against the shore gave him comfort.

It was nearly dark when he returned to the house and placed a phone call to New York.

Katia was in a meeting.

"This is an emergency," Jordan explained to the assistant who had taken the call. He made no attempt to charm; urgency was the only thing he was capable of conveying. "It's Jordan Whyte and I'm calling from Maine. I have a serious problem. It's *mandatory* that I speak with Katia."

"She should be out of her meeting in half an hour."

"I can't wait that long. Will you please get a message to her? See if she'll come to the phone?"

The woman on the other end paused, then said, "Hold on. I'll check."

He alternately shifted from foot to foot, tossed the phone from hand to hand and ear to ear, grumbled and swore for a full five minutes until Katia came on the line. "This better be good, Jordan," she warned without so much as a hello.

"It's not. It's lousy. But I can't help it, Katia. Things are getting out of hand, and I don't know what the hell to do."

"What are you talking about?"

"I need you." The silence that came after his statement was prolonged. "Katia? Are you still there?"

"I'm here," she said wearily. "Look, you dragged me out of an important meeting—"

"*This* is important. I have problems and I need help."

Something in his voice got through to her, because her irritation was reduced to wariness by the time she spoke again. "Where are you?"

"Maine. Didn't the girl tell you that? I specifically told her—"

"What are you doing in Maine?"

"Trying to figure out what's gone wrong with my life!"

There was a pause, then a cautious, "Have you been drinking, Jordan?"

"Not a drop, but I may resort to that if you don't come up."

"Go *there*?"

"Now."

"I can't do that, Jordan! I'm in the middle of one meeting and have another one scheduled after that."

"Cancel it."

"I can't!"

"If you came down with the flu, had a temperature of a hundred and three and couldn't stand on your feet you would."

"I wouldn't have any choice."

"The point is that meetings can be rescheduled and appointments can be changed. I know how much your work means to you, and I know how important you are to your work, and I wouldn't be asking this if I weren't so damned desperate." He was desperate, he realized, and that made him angry. "Remember all the times I was there when you needed me? Remember all the times I held your hand and made you feel better? Damn it, I haven't asked much of you in the past. Have I?"

Katia could have taken his question many ways, but she chose to take it on its simplest level, as, she assumed, he had intended it. "No. You haven't."

"So now, for the first time, I'm asking you to inconvenience yourself a little. After all we've been through is that too much to ask?"

"Oh, Jordan," she sighed, "if I only knew that it *was* urgent. You've already told me that you love me, and *how* you love me. Do you really have anything new to add?" Like what he was going to do about it, the nitwit.

"Yes! Lots! But you're not going to hear a thing unless you come up here tonight. And if you don't come, if you let me down this one time when I'm begging for your help, I'll get the message. So help me, Katia, I will." With that he hung up the phone.

It was after eleven when the helicopter touched down on the beach. Katia climbed out, ran free of the eddy of wind produced by the whirling blades, then watched the craft rise into the air again and head back for the mainland. With its departure went the broad beam of light it had cast on the sand. She found herself in sudden darkness and rain.

Shouldering her overnight case, she looked up toward the house. Its surprising darkness brought home the conflicting emotions she had experienced in the past few hours. She wasn't sure she should have come; Jordan had manipulated her so often in recent months that she felt raw. As long as she had remained in New York it had been easy to hold him at arm's length—well, not easy, never easy given what she felt for the man—but certainly easier than it would be now. But she had been frightened by the near panic in his voice, and even if he hadn't put his request in a you-owe-me-one context, she would probably be standing here now. In the darkness. And the rain.

Belatedly she wished she had worn a jacket, but it had been warm and dry in the city. She had a sweatshirt in her case, but it seemed pointless to dig it out now. Putting her head down against the torrent that had already soaked her hair and clothes, she started across the wet sand. She had gone no further than the boathouse, beyond and behind which were trees and then the open path leading to the house when she stopped.

A dark figure stood in the rain, unprotected by the overhang of the boathouse.

Jordan.

For a minute they simply looked at one another. Then he came forward slowly, transferred the strap of her bag to his own shoulder, and, rain or no rain, as if he couldn't help himself, he took her in his arms and held her close.

"Thank you," he whispered hoarsely.

Katia felt her own arms slip around him. His body was chilled on the surface, but his inner warmth reached out to her as it always had. He was tired; she could feel it in the way his shoulders slumped over her, in the way his head sagged against hers. It occurred to her that he was simply feeling relief, though she suspected that it was a combination of the two, and she was glad she had come.

"I was worried," she murmured against his chest, just loud enough to be heard above rain battered surf. "You sounded awful."

"You're here. I'm better."

"You're soaked."

"So are you. Come on. Let's go inside." But rather than leading her up to the house, he took her hand and loped toward the nearest shelter, the boathouse. Once inside its broad opening he tugged down the garagelike door.

Katia didn't ask questions. Not yet. She wanted to see what Jordan planned to say and do. So she watched, arms wrapped around herself for warmth, while he lit a small hurricane lamp, then dragged cushions from a shelf, tossed them into the hull of one of the small sailboats, and reached for a pair of blankets. He wrapped one around her shoulders, did the same for himself, then helped her into the boat.

Faint amusement lit her features. It was typically Jordan to avoid the main house and burrow instead under a blanket in the hull of a boat.

"Warm enough?" he asked, nestling close beside her.

"Um-hmm."

He nodded and looked off into the darkness, only to look back moments later. "Are you sure?"

"I'm sure."

Again he nodded. Beneath the blanket his clothes were soaked. He knew Katia's were, too. "Would you rather go up to the house and change?"

"No. This is fine."

The hurricane lamp cast a faint golden glow on her face. He studied it. "You're not still angry?"

"No. I guess I left that behind in New York."

"You had a right to be angry. I've been a bastard."

She said nothing.

"It's amazing," he thought aloud as he gazed into the darkness again, "I've always prided myself on being on top of things. Knowing the score. But man, I've really blown it this time." He blew out a breath of dismay. "I assumed things I shouldn't have and reached conclusions I shouldn't have, and now, when things should be coming together, they're falling apart."

Instinctively Katia knew, as she had on the phone, that Jordan had a problem that went beyond their relationship. "What do you mean?"

Katia's mere presence had a soothing effect on him, enabling him to say what he had to with a remarkable degree of calm. "It looks like I may be indicted for Mark and Deborah's murders."

"*What?*"

"I'm the prime suspect."

"That's absurd! Who said that?"

"Cavanaugh. He's a great guy, and I'm convinced he's on my side, but the evidence he has points directly to me."

She turned toward him and clutched the ends of the blanket to her thudding heart. "What evidence?"

As succinctly as possible he told her about the tape with its incriminating threat and about the motive that, with a stretch of the imagination, a jury might believe. He even told her about his alibi.

"She didn't mean a thing to me, Katia," he said quickly. "I'd been with her two, maybe three times before that, and there was nothing to it but sex."

"You don't have to apologize. I haven't been celibate either." Her response had been given softly, but it didn't hide the touch of hurt she felt. It wasn't Jordan's sex life that bothered her as much as the fact that he had never allowed himself to indulge in that luxury with her.

He tugged the blanket closer around him and studied its fraying edge. "I am apologizing. It makes me sick to think of what I was doing at the time Mark died. If I'd been doing it with you it would have been different."

"But you weren't. We don't do that."

He looked at her with a return of the desperation he had expressed on the phone. "We haven't. And now that I finally feel free to I'm facing the prospect of a trial and if I'm convicted a jail term. A *lengthy* jail term."

"Shh, Jordan," she whispered, hearing only the last. All thought of personal hurt was gone. She touched the spot high on his cheek that always twitched when he was upset. "Don't say that. Don't even *think* it."

He covered her hand with his and pressed it closer. "I try not to, but it just won't go away. I think of my entire life being cut off, just like that, and I begin to sweat and shake. Forget my business. Can you imagine what a trial, let alone a conviction, would do to my family? And the Warrens. How do you think they'll feel if they think I was the one who killed Deborah?"

"They'll never think that. They'll know it was a mistake, and they'll do everything they can to correct it." She shivered, realizing that she was thinking ahead, doing just what she had told Jordan not to do.

Jordan caught her shiver. "Cold?"

She shook her head. "Nervous."

"Come here." He opened his blanket and within moments she was enclosed in it, resting snugly against his chest. "Better?" He knew it was for him. The world was still very dark, but not quite as ominous as it had seemed before.

"Yes," she whispered. "But I can't take all this in."

He knew the feeling. "The proverbial nightmare you can't wake up from."

"It's so incredible that it should be laughable, only it isn't. Cavanaugh struck me as being so . . . *reasonable*."

"He is. I told you, he's on my side. He's doing his best to come up with an alternate suspect."

And if his best wasn't enough? "Alternate suspect. It sounds like a game."

"It isn't."

"I know."

"On the other hand, maybe it is—in some warped guy's brain. Someone committed murder, and whether the murderer intended it or not, I'm about to take the fall. Cavanaugh and I discussed the possibility that I'm being framed, but we haven't any more idea of who could be doing it or why than we have of who could have been vicious enough to take two innocent lives in the first place."

"You do trust Cavanaugh?"

"I haven't any choice. He's the least of the evils. From what he's intimated, his boss is the toughie."

"Who's his boss?"

"A guy named John Ryan. Chief of detectives."

"Do you know anything about him?"

"I know that he's a career man who worked his way steadily up in the ranks, that he's as parochial as they come, and that he'd like to nail me to the wall."

"It can't be personal."

"Maybe not, but he wants a suspect brought in and brought in fast. He's given Cavanaugh a week. After that you'll be seeing my mug shot splashed over every paper in the country."

"Oh, God, Jordan, they couldn't—"

"They could and they would," he answered with a spurt of anger. "They're not concerned about the damage a simple indictment can do. Even if the charges are dropped before it gets to the point of a trial, the harm will have been done. Personally *and* professionally. And if I'm tried and acquitted, can you imagine what would happen? I'd walk down a street and people would stare at the murderer who got off thanks to some fancy attorney." He threw back his head and let out a throaty growl. "I feel so frustrated!"

She squeezed him with the arm that circled his waist, then moved her hand higher to rub his back. "Isn't there anything we can do?"

"No." His was the voice of despair. "That's the worst part. From the time I went off to college I knew I wanted to be my own man. When I graduated and went to work I thought: You've got it all in your hands, Jordan, my man. You can do what you want. You're calling the shots." He grunted. "But I'm not any more and it's driving me insane." He paused, lightly caressing her elbow, and spoke in a very quiet voice. "Maybe I've been deluding myself. In some things I've never called the shots."

"What things?" she asked, but she knew what was coming. She had felt his small caress and was increasingly aware of the nearness of his body.

"I've been such a fool, Katia."

Her silence was an effective prod toward explanation, but Jordan wasn't sure exactly where to start. After several moments of internal debate he went with what he thought would be the simplest and most straightforward. "I know this is going to sound stupid," he said, the words racing out, "but for years now I've actually thought you were my sister."

With a hand flattened on his chest, she levered herself so that she could see his face. "Your *sister?*"

"Half-sister, actually."

"Sister . . . half-sister . . . that's ridiculous, Jordan!"

"You're laughing at me," he said more gruffly, because he hadn't missed the small smile that had broken through her astonishment. "It's not funny. I've been in agony. I wanted to love you when you were nineteen years old—no, even before that—but I was afraid. I honestly thought . . . we were related."

Katia did laugh then. She couldn't help it. When he growled in embarrassment, she put soft fingers against his lips. "I'm not laughing at you—well, maybe a little." In truth her laugh was more one of relief, even exhilaration. He had given her the missing piece to the puzzle she had agonized over for years. She would have jumped up and shouted in jubilation had the urge to hold Jordan not been as great. She slid her hand around to knead the back of his neck. "How could you have thought that?"

This was the part he didn't want to go into. So he waffled. "I don't know. Maybe because you were with us so much. Maybe because you were so young at the time and I seemed so old. Maybe because I was just plain dumb."

"I'll second the last," she said, still grinning.

But Jordan was dead sober. "What do you feel, Katia? For me."

"You know."

"I want to hear you say it."

"I've always loved you."

"Do you now?"

"Yes."

"Oh, God," he said, hugging her, "Oh, God, I'm glad."

Katia could have told him she loved him again and again, but she was too busy enjoying the full force of his hug. When he lowered his head and kissed her, she was with him all the way. At first there was a desperation to the kiss, coming as it had on the heels of that more sobering discussion. But desperation inevitably fell

victim to the overpowering and highly emotional attraction between them, which was now enhanced by their declared love.

There was a freedom to their mouths and tongues that had
never quite been there before, and that made the kiss all the
sweeter. And slower. What started with greed and hunger gradually eased into awe-filled exploration.

"Right about now," Jordan murmured somewhat dazedly, "I
was always thinking that I ought to stop, only I couldn't, so I gave
myself another couple of minutes. I'd kiss you again." He put his
words into action, then after a bit went on, "But it would never be
enough. I wanted to touch you and hold you like a man holds a
woman, so I'd give myself another couple of minutes. . . ."

His voice trailed off. In the dim glow of the lamp, his eyes
caught hers and held them while he worked his way between the
blankets until he reached her blouse. His hands were unsteady
and the sodden fabric fought him, so it was awhile before the last
of the buttons squeaked through their holes. But the wait was
worth it, for both of them. Jordan carefully eased the wet cloth
aside and rested appreciative eyes on her breasts, while Katia felt
her flesh swelling into his view.

"Right about now," he went on hoarsely, "I'd be thinking,
you've got to stop, my man. You're treading on dangerous ground.
But I wouldn't be able to stop, because more than anything I
wanted to take off your bra and see you and feel you."

His eyes rose to hers, asking permission. Rather than give it,
Katia released the front closure of the bra herself and drew the
lacy cups away. Instinctively, because everything inside her was
starting to stir, she arched her back. It was an invitation that
Jordan accepted with a low moan.

His hands were gentle, worshipping her as though it were the
first time he had touched anything as beautiful. His long fingers
covered her, outlining her shape and fullness. She was unaware of
the chill in the air; she had begun to smolder from the inside out.
An arc of fire seared her when he touched her taut nipples, and
she cried out at the near painful sensation.

Then she bit her lip, took a deep breath, and whispered, "Right about now, I'd be thinking that if I didn't touch you myself I'd die." Fingers eager, she pulled the bottom of his turtleneck from his pants and pushed the jersey fabric only high enough to allow her hands access to his chest. She loved the hardness of his muscles, the faint abrasion of the dark swirls of hair against her palms. No man she had ever known was quite like Jordan this way, with an outer strength that masked an inner warmth that, in turn, positively captivated her.

She bent to kiss his chest at the same time that he bent toward her breasts, and their heads knocked. Laughing, Jordan simply drew her against him. His eyes closed, he drew in a quivering breath. He moved her around, rolling her breasts against him. "Do you remember when we were on the Vineyard and I did this?"

"I remember." She was having trouble breathing. Everything in her system was going haywire.

"You were half zonked—"

"So were you—"

"But I felt everything, and I thought I was going to make a complete fool of myself by coming there and then I was so hard."

"Jordan, Jordan," she whispered against his throat. "I want to touch you. I've always wanted to, and only once you let me, and after that everything hurt, but I couldn't forget how you felt."

"I was so close . . . and sinful, I thought. . . ."

Her hands were already inching their way down his sides. "Let me do it now . . . unless. . . ." Too clearly she remembered the times he had caught her hand and pulled it away.

But this time when he caught her hand he pressed it to his stomach while with his free hand he unsnapped his jeans. He struggled with the wet zipper, and swore softly when he had to release her to complete the task. The instant the zipper was lowered he brought her hand to him, urging it under the band of his briefs, then moaning when she took him in her grasp. He remembered that day, too, up on the little beach grass throne, only now it was so much better because he *knew* it was right.

Soft gasps mingled with the pounding of rain on the roof, Katia breathing as raggedly as Jordan. She caressed him; he caressed her back. He bared more skin, both hers and his, savoring each new revelation until they both were on the verge of losing control.

"Right about now—" he began with difficulty, because they were naked, kneeling before one another. "But there's never been right about now before." His hands clenched her hips as he swallowed hard.

"In my dreams," she whispered, then shifted up when he urged her astride his lap. "So many times in my dreams. . . ."

Jordan felt near to explosion, and he knew Katia was because he felt her warmth and wetness and quivering when he stroked her. Now, looking into her eyes, he wondered if anticipation could be as heady as consummation. He loved her. He felt the words, spoke them with his eyes, whispered them with the last bit of unfragmented breath he could summon.

Then, very slowly, he lowered her. He nearly closed his eyes; she was tight and hot around him, seeming to grow more so as he penetrated, and the knowledge that this was Katia combined with the physical pleasure itself to make the sensation almost unbearable. A low sound of passion tore from his throat simultaneously with one from hers, but he didn't close his eyes, and what he saw made the effort worth it.

Katia bit her lower lip. Her lids lowered and her head fell back. When Jordan buried himself fully, she dug her fingers into his arms as a dynamic climax shook her. She was madly gasping for breath when she started to laugh.

"My God, Jordan! That's never happened to me! Knowing it was *you* inside . . . everything I felt was so strong . . . I don't believe it!"

"Hold on," Jordan rasped. His eyes were squeezed shut now, his face tense. He withdrew nearly all the way, then surged forward deeply and forcefully into his own prolonged and powerful climax.

Katia, who had sucked in her breath when she realized what was happening, was watching him with every bit of the fascination he had felt moments before. She felt him pulsing inside her, gradually slowing, and saw his features flow from that tight state to a pleasure-pain kind of frown to a more relaxed and utterly satisfied smile.

"Unh, Katia." He opened his eyes and looked at her. With a second grunt he pulled her close, burrowing his chin in her hair, enfolding her tightly in his arms. "Ahh. I knew there had to be more. All those years I knew there had to be."

She might have echoed his words had it not been for the fact that it would have sounded tacky; besides, she knew that he knew what she was feeling. So, with her thighs spread over his and their bodies still joined, she settled against him, basking in his body's warmth and musky smell, even the fine sheen of dampness that had nothing to do with the rain.

"I love you, Jordan," she whispered.

"Say it again."

"I love you."

"Will you marry me?"

"Yes."

"Just like that?"

"*Just like that?* Do you know how many *years* I've been waiting for you to ask?"

Jordan wore a look of happiness, then amusement. "Damn, but I never expected it'd happen this way."

"What way?"

"Here, in this dingy boathouse with the rain coming down in sheets outside and a murder rap hanging over my—"

For a second time that night she pressed her fingers to his mouth. "Shh. Don't say it. Not now."

"Still," he sighed, "I hadn't planned it this way."

"You planned it?"

"No, I didn't plan it," he chided, "at least, not in the sense you're thinking. When I called you today all I knew was that I had to see you. It would have been enough if you had come. I needed to be away from the city and I needed to talk, and you were the only one I wanted to talk with." He went on in a lighter tone. "But let me tell you, I've done my share of dreaming since last Friday—"

"Last Friday? What happened then?"

"That was when I asked my father if he'd ever—if we were— if Cassie and he. . . ."

"If I was your sister?" she asked with a laugh.

"Don't laugh. I honestly believed it at the time."

"I'll bet Jack was thrilled you asked him."

"Yeah. Thrilled. Maybe he had a good laugh about it too."

"Come on, Jordan. I'm only teasing. But I want to know more about these plans of yours."

"My plans? Oh, my plans." He rolled his eyes. "Let's see, there was candlelight and satin sheets—"

She butted her head into his chest. "I knew that would come back to haunt me."

"Actually, it sounded pretty romantic, certainly more so than what you got."

"Are you kidding? Anyone who thinks that making love on cushions in the hull of a boat in a boathouse with a hurricane lamp for atmosphere isn't romantic doesn't have a sense of adventure."

"Whoever that is may be smarter than me." He shifted. "These cushions are none too comfy."

"Uh-oh. You're sore." He had been, and still was, bearing the brunt of their combined weight, and beneath the cushions were hard wood spines.

"Actually . . ." He grinned, and she knew exactly what he meant. That little shift he had made had moved him inside her the tiniest bit, creating the sweetest ripple of sensation. "No," he said firmly. "This time we'll go up to the house and make love in style."

But when he would have withdrawn Katia clamped her fingers on his hips. "Oh, no, buster. You've done this to me once too often." She undulated her bottom. "Mmm. This time you're going to finish what you've started."

"What *I've* started?"

"Yes, what you've started," she retorted, but it was feeble as retorts went, because what was inside her was growing by the minute, and its mere presence was enough to take her breath away.

Much later, they got ready to dash through the rain to the house. Their arms were laden with clothes and Katia's case, and the blankets they had wrapped around themselves were blowing in the wind through the open door of the boathouse, exposing an arm here, a leg there, even a bun or two in the process.

"This is insane," Katia said. "George will think we're crazy."

"George is in his cottage, probably sleeping. And even if he weren't, he's sure as hell not going to be patrolling the grounds in the pouring rain. He knows I'm here. Nothing I do can shock him anymore."

"Well, I don't have your scandalous reputation, Jordan Whyte. What'll he think of *me* if he sees me running half naked through the rain?"

"He's not going to *see*, and besides, the little nothings you wear by the pool aren't exactly prim."

"That's by the pool."

"You're stalling."

"You're right."

"Come on. The sooner we leave the sooner we can get to the house. I could use a hot shower, and I haven't eaten all day, and I didn't sleep a wink last night, and I want to love you on nice, soft sheets."

"In that order?"

"Not necessarily."

Katia peered out at the gusting rain. "I don't know, Jordan. I'm not sure anything's worth going out in that."

To which Jordan responded by grabbing her hand and dragging her onward. When they reached the house, showers were, in-deed, the first order of business. They were chilled. The hot water helped, as did the fact that they shared it.

The second order of business was food. They ate as though they had been starved for days, then left the dishes, pans and mugs for morning and went to bed.

Sleep, however, was not the next order of business. Jordan proceeded to love Katia as he had dreamed of doing so many times. There wasn't an inch of her body that his hands didn't touch or his mouth didn't taste. And if some of the things he did stunned her, she had only to look down at his dark head or meet his impassioned gaze to realize that this was Jordan, *this was Jordan*, and she was in heaven. It was the fulfillment of a dream for her as well.

Come morning—very late morning—they awoke in each other's arms, where they lay, comfortably and peacefully, while they talked.

"I've always known you loved me," Katia mused, almost afraid of the happiness she felt.

"You have, have you?"

"Umm-hmmm. But I never knew in what way."

"Brother or lover?"

She nodded against his chest. "I was confused."

"*You* were confused? Think of what *I* felt. When I was twenty-five you knocked my socks off. All of a sudden the little girl I'd adored like a sister was a gorgeous woman."

"I was only sixteen—"

"Mmm. Trouble there. You sorely tried my patience. When you were nineteen and did that seduction bit—"

"I did not! You were the one who suggested we go for a swim in the middle of the night! You were the one who made the first move!"

"Yeah. But you weren't fighting me."

"No," she said more softly. She put her cheek to his chest so that she wouldn't have to look him in the eye. "Know what I did after that fiasco? I went back to New York and promptly went to bed with the guy I was seeing. It was awful. It hurt, and it was messy, and I was so angry afterward—mostly at myself, though I never told John that—that I accused him of being the most inept lover in the world." She moaned. "I was cruel. I don't think I've ever been that mean to anyone, but I was hurting, and what I'd done had been done to spite you, and poor John was just . . . there. We broke up soon after."

"Was it better with Sean?"

She did look at him then, propping her chin on his chest. "Better, yes. But it was never what I always *felt* it should be. I mean, he was wonderful in his way—warm, considerate, intelligent. I tried to convince myself that I loved him, but how could I do that when all along I was loving you? I knew the jig was up when Sean insisted on marriage."

Jordan said nothing, but the look of gratitude in his eyes was enough to propel her on.

"I think he knew I'd never settle down with him. He was no dummy. He used the issue of marriage to force me into taking a stand." She stroked his chest. "Ah, Jordan. Nothing I felt with Sean remotely resembled what I feel with you."

He grinned. "You're good for my ego."

"Your ego doesn't need my 'good.'" There was more than a little accusation in her voice.

"That's not true," he said with such boyish innocence that she had to laugh. But her laugh died when he grew somber. "Right about now I need all the help I can get."

She knew he was thinking of what awaited him on the mainland. "Let's get married now."

"Now?" He looked around the bedroom. "I think we're missing a few things, like a minister, uh, judge—"

His word switch diverted her for a minute. "I went to temple a lot when I was in college. I never told you that, did I?"

"No."

"I would have done it after Kenny died, but I was young, and when I was old enough I didn't want to do it because I was afraid of upsetting my mother. When I got to New York I couldn't resist the temptation."

"And?"

"It was inspiring. Beautiful services. I did a lot of reading."

"And?"

"I came to the realization that I'd been brought up with pretty universal values. I'm not sure that the specifics of any one religion are as important as overall decency. The most pious Jew, or Protestant or Catholic, for that matter, can be the scum of the earth if he chooses to say one thing and do another."

Jordan pulled her close with arms that trembled. "You are one remarkable lady."

"So when are you gonna make an honest one of me? We could go back to the city today—"

"No. Not yet. I need a little more time alone with you."

"I have to be back in the office on Monday."

"So do I."

"Why don't we do it Sunday night?"

"Because there are little details like blood tests and a license."

"Come on, Jordan. You must have clout in one of the right places. Can't we get those waived?"

He shook his head. "I'm afraid to rush it right now."

"Because of Cavanaugh's dirty business?"

"It's not Cavanaugh's. It's mine." He rolled swiftly, setting her on her back and leaning over her. "I'd pull every string in the book to marry you today, or tomorrow, or the next day, but how can I do that when my future is a big fat question mark?"

"You asked me to marry you."

"Maybe I was dreaming," he said quietly.

"Damn it, Jordan! Don't *do* this to me!"

He kissed her silent, let his lips linger longer, then raised his head and studied her sadly. "What worries me is what I'd be doing to you if we get married now, and within a week I'm charged with murder."

"I don't care!"

"Well I do. There would be ugly words and even uglier publicity. I'd be up to my armpits in shit—"

"I don't care! I love you. Do you think it would be any better for me sitting on the sidelines watching? I want to be there with you, *for* you."

"You can do that from the sidelines. I don't want you exposed to the muckrakers or the whoresons—"

"I am not a weakling, Jordan," she vowed, pushing him back when she came up on her elbows. Her face was set in a stubborn mask. "Marriage is for better or worse. I'd come forward to defend you whether we were married or not, so if you're trying to protect me you're wasting your breath. I can be just as poised in the line of fire as your mother or Lenore ever were—"

"Yeah. They've never been in quite the same line of fire, and even then, look at the toll it's taken on them—"

"Because their marriages weren't as strong as ours would be. We're in this together, Jordan. If—and it's a big if—this ever comes down to a trial, it would be good for the jury to see your new wife sitting right behind you in the courtroom. Don't tie my hands. Please?"

Jordan couldn't take his eyes from her. He thought he had seen every facet of the woman, but he had been wrong. He had known she was strong; perhaps it was just that he'd never seen that strength channeled toward him, as it was now.

"You drive a hard bargain," he murmured at last.

"Only when I believe in something as strongly as I believe in this."

"You really think we should get married right away?"

He was weakening; she tried to curb her excitement. "As soon as possible."

"Just a small ceremony in a judge's chamber?"

"No. Just a small ceremony at your parents' house in Dover. I want them to be there, and my mother, and Gil and Lenore."

"You have it all planned," he said, lips twitching at the corners.

She nodded. "Right down to the wedding ring I want. It's going to be a wide gold band. Shiny, but simple and unadorned. Saying only that we're married. The rest I can say myself."

On the following Wednesday morning Katia and Jordan were married. As Katia had stipulated, the ceremony took place in the Whytes' living room. Not only were the Whytes and Cassie and the Warrens there, but their children and grandchildren had rushed to the scene, as though jumping on the happiness of the event as an antidote for the loss of the summer before.

Unfortunately, the happiness was short-lived. The following Monday, Katia's husband of five days was charged with the murders of his brother and sister-in-law.

At eight o'clock in the morning Cavanaugh appeared at the door of Jordan's condominium. Jordan and Katia were finishing breakfast before leaving for work; all thought of food or work vanished the minute they saw the detective's grim expression.

Apparently, Jordan's alibi witness could swear she had been with him on a Monday night rather than a Sunday night. Moreover, investigators had learned that on the morning of the murders, Jordan had visited an automatic teller on Madison Avenue and withdrawn four hundred dollars in cash, more than enough to cover the rental of scuba equipment and a car. Cavanaugh's vote had been overridden.

There was a brief rendition hearing in a Manhattan courtroom, then the drive to Boston. If Jordan thought the trip tedious, it was nothing compared to what followed. Not until very late that night did he and Katia finally make it to Dover. Jordan had called his father from New York soon after Cavanaugh had arrived. Jack had called Gil, who had quickly flown in from Washington, and together they had broken the news to their wives. All four were waiting when the couple arrived home.

Natalie was immediately on her feet. She opened her arms to Jordan and held him tightly, releasing him only because the other three were clamoring for attention behind her.

"What the hell is this nonsense—"

"Who do they think they are—"

"I don't believe it—"

These outbursts came from Jack, Gil and Lenore respectively. Nor could they stop.

"Someone's going to pay—"

"That Holstrom is a no-good son of a bitch—"

"I don't *believe* it—"

"Believe it," Jordan said, directing his quiet words to Lenore. It took every bit of his effort to keep his voice steady, but still he could not have managed were he not holding Katia's hand tightly in his own. "Someone's got a grudge. It looks like we'll all be bleeding a little."

Natalie came forward, pale and shaky. "Was it true—what they said on the news—about what Mark was doing?"

"It was true."

"You tried to stop him?"

"Sure I did. And look where it got me. Mark and Deborah are dead anyway, and they're saying I did it."

"Well, we don't believe that," Jack blustered.

"Of course not!" Gil raged.

Lenore whimpered, "Who could be so cruel as to commit murder—"

"And put the blame on *you!*" Natalie finished heatedly. The upset she felt at learning of Mark's activities was momentarily supplanted by anger. "It's an insult to *all* of us!"

Jack stepped in front of her and spoke in his most officious voice. "I've already spoken with the mayor. I bring a hell of a lot of business to this city, and if he can't keep his police department on the up and up he's not getting another dime from me."

"It's not a matter of corruption," Jordan protested. "The police are just doing their jobs—"

Gil interrupted him. "Not this way, they're not! They're green with envy, the whole lousy bunch of them. They can't stand it that we have more than they do. They've probably been waiting for years for something like this, and no doubt they're toasting it up right now in some Southie bar. I'm holding a press conference in the morning—"

"No, Gil," Jordan stated firmly. "No press conference. Not yet, at least. We're all angry and upset. Something said under conditions like these could be more damaging than not." He took a deep, steadying breath. "Katia and I have been with VanPelt for the past six hours—"

"Good defense man—"

"Dramatic as hell—"

Jordan looked from one man to the other. "He's confident that we have a good chance in court. The evidence is circumstantial. There's plenty of room for planting doubt in the jurors' minds."

Lenore's high voice followed his words. "Trial? Everything will come out in a trial. What Mark was doing—"

"It's out now," a blustery-faced Gil reminded her. "You can be sure that every paper in the country will have front page articles in the morning." He turned his scowl on Jordan. "The press eats up this kind of thing."

Jordan said nothing. He could still see the flare of the flashes, feel the thrust of microphones under his nose, hear the endless questions. The knot in his stomach tightened.

"How can they *do* that?" Lenore asked, much as Katia had once done.

Natalie was equally worried. "How can you possibly get a fair trial with that kind of publicity?"

"A gag motion. That's what we need," Jack instructed Jordan.

"VanPelt's already filed for it."

Gil was bristling. "The question is how much damage has already been done. Thank God they didn't give you any trouble with bail. That surprised me."

Jordan shrugged. "I don't have a record. Given that and who I am, they had no choice."

"What happens now?" Jack looked from Jordan to Gil—which was ridiculous, since Gil's expertise in law was strictly on the corporate level—and back.

Jordan was the one to answer, having been well tutored by his attorney. "The arraignment today was in the district court, but that court doesn't have jurisdiction over murder cases. Normally there'd be a probable cause hearing in the Boston Municipal Court to see about binding the case to the higher court, but the prosecutor will probably waive it and go directly to the grand jury for a superior court indictment. When that takes place, probably in a couple of weeks, I'll be arraigned again."

"And a trial date?"

"Set within a month or so after that."

"Then we have time," Jack mused. "We have to get an investigator on the case. Some bastard's out there having a good laugh for himself. If the goddamned cops can't find him we'll have to do it ourselves."

Standing before them was growing harder for Jordan by the minute. "Look," he said with a tired sigh, "VanPelt will be on top of all that. We have to work with him. He knows what he's doing. Right now I think I'd like to go upstairs. It's been a long day." Still holding Katia's hand, he turned and headed for the stairs.

"We'll get you out of this, Jordan!" his father called after him. "Everyone's coming over tomorrow morning—Nick and Peter and Laura and Anne, even Emily from New York. We'll figure out something."

"More than that," Gil added in a voice laced with fury, "we'll see that whoever's responsible gets his ass kicked to hell!"

"Fine," Jordan murmured to himself, but he was too drained to do anything but see that one foot followed the other up the stairs. When he and Katia reached the room that had been Jordan's as a boy—where they had stayed on the eve of their wedding six nights before—he drew her in, closed the door and sagged back against it.

The head he had held with dignity through the nightmare of a day dropped forward. The shoulders he had held straight slumped.

At that moment, when dozens of other emotions could easily have been dominating her mind, Katia was aware of feeling nothing but a tremendous pride in her husband. She came close to him and combed the dark hair from his forehead with her fingers.

"You did well, Jordan," she said softly. "You endured it all as no other man could have. You showed them the stuff you're made of, and you showed me, even though I've known it all along. I was very proud to be there by your side."

"Oh God, Katia," he moaned, then leaned forward and wrapped his arms around her. "Oh God. . . ."

His entire body was shaking. Katia held him tighter.

"You have no idea how humiliated I felt." His whisper was a hoarse one, rife with the same pain that continued to shake his body. "Being handcuffed . . . led into the station . . . finger-printed . . . having mug shots taken with that . . . that identification thing in front of me . . . You have no idea . . . no idea."

Wrapping an arm around his back, Katia steered him to the bed. She sat close beside him, never once letting go. "Cavanaugh was suffering, too, not that that's any solace."

He moaned again, this time wrapping his free arm around his stomach. Katia was worried that he was going to be sick he looked so pale.

"It hurts, damn it," he managed through gritted teeth. "I knew it was coming. I sensed it in my gut. But knowing didn't help. Nothing could have prepared me for that."

She stroked his face, feeling as helpless as he. "But it's over. That part, at least." She kissed his shoulder. "Can I get you anything? Are you hungry?" VanPelt had had dinner brought to his office, but Jordan hadn't eaten a bite.

He shook his head.

"How about some aspirin?"

He nodded.

Reluctant to leave him, she kissed his forehead, then hurried down the hall to the bathroom, returning moments later with the pills and a glass of water. Jordan had taken off his blazer, a pocket of which held the tie he had stuffed there while they had been with the lawyer, and he was working on the buttons of his shirt. While he took the aspirin, she released the remaining buttons, then pulled back the bedspread while he finished undressing.

Only after she saw him crawl into bed and stretch out with a groan did she start undressing herself. Moments later, she slid beneath the sheets.

His eyes were closed, his features tight. She was wondering if he would be able to relax enough to sleep when he extended an arm to her in invitation. Without pause she tucked herself against him, satisfied when he closed the gate around her.

She kissed the soft spot adjacent to his armpit that she so adored. "I love you, Jordan."

With a wrenching moan he tightened his hold on her. She could feel the beat of his heart reverberating through his body; its strength remained dominant over the ordeals of life, and it was but another thing to love about him. Brushing her cheek against his chest, she began to press soft kisses to his skin.

"Mmm . . . better than aspirin . . ." he murmured.

"It's the power of love." She drew herself over him. Her kisses spread, open and moist on the dark swirls of his chest hair, the corded column of his neck, the slightly raspy but thoroughly appealing contours of his jaw and the smoother, more gentle lines of his face. They held no pity, only love and desire, but it was perhaps the indignities he had suffered that day and the way he had weathered them that made her want to show the phenomenal strength of that love and desire.

It wasn't difficult. Touching Jordan had always affected Katia deeply. Now, knowing that he was her husband, knowing that she

was free to express her feelings, she let herself go without restraint.

Her hands roamed widely and with purpose, caressing his
hard body. Very slowly, as her fingers worked the muscled expanse of his chest, the lean plane of his stomach, the roped sinews
of his thighs, she felt the tension of the day fade. Very slowly, as
her mouth went the way of her hands, she felt a different tension
begin to build. His skin grew heated. Anchoring his fingers in her
hair, he hoarsely whispered her name. His breath came more rap-
idly and his muscles began to quiver.

"I love you," she vowed against his stomach, "I love you. . . ."

When she slipped lower and took him into her mouth, he
caught in a ragged breath. Her sandy hair swirled lightly over his
groin, but it was the deeper sensation that brought his hips straining upward. Her tongue worked wonders, erasing all thought
from his mind but the one that mattered most—that Katia was his
wife, accepting him fully. Her lips added to the sweet torment,
proclaiming her the ultimate lover as well. His muscles grew taut
and trembled with restraint; what she was doing was so intimate,
so intense that, looking down at the gentle movement of her head,
he knew the immediacy of explosion. A low, raw sound came
from his throat seconds before he bucked back into the mattress.

With a single deft movement he drew her up and flipped her
over, then surged forward into a fluid penetration. He plunged
more deeply with each stroke, and with each stroke she felt more
possessed. His mouth muffled her cries of delight, swallowing her
breath, offering his own in exchange.

Katia realized then that their marriage would always be a two-
sided affair. As much as she wanted to give that night, Jordan did
too. It was his need, and she accepted it, loving him to distraction,
soaring with him to the far reaches of passion. And when they had
finally returned to earth and caught their breath, they settled
snugly against one another, as was meant to be.

They didn't sleep, but lay quietly for a time. At last Jordan
murmured a broken, "Thank you, sweetheart."

"No thanks necessary."

"They are. You were with me today. You stood by me. I feel guilty as hell putting you through—"

Her hand covered his mouth. "Don't say it. I wouldn't have been anywhere else."

He tickled her fingers with his tongue until they retreated in self-defense. Then he slanted her a one-eyed glance. "Not even on a honeymoon in the Caribbean?"

"Nah. It's too hot there now."

"Then London? Or Paris? Or Sydney, Australia?"

"Australia? I'd love to go there one day."

Jordan wanted to say that she would get there, that he would take her there, but he couldn't get the words out.

Katia knew what he was thinking. She also knew that to protest his thoughts would cause him more anguish than it was worth. He was tired and tense and very pessimistic at the moment. He would feel better in the morning. He would feel better once VanPelt crystalized a plan of attack. And she would feel better once Jordan felt better, because the one thing she couldn't do was allow herself to think of what might happen if he was actually convicted.

Chapter 17

CAVANAUGH SAT ALONE AT HOME that night feeling like death. What he had been forced to do that day had gone against every instinct he possessed. For the first time in his life he truly despised his job. He also despised himself, because he was sure that Jordan was innocent, yet he hadn't been able to prove it. And now, theoretically, he was out of the case. Aside from testifying during the hearings and trial to come, his job was done.

He couldn't blame the commissioner for being pleased; it was a feather in Holstrom's cap to have an arrest in any murder case, and he wasn't involved deeply enough with this one to feel what Cavanaugh did. The same held true for the DA, who would only be doing his job by prosecuting the case.

But Ryan bothered Cavanaugh. The pleasure in the man's eyes that day had been enough to turn his stomach. How could someone take pleasure in seeing a human being humbled as Jordan had been? How could any man, much less a policeman, gloat that way? But it was consistent with everything else Ryan had done regarding the case. Since the day the bodies had been found he had been itching to arrest a family member. If it hadn't been Jordan it would have been one of the others. Ryan had been so sure that they were involved. *How had he been so sure?* How had he known the tapes existed? And why had he been so damned eager to rush the arrest?

They were questions with no answers, which frustrated Cavanaugh beyond belief.

His gaze skirted the apartment. It was quiet and still. Jodi had flown to Atlanta two days before to be with her mother, who was in the hospital with a broken hip after an automobile accident. It occurred to Cavanaugh, suddenly and with some surprise, that he would have really liked to talk his feelings out with Jodi. She could assure him that he had done everything he could. She could help him put things into perspective.

But she wasn't there. He was on his own as he had always been. The fact that for the first time it bothered him was interesting. Maybe he was getting old, or mellow. Then again, maybe Jodi, with her independence, her intelligence and her warmth, had simply wormed her way into his life as no other woman, including his ex-wife, had done. He should be annoyed, he told himself, but he wasn't. At least not on that score.

Which left the matter of Jordan's arrest. Cavanaugh tried to imagine what Jodi would say if she were there. Yes, she would say that he had tried his best, but she would go further. She would ask about his feelings toward his job. She would talk about commitment—not so much to that job, per se, but to general beliefs. She would explore the issue of John Ryan in search of the possible motivation or justification for his behavior. She would tell Cavanaugh that if he had serious doubts about Jordan's guilt he should do something about it, rather than sit around the house like a . . . mummy.

He smiled fleetingly. Yes, that was what she would say. And she would be right. He couldn't formally reopen the case, but he damn well could keep his eyes and ears open, and he damn well could continue to ask questions on his own. The answers had to be somewhere. They *had* to be.

Natalie suffered as much in the days that followed as Jordan and Katia. She ached for them. She had suspected that Jordan had been in love with Katia for years, and though she still didn't know what had kept them apart, she had never seen such a radiant bride and groom on the day of their wedding. They were good for each other. They were both mature, as perhaps she hadn't been when she had married Jack, and they were both financially secure. They had all the things going for them that she hadn't had. To have it all snatched from their hands was a twist of fate of the cruelest sort.

She also ached because she knew with profound conviction that Jordan was totally innocent of the charges against him. She was his mother. She had raised him and knew him well. Where Mark had been more elusive, Jordan had always been there in every sense of the word. Jordan had loved Mark; they might have argued, but Jordan loved him. For Jordan to be accused of any murder was obscene; for him to be accused of Mark's murder, let alone Deborah's, was insane.

Then too she ached as only a mother could when told her child had been involved in something as horrible as child pornography. She still couldn't believe it. Nor could she understand it. She had to accept that it was true, since Jordan had seen it first-hand, but she spent hour upon hour wondering where she had gone so far wrong with Mark.

Finally she ached for Jack, because she knew that he was hurting too. He had begun to come to her as he hadn't done in years. He had canceled the business trips that had been on his schedule and went into the office for no more than four or five hours a day. The rest of the time he was home, more often than not choosing to sit in the very room where she was. They talked more than they had in ages, about the children and the grandchildren, and, yes, about Mark and about what Jordan was facing. It was, indeed, what they all faced, because despite their differences Jordan was Jack's son. His indictment was an indictment on Jack as well as Natalie.

Though Natalie wished that the closeness she and Jack were finding was caused by anything but the present circumstances, she was grateful nonetheless. She and Jack were both getting older. Too often she had looked back on the years and seen stark voids where her relationship with her husband was concerned. She knew there had been other women and it had hurt from time to time, but the needs she had now were emotional, not sexual. When it came to her husband's company, she found that she wasn't a prideful person. She didn't care why he had returned to her, just that he had.

And, yet, with all this pain tearing at them, Natalie and Jack seemed to be taking the situation better than anyone else.

Lenore worried. She tried not to do it—she had been better in the past few years—but she couldn't help herself. Deborah's death had been bad enough, but Jordan being accused of it was the twisting of the knife.

Her children had taken Jordan's indictment even harder than they had taken Deborah's death. Laura was drinking more; Lenore could see history repeating itself and she didn't know what to do about it, so she did nothing but worry. When Emily was in Dover she stormed about the house in a perpetual dramatic rage, which Lenore would have been unable to handle under any circumstances much less the tormenting ones of the present, so she simply wrung her hands each time Emily passed. Peter vacillated between fury that someone could possibly think Jordan a murderer and shock at the ramifications for his own personal career; Lenore agreed with both, so she wasn't much help at offering comfort.

More than once in those tense days immediately following the indictment she headed for the living room bar, but on each instance she stopped just short of it. She didn't want to drink. When she drank she felt ill, and when she felt ill she went to her room, and when she did that her husband was justified in thinking the worst of her.

It mattered to her what Gil thought. After that day in the attic years before, when Natalie and Cassie had managed to talk her out of despondency, she had decided that they had been right in suggesting that she had given Gil cause to seek company elsewhere. Not long after that she had started to work in Gil's office—

albeit the Boston, rather than the Washington one, and only several afternoons a week—but something very strange had happened. It wasn't that Gil began to look at her differently, but that she began to look at herself differently. She wasn't stuffing envelopes or typing letters; she was greeting people. Granted, many of the constituents who stopped in came with problems that she farmed out to Gil's paid staffers, but even then she felt she was doing something constructive.

Unfortunately, she hadn't yet managed to fully transfer her improved self-image to the home front. She wasn't needed there. Cassie took full control of the house. Gil took full control of the finances. The groom took full control of the stables, the groundsman took full control of the property. There didn't seem to be anything she could do at home to exert herself. And in the present situation, with the rest of her family so full of opinions and emotions, she took her customary place in the background. And worried.

Gil, in particular, caused her worry. He was looking unusually tired. Like Jack, he had been in Dover more of late than ever before, but those hours were spent, of choice, alone in the library. He looked older. He moved slower. Lenore shouldn't have been surprised; after all, he was seventy-four. But he suddenly lacked vitality. There was something beyond his age, something to do with the look of defeat she saw on his face from time to time that disturbed her most.

"Are you feeling all right?" she asked one night at dinner.

"Fine. A little tired. But I'm fine."

"Gil?" She had been thinking about something as she had watched him come and go before her in the past few weeks. "Will you be running again next year?"

He looked up in surprise, perhaps even annoyance. "Of course I will. Did you think I wouldn't?"

His tone stung. She had hoped it would change with the effort she had made to be more accommodating, but it hadn't. Gil seemed to pride himself on being an icon of strength before her, and while she wanted to tell him it wasn't necessary all the time, she feared his reaction. "You'll have been in the House for twenty-four years when this term expires. You seem tired. I was wondering if you've ever given thought to retiring."

"Not particularly. I may be slowing down on the outside, but up here," he tapped his head, "everything's shipshape."

"Still . . . lately—"

"Lately I've been worried about Jordan and Katia. What they're facing—what we're all facing—is enough to make any man tired. Despite what Peter says, VanPelt seems to be doing everything right." His features tightened in frustration. "I was hoping the investigator would find something before the case was bound over to the grand jury, but it looks like that won't happen. And when Jordan is rearraigned, it'll be as unpleasant as the first time. They shouldn't have to be facing that—Jordan and Katia shouldn't—at this point in their lives. They should be thinking of buying a house in the country and having babies."

Lenore rather envied Jordan and Katia for the concern Gil felt for them. "Katia's still working."

Gil's smile held a touch of smugness. "That I can understand. How else can she keep sane in a world that's gone mad? Work is her salvation." *As it always was mine*, she could hear him say. Indeed, he was shaking his head and continuing as though he had said just that. "No, I can't retire. If I were to do that I'd be dead in a week."

But it was only three days later that Jordan received a phone call from Boston. Within minutes he was on his way to Katia's office. One look at his drawn face and she was on her feet. "Something's wrong," she murmured, though she had no idea what more could possibly be wrong.

Jordan took her hand. "It's Gil. He's had a major coronary. I just got the call."

"Gil?" she echoed in a tiny voice. Then, without another word, she reached back for her purse and left with Jordan.

Two hours later they were landing in Boston and taking a cab to the hospital. Though they had held hands all the way, neither had said much during the flight or cab ride to the hospital. After a brief elevator ride and a slightly longer and more frustrating search for Gil's room, they turned a corner and saw, waiting in the hall just beyond, the scattered gathering of Whytes and Warrens.

"How is he?" Jordan asked to the group in general.

A solemn Peter came forward. "He's resting."

"What do the doctors say?"

"That the next few days are critical. If he can survive them he has a fair chance. In any case he's going to have to start taking it easy."

"Can we see him?" Katia asked shakily.

"We've all taken turns, but just for a minute or two. My mother's with him now."

Dropping Jordan's hand, Katia moved slowly to the glass window and looked into the room. Gil lay on the bed, his face nearly as white as the hospital sheets. Oxygen tubes ran from his nose, an intravenous from his hand. Visible above the sheet were monitors on his chest, connected in turn to machines by the bed.

Lenore sat in a chair close by Gil, her face reflecting the same fear that Katia felt deep inside.

Jordan came up behind his wife. He looked at the man in the bed, then down at Katia, who tore her gaze from Gil's face long enough to cast a beseeching glance at him. "I want to see him," she whispered. "I have to see him."

Jordan studied her for several minutes before nodding, but even before he had moved Lenore rose and came to the door.

She held it open for Katia and Jordan, then stepped outside as soon as they had entered.

For a minute, as the door closed quietly behind her, Katia couldn't move. Her knees seemed locked in spite of the fine trembling that shook the rest of her. Then Jordan took her hand, and giving it a squeeze, cocked his head toward the bed.

"Katia?" It was Gil's voice, hoarse and frightfully frail.

"It's me," she answered unsteadily. Her legs started working again. Crossing to the far side of the bed, she took the hand Gil weakly offered her. "Jordan and I just got here. How are you feeling?"

"Not great."

She swallowed down a wail and forced a crooked smile. "Your timing couldn't have been worse, Gil. If you had to have a heart attack you could at least have waited until the end of the legislative session."

At another time Gil would have given a robust laugh and said something about how the damned fools would be struggling without him. But his face was devoid of humor as his eyes held hers. "Jordan will be cleared, Katia. I want you to know that . . . and be strong."

"I'm trying," she said, feeling weaker than ever, torn by the sight of him lying in bed and the strange sound of his voice.

Gil's gaze darted briefly to Jordan's face before returning to Katia's. "Jordan will take care of you. I feel better knowing you've married him." He took a sharp breath and winced at the effort. "I've worried. There was so much I'd like to have done—"

Katia's fingertips flew to cover his mouth. She gave several short, firm shakes of her head. "You shouldn't be worrying about me."

"I do. I always have. You mean more to me—"

Again she silenced him. "Please, Gil. Just concentrate on getting well."

But instead Gil shook his head, slowly and with resignation. "I don't think that's going to happen." He faltered. "I've lived a long life, fuller than most . . . and I've tempted the devil once too often to get . . . away with it this time."

"You should rest," she whispered, terrified when he seemed to be fading before her eyes. He had always been so strong. "All this talking is only tiring you out."

"Talking's what I do best," he came back with a surge of

strength that was gone in the next breath. "It's what I've always done best. I think I've let some of you down because of that."

She squeezed his hand. "You haven't let us down. We love you. Don't you know that?"

"Do you?" he asked sadly.

Her voice was the faintest of whispers. "Oh, yes."

Weakly, he raised her hand to his mouth and kissed it. Then, even more weakly, he reached up to brush his fingers against her cheek. "And I've always loved you," he whispered before he closed his eyes.

Katia gasped, but Jordan was close by her elbow. "It's okay, sweetheart. The monitors are fine. He's just resting."

Nodding dumbly, she leaned forward and brushed a kiss on Gil's pale cheek. "Sleep well," she murmured brokenly. "I'll be back."

Straightening, she let Jordan lead her from the room, then down the hall until they were out of earshot of the others. She sagged against the wall, then against Jordan when he drew her into a protective embrace.

"You knew," he breathed by her ear.

She nodded, but it was another minute before she could speak. "I've known for years."

"How?"

"My artwork . . . and Gil's. The way my mother looked at him. The way he looked at me."

Jordan rubbed his cheek against her hair. "You were quicker on the uptake than I was. It wasn't until my father denied his involvement that I put two and two together." He had known there had to have been an explanation for the conversation he had overheard so many years before.

"Why didn't you tell me that night in Maine?"

"My mother and Gil chose not to say anything. I wasn't sure it was my place to."

"But he's your father!" Knowing that she knew explained why

she had been so adamant about a wedding at which both Cassie and Gil were present.

"And now he's dying. He is, isn't he, Jordan?"

"We don't know that," he answered very softly. "Modern medicine can work wonders."

But she was shaking her head against his chest. "It sounds like he's given up the fight, which is so unlike him that it's almost unfair. How can he do this to us?"

"At some point we have to stand on our own two feet. We've been doing it for years you and I, but knowing that Gil and my dad were there helped. What bothers me is thinking that something about my whole situation," he couldn't get himself to be more blunt, "was what brought this on."

Katia immediately drew her head back and looked up at him. "No, Jordan. It was nothing you did, or Mark did, or any of us did. It was life. Gil's lived hard. We both know that. He's weathered many another storm without a heart attack. You can't blame yourself for what's happened now."

Jordan wasn't quite convinced, but then his thinking processes seemed to have been screwed up for days. "Well, I guess that's water over the dam. All we can do is to hope that Gil recovers."

Gil didn't recover. Twenty-four hours later he suffered a second, fatal attack. Katia and Jordan were at the hospital—as they had been for the majority of those hours—along with the other Whytes and Warrens when the doctor emerged from the room and shook his head.

The funeral was nothing like Mark and Deborah's. For one thing it was strictly private, kept so by the fact that only the immediate family and friends were notified of the arrangements. For another, a stiff fall wind was blowing, causing the mourners to raise their collars against it. For a third, Lenore had taken charge.

This last was the most profound difference. Something had happened to Lenore at Gil's death. At first she had wept and

started to crumble, then she had caught herself, and to the astonishment of her family she pulled herself upright. Before anyone
quite knew what had happened, she had begun in her own quiet
way to assert herself.

And she had stood firm. When Peter had argued that a private
rite would exclude the many people who had been part of Gil's
life, Lenore had insisted that the mourning ritual was for the sake
of family and that she, for one, wanted to have Gil to herself for a
change. When Laura had pointed out that Gil's colleagues and
constituents would want to do something, Lenore had announced
that there could be a memorial service in Washington during the
week after the funeral and that anyone else who cared to do something could make a donation in Gil's name to the charity of his or
her choice. When Emily had warned that the press would be sniff-
ing around for coverage, Lenore declared that the Whytes and
Warrens had given them too much, particularly recently, to sniff
around for and that if the press couldn't observe common decency
they could stew.

Lenore had her way, partly because deep down the rest of the
family agreed with her and partly because they were so stunned
by her sudden show of control and strength that they couldn't
muster the words, much less the heart, to defy her. She stood far
more strongly at the funeral than anyone would have expected,
certainly more strongly than her children, Natalie and Jack, or
Katia.

Or Cassie. Standing off to the side, head bowed, cheeks damp,
she was a figure draped in sadness. Katia and Jordan stood by her
side, but for the most part she seemed oblivious of their presence.
Only when they had returned to the house and Cassie had tried
to help serve dinner, though her hands were visibly shaking, did
Katia slip away from the table and take her mother back to the
cottage.

There they held each other, crying softly for the man they had
both loved but who had never been fully theirs. For the very first

time Katia acknowledged what she knew, just as Cassie acknowledged what she felt.

"Most people would have thought I was crazy to stay with him all these years," she murmured as she dabbed at her eyes with a handkerchief. "But they didn't know him as I did. They didn't know how truly kind he was and how much he suffered inside sometimes. They didn't know the feeling of coming suddenly alive when he entered the room."

"You loved him deeply."

"Too deeply for my own good, maybe. It's possible that I could have done more with my life if I'd been willing to leave him, but I wasn't. Just seeing him from time to time, or talking together as we used to do was enough to keep me going."

Katia thought about that as she stroked her mother's back. "What about Henry? What did you feel for him?"

"I was fond of him. I never told him what I felt for Gil, but I'm sure he knew. I'm sure Lenore does, too." A broken laugh emerged through her tears. "It's a miracle either of them kept me around."

"They both needed you. Just like Gil did."

Cassie dropped her eyes to the handkerchief she was fingering. "Well, I don't know how much he *needed* me. But he did love me. I'm sure of that. Love goes a long way toward forgiving a world of other sins."

"We're all guilty of sins, Mom."

Cassie looked up. "What are yours?"

"I've spent the last few days crying on Jordan's shoulder, clinging to him as though he's going to be taken away from me any second. I've been ranting about how unfair life is, pretty much feeling sorry for myself." Her voice cracked. Self-mockery wasn't working. She was perilously close to tears again. "It's so *hard*— this on top of everything else. I'm growing superstitious. Things just aren't going my way."

Smoothing the hair from Katia's damp cheeks, Cassie reminded her softly, "You have Jordan."

"But he's going to be arraigned before the superior court next week." One tear, then another trickled down her cheek. "He'll have to stand trial. Nothing's come up to counter the charges against him."

"There's time—"

"But *nothing's* come up. No tips, no leads, nothing. If he goes to trial, he'll be convicted—"

"That's not necessarily true—"

"But that's how I'm seeing things right now!" She was crying freely. "And if he's convicted I'll be spending the next hundred years of my life loving him from a distance, which was very much what you had to do with Gil. You must be that much stronger than me, because I don't think I could bear it! I've waited so long, so long for Jordan, and to have it all taken away again. . . ."

Cassie took her in her arms and crooned to her, "Shh. You're thinking too far ahead, assuming things that might never happen."

"I have to be prepared," Katia gulped between sobs.

"No you don't! Jordan will *not* be convicted. You will *not* have to live without him."

"You can't know that. No one can."

"You're right. But if there's one thing I've learned in life it's that pessimism is self-defeating. If I'd given in to self-pity when I first came to this country I'd be just like some of the others who feel that the world owes them because of what Hitler did. So they walk around with chips on their shoulders and they're never happy. If I'd given in to self-pity when I realized that no matter how much I loved Gil he'd never be mine I'd never have known Henry or had Kenny, and even in spite of what happened to each, for a time they made my life richer. If I'd given in to self-pity when I realized I had a daughter who would never fully be able to take the place she deserved I'd have warped you in the process." She held Katia back and looked her in the eye. "My God, Katia, life is worth more than that. Right now you should be thinking of everything you *do* have. If you dwell on what you might lose tomorrow or next week or next year you'll never be happy."

"Have you been happy?" Katia asked, sniffling.

Cassie straightened her shoulders, but her hands never once left Katia nor did her gaze stray. "Yes. In the long run, yes. I have a good job, a good home, wonderful memories of the man I loved. And I have you. Do you know how much pleasure I get when I look at you and know that Gil and I made you? Your marriage to Jordan was destined to be, which is why I simply can't believe that anything will happen to take him from you. You're the best of the Warrens and Whytes, you and Jordan, and one day you'll have children, my grandchildren, who will make all of us proud."

"You sound so *sure* of things," Katia said with a bit of awe.

"I've had a lifetime of practice."

"But what happens when things don't go the way you were sure they were going to?"

Cassie quickly shook her head. "It's irrelevant. It doesn't matter. Don't you see? A life spent fearing the worst isn't worth living. It doesn't matter whether your dreams ever come true. It's the dreaming that counts. A person without dreams is a very, very sad creature."

Katia thought about what her mother had said, but she found dreaming difficult when she saw the prospect of a nightmare ahead. Jordan was, indeed, rearraigned at the superior court, and the horror of lead stories and headlines went on. In the days that followed meetings with VanPelt occupied much of his and Katia's time. They shuttled back and forth between New York and Boston at least twice a week, grateful that while the court had seized Jordan's passport, it had given him permission to travel within the northeast. Given the circumstances he had no desire to travel farther. After his initial arraignment he had appointed his second in command to take over the visible aspects of the business, believing with just cause that his name had a certain notoriety to it now that could do more harm than good. Moreover, what with meeting with VanPelt and spending as much time with Katia as possible, he had little energy left for travel.

Thanksgiving was a strange affair. Coming within a month after Gil's death, it was the families' first general reunion since the funeral. As had always been the case a lavish turkey dinner was served at the Whytes. But while Thanksgivings of the past had been jovial, this year the smiles were solely for the benefit of the young children.

Natalie, who had been a huge help to Jack in dealing with the death of his dearest friend, was reaping the benefits of that effort. Jack and she were closer than ever. She would have actually been happy had it not been for Jordan's impending trial.

Lenore, who had mourned Gil by becoming at last and fully the type of woman he would have loved, was similarly burdened. She had come to understand that taking command of her life was critical to her emotional well-being, but in the matter of Jordan's predicament, which she took nearly as personally as Natalie, she felt totally powerless.

Ironically, many of her worries focused on Katia. She told herself that she was a fool, that another woman wouldn't care about Katia, given her parentage. But she did care. Maybe she felt guilty for having shunned Katia for years. Maybe she was rebelling in her own way by doing exactly what another woman wouldn't. Maybe she was respecting the fact that Gil had loved Katia.

Then again, maybe she was simply a human being feeling sorry for another human being at a difficult time. She could empathize with the frustration Katia had to be feeling watching Jordan's torment, knowing it could get much worse, trying to think of ways to help but coming up short. She could empathize with the fear Katia had to be feeling knowing that she could well lose that which she held closest to her heart.

It was for many of these reasons that Lenore graciously invited Robert Cavanaugh into the house when he showed up on the doorstep one day in early December.

"Thank you for seeing me, Mrs. Warren," Cavanaugh said somewhat uneasily. "I know this has to be a hard time for you. You may well see me as the enemy."

"No, Detective. Jordan has spoken highly of you. I trust his judgment." With quiet dignity she led Cavanaugh into the living room and gestured for him to sit. "Would you like something hot to drink, coffee or tea?"

"No, thank you." He placed his overcoat on the arm of the sofa. "Uh, on second thought, a cup of coffee would be nice. If it's no trouble."

Lenore cast him a you-should-know-I'd-never-be-doing-the-work-myself look as she swept by. When she returned, she settled into the wingback chair opposite him. "Cassie will bring coffee. I'd like her to sit with us if you don't mind. Also, I've told her to call Mrs. Whyte. I believe that they'd both be as interested in what you have to say as I am. As a matter of fact, I'm not quite sure why you've sought *me* out."

Cavanaugh hadn't expected such forthrightness from Lenore Warren. He'd been led to believe that she was the weak link in the family, but that belief was now open to reconsideration. "For the record, I'm here to pay a belated condolence call. Off the record, I'm here to ask you about Deborah."

Lenore frowned. "But I thought your investigation was done."

"Technically it is. I'm here in an unofficial capacity."

For a moment she misunderstood. Her composure wavered. "Don't tell me you're looking further, that you think more of us were involved!"

Smiling, he shook his head. "No, no. I don't think even Jordan was involved. He must have told you that."

"He did. But that doesn't preclude you suspecting someone else in the family."

"I don't. Please believe me. I don't think *anyone* in the family was involved, and I feel a certain responsibility for Jordan's problems."

"You feel guilty?"

He nodded. "I didn't speak with you earlier this fall because I thought you'd be too upset, and then things came out that forced the indictment, so it seemed a moot point. I know you may be every bit as upset now as you were then, but," he hesitated for a minute before continuing with conviction, "I'm sorry. I can't just let things rest as they are. There has to be something I'm not seeing. I was hoping you'd be able to give me a clue."

Lenore sighed. On the one hand she was relieved, on the other stymied. "I don't know, Detective Cavanaugh. I've searched— we've all searched—for clues, but we haven't been able to find any. I have no idea who could have possibly wanted to murder either Deborah or Mark, or why."

"Okay." He rubbed his hands together. "Let's look at it from a different slant then." He'd opened his mouth to go on when Cassie appeared at the open archway, where she hesitated, not knowing what she was interrupting.

Lenore gestured to her. "Come on in, Cassie. Have you met Detective Cavanaugh?"

Cassie came forward and set the silver service on the coffee table. "Yes. We spoke a while back. How are you, Detective?"

"Just fine, Mrs. Morell."

She nodded, then poured coffee into two of the three cups that stood on the tray. Lenore counted the cups before gently reprimanding Cassie.

"We'll need a fourth."

"That's all right," Cassie answered quickly. "I had my own not long ago."

"Did you call Mrs. Whyte?"

"She said she'd be—"

"Right here," Natalie herself finished, slipping off her own coat as she entered the room. "Has something come up?" she asked with that odd blend of fear and hope that had become so common in recent days.

"No. But the detective is still working on it."

Cavanaugh stood and extended his hand. "Mrs. Whyte. I don't believe we've met."

Natalie put her hand in his. "By rights I should be cursing you, but I'm afraid that what happened to Jordan would have happened regardless of who'd been doing the investigating. I'm grateful that you treated Jordan as well as you have."

"Jordan's a likeable man. But the fact that I like him has nothing to do with my being here." He waited until Natalie had taken a seat before returning to his own. "I'm still trying to find the piece of the puzzle that's missing. Mrs. Warren has said that you're all in the dark as to who could have wanted Mark or Deborah dead. I wanted to talk about that a little."

All three women were seated and waiting with varying degrees of anticipation.

"For the most part," Cavanaugh began, "we've gone on the theory that someone had something against Mark. When the evidence began to point to Jordan, he and I discussed the possibility that he'd been framed, which could mean that Jordan was the ultimate target, and Mark and Deborah innocent victims."

"We've discussed that possibility," Lenore admitted, "but we're still in the dark."

"That's okay, because I'm not sure I can accept the theory anyway." He had talked it all out with Jodi when she had returned from Atlanta, and they had reached the same conclusion.

Natalie was watching him intently. "Explain, please."

"Hypothetically it would work. Someone wanted to get back at Jordan, so he—or she—murdered Mark and Deborah, then framed Jordan. Slow torture. That's certainly what Jordan's suffering."

"But—"

"It's too pat. In the first place," he held up a single finger, "Jordan's clean. We did an in-depth workup on him. He hasn't done anything criminal, and I can't buy the fact that someone would go to such violent extremes simply to avenge a business disagreement or a thwarted love affair or the fact that Jordan drives a bright red Audi. In the second place," another finger joined the first, "Jordan's indictment was so spectacular that it was bound to shift attention. The perfect red herring. If someone legitimately had a quarrel with Mark and could throw the blame for the mur-

ders on Jordan, or any one of you, it would be the perfect diversion. And in the third place," one more finger went up, "much as
I hate to say it, Mark was the one in a barrel of trouble."

"There's always the possibility," Lenore proposed, "that Mark
and Deborah were killed and Jordan framed for it to get revenge
on another one of us. It sounds far-fetched, but if that was the
killer's goal it was effective. We're all suffering. Look at what happened to Gil. I'm not saying that his heart attack was directly
brought on by Jordan's indictment, but I'm sure the anger he
felt—not only about Jordan's being framed but also the murders
themselves—had to have affected him."

Cavanaugh had dropped his hand to his lap. "I've spoken with
Nick and Peter. As a matter of fact, in the past few weeks I've spoken with all of the Whyte and Warren siblings. People may be
jealous of them. People may have gripes here and there. But nothing I learned from them or from the snooping I've done myself has
revealed anything heinous enough on their part to warrant this
type of revenge." His voice lowered. "Which is one of the reasons
I'm here now. Can either of you," he looked from Lenore to Natalie
and back, "think of a reason why someone would hate either of
your husbands that much?"

He knew how much he had hated them himself when he had
first begun work on the case. True, his feelings had been modified
by what he had learned, but even before that he would never have
considered murder. Nor would his father have, though the man
threatened it in anger any number of times—just, Cavanaugh realized, as Jordan had threatened Mark.

Natalie and Lenore were looking at each other. Ironically, it
was Cassie who spoke. "I'm sure you understand, Detective, that
men don't reach the places of power that Mr. Whyte and Congressman Warren reached without making a few enemies along
the way."

"I do understand that. But what I'm looking for is someone
who *really* had a gripe. Someone who may have threatened either

man or his family. Someone they may have known who was prone to violence."

Lenore shook her head. "Only a crackpot. A nameless, faceless crackpot."

Natalie shrugged. "I'd have to agree with that. I can think of many people who dislike my husband, but not one of them would resort to the kind of violence we're dealing with."

Cavanaugh remained silent for a minute, gnawing on his lower lip. He released it at last and spoke quietly. "Do either of you or your husbands know a man named John Ryan?"

"Isn't he with the police department?" Lenore asked.

"Then you have heard of him?"

"Only through this case."

"Had you ever heard the name before all this came up?"

Lenore and Natalie exchanged equally puzzled glances. "Should we have?" Natalie asked.

Cavanaugh let out a breath. "Nope. Forget I asked. Okay then. Let's go back to Mark. I know that he didn't bring his friends here much, but did he ever mention them to you?"

"Only in passing. He dropped names, but I rarely recognized them. If you were to ask me to recall them now I couldn't."

"Did he ever mention any trouble?"

Natalie sighed sadly. "Real trouble? I'm afraid that I'm the last person—no, I'd take next-to-last place before my husband—who he would have mentioned trouble to. Mark was sensitive about success and failure. He knew that he'd disappointed us over the years. We knew things weren't always smooth, but when he told us anything it was always in glowing terms, probably exaggerated, I'm afraid to say."

"There's nothing you can think of? No one person he might have felt was the bane of his existence?"

When Natalie shook her head, Cavanaugh turned to Lenore. "What about you, Mrs. Warren?"

"Mark wouldn't have come to me any more than he'd have gone to his parents."

"Then what about Deborah? Did she ever mention any particular problem to you?"

"Oh, yes," Lenore said more softly. She shot a nervous glance
at Natalie but went on. "There were money problems. We gave
her some from time to time, but it always seemed to vanish, so in
the end we put our foot down. We told her that if we didn't know
where the money was going we wouldn't keep handing it out."

"She wouldn't tell you."

"No."

"Any other problems she mentioned?"

Again Lenore glanced at Natalie, this time apologetically. "She
was discouraged sometimes. The people they moved with frightened her."

"Did she ever mention anyone specific?"

"No. Just a general kind of thing. She wasn't wild about the
parties. Or," this time she didn't look at Natalie, "the other
women."

"Were there steady ones? I mean, was Mark spending his time
with any specific woman?" When Lenore shrugged, he prodded
gently. "I know that there were parties. Wild parties."

"Orgies," she said, to which he smiled.

"I was trying to be tactful, but that's pretty much what they
were. Did Deborah take part in them?" He hadn't been able to see
that from the tape, though in truth he'd been so disgusted that he
hadn't looked all that hard. It occurred to him now that he should
have.

"I don't really know," Lenore answered. She was clearly uncomfortable with the thought of her daughter being a sexual
groupie. "I'd like to think that she didn't, but she never talked
against the parties per se. She did talk against the women who se-
duced Mark into tidy little affairs."

The fact was, Cavanaugh mused, that Mark may well have
been the seducer, but he wasn't about to argue with Lenore's
choice of words.

"If we want to talk possible scenarios, here's one. What if

Mark had an ongoing thing with a woman who just happened to be married? What if her husband caught on? What if that husband knew about the tapes, was even close enough to Mark to know about his argument with Jordan *and* about the existence of the tape confirming it? What if that husband then decided to do Mark in, knowing that Jordan could easily be framed, in which case the heat would be off him?"

Cassie stirred in her seat, going along with Cavanaugh's reasoning only to a point. "You've supposedly interviewed everyone on the west coast who had dealings with Mark and Deborah. Did you speak with anyone who could possibly fit?"

"No. We could have missed someone, though. I even spoke with Deborah's therapist, but he wasn't much help." He looked back at Lenore. "Was there anything Deborah might have told you—anything at all specific that could have relevance?"

Lenore lowered her head and squeezed her eyes shut. She tried to think, to remember. "I wish I'd listened closer," she murmured, "but I used to get upset and try not to hear her." There was something. She felt it nagging at the back of her mind, where it had been pushed a long while before. She tried to draw it forth, but it eluded her, and that in turn angered her. She didn't like feeling powerless. At Gil's death she had emerged from the shadow. She had a stable life now, a solid fortune. She knew she would never lose it, but now she needed more. She needed to do, to act, to take fate in her own hands.

Then it came. Calmly she raised her head and eyed Cavanaugh. "Deborah did mention one girl. Mark had an affair with her, she'd gotten pregnant, then had an abortion. Deborah was nearly as upset about the abortion as she was about the affair. She'd wanted a baby so badly herself."

"When did the affair take place?" Cavanaugh asked quietly.

"I'm not sure. Deborah told me about it a year ago. No, I think it was less than a year ago, though I don't know how long it had been going on or how long it went on after that."

"What happened to the girl?"

"I don't know."

"Did Deborah mention a name?"

Again Lenore felt a wave of helplessness, but she fought it, digging, digging into her memory bank. "Jane . . . June. No." She took a breath. "Julie. I think that was it. Julie."

"No last name?"

"No."

"What are you going to do?" Natalie asked.

"Find out who Julie is. We haven't interviewed anyone by that name. She may open up several new doors. In the meantime," he looked from one face to the next, "If any of you think of anything else, I'd appreciate your giving me a call. This Julie person may lead us nowhere, but it's worth a try."

None of the three women could argue with that.

Chapter 18

JULIE PROVED TO BE JULIE DUNCAN and beyond Cavanaugh's reach. On a visit to her Bakersfield home, Cavanaugh learned that her husband was a paraplegic confined to a wheelchair, while Julie herself had died several months before of a drug overdose.

John Duncan was a figure who evoked Cavanaugh's deepest sympathies. He was a broken man. He told Cavanaugh of the reluctance he had had in inflicting his condition on someone as vibrant as Julie, had even admitted that he hadn't faulted her for seeking pleasure elsewhere. His biggest mistake, he said, had been in assuming Julie had been stronger than she was. Having an abortion had been her own decision. He would have had the baby since he wasn't able to father one himself, but Julie hadn't wanted the added responsibility. Unfortunately, the abortion had gone against her deeply ingrained religious principles, which after the fact had torn her apart, as had, apparently, the dual life she had led.

If Duncan blamed anyone for his wife's demise it was himself. Though Cavanaugh had every intention of checking it out, his cop's instinct told him that the man was not mentally, much less physically capable of murder.

Well apart from Duncan, there remained a niggling in the back of Cavanaugh's mind. An elusive instinct told him that the clue to the murders was within his grasp, but he couldn't seem to close in on it. What he did close in on was the rest of the tapes Mark had made. He brought them back east with him and stopped in New York for an exclusive viewing with Jordan, who was more than grateful to feel that he was doing something with potential relevance to his case.

"Just watch," Cavanaugh said quietly as the first of the pictures appeared on the VCR. "See if anything strikes you. Anything at all."

So they watched. Katia joined them after a time, and though Jordan was ashamed enough of what his brother had done to want to send her away, he couldn't. He felt guilty about the spurts of moodiness that had made him difficult to be with of late, and selfishly, he took comfort having her by his side.

For long hours the three of them sat, eyes glued to the set as one tape after another rolled. From time to time they would replay a section when a question arose, but the results were sadly unproductive. Then came the tape of the orgy, and Jordan did turn to Katia. "You don't want to see this," he whispered.

"Are you kidding?" she whispered back. "After those other boring ones you want me to leave now?"

"They're disgusting."

"Come on, where's your sense of adventure?"

"Adventure? You call this adventure? I call it—"

"Disgusting. I know." She leaned closer to his ear. "If I didn't have firsthand knowledge to the contrary, I'd think you were a prude."

Jordan's lips twitched, but he couldn't quite smile. Knowing that his brother had not only taken part in what they were watching, but had filmed it did something unsettling to his stomach. In fact, it had the same effect on Katia, who had resorted to humor as an antidote.

Cavanaugh was beyond feeling unsettled. He stopped the tape at one point, reversed it for a minute, then ran the particular segment again. "Who *is* she?" he muttered under his breath.

"Who?" Jordan asked.

"That girl. The one off on the right." He stopped the tape at the spot. "Dark-haired girl with a dark-skinned guy. Something about her is familiar. I saw it when I was watching before, and I feel the same thing now. Does the face ring any kind of bell with you?"

Jordan studied it. "No. Looks like she's very much into the thing." Her eyes were closed, her lips parted.

"Either she's high on something," Katia remarked dryly, "or this really is her style. How old would you say she is?"

Cavanaugh continued staring at the face in silence. It was Jordan who answered. "It's hard to tell from the distance and with all the makeup she's wearing, but I'd say she's about twenty-five, maybe twenty-six."

Cavanaugh took a quick breath. "Twenty-four," he said with sudden conviction. "If I'm not mistaken that's Julie Duncan. Her husband showed me a picture. It was a profile shot of the two of them, soft focused, a little fuzzy. Yeah, she's more made up here. She looks older. I guess I was so taken with Duncan's story that nothing registered when I was with him."

"But it does now."

"Right."

Katia was looking appalled. "She's the one who supposedly got pregnant by Mark? That's not Mark with her there. How could she possibly know the baby was his?"

"Deborah knew, so Mark must have told her. If he did there must have been some truth to it."

Cavanaugh's mind was elsewhere. "But why did I recognize her the first time I saw this tape? That was before I'd met Duncan or seen the picture." He paused, wracking his brain for the proper placement. "Julie . . . Julie." He frowned. There was something about the nose. "Julie Duncan." And the mouth. "Julie. Julie Duncan. Julie— Oh, shit."

"What is it?"

"Julie Ryan."

"Who's Julie Ryan?" Katia asked.

Cavanaugh sagged back in his seat. "Julie Ryan. Originally from Boston. One of six kids—and only daughter, now deceased—of John Ryan."

"John Ryan," Jordan said quietly. "Your superior?"

"Right. My superior." The man who had assigned Cavanaugh the case. The man who had hinted right off the bat that one of the Whytes or Warrens had committed the murders. The man who had known that the tapes existed.

Jordan was sitting forward. "What do you think?"

Hell of a coincidence was what Cavanaugh thought, but for a moment he said nothing. He rubbed the bridge of his nose, then the crease between his eyes. "I think," he began slowly, "that I'd better be careful. We're playing with fire here. It could be something or nothing." But damn, it would almost make sense.

"Are you sure that's the same girl?" Katia asked.

"No. It's been years since I've seen Julie Ryan, and maybe I'm imagining the resemblance to John. I'll have to check it out. A simple question to one of the other guys on the force about the married name of Ryan's daughter should do the trick."

Jordan's expression was grim. "And then what?"

"Then I'll have to think." He thrust a hand through his hair. "Christ, the implications are mind-boggling."

Jordan and Katia were thinking the same thing. They discussed it into the early morning hours, long after Cavanaugh left, and they grew hopeful, angry and incredulous in turn.

"I think you should call VanPelt," Katia finally announced.

"No. Not yet."

"Jordan, this is a *lead*."

"Not unless the name checks out."

"But if it does, VanPelt should know about it."

"Not *yet*."

Jumping from the sofa, she paced to the far side of the room, then whirled to face him. "What's *with* you, Jordan? Don't you *want* to find the real killer?"

He shot her a hard glance. "You should know better than to

ask me that. Of course I want to find the real killer. But I think I owe it to Cavanaugh to let him do his thing first."

"And just how is he going to do it with Ryan breathing down his neck? Do you really think Cavanaugh's going to jeopardize his career by accusing his superior of murder?"

"He won't accuse Ryan of anything unless he finds evidence to support it. Right now all we can do is speculate. Suppose the name does check out? All we'll really know is that John Ryan's daughter had an affair with Mark, got pregnant, had an abortion, then OD'd on drugs."

"But that would give Ryan a motive for killing Mark. Hatred. Vengeance. Don't you see? It's a more plausible motive than the one they claim was yours."

"Cavanaugh needs solid evidence to prove Ryan committed murder."

"He doesn't have that kind of evidence on you."

"He has a threat. He needs something like that on Ryan."

"And if he can't get it?"

"*Then* I'll tell VanPelt."

"Then it may be too late! You may have already gone to trial!"

"In which case VanPelt can use the matter of Julie Ryan Duncan—if that's her name—to raise doubt in the jurors' minds. Listen to me, Katia," he sighed. "I want to get out of this every bit as much as you do, but when I do, I don't want there to be a single, possible doubt in the world about my innocence. I want to be utterly and completely vindicated. If that means I have to stand a little more pain it'll be worth it in the end. Hell, we've already suffered. It's not like I can turn the clock back and erase all that's happened. But I do trust Cavanaugh. I'm willing to sit back and wait awhile longer."

Katia stood very still. "This isn't like you, Jordan. You were always aggressive. You'd have taken the bull by the horns rather than waiting around for it to gore you."

"Maybe I've changed."

"I'll say. There are times when you sit here and I could just as well be a—" she gestured wildly, "a picture on the wall. It's like I'm not even here. You draw into yourself. You don't talk to me."

If Katia had reached the end of her tether, so had Jordan. "Hell, Katia, what do you want from me? I feel bad enough putting you through all this. Do you really want to know all the dark little thoughts I have, all the contingency plans I'm making for what I'll do if I'm convicted? My God, it's not like I don't have a thing on my mind!"

"*Share it with me!*" she cried. "That's all I ask. Share it with me and then I won't have to hold everything in myself. I won't have to sit here wondering what you're thinking, wondering whether you'd rather be alone, wondering whether you regret having married me, wondering whether you resent the way I rushed our marriage!" Not wanting him to see her tears, she stormed past him and headed straight for the bedroom. There she tore off her clothes, yanked on a nightgown, threw herself on the bed and buried her face in the pillow.

She was exhausted. And discouraged. The past weeks had been like years to her. She loved Jordan more than ever, which was why his silences cut her so deeply. She hadn't meant to lose her temper, but strain had gotten the best of her.

"Katia?" Jordan's voice came softly through the darkness, his approach silenced by the carpet. The mattress gave beneath his weight, then heaved again when he stood back up.

Katia lay still, unsure what to do. She heard the rustle of cloth when he removed his shirt, then the rasp of a zipper and slither of denim down his legs. Moments later his weight returned to the mattress, and he curled himself half over her.

"I'm sorry, babe." His breath was by her ear. "I know how hard this is on you. That makes it even harder for me."

"I'm so ashamed." Her whisper was muffled in the pillow. She couldn't face him. "I sounded like a shrew. I shouldn't have yelled at you like that. You have enough to worry about without adding my frustration to the list."

"But it's there. I know you're frustrated and angry and impatient. I'm feeling the same things. And I do worry about you." He ran his hand along her upper arm. "I don't want to have to put you through a trial. It was bad enough with the arraignments."

"Are you sorry we got married so quickly?"

His hand wandered to her hip, caressing it through the silken fabric of her nightgown. "Oh, no," he murmured. "It's meant the world to have you with me, Katia. Even in that I'm a selfish bastard. But you've been the only thing that's seemed real these past weeks." He kissed her ear, drew away, then, unable to resist, returned to run his tongue along its edge. "But I do feel guilty—"

"Don't say that."

"It's what I feel. You don't deserve all this."

"Neither do you," she argued, but her voice was wispy, as it always was when his bare body was near. "Half of my frustration is in not being able to do more to help you. Then I go and sound off like a witch—"

"Shh. You could never be a witch," he whispered. His mouth drifted to her neck, then her shoulder. "You're human. Like me." He slipped his hand between her legs, pushing her nightgown up as he went. When he began to caress her, she sucked in a breath. "Relax. That's it."

"Jordan. . . ."

"Mmm. Like that?"

"Oh, yes." She felt she had been injected with a sensual brand of morphine. Pleasure flowed through her body.

His fingers delved softly, deeply, while he kissed her cheek, her neck, the sensitive spot beneath her earlobe. She started to turn, needing to hold and touch, but he held her there on the bed.

"I love you," he whispered, and she could only sigh her response, because his fingers were magic, sweeping her mind clean of everything but the fire he stoked. Gently, he raised her hips and spread her thighs, then just as gently eased into her.

Katia's fingers clenched around the softness of the pillow. Jordan had never made love to her this way before, and while moments earlier she had wanted nothing more than to face him, she found that there was something to the deprivation that heightened her other senses. With vivid clarity she felt his slow withdrawal and more forceful return. With a repeat she heard the sound of his breathing growing shorter, more ragged. The press of his body against her back created a line of heat that broke only on the recoil of his thrusts. His gentle caress of her breasts kept time with that lower, deeper stroking.

Blindly she reached for one of his hands, twining her fingers through his and anchoring them by her lips on the pillow. Then she held on for dear life as the heat within rose and crested. Only when Jordan, too, had reached his climax and slumped against her did she make another effort to turn. This time he allowed it. He took her in his arms and cradled her close.

"You're the best thing that's ever happened to me," he said brokenly. "The best thing."

At that moment she knew that regardless of what the future held these moments of closeness made it all worthwhile.

Cavanaugh was thinking similar thoughts several nights later as he and Jodi walked, arm in arm, along the waterfront. In the past days they had been closer than ever, which was an irony, Cavanaugh mused, when professionally he was in such a quandary. He would have expected his problems to drive them apart, but they hadn't. Between Jodi's persistence and his own love for her he had discovered that there was, indeed, more to his life than being a cop. Oh, he still had his moments of withdrawal, when habit locked his worries inside, but she was understanding even as she gently pried and he had learned that he actually felt better for opening up. Better . . . freer . . . more adventuresome, which was perhaps why he had dragged her from their apartment so late to grab an impulsive midnight snack in the North End.

Bellies filled, they had walked a bit, then stopped at a bench facing the harbor and sat down. The night was cold and still. Even the rank smell of the harbor was mellow. They leaned into one another, watched their breath mingle in the air, then dissipate. From an occasional boat or townhouse window a Christmas light blinked, but the only sound was that of the water lapping against the hulls of the boats that swayed in the breeze.

"That's where it happened, isn't it?" Jodi asked, looking toward the pier.

"Yup."

"Right about this time, too."

"Yup."

"How do you think he did it?"

"Ryan?" Cavanaugh frowned. He had quickly learned that Julie Duncan was John Ryan's daughter, but beyond that he had been stewing for clues. "I don't know. One thing's for sure. He didn't do the killing himself. There's no way that tub of lard could have made it through the water, much less hauled himself up over the side of a boat."

Jodi didn't miss the hardening of his voice or the bitterness in it. "You never did like him, did you?"

"There was always something about the guy that bugged me. An arrogance, maybe. An air of superiority. Right about now I've got damn good reason to hate him. He used me. He set me up to pin a rap on someone who is innocent. I don't like that."

"Still, he asked you to do the job."

"Yeah. He assumed I'd only go so far with the investigation. What does that say about his opinion of me?"

"What does it matter? Knowing you did your job better than he'd planned has to give you some satisfaction."

"Not yet. Not until I clinch it."

Her elbow tightened around his. "There has to be evidence somewhere. Ryan had to have hired someone. Who would have done his bidding without demanding something powerful in return?"

"Beats me."

"Are there any signs that he's compromising himself on other cases?"

"Nope."

"Then he had to have paid someone outright. Have you checked his bank?"

"Oh, yeah. There was nothing. But let me tell you, it was touchy enough doing even that."

"Holstrom's on your side."

"Fortunately. But everything has to be kept so damn quiet. It's like I'm walking on eggs. I don't dare breathe a word about this to anyone else in the department. I'm just not sure who my friends are."

"Or who Ryan's friends are."

"Bingo. In some respects I'm surprised Holstrom went along with me."

"He *had* to. There was one coincidence too many where Ryan's involvement with this thing is concerned. Even if, by a long shot, it turns out that Ryan had nothing to do with the murders, he should have steered clear of this case. He was too emotionally involved."

"I wasn't all that pure myself," Cavanaugh pointed out.

"Yes you were. From the first you were determined to do the job right."

"There are some who might say the same about Ryan."

"But he was dishonest. He could have come clean at the start. He could have told you about his daughter. Was there ever *any* mention of what caused her death?"

"There was very little mention of her death at all. It came and went. Julie was buried in California quickly and with little ceremony from what I've learned. At the time Ryan didn't welcome more than the token expression of sympathy. And he wasn't the type you'd approach and question, particularly about something like that."

Jodi thought about that for a minute. "It fits in with what you said about his maintaining strict barriers between the office and his home. But if your suspicions are correct, he crossed them himself."

"If my suspicions are correct he's as sick as they come."

"He's sick anyway. If he was innocent he should have told you about Julie after Mark and Deborah were murdered. And he should have come right out and told you about the existence of the tapes rather than coyly dropping hints." Consternation dominated the expression on her face. "What I don't understand is why he'd want the tapes found if he knew his daughter was on them."

"He may not have known that. We don't know what she told him other than that Mark did make the tapes."

"How could she have known about the argument between Mark and Jordan?"

"Either she saw the tape herself shortly before she died or Mark must have told her."

A new thought brought Jodi's eyes wide. "My God, Bob. Do you think it's possible that Mark had something to do with her death?"

Cavanaugh was shaking his head even before she had finished. "I checked it out with the department in Bakersfield. She'd taken a room in a small hotel for the night. No one met her there. No one saw her after she'd locked herself in. It wasn't until the next day, after her husband got worried, that the police traced her to the place and broke down the door. Mark was one of dozens of people who were later questioned. He was in Boston on the night of her death and had been here for the two days preceding it. A solid alibi, and no evidence to suggest that he supplied her with the stuff."

"I suppose we should be grateful for that," she mused. "You know, it's interesting from a psychological standpoint that Julie chose to marry a man named John."

"Pure coincidence."

"Not necessarily. John Ryan must have been a powerful force in her life. When she moved to California—why *did* she move to California?"

The darkness couldn't hide Cavanaugh's why-else look. "To be an actress."

"Wonder what Ryan thought of that," she mused, then went on. "When she moved there, she may well have felt the loss of a stabilizing force. It's possible she married John Duncan to counter that loss. Handicapped or not, you said that he was pretty down to earth."

"I did. I don't know—maybe you have a point. It seems she was hung up enough on religion. She could have been hung up on her father. In the months before her death he made quite a few trips out there—quick weekend trips so no one here knew."

"How did you?"

"Clever sleuthing this morning," he told her, but the wry twist to his lips quickly straightened. "If, around the time of the abortion, Julie was disturbed enough to have broken down and confessed her sins to her father, she could well have told him about Mark and the coke and the parties and the tapes. It's easy enough to envision a discussion between father and daughter about the evil Whyte family. Julie may have mentioned the argument between Mark and Jordan in passing, even in defense of the family. Whether or not she saw the actual tape, if she knew of Mark's fetish, she may have just assumed that the argument was there."

"Or Ryan assumed it."

He sighed. "Whoever planned the murders certainly knew something. If I could only close in on the scene of the crime. I'll have to do that if I'm ever going to nail Ryan. Without some kind of evidence regarding the actual murders I've got nothing."

"You don't have evidence like that on Jordan."

"And he'll probably be acquitted because of it. I told Ryan that, but he insisted on making the arrest. At the time I was tempted to make a stink, but he'd only have assigned someone else to the case, and I didn't want that."

"A grand jury returned the indictments."

"Yeah, but grand juries aren't immune to rhetoric, particularly when they only hear one side of the story. The prosecutor made an emotional case, and the kinds of people listening weren't exactly the kind who'd identify with a Whyte or a Warren." He stared off toward the darkness of the harbor. "I need something. It has to be here. Someone has to have seen something that night."

Jodi looked around. "I don't know, Bob. It's pretty deserted right about now. I don't see a soul."

"Maybe one," Cavanaugh murmured. His eyes were suddenly focused on the far end of the pier. It took Jodi a minute to see the lone figure who stood like a dark shadow against a post.

"Fellow looks lonesome," she mused. "I wonder what he's doing out there all by himself at this time of night."

Cavanaugh drew her up beside him. "Might be worth a stroll to find out."

"We can't do that, Bob," she scolded in a stage whisper, but, not about to be left behind, she was pacing herself to his leisurely strides. "We'll be intruding on his privacy."

"Nah. Residents of the waterfront are pretty proud of their turf. If we tell him we're thinking of moving here he won't turn us away. We're a pretty respectable looking couple, don't you think?"

"Oh, sure. Looking over real estate at one in the morning. Not to mention the fact that the day we can afford one of these will be the day we win the lottery."

"He doesn't have to know we haven't already won." They had turned onto the pier and were moving slowly toward the figure.

"How do you know he's a resident?" she whispered out of the side of her mouth.

Cavanaugh answered in the same fashion. "If he isn't, I'll be justified in investigating."

"It's a free country. Anyone can walk here."

"Right, which is why we are. Just keep cool. Smile. Act like you belong."

"This is insane, Bob. He could be a criminal. He could have a knife or a gun, and we have nothing." For once, she actually wished he had worn his shoulder holster. But under the circumstances of their leaving the apartment, that would have been absurd.

"Then look at it this way," Cavanaugh said even more softly, because they were nearing the man. "If he mugs us he won't get much cash."

"Some solace—hey, he's leaving."

"Yeah. Running." Even before the words had left his mouth Cavanaugh dropped Jodi's arm and broke into a run himself. As far as he was concerned, when a man took off like that he was worth chasing.

Cavanaugh might have been off-duty and unarmed, but neither of those facts blunted the speed with which he followed, then reached the man, who was trying to scramble up a series of pilings in hope of escape. Cavanaugh clamped a hand on the collar of his heavy denim jacket and hauled him back down.

"In some rush, aren't you, buddie?" he growled. A panting Jodi arrived just as he turned the man around, at which point they both discovered that they were dealing with a boy of no more than fifteen. Though he nearly matched Cavanaugh in height, he was spindly.

The boy held up both hands. "Hey man. What's the problem?"

His voice was at the changing stage, not high, not low, but in the netherland between. Jodi wasn't sure how much of the warble had to do with fear, which was clearly written in the boy's eyes.

"Why did you run?" Cavanaugh asked more quietly.

"I wanted the exercise."

"All of a sudden?"

"Yeah."

"Do you live here?" Jodi asked. She had already taken in the boy's hair, spiked on top, falling to his collar in back, and the gold stud in his left ear. He wasn't exactly the type of kid she would expect to find living in an expensive condominium on the waterfront.

The boy looked wide-eyed from Cavanaugh to her and back, then tried to shrug off the hand at his shoulder. The detective simply grasped more of the denim.

"Where do you live?" he demanded.

The boy tossed his head toward the townhouses behind him.

"With your family?"

He nodded.

"Do they know you're out here at this hour?"

"No, man! Why do you think I ran? If they find out they'll kill me!"

"What were you doing here?"

"Gettin' air."

"Do you do it a lot?"

"Hell, man, I don't know."

"Look, I asked you a simple question—"

Jodi's hand on his arm stopped him. "What's your name?" she asked gently.

The boy gave the same one-shouldered shrug he had given moments before.

"The lady asked you a question," Cavanaugh prompted, keeping his tone calm for Jodi's sake alone. "What's your name?"

After a minute the kid answered grudgingly. "Alex."

"Alex what?"

After another little while there was an even more reluctant, "Petri. Look, I live here, okay? I was gettin' some air. But I wasn't doing anything illegal, so you got no right to stop me."

"Who said anything about illegal?" Cavanaugh returned with a more natural calm this time. And a creeping suspicion. "Do you know me?"

"No," Alex said quickly. Too quickly.

Cavanaugh's fist tightened around the boy's jacket. "That's good," he said smoothly. "Then you won't be able to identify me after I beat you to a pulp for being a punk kid. I don't like punk kids. I don't like kids period."

"You wouldn't beat me," Alex gloated. "Not with your lady standing here watching."

Jodi was almost enjoying herself. She had never seen her man in action, and knowing that he would never harm the boy, she was curious as to what he would do next. She had the same suspicion Cavanaugh did. Alex Petri recognized him.

"But she's part of the scam," Cavanaugh went on. "She's trained in the martial arts, knows just where to kick so it hurts."

"Come off it, man. She won't touch me."

"Why not?"

" 'Cause that would be assault. She's not the type."

"But I am?"

"You're a friggin' cop—"

Cavanaugh smiled. And Alex realized what he'd said.

"Okay," he grumbled. "So I know. It's easy enough to spot a cop."

"I'm not in uniform."

Alex aimed a disdainful glance at Cavanaugh's conservative slacks, sweater and topcoat. He might have said, Oh, no? Instead he said, "You smell like a cop."

Cavanaugh looked at Jodi. "Do I smell like a cop?"

Innocently, she shook her head, at which point Cavanaugh returned his gaze to Alex, who shifted from one black booted foot to the other. "All I smell," Cavanaugh said slowly, "is a rat, and I know it's not me, and I know it's not her, so it must be you. Why were you running?"

"I told you. If my parents find out I'm out here—"

Cavanaugh's fist tightened, bringing Alex up higher. "You said you weren't doing anything illegal. If you'd just stayed where you were we wouldn't have noticed you."

"You were heading straight *for* me."

"We were walking."

"Right at me."

"So speaks the voice of guilt. And you ran. Why did you run? Were you smoking something?"

"Did you see me smoking something?" he asked nervously.

Cavanaugh honestly hadn't, but he was certain from the way he was acting that the kid had come out to smoke a joint. That would explain his panicky fear of his parents. Cavanaugh was also certain the kid had dumped anything illegal he had with him in the harbor before he ran. But that didn't stop the detective from realizing he had the leverage he needed to get the kid to talk.

"It's dark," Cavanaugh said brusquely. "I can't see everything. Maybe I should search you. Carrying a stash?"

"No. I got nothing. I wasn't smoking."

"Then why did you run when you saw a cop? What are you hiding, Alex?"

"Nothing. So help me God, nothing." But the high pitch of his voice said the opposite.

"Maybe I should bring you to the station and question you there. What's a few hours more or less? Your parents can pick you up in the morning."

"Hey man, don't do that. I'm not hiding a thing. I got nothing to tell you. I didn't see nothing that night. I swear it. Nothing."

Cavanaugh relaxed his hold on the boy's coat. "Now we're getting somewhere. You recognized me from the time I was here questioning people." Alex's silence was ample confirmation. "Were you here on the pier that night?"

"How the hell should I know? I come out lots of nights."

"Your parents would love to hear that."

"Well, you're probably gonna tell them anyway. I'll just deny it."

"Tough guy, aren't you? How would you like to be subpoenaed? What would your parents think about that?"

"They'll think you're nuts."

"Not if I tell them that their son may have been the only witness to a double murder."

"You already got the guy who did it. What do you need me for?"

"Evidence, Alex. The way it stands, the guy we've arrested may get off, and if that happens he may come after you to make sure you don't talk later."

"I'm not as dumb as you think," Alex fumed. "There's something called double jeopardy. If the guy gets off he can't be tried again."

"But if there's new evidence he can be tried for perjury. He'll do anything it takes to keep that evidence from coming out. The guy's already committed murder. Twice. Are you willing to spend the next few years of your life looking over your shoulder?"

Alex's jaw was set. "I got nothing to say."

Jodi, who had been watching the exchange quietly, felt it was time to step in. "You know, Alex, that will only buy you a little time. The detective here is determined to find a witness to those murders, and he will subpoena you if he has to. It would be much easier if you'd be straight with us. Your parents might not want you out here late at night and you might not want to tell them why you came out here, but if you come forward and give evidence that can lead to justice, I'd daresay they'd be proud of you."

"You don't know my parents."

"You're right. But I know lots of others, and I know that parents can sometimes surprise their kids. But forget your parents for a minute. Think about yourself. If you were out here that night, and if you did see something, wouldn't you like to feel that you were the one to step forward?"

"I don't want to be a hero. If I say something I'll have double trouble. Not only will my parents be on my back, but the guy who did the murders will be after me." He tossed an accusatory glance at Cavanaugh. "Just like he said."

"It doesn't have to be that way," Cavanaugh suggested. "If you tell us what you know we can protect you. If what you know leads to the evidence I need, the guy will be put away for a good long time. There might never even be a trial. If he knows we have an airtight case against him he might plead guilty, and no one but the three of us would be any the wiser to your involvement. Think of yourself as a high-class informant. I'd be willing to promise not to reveal your identity." Cavanaugh knew that last offer would clinch it.

"You wouldn't tell my parents you saw me out here?"

The detective shook his head.

"How do I know I can trust you?"

"You seem like a smart kid. What's the alternative? I'm granting you immunity in exchange for information. If you don't talk to me now I'll just have to take you in."

Alex held up an awkward hand. It occurred to Jodi that he hadn't yet grown into his body. "Look man," he rushed out, "I don't know if I have the information you want. I was just standin' out here—"

"On the night of the murders?"

"Yeah."

"What did you see?"

"A figure. All in black. That's it."

"Black suit?"

"Wet suit. With scuba gear."

"What did he look like? Size? Build?"

"It was dark. He was dark."

"Alex . . ."

"Okay, okay. He looked hunchback. Tall and thin with that stuff on his back."

"Where was he?"

"On the boat."

"Standing? Walking?"

"Climbing up the side of the boat. Going inside. I didn't think nothin' of it. I thought he belonged there."

"But you changed your mind at some point?"

"No."

"Then why are you telling me this?"

"'Cause you asked what I *saw* that night." He screwed up his face, then gave a single rough headshake. "Ah, shit, two bodies turned up on the boat."

"What time was it when you saw the guy?"

"Twelve-thirty. Maybe one."

"Did you hear anything?"

"Like gunshots? No."

That was okay. The killer used a silencer. "Then what?"

"Then he went back in the water. I thought he'd gone into the boat to get something—a piece of diving equipment or something he'd forgotten."

Cavanaugh wasn't ready to be optimistic just yet. Alex had only confirmed what he had suspected all along. If there was going to be a break in the case he would need more. "Did you watch him after he got back in the water?"

"Yeah. I wanted to know what he was doing."

"What was he doing?"

"Swimming."

"Underwater?"

"Yeah."

"It was dark. Cloudy. There wasn't any moon that night. How could you see?"

"The waterfront lights. They reflect off the clouds. And the air bubbles."

"How far did you follow the bubbles?"

"Till the guy got out of the water."

"Where? Where did he get out?" The questions were coming with increasing speed.

Alex peered off toward the harbor, then pointed. "There. That dock way over there. He climbed out, then fuckin' disappeared behind the building."

Cavanaugh followed the pointing finger, which took his gaze diagonally across the harbor to a building not far from the USS *Constitution*. "That one with the neon strip?"

"Yeah."

He let out a breath but kept his jubilation tightly in check. "What did you see then?" he asked calmly.

"Nothing. I stayed for a few more minutes, then left."

"You went back inside?"

"Yeah. Hey, it's not like I'm out here long. I just need to get air sometimes. I feel so damned cooped up in there—"

"You know, Alex," Cavanaugh said, this time giving the boy's shoulder a kind squeeze, "you're not bad for a kid. But let me give you a tip." This he said softly, conspiratorially, moving closer to Alex as he shot a glance at Jodi. "Your mouth is a little foul. If you want to attract women, real women, you'll have to ease up on the swearing." He drew his head back and peered at the boy. "You may want to get rid of the earring, too. Wouldn't want someone to mug you for it."

"Shit, it's not worth much," Alex said, then had the good grace to shoot Jodi an apologetic glance before looking back at Cavanaugh. "Are we done?"

Cavanaugh dropped his hand and stepped back. "We're done."

"I'm free to go?"

"Depends where you're going."

"Up there," Alex said, indicating the townhouse. "My tape's just about run through. If I'm not there to turn it off my parents are gonna hear the same conversation twice."

"Conversation?"

"Yeah." He grinned, proud of himself. "If my parents wake up they hear me talking to my girl."

Cavanaugh stared at him for a minute, then shook his head. "Okay. Go on."

Alex took several steps sideways, as though afraid to turn his back on the cop. "You won't tell?"

"I told you I wouldn't."

"Are you gonna be back looking for me?" He kept moving sideways.

"Not if I can help it."

"Did I do any good?"

"Keep your eyes on the papers. You'll see for yourself. That is, if you can read."

"That," Alex declared with a look of disgust that was terribly adult, "isn't even worth answering." Turning, he raced back along the pier, swung himself onto the walk, and within minutes disappeared behind the door of his home.

Cavanaugh watched until he was safely inside, then locked his elbow through Jodi's and set off at a jaunty pace.

"I don't believe it!" she whispered. She was grinning and kept darting incredulous glances over her shoulder.

Cavanaugh was grinning too. "Oh boy," he hummed. "Oh boy . . . oh boy." His pitch rose with each repeat and his pace quickened.

"He was *there*. We *found* him."

"Oh boy."

They reached the end of the pier and turned, all but flying past the bench on which they had sat earlier, heading straight for Cavanaugh's car. When they reached it he swept her into his arms, hugged her from side to side, then swung her in a full circle.

"It's what I needed, babe! Couldn't have been better!"

"That's the dock I think it is?"

"Damn right. The guy climbed off the boat and swam to the fuckin' *police* dock!"

She laughed, then sighed. "Poor Alex. He had no idea what he was pointing to."

"Makes sense. The kid can't see the dock from his window, so he wasn't familiar with it. It's visible only from the end of the pier where he was standing, and from that angle all you can see is the slash of neon where it says Boston Police Harbor Unit. When the tides are right you can't even see the police boats."

For a minute they both wondered what would have happened had Alex known where the diver had gone. Then Jodi wondered something else. "Why didn't the diver see Alex?"

"Preoccupied, I guess. And it was dark. Alex could easily have blended in with that post he was glued to and he's not the type that wants to be seen."

"But still, you'd think the guy would have been cautious."

"Arrogance overrides caution sometimes." Cavanaugh held Jodi within the circle of his arms, his hands clasped at the back of her waist. "But it wasn't Ryan himself. We suspected that, and Alex's description confirmed it."

"So who was it?"

"Someone with the department, probably with the Harbor Patrol Unit itself. It'll be easy enough to find out who was on duty that night."

"You think it was someone on duty? That would have been *really* stupid."

"Not necessarily. There have to be two guys there at any given time, a boat operator and a scuba diver. Suppose the boat operator fell asleep—it's been known to happen at one in the morning—and the scuba diver did his thing. He'd have been gone for half an hour, maybe a little more. The boat operator would never have known he'd left."

"They don't have to sign out equipment when they use it?"

"Not when they're on duty. And even if they had to, what's a little slip-up on paper when murder is the name of the game?"

"Why would a cop—a *cop*—do it?"

"Promise of future advancement? Blackmail? I don't know, but I'm sure as hell going to find out."

Chapter 19

CAVANAUGH MET WILLIAM HOLSTROM the next day in a small coffee shop in Brookline. It was a different shop from the one they had met in several days before, which in turn had been different from the one they had met in several days before that. All were far enough from the city limits to ensure secrecy. Neither man wanted to be seen with the other. At least not yet.

"What have you got?" Holstrom asked directly.

Cavanaugh spoke quietly. "I have a witness who saw a diver climb from the harbor onto the boat, go inside, come out, slip back into the harbor, then swim across to the Harbor Patrol Unit."

"You're sure?"

"The witness pointed straight to the dock and he didn't even realize what it was. I did some work this morning. On the night of the murders, there were two men on duty at the unit. One was Anthony Amsbury, the boat operator. The other was the scuba diver, Chip Ryan. Officially, John Ryan, Jr."

Holstrom closed his eyes for a minute. When he opened them he was ready for battle. "You'll have to speak with Amsbury."

"I did. He wasn't feeling well that night."

"But he was on duty."

"He was fine when he came on, but after he and Chip had something to eat he began to feel woozy. He slept for two or three hours, right at his desk."

"Drugged."

"Probably. We can't prove it, though. The evidence is long gone."

"Did he have any trouble after he woke up?"

"A headache. It passed."

"Did he notice anything amiss with the equipment?"

Cavanaugh shook his head. "Not that he was looking for anything strange, but Chip must have wiped everything down. And if there were wet towels where they weren't supposed to be, Amsbury didn't notice. They would be long gone, too." He let out a breath. "I hadn't even realized Ryan had a boy on the force."

"I knew it, but I'm glad I didn't say anything earlier. You found out on your own. It adds credibility to the investigation. It also explains why he didn't have to pay someone off to commit the murders. If the girl killed herself over the abortion, you can imagine what the rest of the family felt on both counts. They're pretty devout." He sat back, but his fist was as tightly clenched as his jaw. "Okay we have motive and opportunity. Let's bring them in."

But Cavanaugh had something else in mind. "Let's get Chip first. He's young. He can't be as sure of himself as his father is. We may have an easier time cracking him, while Ryan could brazen it out."

"They could both do that. They could deny everything, call it a setup."

"The evidence is solid. Much more so than it ever was on Jordan Whyte."

Holstrom shifted in his seat, clearly uncomfortable with the mention of Jordan's name. "I don't like making mistakes. It doesn't look good for the department, and it doesn't look good for me. This time around I've made two—arresting Whyte and trusting Ryan. I was the one who made him a deputy superintendent."

"The man's been on the force for years. His record is clean. You had no way of knowing he'd go off the deep end on a personal matter."

"But I want it cleared up. And soon."

"So do I. If nothing else we owe it to the Whytes. But I've always believed in doing things right. If we're going to worm our way out of embarrassment we'll have to make sure we have Ryan cold."

"Is there any chance," Holstrom asked slowly, "that Ryan's boy was acting on his own?"

Cavanaugh had forced himself to consider that. "No. Ryan knew about those tapes. He all but told me where to find them. And Ryan masterminding the murders explains his obsession with this case. When he first assigned it to me he handed me a huge file. I assumed he had just been a Whyte-Warren follower over the years. It seems, though, that he put that file together over the last six months. Must have started it around the time of Julie's abortion. One of the more lowly department secretaries confessed to having spent a lot of time in both the library and the department archives at Ryan's request. She didn't think to question it. So Ryan put together a file that was just thorough enough to look condemning, just condemning enough to give me food for thought."

Holstrom pressed his lips together and shook his head. "This one really *is* an embarrassment."

"Much less so if we can guarantee convictions."

"Mmm. You think you can get a confession out of the boy?"

"I don't know. I've never met him. I'll try my best."

"All on the up and up?" Holstrom asked, arching a warning brow.

For the first time Cavanaugh grinned. "Always."

It was very, very late that night when Cavanaugh put through a call to Jordan, who picked up the phone with a groggy, "Yuh?"

"You were sleeping."

"Cavanaugh?" He hoisted himself up.

"Sorry to wake you, but it's important."

"You didn't wake me from anything deep. There's this problem I've had lately—"

"I think I've solved it."

Jordan's spine straightened at the very moment a sleepy Katia sat up. "You have?"

"How early can you get up here tomorrow?"

"There's a six-thirty shuttle. What's happening?"

"Take that flight. I'll meet you at Logan at seven-thirty. I'll tell you then."

"Tell me now, Cavanaugh."

"Too late. Not safe. But the word's good."

"As in freedom?"

"Bingo. Tomorrow morning. Seven-thirty. Be there."

Jordan was, along with Katia, who couldn't have cared less if she lost her job for missing another day of work, she was so determined to hear Cavanaugh's news firsthand.

As promised, Cavanaugh met them at the airport, then took a circuitous route back into the city to allow the time he needed to explain what had happened and what was yet to be done.

"I'm going, too," Katia declared after Cavanaugh had set forth his plan.

"You are not," Jordan stated.

"But I'm part of this. By hurting you Ryan hurt me."

"You're not going."

She turned her attention to Cavanaugh. "Is there any reason I can't be there?"

"It'll be dangerous," Jordan insisted.

"Bob, is there?" When Cavanaugh simply shrugged, she pressed on. "We'll be in Police Headquarters. What could be safer?"

"You'd be surprised," Cavanaugh quipped.

Jordan was more specific. "Ryan could see that he's cornered, pull out a gun and decide to take all of us down with him."

Cavanaugh chuckled. "Another 'Miami Vice' fan?"

"He's right, Jordan. What you've described is a scene from a TV script. Please. I want to be there. It's possible I could even help. Seeing me will make what he's done to you that much more real to him. I'm not that much older than his daughter was. My presence could weaken him."

"She has a point, Jordan."

"Christ, Cavanaugh, where's your common sense? That office, under those circumstances, is no place for *my wife*. As a matter of fact, this whole thing is a little melodramatic. What you're doing isn't exactly common police practice."

"No, it's not, but I'm loving it. For seventeen years I've gone by the book. I've lived and breathed standard procedure. Sure, there's creativity involved in psyching out a case, but when you want to work your way up through the ranks you have to keep that creativity in check. Never let the guy above you know you're more clever than he is—it's an unwritten rule. Well, this time I'm going to let him know that he's not more clever than the rest of us, and I'm going to enjoy doing it." He shot a glance at Jordan, who was sitting in the passenger seat. "Remember the discussion we had once about the little unexpected twists in life that make things exciting? When I first got this case I never dreamed it would turn out the way it has. The twists have been unexpected, that's for sure." He refrained from saying exciting; after all, Jordan's brother and sister-in-law were dead.

"Let me remind you that this is my future you're playing with."

"I'm not playing. I'm telling you, we've got the guy."

"So why do you need us along?" Jordan asked, but he was thinking more of Katia than himself.

"For the sheer pleasure of it." Cavanaugh grinned. "After all you've been through do you really want to miss out on the final coup?"

No, Jordan didn't. Nor did Katia. He understood that, which was why he finally gave in and dropped his objections about her accompanying them. Still, he was nervous, and he told her so during the minutes they were alone, when Cavanaugh stopped at a pay phone to make a call.

"I don't like this, sweetheart. If anything happens—"

"Nothing's going to happen," she insisted, sitting forward in the backseat and reaching for his hand. Her eyes were brimming with anticipation. "Bob has it worked out. Nothing's going to happen."

"I want you to stay by the door. If there's the slightest sign of trouble, get out."

She smiled sweetly. "Yes, Jordan."

" 'Yes, Jordan.' Why doesn't that reassure me?"

"Because you love me so much that you're determined to worry."

"Will you be careful? Just stay in the background?"

Taking pity on him, she simply nodded this time, doing her best to look sincere. Deep inside she knew she'd gladly strangle Ryan if he didn't give them the satisfaction they sought, but she wasn't about to tell Jordan that. Then Cavanaugh was back, preventing her from telling him anything.

"All set. Ryan's in. We're on our way."

Fifteen minutes later the three walked down the hall to the squad room. They ignored the few curious glances that were thrown their way and proceeded directly to Ryan's office. The door was ajar. Cavanaugh leaned around it and rapped. Ryan looked up.

"Got a minute?" the detective asked. His gaze fell to the newspaper open on the chief's desk. Ryan closed it, shoved it aside and nodded. His eyes barely widened when he saw Jordan and Katia on Cavanaugh's tail.

Cavanaugh waited until they were all in the office before closing the door. Then he tucked his hands in the pockets of his slacks and turned to Ryan.

"I think we have a problem," he began. Behind him and to his left Jordan and Katia stood studying the man who had wreaked such havoc with their lives. Jordan was feeling pure hatred, Katia pure disgust. To her, Ryan looked like an overweight and aging porcupine.

"Mr. Whyte," Cavanaugh went on, "is under indictment for a murder he didn't commit."

"Isn't that for a jury to decide?" Ryan asked. His voice was high, its tone bland, disinterested.

Cocksure son of a bitch, Jordan thought.

Pompous porcupine, Katia thought.

"It shouldn't have to go to a jury," Cavanaugh said. "The case shouldn't even come to trial. We were wrong in arresting him when we did. The indictments were a travesty."

Ryan was staring at Cavanaugh. "You were instrumental in that arrest."

"Under pressure from you. I wanted to wait. There were too many questions."

"A grand jury took the matter out of our hands," Ryan said with a shrug of dismissal. "They seemed to feel there was enough evidence to warrant an indictment."

"They only heard what we gave the DA. It's a one-sided affair, a grand jury hearing. There's no chance for rebuttal."

Again Ryan shrugged. "That's the system. There's nothing we can do now."

"I believe there is," Cavanaugh stated. All along his voice had been low, and it remained so. "I believe we can make up for our shortcomings of the past."

"This is beginning to sound like a revival meeting. Do you have something to confess, Cavanaugh? You were in charge of the investigation. Are you saying you did a lousy job?"

If he had expected to rile Cavanaugh he failed. At the moment nothing could have riled the detective. He had his prey right where he wanted him. "Not at all. I've finally got the answers."

For the first time Ryan's composure wavered, but only for a moment with a frown and the flexing of his fingers. "Well? I haven't got all day."

Leisurely—all the better to annoy him—Cavanaugh strolled to the far side of the office. He wanted to put distance between himself and Jordan and Katia. If Ryan panicked and tried something he would have widespread targets.

"From the start I had questions about Jordan's supposed motive in killing his brother," Cavanaugh said slowly. "It didn't ring true, not when I got to know him."

Ryan didn't blink. "You were taken in. I'd have expected you'd be more professional than that."

"I was professional, all right. I began to wonder about those tapes. You knew about them."

"Of course I knew. You found them. You told me. So I knew."

"You knew about them before I found them. Don't you remember getting nervous when it took me awhile? Was that why you kept urging me to go back to L.A. and look? Look everywhere? Take the place apart?"

Ryan stood with greater speed than Cavanaugh had ever seen in him. "If there are problems with the way you handled the case it will be taken up before a board of inquiry. The department doesn't air its dirty laundry in public." The look he sent Katia and Jordan clearly branded them public.

Cavanaugh was as calm as ever. "I don't think you'll want a board of inquiry to hear what I have to say. And as for Mr. and Mrs. Whyte being here, I think you owe them. We all owe them."

"We don't owe them a thing! We did our jobs, and if they've suffered they had it coming."

Something about what he said and the way he said it struck a dissonant chord in Jordan. "Why?" he pressed, entering the conversation. "What did we ever have coming?"

Ryan opened his mouth, then shut it again. Katia was in the process of amending her vision of him to one of a flounder when he sat down, obviously in what he felt was a show of dignity. Katia felt it was a show of arrogance.

"You killed your brother and sister-in-law," he said. "You cold-bloodedly murdered them."

"No, Ryan. I didn't do that. *You* did."

Ryan studied Jordan for a minute longer, then swiveled his fat head toward Cavanaugh. "I want him out of here. I don't like him."

"Is that why you set me up?" Jordan shot back. "Because you don't *like* me? Or was it something about my family, or about the Warrens? Would any one of us have been right for the fall?"

Katia put a restraining hand on Jordan's arm. "Let's let Bob continue," she said softly, but Ryan heard.

"Bob?" he echoed. "So it's Bob? You're on a first name basis now?" He glowered at Cavanaugh. "You have a lot to answer for. If you thought you were in line for Haas' job you'd better think again."

A promotion was the last thing on Cavanaugh's mind. "Right now I'm thinking that I really want to tell you about what happened after I found those tapes." He didn't give Ryan time to argue. "I viewed them carefully, like a good detective would, and I found the one with Jordan's threat. But I found another one. This one was of an orgy, with bodies all over the place, faces sticking up in between. One of those faces looked familiar, a woman's face, young, maybe twenty-four, but I couldn't place it." He thought he saw Ryan pale, but his complexion was such a pasty color anyway that it was hard to tell. He had the older man's attention, that was for sure. So he went on.

"It bothered me, that face. It also bothered me that you'd known about the existence of those tapes before I did."

"I'm a better detective than you'll ever be, Cavanaugh. You lack imagination."

"I wouldn't say that," was the detective's smooth reply. "I started imagining all kinds of things, particularly when I learned that Mark Whyte had had an affair with a girl named Julie Duncan."

"He had affairs with lots of girls."

Cavanaugh began to close in. "Not ones who got pregnant, had abortions, then committed suicide. Not ones who were married, and whose maiden names were Ryan, and whose father was you."

More warily, Ryan glanced at Jordan and Katia, then back at Cavanaugh. "So? My daughter did something foolish. She paid for it with her life."

"Why didn't you tell me, Ryan?"

"It was none of your business."

"It had direct relevance to this case."

"I decided it didn't."

"Was that before or after you had my brother killed?" Jordan demanded. Katia felt the tendons in his arm straining against her hand. She suspected that he shared her opinion on strangling Ryan, and she was grateful that Cavanaugh was along to prevent it.

Cavanaugh, bless him, stayed cool. "It gave you a motive, John. But I knew I'd have to find out how you did it if I was to have any chance of nailing you."

"You won't find out," Ryan said lightly, "because I didn't do it."

"I know that now. Chip did."

"What does Chip have to do with this?" Ryan asked, but his smugness of moments before was gone.

Cavanaugh scratched his head. "It seems that Chip was on duty at the Harbor Patrol Unit that night. He used the scuba gear there." He grinned at Jordan. "You hit it on the head when you said that the only people who swam through the harbor were nuts or cops. Chip is both."

"Now wait just a minute." Ryan rose to his feet, but awkwardly this time. "That's my flesh and blood you're talking about. He's a damned good cop, and a damned good son."

"No, John. If he was either he'd have talked you out of this scheme."

Ryan was shaking his head. His lips were pursed, his eyes filled with what could only be called murder. "If there's a nut around here he's standing in front of me now. I think I've heard enough, Cavanaugh." He reached for the phone, but the detective was suddenly there, slamming both Ryan's hand and the receiver back down. It was his first and only sign of anger. When he spoke, his voice was evenly modulated.

"Chip talked, John. It's all over."

"Chip didn't talk. He had nothing to say."

"Would you like to hear the tape?" He took perverse pleasure in the other man's recoil. "Filmmakers aren't the only ones who record things. Cops do it too. I spent five hours with Chip last night."

"You couldn't have. He was on duty."

"Only until we brought him in for questioning. When he realized we had him right down to the foot powder he uses he spilled it all."

Ryan yanked his hand from beneath Cavanaugh's. "You forced him. I know the methods. I've used them often enough myself." Which reminded him of something. "And who the hell are *you* to take it upon yourself to do an independent investigation? Under whose authority did you drag my son in to ask him questions about some murder?"

"Not *some* murder," Jordan grated, taking an ominous step forward. "My *brother's* murder."

Ryan ignored him. "I'll have you kicked off the force, Cavanaugh. And that's just for starters. I have friends all over this city. You try to get another job here and you'll be laughed to kingdom come!"

"I don't think so," Cavanaugh returned. He walked to the window and glanced out. For a minute the only sound in the room was the faltering click of a distant typewriter. Katia shivered at the eeriness of it.

Then Cavanaugh's voice came quietly. "I've been working with Holstrom. He authorized my actions. Right now he's waiting in his office for your confession." He turned in time to see Ryan's cheeks, pasty earlier, turn red with rage.

"*Holstrom? Confession?* What do you take me for, some kind of fool?" His eyes narrowed. "You really are going for that promotion, aren't you? You're determined to do it with a bang and at my expense. *Well, I won't have it!*"

"You don't have any choice, John." Strangely, some of the pleasure had gone out of it for Cavanaugh. He saw the signs of rage as synonymous with desperation, and there was something very sad about desperation, even in a man he disliked as much as he had come to dislike John Ryan. "We have Chip's confession, taped, typed and signed. You can claim your innocence for as long as you want, but if you come clean now there won't have to be a trial. If you're talking about bangs, spare yourself one."

"You don't have a case," Ryan scoffed. He plopped back into his chair. "We'll prove that you manipulated Chip into that confession. He's not old enough to know that he can't be forced."

"Which is why he did your bidding, I assume. You know, John, I have to hand it to you. You planned it well. You bided your time, then pounced, and Chip did okay, too. He even knew enough not to use his own revolver. Then you started making mistakes. Your first one was in assigning me to the case. I was honored. I thought you'd done it because you thought I was good. And I am, but in my own sweet time. Then you got impatient. That was your second mistake. After all that waiting you got impatient. You started pushing, and that puzzled me."

"It was an important case!"

"We've had other important cases, but you've never stuck your nose in so much. It was your harping on the tapes that really did it."

"If I hadn't harped, you'd never have found the tapes and *he*—" Ryan rolled his head toward Jordan, "wouldn't have been caught."

"Did you know Julie was on the tape? Did she tell you that?"

"You're bluffing there, too. She wasn't on any tape."

"I saw her."

"You haven't seen her in years."

"I talked with her husband. He showed me a picture. It was the same girl who'd looked so familiar to me on that tape."

"My daughter wouldn't have gone to an orgy."

"Would you like to see the tape?"

"She wouldn't have gone. She wasn't on that tape. She wasn't on any tape. She told me she wasn't—"

"Ahh." A break at last. "She told you. She told you about the tapes, but she assured you she wasn't on them. Or did she die before she could get to that part?"

Ryan gave a convulsive little shake of his head, and each of the three others in the room felt a moment's sympathy. But only a moment's.

"Apparently she underestimated the filmmaker," Cavanaugh said quietly.

Ryan's upper lip twitched and curled. "She knew him for the scum he was. That was why she had the abortion. She couldn't bear the thought of carrying any part of him, much less bringing it into the world."

Jordan started forward, restrained first by Katia's hand, then by Cavanaugh's retort.

"But the abortion did her in. She should have been relieved afterward. Instead, she cracked."

Nostrils flaring, Ryan shifted his gaze to Jordan. "Your brother did that to her. He deserved to die. He wasn't worth the ground she walked on."

"And Deborah?" Jordan goaded angrily. "Did she deserve to die?"

"She was as bad as he was, going along with that sicko group! She was at the parties. She took drugs like the rest of them. She stood there saying nothing while her husband took obscene pictures of little kids! The *two* of them deserved to die!"

Jordan struggled to keep his fury in check. "And me? What did I do to deserve to be framed?"

Ryan was beyond caution. "You're a Whyte! The whole bunch of you—Whytes *and* Warrens—are disgusting! You walk around like you own the world and you don't give a damn who you trample in the process. Well, my daughter didn't deserve to be trampled. It was a Whyte who introduced her to drugs, a Whyte who made her pregnant, a Whyte who forced her into an abortion and suicide. An eye for an eye, so they say. He deserved to die, and you—as far as I'm concerned a life sentence wouldn't be long enough!"

"Tell me one more thing, Ryan," Jordan persisted. "Why me? Why not my brother or my sister?"

"You were a perfect patsy," Ryan spat and turned his face away as though the sight of Jordan turned his stomach. "You had a reputation for brashness. You were visible. And you threatened Mark. When I learned about that I knew I had it made."

"You learned about that before Julie died," Cavanaugh remarked. "Were you planning on murder even then?"

Ryan sent him a venomous look. "There was plenty to justify murder even before her death. And after—all I needed was the right fall guy. Whyte here was ripe for the picking. It was too good to believe."

"I think we have enough," Cavanaugh said softy. His gaze slid from Jordan to Katia, then back to Ryan, whose venom had mellowed to something akin to confusion. Cavanaugh drew his blazer open to reveal the tiny microphone fastened to the breast pocket of his shirt. "We have it all, John."

Ryan was very still for a long minute—disbelieving, dismayed, stunned. But the minute passed. "I don't think so," he murmured. "I think I'd like to put something down on paper." Laboring around his protruding belly, he opened the side drawer of his desk.

A second too late Cavanaugh realized what he was up to. He had barely drawn his gun before Ryan put his to his own head. It was a twist Cavanaugh hadn't expected.

Katia gasped and grabbed Jordan's elbow when he stepped in front of her.

"Put it down, Cavanaugh," Ryan said with the calm of one truly mad. "Put it down or I'll pull the trigger."

For the sake of the audience listening in another room, Cavanaugh said quietly, "Ryan is holding a gun to his head." Then, to Ryan, "You won't do it."

"Why not? I have nothing to lose."

"Your life is nothing?"

"Thanks to you. Put down the gun."

If he had been alone, Cavanaugh would have done so in a minute. But he was worried about Jordan and Katia. The last thing he wanted was for Ryan to turn his gun on them. So he held his own steady and said, "Suicide isn't your style."

"Oh?"

"It's against your religion."

"So is abortion. And murder. My daughter committed suicide. Apparently she found it painless."

Jordan was slowly shaking his head. "Don't do it, Ryan. For your family's sake, don't do it."

The wheels on the chair moved as Ryan's stocky legs slowly maneuvered it free of the desk. "Do you think my family's going to enjoy seeing me suspended and put on trial?" He was pushing the chair steadily back into a corner so that he faced diagonally into the room. Though his head was slanted toward Jordan, he didn't take his eyes from Cavanaugh for a minute. The short barrel of the revolver remained firmly pressed to his temple.

Jordan swallowed hard. "They'll understand that you did what you did out of love for your daughter."

"Do you understand it, Whyte? Do you forgive me?" Both questions were laden with such sarcasm that it was all Jordan could do not to lunge.

"That's asking a lot," he answered tightly.

"Perhaps," Ryan agreed, then his voice hardened. "Put it down, Cavanaugh. Put it down now or I'll shoot. Do you want your friends here to see my blood all over the place? Do you think the memory of that will give them sweet dreams for years to come? Do you want my death on your head?"

"Your death will be on no one's head but your own."

"Moot point. Mine will be blown apart."

"You won't do it," Cavanaugh repeated, praying he was right, but Ryan was proving to be a complex man.

"Want to try me?"

Cavanaugh didn't. He'd been half hoping Ryan would have remained at his desk, where a sharpshooter would have had a chance through the window—if it came to that. But, shrewdly, Ryan had moved. He was cornered, but protected. And he refused to look away, even for a minute. Another shrewd move. Cavanaugh would have disabled him himself given the briefest lapse of attention.

Realizing that his only hope was in hurtling toward Ryan if the man aimed at either Jordan or Katia, Cavanaugh started to return his gun to its holster.

"Uh-uh," Ryan prompted. "Over here on the desk."

Cavanaugh put it on the corner farthest from Ryan.

"Closer. Slide it over."

"I can't. There's too much crap on your desk."

Ryan was undaunted. One fat forefinger pointed to where his feet were flattened on the floor. "Toss it here." A second fat forefinger tightened on the trigger in warning that if the toss were anything but gentle and to his feet he would shoot himself.

Cavanaugh tossed the gun, then stepped back, away from Jordan and Katia. But Ryan saw through that move as well. The same finger that had pointed to the floor now wagged toward Jordan and Katia.

"With them. Over there." When Cavanaugh hesitated he put pressure on the trigger. Cavanaugh moved, but only a few feet.

"This isn't necessary, John. A judge will be sympathetic. It's not like you have a record."

"Don't be patronizing. There isn't much sympathy for murder."

"Why did you *do* it?" Katia asked, very much on impulse. "Your daughter knew what she was doing when she went to bed with Mark—"

"She did not! She was conned by him. She was conned by that whole crowd. I don't like cheap thrill seekers. I don't like users."

"Listen to me, John," Cavanaugh said quickly. He didn't want Katia talking. He didn't want her in the room. But there wasn't time to berate himself for his stupidity in allowing her to come.

"This is absurd. Why don't you let these two leave? You and I can talk in private."

"I wanted that before but you wouldn't have it. Now it's a little too late. I want them to stay."

"They don't need to be here."

"I like having them here."

"What do you plan to do?"

Ryan pushed his lips out as he thought about that for a minute, then answered flippantly, "I'm not really sure."

Cavanaugh half believed him, which was why talking seemed the smartest thing to do. If he could wear Ryan down, get him to crumble, even for a minute . . . "You don't have many choices. It's between shooting or leaving."

"I'm thinking."

"You shouldn't have brought out the gun. You could have surrendered quietly."

"But I did bring out the gun."

"You could still put it away and leave peacefully."

"Leave? Are you kidding? There are probably a dozen guys with their own guns in the squad room right about now."

"They won't shoot."

"You're right. They'd rather see me suffer. They don't like me. They've always been jealous."

"What are you going to do about it?"

"I'm thinking."

"You can't sit here forever with a gun pointed to your head."

"I can do whatever I want. I'm the one with the gun."

Jordan decided to give it another try. "Think of your daughter, Ryan. Is this what she would have wanted?"

"She sure as hell wouldn't have wanted to see me in prison. Try again."

He did, this time wearily. "Turn over the gun. None of us wants you hurt."

"There's hurt and there's hurt. You'd be more than happy to see me locked up for life, yet you don't want me to kill myself. It's ironic when you think of it." He laughed, but it was an ugly sound. "You won't budge, none of you, because you don't want to see a man die before your eyes. You don't want to see me die—me, who was responsible for two deaths. What's a life worth, anyway? Just a breathing body. Easily replaced by another sucker."

He rocked back in his chair, but the gun remained at his head. "I should have been named commissioner. You know that? I had the experience. I should have been named commissioner. But no. The mayor brought someone in from Baltimore. You wouldn't have stood for anyone doing that to you, would you, Whyte?"

Jordan simply said, "Put the gun down."

"What? When I'm beginning to enjoy myself? There are guys all over the squad room right now. There are more at the other end of Cavanaugh's little microphone. And then there's Holstrom, sitting in his office, waiting for my move. I don't think I've had this much attention since I nabbed the dwarf who was plotting to kill the Pope when he was here."

Jordan was sickened, but he forced himself to talk. "If it's attention you want, think how much more you'll get when you walk out there. The press will be all over the place. They'll take your picture, trip over each other to ask you questions. You'll be a celebrity. I know. I've been there."

"You've been everywhere," Ryan drawled disdainfully. "It's always you first and everyone else second. Now, if I were to kill myself, that would be something you've never done."

Jordan said nothing. He darted a glance at Cavanaugh, who seemed as frustrated as he. Meanwhile, Katia was standing behind Jordan's shoulder, fed up with the whole scene. She wanted to be celebrating with Jordan and the rest of the family in Dover. She wanted to be making up for all the smiling and laughing she had missed in the past weeks. She wanted to be able to hug her husband, knowing for the first time that their future was free.

She thought of Natalie, who had watched the years roll by as she silently waited for that which she had wanted most.

She thought of Lenore, who had realized too late what she had wanted most and then not quite known how to fight for it.

She thought of her mother, who had conceded defeat and settled for trying to make the most of it.

And she thought of herself. Too much time had been wasted. If she had confronted Jordan years ago as she should have, instead of taking his repeated rejections in silence, the matter of her parentage would have been brought to a head and they would have been married much sooner.

Now, suddenly, she was impatient. She didn't want to wait silently for fate to make its play. She knew what she wanted and wasn't afraid to fight for it. And she had no intention of suffering defeat.

Darting free of Jordan, she threw her hands in the air. "That's it! I've had it!" she screamed, sounding for all the world like a woman abruptly gone mad. "It's senseless! *All* of it—"

"Katia!" Jordan reached for her, but she threw him off, her eyes wide and wild, and held her hands up, palms out.

"Don't touch me!" She jerked her head once, then again, as though shaking off a spider. "Don't lay a single finger on me!"

Cavanaugh had taken a step forward, but he too halted in shock.

"I can't stand this a minute longer!" she yelled as she turned and advanced on John Ryan, who was every bit as taken aback as the other two men. "You," she said, pointing a furiously shaking finger, "are *cruel!* Just who do you think you are that you can do this to me? I never did anything to you! I never hurt you! But I can understand why your daughter must have gone mad!" She had come to a stop and was bending over with her hands on her hips, gasping for breath, nose to nose with a stunned Ryan. "She loved you! She wanted to please you! You were the one in control of her life!" Her hands shot out, flailing. "It's not fair! You can't *do* this to people—"

Before Ryan knew what hit him, she had smacked the gun from his hand. Jordan scrambled for it while Cavanaugh dove for his own revolver. The two men straightened, guns pointed toward Ryan, eyes riveted on Katia.

Stepping safely away from Ryan, she drew herself up to her full height, set her shoulders back, took a deep and audible breath, then smiled broadly at Jordan. "How'd I do?" she asked calmly.

Jordan stared. Cavanaugh stared. Ryan was the only one to lower his eyes and slowly, sadly shake his head.

The celebration in Dover that night was one of true victory. Amid trappings of the upcoming holiday, three families ate and drank, talked and laughed and hugged one another spontaneously. It wasn't that it was the first time they had overcome adversity or the first time they had had cause for celebration, but the dropping of charges against Jordan seemed symbolic of the start of a new chapter in the Whyte-Warren chronicles.

Gil was gone. In his stead Lenore had emerged as the cornerstone of the Warrens. She felt strong and vibrant and looked toward the future without dread. She knew there would be problems. Laura's drinking wasn't going to stop with Jordan's release; Peter was as egotistical as ever; Emily as dramatic. Lenore fully expected there to be ups and downs with the grandchildren as well, but for the first time in her life she was willing to meet them head on.

Natalie had Jack and the knowledge that he would be beside her when she awoke the next morning. And if she was rosy-eyed about that particular relationship she saw all too clearly the stumbling blocks her children would have to face. Nick, while having taken over at the office with aplomb, was far from faithful to his wife; she knew that the very modern Angie would have less patience with his dalliances, if they continued, than she had had with Jack's. She also suspected that Anne, an eighties woman as well, was going to have times of trial in the struggle to maintain a satisfactory balance between her career and her family. Even Jordan and Katia would face challenges. But life was like that.

Mark's death notwithstanding, Natalie felt certain for the very first time that the children she had raised could cope.

Cassie was ecstatic with the turn of events, not the least of which was the fact that, of her own free will, Lenore had thrown her arms around Katia and held her close. For the first time in years Cassie was almost willing to concede that there was God and a method to His madness. From heartache came strength, from strength, satisfaction. Cassie was satisfied. She had what she had always wanted, the promise of happiness and security for her daughter.

And Katia—Katia could do nothing but smile with delight from where she sat within the comforting circle of Jordan's arms.